AM I NOT A MAN?

Tho Dred Scott Story

AM I NOT A MAN?

The Dred Scott Story

by

MARK L. SHURTLEFF

Valor Publishing Group, LLC

This is a work of historical fiction. The characters and places are real, and the incidents are based on historical accounts. However, for the sake of storytelling, the author has taken some liberties with dialogue and certain incidents, and takes full responsibility for any errors or omissions as a result thereof. Likewise all views expressed herein are the sole responsibility of the author.

Am I Not A Man? The Dred Scott Story

Published by Valor Publishing Group, LLC
P.O. Box 2516
Orem, Utah 84059-2516

Cover art copyright © 2009 by Cash Case
Cover design copyright © 2009 by Valor Publishing Group, LLC
Book design and layout copyright © 2009 by Valor Publishing Group, LLC

Valor Publishing and the Valor Sword & Shield are registered trademarks of
Valor Publishing Group, LLC

Regular hardcover edition ISBN: 978-1-935546-00-9
Limited heirloom 1ˢᵗ edition ISBN: 978-1-935546-01-6

Printed in the United States of America
Year of first printing: 2009

10 9 8 7 6 5 4 3 2 1

Acknowledgments

The only known interview of Dred Scott took place in June of 1857, when a reporter from the celebrated *Frank Leslie's Illustrated Newspaper* convinced him and his family to sit for a daguerreotype. It is noteworthy that Dred expressed his desire to make a little money so he could pay back the attorneys who had represented him without charge in his long fight for freedom.

In March of 1853, Frederick Douglass wrote a letter to Harriet Beecher Stowe to thank her for writing *Uncle Tom's Cabin,* to which his oppressed people owed "a debt of gratitude which cannot be measured."

Let me here measure and acknowledge those without whom, this book would not have been possible.

I am grateful to have been blessed with a wife who, like Harriet Scott did for Dred, motivates me to be my very best, encourages me to dream and "tilt at windmills," and keeps me humble. In addition, my sweetheart, M'Liss, shoulders much responsibility at home so I'm able to serve as an elected official and share my heart and spirit through my writing. I'm thankful for my five children: Ambra, Heath, Danielle, Tommy, and Annie, who give my life purpose and bring me joy. I acknowledge and thank my amazing parents, James and Sandra Shurtleff, who by their example instilled in me a love of literature, an appreciation for history, and a commitment of service to God and country.

Dred Scott could not have sued for his freedom without the support and help of friends. Likewise, I would not have finished this project without the same from many friends. A few require special mention. Steve Hasler provided persistent but gentle prodding, a rare Lincoln or Dred Scott book to educate and inspire, and the use of his remote cabin when I needed it most for the inspiration that sometimes only solitude can provide. Tim Lawson introduced me to Harland and Shirley Stonecipher, motivated me with his "no holds barred" approach to life, and relaxed me with his humor when I needed it most. New friends Gil and Marilyn Salinas lent me their beautiful Laguna Beach bungalow when only the sun, sea breeze, and bougainvillea could pull me out of a funk and put the end within my grasp. My dear friend and long-time Executive Assistant Helen Petersen always got me where I needed to go and made sure that I never let down in my responsibilities as Attorney General while researching and writing Dred's story. I am grateful to my Chief Deputies Kirk Torgensen and Ray Hintze, and Director of Communications Paul Murphy for their commitment to justice and service to the people of Utah and for helping me be the best Attorney General I can be.

I thank my publisher Candace Salima and editor Tristi Pinkston for their extraordinary literary expertise and for instilling confidence in an amateur writer that others would actually pay money to read what I wrote.

I walked the humid cotton fields of The Olde Place plantation in Southampton County, Virginia where Dred was born; prayed at the slave cemetery in Huntsville, Alabama; twisted my ankle on the same uneven bricks of the riverboat levee in St. Louis that Dred trudged up and down thousands of times; rode riverboats on, and swam in, the turbulent waters of the Mississippi; felt Dred's strength at Ft. Armstrong on Rock Island, Illinois; wandered the snowy grounds of Fort Snelling in Minneapolis-St. Paul where Dred and Harriet fell in love; meditated in the St. Louis courthouse and mourned on the eastern steps where slave auctions took place; and wept at the grave of Dred Scott.

But I never really knew Dred and Harriet until I looked into the eyes of their great-great-granddaughter, Lynne Jackson of St. Louis, listened to her kind voice, and felt her unsurpassed spirit.

Thank you, Lynne!

Introduction and Dedication

In law school, I studied the infamous case of *Scott vs. Sandford* where the focus was primarily on the significance of the Supreme Court overturning an act of Congress in the Missouri Compromise. Years later, while researching famous legal decisions, I again came across the Dred Scott case and this time found myself wondering, "Who was this man, Dred Scott, a slave, who thought he could sue for his freedom in the white man's courts?" My interest then was mainly academic.

Then in 2002, I met an extraordinary man named Harland Stonecipher, founder and CEO of Pre-Paid Legal Services, and was invited to speak at their annual convention in Oklahoma City.

As Utah Attorney General, I had just redesigned the Seal of the Office around the theme of justice when a friend introduced me to Pre-Paid Legal Services. I was intrigued by a company offering legal insurance founded on the principle emblazoned on the front of the United States Supreme Court, "Equal Justice Under Law," made real by offering all its members direct access to representation by some of the best law firms in the country.

I was so impressed, I asked to meet this man whose vision it was to focus, as I had, on justice.

That evening after my speech, I sat with Harland and his lovely wife, Shirley. I marveled as I discovered that many of the highest achievers in sales and organizations were minorities—in particular, young African Americans. I asked Harland why that was.

He gave two reasons:

1) They have personally experienced injustice and have lived the reality that, too often, money buys access to justice in the courts, and,

2) Many of them are hungry for success, and when given an opportunity to bring justice to their family, neighbors, and associates, they catch fire with enthusiasm.

I noticed a tear in the corner of Harland's eye as he continued, "I am so proud of their success and so grateful to have been inspired to build a company that is based on the true principle promised by the Constitution—'equal justice for all.'"

I returned home to Utah burning with inspiration from Harland Stonecipher and determined to answer my original question.

After five years of research, including travel to all the places where Dred and Harriet Scott lived, I began writing this inspirational story of a man who would not rest until he found justice and freedom in the courts. It is, at the same time, a daring story of the grown children of his first master who loved Dred and risked losing everything in fighting the most powerful pro-slavery families in America—all the way to the United States Supreme Court.

I had to share my hero, Dred Scott, with the world. His is the story of an undying crusade for equal access to justice.

I therefore dedicate this novel to my friend and mentor, Mr. Harland Stonecipher, who today tirelessly crusades for the same.

— Mark L. Shurtleff

Table of Contents

Chronology

1638   George Blow immigrates to Virginia from England and establishes the Blow legacy in America.

1799   A baby slave boy is born on the Blow plantation and is named Samuel by his proud mother, Hannah. On this same night, Thomas Jefferson and James Madison are guests of the Blows.

1805   Louisiana Purchase opens up millions of acres to westward expansion.

1813   Sam fights against the British in the Battle of Crancy Island with his master, Captain Peter Blow.

1820   Congress passes the Missouri Compromise, which admits Missouri and Maine as slave and free states respectively. No other territories above the 36th Parallel (southern border of Missouri) can enter the Union as slave states. The Peter Blow family immigrates down the Tennessee River to Huntsville, Alabama, and clears land for a new plantation. Sam changes his name to Dred after an accident involving his brother.

1830   The Blow family moves to St. Louis, Missouri, joining tens of thousands of Americans heading west.

1832	Dred marries for the first time, but his wife is sold away from him. Shortly thereafter, Dred is sold to Army Dr. John Emerson to pay debts left upon the death of Peter Blow.
1833	Dred goes with Dr. Emerson to the military post Fort Armstrong in the free state of Illinois, and, while there, takes upon himself the last name of "Scott."
1836	Dred and Dr. Emerson are transferred further north to Fort Snelling in Wisconsin Territory (modern-day Minnesota.)
1837	Dred marries the beautiful Harriet Robinson, whose master is also stationed at the Fort Snelling and who gives Harriet to Dr. Emerson to keep her with her husband.
1838	Dred and Harriet's first daughter, Eliza, is born on a steamboat while traveling on the Mississippi River.
1840	Dr. Emerson is transferred to a fort in Florida, but leaves his wife and the Scotts in St. Louis.
1846	The Scotts' second daughter, Lizzie, is born, and Dred begins to seek out his freedom, beginning his long fight in the court system. Dr. Emerson dies and leaves Dred and Harriet to his wife, Irene, who asks her brother, John Sanford, to help her manage her affairs.
1847	The courts rule for Irene Emerson, and the Scotts remain in slavery, but prepare for a new trial.

1850	After much waiting and preparation, the court system proclaims Dred and Harriet to be free. Irene Emerson moves away and leaves matters in her brother's hands, and he appeals the court's decision.
1852	The court reverses its decision, and the Scotts are taken back into slavery. Sanford meets up with them later and whips them severely, inspiring the Scotts to try once again to sue for their freedom, this time in the Supreme Court.
1856	Arguments begin in the Supreme Court on the now-famous case, Scott vs. Sandford.
1857	The court renders it infamous decision on Scott vs. Sandford.
1858	Dred Scott dies of tuberculosis.
1863	Abraham Lincoln, 16th president of the United States, issues the Emancipation Proclamation and frees all slaves, having followed Dred Scott's courageous battle in the Supreme Court and being inspired thereby.

Preface

On November 6, 1860, the people of the United States elected the nominee of the infant Republican Party as their sixteenth president. An obscure lawyer from Illinois, Abraham Lincoln had lost his two prior forays into national politics as a candidate for the U.S. Senate, but in a stunning turnaround that garnered 59% of the electoral votes, Lincoln beat Senator Stephen Douglas and three other candidates, including the incumbent vice president. Many Lincoln scholars and historians believe, as do I, that the single greatest reason for his extraordinary victory was a notorious 1857 decision by the United States Supreme Court in *Scott v. Sandford*.

In a brutal decision that has been called the worst in the history of the court, Chief Justice Roger Taney ruled that a black man was not a man and had no rights a white man was bound to respect. In the famous Lincoln-Douglas debates of 1857, Lincoln made Taney's abhorrent decision the basis of his "house divided" speech.

> *"A house divided against itself cannot stand. I believe this government cannot endure permanently half slave and half free."*

Douglas and the Democrats supported the Supreme Court decision.

In a speech on the case, Lincoln said,

> *"The Republicans inculcate, with whatever of ability they can, that the negro is a man; that his bondage is cruelly wrong, and that the field of his oppression ought not to be enlarged. The Democrats deny his manhood; deny, or dwarf to insignificance, the wrong of his bondage; so far as possible, crush all sympathy for him, and cultivate and excite hatred and disgust against him."*

Northern Democrats and Whigs agreed with Lincoln. They flocked to the Republican Party in the next presidential election and chose the man who would become The Great Emancipator and fight a war to free the Negro. Therefore, it can be claimed with authority that, but for the slave Dred Scott, there would have been no President Abraham Lincoln.

Who was this illiterate slave Dred Scott, born and raised as Sam Blow in southern Virginia, and as a man barely passed five feet tall and a hundred pounds soaking wet; who had the audacity, courage, and faith to persevere for ten years in state and federal court to gain his freedom? What moved him to endure whippings and vile threats and stand erect before a jury of white slaveholders, defiant in appealing the decisions of lofty appellate judges?

The life of Dred Scott is the story of America from the beginning of the 19th century through the Louisiana Purchase, the War of 1812, the Missouri Compromise, The War with Mexico, Bloody Kansas, and culminating in the War Between the States.

It is also a moving personal tale of the life of a slave who wanted to be treated as a man, and, when he became a husband and a father, would stop at nothing in his quest for freedom for the girls he loved more than his own life.

Part I

DEEP RIVER

"Deep River, my home is over Jordan,
Deep River, Lord; I want to Pass over to Camp Ground."

- Slave prayer on marker stone at slave
cemetery on site of Peter Blow Plantation,
Oakwood College, Huntsville, AL

"The source of the American River is the pure, clear,
dream of freedom, and justice and mercy; the lifeblood
of a visionary embodiment of human hunger for a
better life; the powerful current of this notion, this
nation, indelibly carving its course into the landscape
of the world."

- Kris Kristofferson, <u>The Source</u>, from the
album "American River," by Jonathan Elias

Dred Scott

Chapter 1

Let My People Go

St. Louis, 1852

To him, the river sang. It intoned but one word, repeated with every ripple and lap and tide. One word that began with a gurgle far to the north, crescendoed through the heart of a nation, and climaxed in the Deep South with such force that no power on earth could hold it back. One word that bled from every pore. One word: *FREEDOM!*

The Father of Waters sang, not with the splash of waves lapping against the levee, for the Mighty Mississippi was wide and thick and slow. It slid like a solid mass of glacial mud that had been moving toward the sea since before the Fall of Adam. It was ancient by the time Moses led the children of Israel out of slavery in Egypt. No, its melody was something more profound and timeless, and it harmonized with something deep inside Dred and filled his very being so he was powerless to ignore it. He turned toward the river, closed his eyes, and whispered the song of the slave.

"Go down Moses. Way down in Egypt land.
Tell ole Pharaoh,
to let my people go!
When Israel was in Egypt land,
Let my people go!
Oppressed so hard they could not stand.
Let my people go!

"Thus spoke the Lord, bold Moses said.
If not, I'll smite your firstborn dead.
Let my people go!
No more in bondage shall they toil.
Let my people go!
Let them come out with Egypt's spoil.
Let my people go!"

Dred's pearly smile widened as he contemplated the wide brown expanse. "That old Moses sho' 'nuff wouldn't have to part the Mississippi like he done the Red Sea to lead his people to freedom. I reckon they could've walked right across it, so thick is that river with silt and trees and wrecks of a thousand steamers."

He turned the key to lock the back door of the law offices, returned it carefully to its secure spot with the three other keys on the chain around his neck, tucked it under his shirt, and patted their form against his chest—just to be sure. He closed his eyes and breathed in deeply, wondering if what called him was more earthly than spiritual. He had to admit he loved the pungent odors that rose up Market Street, lifted by a breeze out of the east. Many newcomers to St. Louis were nearly overcome by the feral scent of muskrats and turtles, churned with loamy mud and moldy rot, roasted in the greasy smoke and oily pitch from the scores of steamboats lining the quay, sometimes three deep, for a mile up and down the river.

Others might hold their noses, but not Dred. He had spent most of his life on or near great rivers and small streams: from the swampy Gum Branch of the Nottoway river in southern Virginia where he was born, down the wild Tennessee, and up the stately Ohio, to now—nearly two decades on the greatest of them all— "that old brown man," the Mississippi. It sounded kind of funny, but he thought it smelled downright delicious. He often kidded with the girls that whenever he got "a-hungering, I love to cut me a slice of Mississipp' and fry it up with onions and okra." Then he'd send them into peals of laughter as he danced a little jig, bouncing from one foot to the other and crying, "Oh Lordy, I've et so much river mud that if my feet touch the ground too long, they will grow roots right into the floor!"

The thought of onions and okra set Dred's middle to rumbling, and he turned his attention immediately toward home where Harriet was sure to be putting the final touches on a thick, juicy dinner. He leaped off the porch like a man half his age, stuck out his chest, and stretched out his short legs in a stride that he had manufactured twenty years earlier at the time he changed his last name to Scott in mimicry of the stride and the pride of General Winfield "Great" Scott. Although the general was a foot taller and two hundred pounds heavier, Dred had always believed deep in his heart that he, too, was destined for greatness. Though he was a tiny slave, why not act the part of a great man, he'd reasoned. He slowed up a bit when three large men passing on the opposite side of the street eyed him evilly. His left cheek twitched in memory of the times this manner of walking had gotten him thrashed.

The setting sun glistened off his taut skin and reflected a golden brown on the left side of his face as he moved along Third Street past the solid St. Louis Cathedral. He'd worked hard that day polishing all the brass at the offices of his employers and smiled in anticipation of the praise he'd hear in the morning for a job well done. "My 'employers,'" he chuckled as he patted once again his chest and felt the firm outline of the keys. "Thank'e Lord Jesus!" he exclaimed, not caring that a covey of solemn white ladies scowled at him, and he turned quickly toward the cathedral. He couldn't have been prouder had he been carrying the Holy Grail because of what those tiny skeleton keys represented.

Just over two years had passed since that January day in 1850 when a jury of white folk—most of them slave owners—had declared that under the laws of the state of Missouri, since he and his wife had been taken to states and territories where slavery was outlawed, and therefore since they were once free, they were thereafter always and forever free. A man of great passion, Dred clutched his breast and shouted "Hallelujah" at the thought. As a free man he was paid for his labors. More importantly, he was trusted to clean, care for, and secure the property of white men, and he would be recognized and even praised for his efficiency and attention to detail. That was to Dred a miracle when he considered that from the moment his mammy brought him screaming into this land of sorrow, he had been the property of white men.

If only old Hannah could see him now! What joyous rapture would overcome her to see that he was in body the man she always told him he was in the Lord's eyes. A *man!* Not the beast of burden she had often bemoaned bringing into a world of degradation and despair. She taught him all the stories of the Bible, but the one that moved him most was of Moses and the Israelites. Surely the mighty miracles of God that freed His people from the Egyptians could not have been greater than the miracle of a skinny, illiterate slave who, having been the property of white men for over forty years, would be freed by white men in a court of law in the slave state of Missouri—then handed the key that opened the door to the white man's world!

As Dred crossed wide Market Street and turned to look down its gentle slope to the river, he caught his breath at the giant shadow he cast. "Go down Moses," he began again. "Way down in Egypt land. Tell ole Pharaoh, to let my people go!"

Then just as suddenly, his shadow disappeared into a larger, darker shade, for the sun had set behind the massive dome of the St. Louis courthouse. He would never be rid of that familiar chill that shot through his limbs and out the top of his head, causing even his thick black hair to tingle and stand on end. He tried to swallow as he turned to gaze at the east entrance, but he had no spittle. He felt cold perspiration on his forehead, and he was suddenly damp under his arms.

"Dred Scott," he chastised himself, "shame on you! You needs to get shet of that old feelin' of bondage. That edifice be the place of you' freedom!"

Indeed, Dred was troubled by the spontaneous apprehension he felt whenever he walked past that beautiful symbol of justice, in which he had successfully trusted. And what a magnificent structure it was. It dominated the St. Louis skyline at the crest of the hill that gently rose from the banks of the river, and declared to all the world travelers who had gaped in wonder as trade had passed up and down the river that this was truly the gateway to the west and a city with which to be reckoned.

It angered Dred that he still felt fear whenever he passed this monumental embodiment of the United States of America, for he had been taught by his former masters of the promises and ideals it represented. He had been in many courthouses, especially in Virginia and Alabama with his first master, Peter Blow. And it was

Master Blow who taught him it was only in such buildings that men could seek the justice, opportunity, and equality promised by the Founding Fathers. He would never forget the day they were leaving the courthouse in Jerusalem, the seat of Southampton County, Virginia, when Master Blow turned to him and told him that Thomas Jefferson himself, the author of the Declaration of Independence who penned the "self-evident truth" that "all men are created equal," had visited the Blow plantation at The Olde Place the night Dred Scott was born as Sam Blow. Master Blow was always quick to point out that Jefferson, and the Declaration, were not speaking of the black man, but Dred felt for himself that one could indeed find satisfaction and fairness inside a court, and he had never stopped believing the day would come when *all men* would be granted that blessing.

Dred's mammy, Hannah, had always taught him that "not one sparrow ever fell to the ground without God knowin' it, and He numbered every one of the hairs on you' head."

Dred believed it was no small coincidence that his first experience with a courthouse was in a city named after the place where Jesus himself walked and taught of justice, mercy, and freedom from "that ol' stick," the devil. Indeed, it must have been divine providence that he had been born halfway between Jerusalem and the little Virginia town of Bethlehem. It was Dred's journeys to Jerusalem with Master Blow that bred his conviction that in the hallowed halls of the courthouse, he and his people could someday find equality, fairness, and freedom.

And so it had been for him in a magnificent building that could house four Jerusalem courthouses. He forced a smile on his lips and tried to keep his eyes on the wonderful dome wreathed in sunlight, but he could not stop his eyes from dropping into the shadows of the east steps where earlier this very day his people had been poked, prodded, pinched, and fondled like animals; where large and powerful men could not gaze into the eyes of wizened slave traders without fear of the lash or the stick; and where, most horrible of all, children had been ripped from the breasts of their mammies and sold away down the river, never to be seen again. Despite his great effort, tears sprang to his eyes, and a soft "Sarah" slipped off his lips. He forced himself to turn away. He realized this frontier marvel to human greatness would always be to him a profound irony. It would forever be the symbol of his greatest joy and deepest sorrow.

Cotton Levee

Chapter 2

Am I Not a Man?

St. Louis Levee, 1852

Knowing he could not go home feeling as he did, he turned instead to the source of his strength. "Trust not in the arm of flesh," he heard his mammy quote. "Trust only in the Lord God that gave you life." God was evident not in the handiwork of man, but was surely evident everywhere in nature, and the Mississippi was to Dred the greatest evidence of God's power. It could be neither controlled nor tamed by man. It brought life to a nation, and it was no respecter of persons. When a steamboat ran aground on one of its constantly shifting sandbars, or a boiler blew, the river sucked white and black, bond and free alike, down to its murky depths.

What's more, while moving upon it, Dred had always been sought after and respected, even as a slave, for his seamanship and ease with knot and line and sounder. And, of course, it was on a steamship chugging up the Giver of Life that his oldest daughter, Eliza, was born. He felt warmth spread over him, and he straightened as he walked from the rapidly dissipating shadow of the courthouse which completely disappeared before it touched the river's edge.

Most of the steamboat commerce of the day was done as Dred stepped onto the rough, angled bricks that formed the levee. In 1852, the St. Louis riverfront was the second busiest port on the Mississippi River. Every day, dozens of steamboats pulled up to the sloping quay, lowered their long ramps—called "stages,"—from their suspension derrick poles, and disgorged passengers and produce to take on more of the same: huge sacks of cotton seed, tobacco hogsheads, barrels of peanuts, beans, black-eyed peas, and all manner of livestock. Dred was glad the human livestock from the day's auctions, in their chains and misery, had already headed downriver. The guilt in his own freedom was often a very brutal master.

He nodded to several giant roustabouts he recognized, and then climbed a pile of sacks full of cotton seeds. He didn't feel much like talking with anyone today. He sat on the top with his legs dangling over and watched the river, letting its eternal movement soothe his soul. He took a deep breath and felt the mystical power of cotton, which to Negroes was a powerful "conjure," or folk medicine. On an urge, he felt in his right pocket for the cotton ball he kept there as a constant reminder of his marriage to Harriet, and almost without thinking, he poked a hole in a sack and scooped out a handful of seeds he would carry for good luck the next time he went fishing. Thoughts of Harriet and fishing put a satisfaction on him that would be hard to break.

He chuckled as a large hog, which had to weigh well over a hundred pounds, squealed and struggled on the shoulders of one giant roustabout. Several other dockworkers lined up, assembly-style, rolling barrels of molasses aboard the steamer *Nodaway*. He smiled at his fond recollection of his boyhood along the banks of the Nottoway River in Virginia and wondered at the name, and the coincidence, of seeing this boat on the quay that day.

The fading sunlight glistened on skin stretched taut over thick muscles chiseled by years of heavy labor. Nearly every back was crisscrossed with the brutality of the lash and the stick. Dred had long ago stopped envying the size and strength of field hands. At five foot four inches and barely a hundred pounds, Dred had been removed from the cotton fields of southern Virginia as a young man and had learned the more refined and less physically demanding duties of a house slave. Working under the gaze of Master and his family, he was spared the predictable cruelty of the overseer. The sudden tingling along the ragged ridges on his chest and arms checked that thought. He flinched as he recalled the one time, twenty-two years ago, that suddenly seemed like yesterday.

He pounded his fist on the sack and rolled over on his stomach—unconsciously snuffing the heat of the embers that still glowed under his own ligatures. It was best to let the mystical cotton seed force those memories back into the closet in his heart. It did him no good to dwell on a past that was gone forever. He was free now, and so were his wife and children; and while he felt pain for those large men who were whooping and hollering after getting the last barrels of the day on board, he found some peace in the belief that his successful case might be a light for others to follow "'cross the River Jordan" to freedom. The embers on his chest cooled, and he rolled onto his back and looked up at the darkening sky.

The thought of Harriet and his girls urged him to get along home, but the very fact that he could lie here, arms crossed behind his head, staring up at the first star of the coming night, feeling the power of "King Cotton," and listening to the sounds of the river he loved, was something a free man could choose to do.

"I am a man." He smiled. "And no other man can force me to move off this here cotton throne against my will!"

The blast of a steam-whistle shook him from his reverie, followed by the familiar cry of the leadsman on an approaching steamboat. "Mark ta-ree!"

Dred rolled and swung his legs over the sacks to watch the approach. Having heaved the lead and sung the marks on several boats himself, he knew what came next.

"Quarter-less-ta-ree!"

The whistle sounded again, the timbre resonating life. He would forever associate that sound with the hearty cry of his newborn Eliza and the fond memory of a kind pilot who let Dred blow the whistle on the *Gypsy* to announce the miracle of birth fourteen years earlier. And most miraculous to Dred was that the tiny infant, though born to slaves, was born on the river north of the state of Missouri, and therefore, born free!

"Mark twain!" The leadsman signaled that the Mississippi bed was two fathoms, or twelve feet, below the bottom of the boat. Dred waited for the call of "quarter-less-twain" as the boat inched toward shore against the strong current, but was surprised instead to hear a familiar voice calling his own name.

"Sam," hollered a voice from Dred's past, the sound of his slave name cracking like the whip of oppression. "Halloo! Sam!"

When he did not acknowledge the salutation, Peter Blow called him by his free name. "Hey, Dred! Dred Scott!"

His heart stopped for a moment when he turned and saw Master Peter waving his arms and stumbling toward him on the jaggedly sloping bricks of the quay. He immediately realized it wasn't his old master, but his younger namesake, Peter Jr., now grown to resemble his father. But Dred's apprehension doubled when he recognized the three men following closely behind: Peter's brother, Taylor, Dred's employer, Edmund LaBeaume, and his brother, Sheriff Louis LaBeaume.

The Blow children had all married well, and to Dred's amazement and deep gratitude, the Blows and their spouses had made it possible for him to sue for, and gain, his freedom. His second attorney was the widower of Martha Ella Blow. The husband of the oldest surviving Blow child, Charlotte Blow Charless, arranged for his third lawyer, and Peter had married into an old St. Louis family, the LaBeaumes, who were highly successful and well-connected. Edmund was a lawyer who urged his partners, Alexander Field and David Hall, to represent the Scotts on their first appeal to the Missouri Supreme Court, which resulted in a new trial that won his freedom. Brother Louis was sheriff of St. Louis, ironically required by law and Mrs. Emerson to jail the Scotts, then hire them out and collect their wages after they sued her and she moved to Massachusetts. Edmund hired Dred to work as a janitor in his and other law firms, and was the person Dred most admired, as one glorious day two years ago he had looked him square in the eyes, man-to-man, put one hand on Dred's shoulder, and pressed the key into his palm.

Dred knew the Supreme Court had reconvened a few days ago and was expected to rule on Missus Emerson's appeal. The approach of the men could only mean that they had decided. Dred jumped down off the cotton seed sacks and nearly gave in to the urge to bolt for the river and never look back until he reached the free Illinois shore. But these men had been his friends and—Dred reached up and grabbed the key through his shirt—they had trusted him. He could now see their faces, and to his dismay, their countenances were dark and sorrowful.

Before Dred could speak, Edmund reached him, enveloped him in his arms, and wept.

"Oh, my dear friend," he whispered in Dred's ear. "I am so sorry, but two of the three justices ruled against you. They have overturned the decision of the jury and have ordered that you and Harriet be returned to slavery!"

Dred felt the life flow out of him. He couldn't move and was certain that if Mr. LaBeaume hadn't been holding onto him so tight, he would've slipped right out of his arms and onto the cobblestones. Peter stepped up and gently urged Dred to sit down on a barrel.

"Charlotte is with Harriet and the girls," Peter comforted, "and we want you to know we will not give up!"

At the mention of his family, Dred felt a flush of anger that steeled his frame and brought him to his feet.

"With all respect, Massa Peter, you been a good friend, an' yo' family looked after me and mine these six years since we first went to court, but I'm done trustin' in the law. Harriet and me could've run from Massa Emerson a dozen times when he left us up in 'Sconsin Territory, and right here in St. Louis. We been free two years, and still we stayed and trusted in the court. Well, I don't trust it no more! No, suh!"

He turned back to Edmund. "How can these judges choose not to follow the law? You and the other lawyers told me that the law in Missura was that once free—always free! Harriet and I knowed a slave gal at Fort Snelling, name of Rachel, who was taken there by her Army massa—just like us. And this here court says she's free. Why not us? No, this ain't right! This here is of the devil, for sho'!"

Dred's tear-filled eyes had grown wide, and he tensed like a wild animal cornered with no way out. The sheriff moved closer, and Dred heard for the first time the unmistakable clank of chains. He flinched at the ring of slavery, took a step back, and then focused on the cuffs and ankle irons dangling from Louis LaBeaume's fist. He began to shake in fear and rage as he looked in the sheriff's eyes, but relaxed as he found there not the anger, hatred, and disdain he had seen in the eyes of most white men, but only sorrow and pity. The obvious compassion disarmed Dred, drained the fight out of him, and resignation crept in.

"You come to chain me up like a mongrel? Why you have to do that, Sheriff?"

"I'm sorry, Dred," Louis replied, "but Miz Emerson's lawyers convinced the judges you would try to run, and I was ordered to put these on and take you to jail until we can figure out what we're gonna do next. I've been your friend too, Dred, and it kills me to do this, but the law's the law."

"Law?" Dred groaned as the tears now burst from his eyes. "There ain't no law fo' the likes of me."

"There is law for you, Dred," Taylor interjected. "I believe that, or I wouldn't a testified for you in the first trial. But these judges have ignored law for political reasons. They claim, 'times now are not as they were.' Times are changing, Dred, and white men will be shedding the blood of white men before too long over the evil of slavery."

"This is a temporary setback, Dred," Peter added. "Taylor and I have talked to our brothers and sisters, and we're going to offer to buy your freedom and that of Harriet and Eliza and Lizzie. I hear Miz Emerson went and married an abolitionist Yankee in Massachusetts. Maybe he'll order her brother, Mr. Sanford, to just free ya'll outright."

Dred felt a seed of hope sprouting as he fished in his pocket for the cotton ball he had carried since that night at Fort Snelling when Major Taliaferro had married him and Harriet in a white man's ceremony. He looked at it, and then clenched it in his fist.

"Harriet has always been my rod and my strength. She kept me fightin' and trustin'. She says if we can't trust the law, maybe we should trust the Lord."

The irons clanked again as Sheriff LaBeaume moved close. "It's gittin' late, Dred. We've got to git you back."

A profound sadness replaced Dred's anger as the sheriff knelt and closed the irons around his ankles. His flesh shrunk away from the cold steel, and just like that, the freedom in which he had so rejoiced and celebrated that very day was ripped from his heart and pulled with the weight of the chains down through the cobbled quay to the gates of Hell. With his freedom, so too went his humanity.

Dred felt for the key, ripped it from under his blouse, and held it out to Edmund. "Am I not a man like you?" he cried. "When I cleans yo' office, do'n' I feel the pride of a job well done by my own hands, just like you when you wins a case?"

Edmund could not reply, but took the key and turned away. A donkey brayed hysterically, and they all turned to see several black roustabouts knocked by the animal off the plank and into the muddy water, cussing and hollering. Without thinking, the white men laughed at the scene.

Dred didn't laugh.

"Am I not a man? Am I like that mule?" Dred implored, turning his gaze back on the sheriff, who averted his eyes as he clanked the cuff shut on Dred's left wrist.

"Why, he don't even know he a beast of burden. But I does, Massa LaBeaume, I does!"

Louis could only mumble a feeble, "Oh, Dred, don't call me Massa," as he locked the cuff on Dred's other wrist. Looking at his thin arms lost in the cruel iron, Dred flinched as he relived the pain and remembered the blood that had run thickly off his hands after he was caught hiding in the swamp. He turned and dropped to his knees before his dear friends Peter and Taylor Blow.

"Am I not a man, and a brother?" Dred held up his manacled hands to Peter. "You seen me bleed, Petey, and you knows I stopped yo' bleedin' many times when you was small and came to me cryin' after a fall. Do'n' I bleed jes' like you?"

Peter could not answer, and Dred turned to Taylor. Tears broke from Taylor's eyes and rolled down his face. Dred tasted salt at the corner of his own mouth.

"Taylor, did my eyes not drop the same tears when yo' big sissy Mary passed when you was only nine? I held you by her grave, and you buried yo' little face against my cheek, and our tears flowed together, Taylor! Was our hearts and tears not one that day?"

Taylor choked and turned away.

The lightning bugs danced about them as Louis lifted Dred to his feet by the arm to lead him back up Market Street to the city jail. Dred watched the last of the roustabouts grab the sacks of cotton seed he had been resting on and muscle them onto their scarred backs for loading on the boats heading down river—down to the cotton plantations, down to the Deep South and the endless days and the whip and the plow and the auction block. He stretched his tethered hands and felt for the seeds in his pocket he had hoped would bring him luck. Pulling them out, he let them drop onto the stones and thought proudly, *At least that's thirty seeds that won't bring no pain, and that's a start, ain't it?*

Dred took one last, long look at the Mighty Mississippi barely visible in the dusk but moving along, powerful and unchanging. The Father of Waters, the Giver of Life. Dred's Jordan River of freedom moved him to prophesy. He straightened up all the way to his five-foot-four frame, squared his shoulders, held his head high, and said to his three friends-turned-masters:

"I will answer my own question. *I am a man!* And there burns within my soul a fire for freedom so fierce that no man, no court, no law, no earthly judge, can ever douse this desire to be *free!* In fact," Dred nodded toward the river, "all the water in that Mighty Mississipp' could never quench this inferno a' burnin' in my bosom!"

Part II

At the Threshold

"How is freedom measured, in individuals as in nations? By the resistance which has to be overcome, by the effort it costs to stay aloft. One would have to seek the highest type of free man where the greatest resistance is constantly being overcome: five steps from tyranny, near the threshold of the danger of servitude."

- Friedrich Nietzche

"For many men that stumble at the threshold are well foretold that danger lurks within."

- William Shakespeare

Harriett Robinson Scott

Chapter 3

I Am a Man!

Old St. Louis Jail, 1852

The spirit power of the river seemed to ebb as night descended and the sound of flowing water was replaced by the skittering of rats. Gone were the broad levees, replaced by jailhouse bars. The embers in Dred's soul glowed hot, but his spirit waned as he sat on the cold dirt floor. What could be worse, he pondered, than to have tasted the sweet savor of freedom, and then to have it ripped away? The loss was nearly more than he could bear. Dred leaped to his feet and rushed headlong into the bars, and cried and beat upon the unforgiving iron.

THUD! "I am a man!" he screamed, but the heavy walls absorbed his protest, and no one heard.

WHUMP! "I ain't no stupid jackass!"

THUD! "I ain't no dumb hog. I knows better!" he moaned. But only a greasy rodent paused to notice, and then scurried away.

He sobbed and pounded until the flesh on his fists tore and the pain in his hands began to overshadow the pain in his heart. He stopped and looked down at the thick, dark blood dripping from his mangled flesh onto the hard-packed clay. It caught the shimmering light of the gas lamp in the corridor and held it for just a moment before it sank into the earth.

"Dust you is, and to dust you will return," Dred quoted from the Bible. "Lord forgive me for thinkin' I was something I was not. Maybe it be better I died than to think I could be the same as a white man. At least then I'd be truly free."

Dred dropped to his knees, cupped his hands, and began to hum. His mammy's music had always quieted his fears and brought him peace. The prayer of the Negro spiritual formed on his lips and he began to softly sing,

> *"Some o' these mornin's bright and fair,*
> *I thank God I'm free at last.*
> *Gwineter meet my Jesus in*
> *The middle of the air. . ."*

He paused as a shudder of defeat spread down through his body. Death would be a welcome relief.

> *"I thank God I'm free at last."*

Dred prostrated himself on the floor, his face on the wet dirt, his tears and blood and mucus fusing with the earth. Broken and contrite, he pleaded, "Please, God, jes' let me die. Please, Lord, take me to yo' bosom. Oh please, Lord, bring me over Jordan and give me rest. Have mercy, Jesus, and jes' take me away and free my soul!"

He wept softly, and then in a final moment of awful, lonely resignation, he remembered his mammy's teachings and humbly added, "Nevertheless, not my will . . . but yours be done."

Silence, and then the merciful shroud of unconsciousness enveloped him.

* * *

"Dred," a tender voice called. Was it his mammy come to carry him home?

"Dred! Dred Scott! Is you alive? Oh dear Lord, Dred! Please come back to me. I need you. The babies need you!"

Dred stirred. It wasn't his mammy. It was his sweet Harriet calling to him. He slowly raised himself out of the dust, blinked away dirty tears, and looked into the chocolate eyes of his soul mate.

"Oh, thank God Jesus!" Harriet proclaimed as she knelt and reached through the bars. "Dred, you give me a fright! I done thought you was gone and left me 'lone with the girls to fight the devil in this sad and evil place!"

Dred smiled despite himself as his knees met hers through the bars and their eyes locked. "Well, looky here, if it ain't my Joan of Arc," he chuckled. "Ready to wrestle that ol' stick, even now!" He grasped the cold steel bars in his battered hands.

New tears welled as Harriet looked down and gently touched his torn knuckles. "Oh, Dred, what they do to yo' hands?" She suddenly turned a flaming gaze at the people just down the corridor.

"Sheriff Louis! What you done to Dred's hands?" She made to rise, but Dred grasped her arm.

"No, Harriet! Nobody did this but me. Leave the sheriff 'lone. He been kind. He jes' do his job."

"But why, Dred?" Harriet asked as she helped Dred to his feet through the bars. "Why you do that to yourself?" Then, with some anger rising in her voice, "Don't tell me you done give up."

Dred laughed and felt his spirits lift slightly as Sheriff LaBeaume came forward with the keys to the cell. "Oh, Lordy, Sheriff, I guess I'm in real trouble now. Maybe you can protect me from Joan here?"

It was Sheriff LaBeaume's turn to laugh. "I think I'd rather face a lynch mob than Harriet Scott!" His cheeks bloomed scarlet the instant the words left his mouth. "Tarnation! I'm sorry, folks; you know I sometimes speak before I think. Come on, Dred, let's get those hands mended. I got a lot of yer friends here who want to talk. We gotta figure out a plan, and we don't have a lot of time. Yer expected in court first thing in the mornin'."

Dred felt revived as Harriet put her arm around his thin waist to help him down the hall to the office.

"You's freezin', Dred," Harriet complained. She removed her burnoose and covered his skeletal shoulders. "I always told you that you needed more fat on them bones," she lightly scolded.

They entered the warmth of the office where the sheriff had turned up the lamps to illuminate several people crammed into the tiny place. The light on the white faces glowed warm with care and concern . . . and something else. Was it hope? Dred almost didn't dare believe it.

"Daddy!" shrieked six-year-old Lizzie as she bolted from behind the bell-shaped crinolines of Charlotte's full skirt. Lizzie rammed into Dred's legs and squeezed with a death grip surprising in one so tiny. "Is you okay, Daddy?" Lizzie looked up, and Dred nearly fainted, so overcome was he with the joy of uncontrollable love.

"Daddy is fine, Lizzie-girl." Dred held her with his forearms, careful not to mar her soft brown curls with his bloody hands.

"Your hands look awful sore, Daddy." Eliza stepped forward. Her fourteen years kept her from rushing headlong into her father's arms, but her love was as powerfully evident in her compassion as was Lizzie's childish fervor. "Come sit here, and let me tend to them," she ordered.

It never ceased to amaze Dred how mature his "Little Gypsy" had grown. She was sweet and caring and motherly. He winced at the realization that she was old enough to be a mother, and now that she was no longer free, she could be sold away to a man, with all the horror and degradation that could entail to one still so young and innocent.

"See, Daddy," Eliza cooed when she saw him wince. "You're in a lotta pain, and I can help."

Dred wouldn't allow himself to react, fighting mightily to hide the source of his real pain as he sat down at the small table and watched Eliza wet a cloth in the basin and begin ever so tenderly to bathe his wounds. He took a deep breath and looked up at the surprising confidence in the faces of his gathered friends.

"It looks like y'all has a plan," he said with a smile. The hopelessness and despair of a short time ago seemed to evaporate. "Mind if I'm a part of it?"

The group did have a plan. Crowded into the small St. Louis jail that early spring evening were most of the key players who had stood by and helped Dred and Harriet through the last six years of legal battle. All of them were related in some way, through marriage or business, to the children of Dred's first masters, Peter and Elizabeth Blow. At forty, Charlotte was the eldest of the Blow children. Her husband, Joseph Charless Jr., had been a partner with her brothers in the Charless, Blow & Co. drug and paint store. He was an officer of the Bank of Missouri, which had enabled him to sign as security for the Scotts on legal documents they had filed.

Also present in the jail that night were the two Blow brothers, Peter and Taylor. They had been like younger brothers to Dred throughout the years in Virginia, Alabama, and in St. Louis until

31

their parents died and Dred was sold to pay the debts left by their father. These Blow boys, very successful businessmen, had joined with their sisters in their attempt to help Dred win his freedom after his return from first St. Louis, then Texas, as slave of U.S. Army surgeon Dr. John Emerson.

Rounding out the meeting that night was the Scotts' newest lawyer, Roswell Field, the sixth, thus far. The Scotts had been represented before the Missouri Supreme Court by David Hall, who had passed away the previous spring, and by Alexander Field, who had recently moved to Louisiana. Needing an attorney's advice on what options remained, Peter's partner and brother-in-law, Edmund, had once again gone looking. Roswell Field had arrived in St. Louis a few years earlier. Although he did not have a lot of experience or reputation, he had three things that gave the group hope: he was ardently against slavery, he was good friends with the sympathetic Scott trial judge Alexander Hamilton and the dissenting Missouri Supreme Court Justice Hamilton Gamble, and, perhaps most importantly, he had agreed to take the Scotts' case free of charge. Roswell and his wife, Frances, had also become close friends with Peter and Sarah, and their two little sons Teddy and Eugene were the same ages as little Annie and Louis-Auguste LaBeaume.

The room remained quiet as all eyes fastened on the tender scene of Eliza gently cleaning and bandaging Dred's hands, Harriet running her fingers through his hair, and Lizzie slumbering safely on his lap. All in the room had invested heavily in this sweet family, both financially and most significantly, socially, as friends and would-be saviors. Although Dred saw hope in the gathering, his white benefactors feared that having lost in the highest court, contrary to several decades of cases favorable to their cause, they were more likely to "catch a weasel asleep" than ever to win the Scotts' freedom. Each one understood all too well that since Dred's owner, Irene Emerson, had moved to Massachusetts, leaving her affairs in the charge of her wealthy, connected, and ardently pro-slavery brother, John F. A. Sanford, the horrors of the auction block and degradation and separation of this lovely family was as close as the courthouse steps two blocks from where they met.

Sanford had married Eugenie, the daughter of Pierre Chouteau, Jr. and thereby became part of the one of oldest, wealthiest, and largest slaveholding families in St. Louis. In 1764, Pierre's grandfather, Rene Auguste Chouteau, traveled up the Mississippi from New Orleans with his step-father, Pierre Laclede, and established the post that would become St. Louis. Pierre's father had a trading monopoly and supplied most of the needs for Lewis and Clark as they set forth on their journey of discovery. Young Pierre, Jr. accompanied them on several expeditions. As an adult, Pierre Jr. built on his family money by investing largely in the American Fur Company, becoming majority owner when John Jacob Astor sold his interest. With his son-in-law John Sanford as a minority partner, he had reorganized the company in 1838 as Pierre Chouteau, Jr. and Company, ultimately extending their business from the Mississippi to the Rockies and from Texas to Minnesota. By proceeding with the Scotts, the small group would be taking on one of the most powerful slaveholding families in the country at a time when pro- and anti-slavery sentiments were heating to a boiling point. That tiny band stood at a threshold as precarious as the ancient Spartans at the Gates of Thermopile, and they weren't entirely certain it could be crossed.

Eliza finished bandaging her pappy's hands, kissed him on a gray-whiskered cheek, then knelt beside him. The Scotts' anxious eyes were on their friends. Roswell Field waited for Peter or Taylor to begin, but sensed they were overcome by both emotion and fear at what lay ahead. As the only lawyer in the room, and knowing he would be required to appear in court the following morning, he broke the awkward silence.

Henry Taylor Blow

Chapter 4

All Men are Created Equal?

St. Louis Jail, 1852

Roswell pulled a paper out of his coat pocket and spoke to his clients. "Dred and Harriet, let me read my notes of what the Justices said yesterday after their shocking decision. They ordered that the jury decision making you free be reversed, annulled, and for naught held and esteemed, 'and that said appellant'—that would be Irene Emerson and now her brother John Sanford—'be restored to all things which he has lost by reason of said judgment.'" He looked at Dred and Harriet. "That would be you. The court then sent this back to the circuit court for further proceedings."

He folded the paper and returned it to his pocket. "Sanford and Emerson's lawyers have requested a hearing before Judge Hamilton tomorrow morning. As executor of Captain Emerson's estate, Mr. Sanford has now exercised ownership over you. At his demand, you were brought to jail this evening. Tomorrow, his attorneys will ask the judge to order payment of the bonds signed by the LaBeaumes and Blows, and delivery of the money Sheriff LaBeaume has collected and held in trust on your behalf, constituting your salary during the last two years as a free man." He paused, looked into the wide-eyed apprehension of the Scotts, and wished he did not have to continue. He took a deep breath. "They will also demand that all four of you be immediately turned over to Mr. Sanford's and Pierre Chouteau's overseer."

"Noooooo!" Eliza screamed and jumped to her feet, embracing her parents. Lizzie startled awake to a room full of cries, and Charlotte rushed to comfort her.

"Please!" shouted Roswell, trying not to lose control of the gathering. "Please! We must try to remain calm in the face of this storm! I have only known you all for a few years, but I have witnessed your strength and felt your love and your faith, and I implore you to hang on a little longer!"

Dred and Harriet were too overcome to speak.

Taylor found his voice. "Charlotte, please take the children outside." He waited until the door had been closed behind them, but Eliza and Lizzie's terrified wails passed through the walls and into their hearts.

"But Roswell, what can be done?" Taylor asked. "We have already been rebuffed several times in our offer to purchase Dred and his family. How can we now fight the might of the Chouteau family? They're the biggest toad in the puddle! You know Missouri law well by now, as it relates to Negroes. As of today, the state of Missouri does not recognize Dred and Harriet's marriage. Married slaves may be subject to separation by sale without notice. By tomorrow, all four of them could be on the slave block! This is why we wanted to meet tonight. I think we should head out full chisel and get them across the river right now and never look back!"

"Taylor, stop. Think! You know the punishment for aiding slaves to escape, and given the notoriety and divisiveness of this case, there are dozens of traders and ruffians who would hunt Dred and his family down and gladly take out years of anger and hatred."

Roswell noticed that Dred had the look of a trapped animal. He could see the ligaments in his neck contract and the muscles on his arms and legs bunch, ready to spring. He knew he only had a few minutes. He turned and placed both hands squarely on Dred's shoulders. He felt his entire body quivering and wasn't at all certain he could hold him. He noticed Sheriff LaBeaume moving closer.

"Dred, please let me appear on your behalf in the court of law," Roswell pleaded. "I must admit, I don't know all the reasons why you have trusted in the courts these six years, but I'm asking you to trust a little longer. You have a sympathetic ear in Judge Hamilton. I believe him to be a friend. He is known to be personally against slavery, and while I cannot guarantee it, I believe he will deny Sanford's motions tomorrow."

"The risk is too great!" Peter interrupted. "I overheard some of the Chouteau muleskinners bragging they was 'gonna get that uppity Scott and fix his flint good.' Even if there were a way to continue to trust in the courts, how do we fight the wealth of Sanford and his daddy-in-law?"

"We can never stop the vile devils whose hatred for the black man moves them to violence. But you know there are many kind, religious people in this town who, while they hold on to the practice of slavery, do so out of a sense of history and principle and do not approve of violence. Dred and Harriet have developed a powerful reputation among those folks who respect them for obeying our laws and trusting in our legal system. I believe we can protect the Scotts, and I want them to trust a little longer."

Roswell felt Dred's shoulder muscles relax just a smidgen, and he pressed his point. "Dred, I've heard you tell the story of the night you were born, that Thomas Jefferson and James Madison themselves visited the Blow plantation in southern Virginia." He saw Peter and Taylor nodding at the familiar tale. He pushed on. "Those men were the fathers of the Declaration of Independence and our inspired Constitution. Jefferson wrote those true words, Dred: 'All men are created equal.' They staked their lives and their fortunes on their declaration that God himself had endowed *all* men with rights that government could not give or take away: Life! Liberty! Pursuit of Happiness!"

"I knows they said that!" Dred fired back, rising to his feet and throwing off Roswell's hands. "They wrote it! And they shook their fists at King George! And then they fought and they beat mighty England to make their point! Not once, but twice, and me and yo' pa done fought them too, at Craney Island!" He held his hands in front of Roswell's eyes. "But did they mean this color when they said *man?*"

The room was silent as all eyes locked on the angry scar on the palm of Dred's left hand. Everyone knew, and the Blow children remembered, the story they had heard their father tell many times around the family fireplace as Dred served them an evening punch. It was the story of the Battle of Craney Island in the War of 1812 when Dred, not his master, had shed blood in defense of their beloved Virginia.

Roswell did not flinch, and the Blows and LaBeaumes in the room at once realized they had a champion and almost dared to hope. The lawyer gently took Dred's arms, and then his swollen hands, in a firm, brotherly grip. He set down Dred's right hand and touched the jagged welt on the left.

"You bled along with free men, and still you were not free. But to answer your question, yes, Dred, I believe our Founding Fathers did mean *all* men! And what's more, they knew the irony of making those declarations in light of their own slaveholdings. But they were inspired men, and they knew that to beat the mightiest nation on earth, they had to be united. They looked to our day, Dred. They dreamed and prayed for the time when the issue would be resolved, the day when their audacious 'self-evident truth' would become a self-evident reality."

He let go of Dred's hand, grasped him by the shoulders, and looked into his bloodshot eyes. "I believe that day is today, Dred! That day is today," he repeated with solemnity. "And I believe you are the man. You and Harriet and your girls were meant for something grand. Someone, somehow, would eventually have to go to the highest court in the land, all the way to the very symbol of justice guaranteed by Madison and his compatriots in penning the Constitution: The Supreme Court of the United States of America. You are not done! What you have started must be seen through to the end. I'm asking you to trust again. Tomorrow, let me use the law to keep you together, and then let me file your case in the federal courts, and we'll be on our way to Washington D.C.!"

There was not a breath in that small jailhouse. The sobbing had subsided. Wind whistled through the chinks around the windows. No one moved. No one spoke. Roswell began to worry, and then Harriet moved. She slid softly up beside Dred, bent, gently brushed his temple with her lips, and whispered, "Go down Moses, way down in Egypt land . . ."

Part III

We Hold These Truths

"*[Slavery] is a perpetual exercise of the most boisterous passions, the most unremitting despotism on the one part, and degrading submissions on the other.*"

- Thomas Jefferson

Thomas Jefferson

Chapter 5

To Be Born a Virginian

Southampton County, Virginia, 1799

To be born a Virginian in the eighteenth century is about as close as one could ever get to American royalty . . . to New World nobility, if you will," the vice president of the United States proudly declared to his traveling companion. He removed a kerchief from his waistcoat and wiped the sweat from his eyes, which he then focused on the hunched slaves picking cotton in the hazy distance. He sadly shook his head. "Unless, of course, your skin is colored, and your mammy is the property of a white man."

It was a sight Thomas Jefferson had witnessed a thousand times, and one he would never get used to: the overseer dozing in his saddle in the shade of a loblolly pine while stooped Negro men, women, and even children—some whose dark, curly tops were barely visible above the ocean of white—swayed through the drenching heat to the rhythm of the cicada. He slowly shook his head, dismounted, and led his horse down an incline to a small, marshy stream.

"Think about it, Jemmy: American nobility. This God-kissed Virginia soil has given birth to men who would be kings had they been born under the right crest anywhere in Europe, or even the world, for that matter. General Washington, noble Virginian to the core, refused the title of Your Majesty, but will always be called the Father of Our Nation. And you, my friend, are already toasted throughout the land—except perhaps in Adams' Boston—as the Father of the Constitution and of the Bill of Rights."

James Madison managed a smile as he nudged his mount's flank and urged her toward the stream. At forty-six and childless after five years of marriage, any mention of fatherhood carried some pain. Never one to wallow in self-pity, though, he forced a chuckle and swung off his horse, landing with a splash in the bog. He laughed at himself and almost heard the soft titter of his dear Dolly contemplating her bookish husband on another rugged botanical dismounting mid-marsh.

"Don't forget yourself, Tom. Dolly loves to refer to you as the Father of the Declaration of Independence. It would also behoove you not to forget that your new boss, President Adams, had a hand in the founding of the country—and he isn't a Virginian."

"Ha, ha," Jefferson laughed as he tossed his hat high among the hickory branches.

Madison wasn't sure if he was laughing at him as warm water poured into his boots.

A shaft of sunlight fell on Jefferson's reddish hair, setting it alight, and his hazel eyes glowed mischievously. "Stout Johnny Adams is not my boss—he certainly didn't pick me to be vice president. Thank the Good Lord for those three electoral votes that made him president over me." Jefferson chuckled. Prior to the

Twelfth Amendment, presidential and vice presidential candidates ran as a team, but electors had two votes and were not required to vote for the ticket. The man with the most votes became president and the runner-up, as with Jefferson in 1796, was vice president.

Jefferson whistled and continued. "But for those three, I would be stuck in Philadelphia right now instead of traveling the length of our lovely Commonwealth with my good friend on another one of our 'botanicals.' But I deviate. You are right, James, that Adams, and indeed many a good man from New Hampshire to Georgia, could be called 'Father' for their role in the cause of freedom. The difference with Federalists like the president and Alexander Hamilton is that I fear they do cling too much to monarchy and aristocracy."

Jefferson picked up his hat and led his horse back up the hill. He noticed a leafy plant he hadn't seen before, pulled his sketchbook out of the saddlebags, and sat in the shade to draw. Madison waited while his horse finished drinking and let the temptation to respond pass. He knew Thomas to be stridently anti-Federalist, and he, Madison, professed the same Republican politics of the prominence of individual and states rights. He had never known John Adams to act the part of aristocrat. Hamilton, his co-author of the Federalist Papers, was committed to a stronger federal government, but was every bit as patriotic as he and Jefferson.

Madison filled his hat with water and poured it over his head. The water smelled somewhat brackish, but in the still-oppressive September heat and humidity of southern Virginia, it felt marvelous. As he rejoined his companion above the bank, he sensed the vice president had turned solemn once again. Madison sat on a log and waited until Jefferson had finished a rather precise depiction of the strange plant.

"The point I wished to make, Jemmy," Jefferson continued, "was that history will recognize the inherent nobility of so many great

Virginians, including our good friends Patrick Henry, Harry Lee, Monroe, Mason, Wythe—all of them noble, not because of royal birthright, but of a God-given right to liberty by the fact of their birth, and the will to use that freedom to shine! That is what we declared on that hot July day in 1776."

The Father of the Bill of Rights was as quiet and shy as Thomas Jefferson was flamboyant and gregarious. His diffident style had always been underestimated, but not his intellect and ability to come out on top at the end of the day. Patience was a virtue he had perfected, and so he continued to wait for his friend and mentor to finish. After all, he knew what was coming next. He had felt the same irony many times since those heady days of philosophical and moral grandeur in declaring and codifying a nation based on the inalienable rights of men.

Jefferson stood and, after replacing his artwork, mounted, turned his horse, and stared hard at the slaves in the cotton field. Madison stood also and felt the same regret.

"But what of those Virginians, Jemmy? We declared . . . *I* declared, with my own pen, that all men are created equal. But that truth is certainly not a reality, and I tremble for the country I help lead, and for myself, when I reflect that God is just, and His justice cannot sleep forever when the very rights of human nature are deeply wounded by this infamous practice of slavery."

Madison strode to his friend's side and grasped his knee. Looking up into his eyes, he could read the turmoil there. "Tom, we've had this conversation before. You know I consider slavery to be evil, and although both of us are guilty, I believe we must use whatever office, power, or influence we gain in this life to end the practice. Do you recall when Joseph Jones wrote me with the idea of offering a slave to everyone who would enlist in the war for independence?"

Jefferson smiled. "I remember your letter to me in France recounting his request. Tell me again of your response."

Madison reached for his reins, put his left foot in the stirrup and swung himself up into his saddle. "I congratulated Joe and the legislature for their persistence in the cause of recruiting their line of army for the war, but asked rhetorically if it might not be better to liberate the blacks and make them soldiers. I pointed out that it would certainly be more consonant to the principles of liberty which ought never to be lost sight of in a contest for freedom."

"Huzzah! Well said, Jemmy!" Jefferson cried as he reined his mount over and clapped Madison on the back. "Too bad we all didn't follow your advice. We might have won the war sooner. We both know the accounts of many brave free blacks who fought side by side with whites. And if they fight like they work—just imagine! Come, it's getting late. My friends await us." He spurred his horse to the Bethlehem crossroad and reined in. When Madison caught up, Jefferson continued.

"Numerous sections here in the center of Southampton County have been in the possession of various members of the George Blow family for generations, going as far back as the 1630s. To the north lies Tower Hill and The Quarter, to the east is Rose Hill, and beginning right here and running more than a thousand acres to the south is The Olde Place. These Blow plantations form the outline of a diamond sitting midway between Jerusalem, where we crossed the Nottoway River on the Flowers Bridge, and the village of Bethlehem to the west. The Olde Place borders Cross Keys, and then it's North Carolina. Blow lands are some of the oldest, continuously operated interior plantations in Virginia. Before the Blows, this same diamond parcel was the ancient home of the Nottoway tribe of Indians. Think of it, Jemmy—for centuries, this land has fed and provided abundantly for the men and women who lived on it, but it took the Blows to make it produce food and raiment for others well beyond its borders."

From where they sat on Barrow Road, it was difficult for Madison to see much of the land other than the towering oak and hickory draped in various shades of green moss and tangled vines. To have cleared hundreds, and even thousands, of acres out of this dense wilderness was certainly Herculean, and then to make the land produce large quantities of cotton, tobacco, corn, and beans, was to James almost divine.

"These Blows might not be nobility, but they must certainly be Titans." Madison gave voice to his thoughts.

"Indeed, Jemmy," Jefferson replied, "you'll meet several of them tonight. We may be considered part of the illustrious First Families of Virginia, but I understand these Blows go back nearly to the beginning, truly F. F. V. I know you prefer the environment of the library to that of the field, but I also know you share my love for the land, and you've heard me say that those who labor in the earth are the chosen people of God. Well, something tells me the people who made this wilderness between Bethlehem and Jerusalem to blossom as the rose must truly be among the chosen ones!"

Chapter 6

Fathers of the Declaration

Blow Plantation, Southampton County, Virginia, 1799

The two men had been traveling two days since leaving Richmond, through dense forests and across several rivers and swamps. Madison marveled that hearty pioneers had come so far inland and had, by brute force, made this land productive within just a few years of the establishment of Jamestown, where it had all begun.

"How did George Blow and his kin do it, Tom? How could they have tamed this land and made it produce?"

They turned their mounts south toward the main buildings of The Olde Place, where the descendents of George had gathered to receive the distinguished guests. "I'm told that the first George—who, by the way, was cousin to the famous English composer Dr. John Blow whose tomb I've visited in Westminster Abbey—

imported many indentured white servants, but eventually turned to slavery with the rest of the South for economic and manpower reasons. So the story is the same. Slavery is both the boon and bane of our national success."

Keenly aware of the recent slave revolts in Richmond and Fredericksburg, Madison queried, "One wonders if the Negroes will ever succeed in rising up against their masters and shaking off their chains. Can you imagine, Thomas, if they became educated and learned to organize? Aren't there some 350,000 slaves in the Commonwealth alone?"

"That's right, constituting about forty percent of the total population. And if it is ever to be successful, it might start here, where blacks have outnumbered whites for a half-century. You'll recall that, earlier this year, two slave traders were killed right here in Southampton County!"

Jefferson slowed and stopped his horse in front of a lane leading to a large two-story plantation home. They were now directly across the road from the cotton field they had seen from the distant hill. Some of the children stopped picking to stare at the tall rider and his shorter companion. The sun had set behind the large oak trees to the west, but there was still an hour of daylight, and the older slaves didn't let up on the rhythm of the harvest. Jefferson could not pull his eyes away from one emaciated slave who was moving methodically, though somewhat slower than the others, down her row. He hadn't noticed from the distance, but could now tell she was great with child, though delicate of frame. He felt a heaviness of heart returning.

"Have you ever marveled, Jemmy, at how they can work bent over like that for hours with their eyes cast down, fingers burning, backs aching, never stopping to look toward heaven or gaze around them at the beauty of this land?"

"They sure do know how to work," Madison replied, once again feeling a wave of depression and regret start to settle over him. "But it's not their land, and all it has ever brought them is pain, despair, and a weariness that must pass through their bones and penetrate deep down into their very souls."

"So you do truly believe they have souls—just like you and me?"

Madison was somewhat startled by the question. "Most certainly," he declared. "Do you not so believe?"

"Oh, well, of course I do," responded Jefferson, thinking of the slave boy who had been his best friend and companion growing up, and, to this day, managed his stables at Monticello. He stroked his mare's mane which was usually beautifully tended, but had grown matted and tangled during the long trip. He saw Madison watching him.

"Jupiter will have this mane as smooth as silk within an hour of our return. You knew, didn't you, that Jupiter was born the same year as me, and we grew up running the hills, swimming the streams, and climbing the trees together? We were inseparable as lads and remain friends, but we will never get past the fact that I am master, and he, my property. Oh, I am indeed a damned hypocrite!"

"We have trod this path so oft, the rug has truly grown thin, Thomas."

"And it is a path I will wear to my grave," replied the man who had concluded his original draft of the Declaration of Independence with his strongest attack against "the Christian King of England" who was responsible for forcing slavery on the American colonies, and thereby violating "the most sacred rights of life and liberty in the persons of a distant people who never offended him."

"I tried to include the Negro and his plight in the Declaration," Jefferson continued, "but my fellow slaveholders, most notably the delegates from Georgia and South Carolina, insisted it be removed, thus beginning the great 'compromise' that would be carried into your Constitutional Convention committee of eleven. I know I am a hypocrite, James, but I do believe the black man was created by the same God and endowed by that Creator with the same unalienable rights of life, liberty, and the pursuit of happiness. I had hoped the practice could have been ended through the process of establishing a Constitution. But I know how hard the debate was and that a practicable solution could not be agreed upon."

"You know not how true that is," interrupted Madison, slightly surprised at his bravado, but both men recognized James was the ultimate authority on the Constitutional Convention. He wasn't about to let Thomas enjoy the pity party alone. After all, it was he who was there in Philadelphia, not Thomas, who had been in France negotiating for crucial support of the newborn nation. It was James Madison who became the leader, the deal maker, the intellect, and the "author" of the Constitutional Convention. And James knew that when it came to the issue of slavery, there was plenty of hypocrisy and regret to go around.

Notwithstanding the fact that many of the delegates from the North were, or had been, slaveholders, they were firm in their belief that slavery was both evil and certainly contrary to the freedoms they had fought for in the Revolution. Many still felt the bitter taste of irony as they recalled the criticisms from across "the Pond," such as that from one Samuel Johnson who had cried, "How is it that we hear the loudest yelps for liberty from the drivers of Negroes?"

These delegates counted as chief among their goals for a national constitution the immediate cessation of the slave trade, a requirement that a state must outlaw slavery before it could be considered for entry into the Union, and the establishment of a plan and a timetable for the abolition of slavery. Delegates were inflamed with the righteousness of their cause and declared loudly, and often, that slavery was a "curse." In the words of John Adams, slavery was "a foul contagion of the human character." Men like Adams, who recognized that this intransigent position would prove the greatest stumbling block in the path of "we the people" in forming "a more perfect union," sought to win over the Virginia delegation by reminding them of the words of their *in absentia* leader. He claimed Jefferson's passages against slavery in *Notes on the State of Virginia* were "worth diamonds." Adams felt that Jefferson's words, penned while his slaves worked in the fields, might bring some compromise from the other slave-holding delegates. He quoted from memory, "The whole commerce between master and slave is . . . the most unremitting despotism on the one part, and degrading submission on the other. . . . If a slave can have a country in this world, it must be any other in preference to that in which he is to be born to live and labor for another . . . or entail his own miserable condition on the endless generations proceeding from him. . . . Indeed, I tremble for my country when I reflect that God is just: that his justice cannot sleep forever."

Although Jefferson was in France and would not participate in the Convention, his words and his reputation as the Father of the Declaration had a persuasive effect, but mostly with those who happened to agree. Both sides used his reason to support their goals for drafting the Constitution. For that reason, the Southern delegates were unmoved by his attitude about slavery and easily dismissed it as lacking persuasive effect, given the fact that he owned more slaves than any of them. So they fired back with their own select offerings from Thomas Jefferson, primarily his focus on the preeminence of individual rights and that the greatest power ought to lie with the states, and not with a federal government that would tell them whether or not they could choose to continue to own slaves as essential to their economic growth. They were inflamed with the passion of their own self-righteousness built on the foundation of their God-given rights to own property, and their individual rights to be free from the oppression of the national government. After all, hadn't they just bled and died to rid themselves of the oppression of a strong, unbending, Federalist power that wanted to control every aspect of their lives? Given the chasm that existed between the delegates, it is no wonder that so many have referred to the success of that Constitutional Convention as "the Miracle at Philadelphia."

What was miraculous was that these delegates, who were committed to forming a more perfect union and a new nation, conceived in liberty, were able to reach a compromise that would allow each to claim victory and give birth to a new nation that, in theory, was based on justice, but avoided the issue of slavery altogether. Some would say that the Northern delegates gave up their principles, but in fact, in exchange for leaving the question of slavery unaddressed in the Constitution, they—or rather those serving on the last Confederation Congress that was meeting at the same time—were to pass the Northwest Ordinance which prohibited slavery north of the Ohio River. Those from the North could therefore boast that they had moved significantly down the road to prohibiting slavery in all new states, and the politicos of the South could argue back home that they had drawn a line and persuaded the Yankees to leave them to self-determination and thereby tacitly approved Southern slavery.

Of course the delegates to the Constitutional Convention knew they could not take complete credit for the actions of the closing Confederation Congress, and so the great compromise of the convention delegates was for those from the South to give in to the demands of the New Englanders to only require a majority vote of Congress on issues relating to the regulation of commerce, as opposed to the two-thirds majority demanded by the South. Shipping was so critical to the economic survival of the Southern states that they greatly feared Congress could too easily pass laws regulating sea-born commerce that would hurt them. Nevertheless, they agreed, but only upon the Northerners' agreeing to their demand that Congress extend the slave trade another twenty years, and that non-white inhabitants would only count as "three-fifths" of a person for purposes of apportioning seats in Congress.

And so it was done. The great divide was bridged, if only for a season, but having crossed that span, the delegates were free to concentrate on drawing up a governmental structure and a legal charter that would give this great new experiment in democracy and the rule of law a chance to succeed.

And succeed it had. The first decade had seen the peaceful transition of the presidency from the giant, nearly mythical hero and father George Washington of Virginia, through a tough partisan battle of Federalist and anti-Federalist ideologues, to the short, stout, intellect John Adams of Massachusetts. Thus the new nation had weathered the first great test of any government, and one that so many nations had failed—an orderly transfer of power without violence or bloodshed.

And here in Virginia rode two friends who had played so pivotal a role in the creation of America, but had lost in their first contest to lead the United States from their political perspective. They traveled, not to inflame their fellow countrymen to revolt, but to visit and learn and study the land and the people, to look to the future and another election, perhaps the opportunity to yet lead.

Thinking back on what they had accomplished in Philadelphia, what they had sadly left undone, and what the future might portend, Madison next did what he was known for. He summed up the birth of a nation with its beauties and its sorrows. "I know how much importance you have put in the Great Compromise

55

between large state and small state representation, Thomas, but to me, the Sectional Compromise might be even greater. Had the slavery debate not been taken off the table, we would not have succeeded in finalizing a Constitution, and this glorious union of states would not have been possible. Still, I walked out of that convention unsatisfied and have hungered for a solution these ten years. It hurts that we acquiesced to evil—a necessary evil, but evil nonetheless. I have committed by all I hold dear that I will do all I can, before I return to my Creator, to put an end to that evil."

Jefferson felt the sting of that unintended rebuke and was glad the conversation was at an end. With a click of his tongue, he signaled his mount to turn and head down the lane, lined with several small slave cabins, to the Blow's stately Olde Place plantation home. On an impulse, he turned one last time to stare at the pregnant slave, her left hand holding up her bulging stomach while the right continued to pick cotton.

"*Mea culpa*," Jefferson added, "but I will echo your pain and your resolve, Jemmy. There is nothing I would not sacrifice to find a practicable plan of abolishing every vestige of this moral and political depravity. We are indeed two very tired and sorry men." He laughed. "Come, let's go in and share the hearth with my good friend Lt. Richard Blow and his family. But be prepared—after they fill your belly and your pipe, they're certain to fill the rest of you with 'The History of Virginia' as seen through the eyes of the 'Blow-hards' of Virginia."

With a chuckle and a sigh, and an acknowledging grin from James Madison, Thomas Jefferson turned forward a final time in the saddle and quietly prophesied. "Alas, with all the great and noble men who have acknowledged the evil of slavery, and failed to take steps to abolish it, a Virginian greater than us all will be necessary to make real that truth we piously called self-evident."

* * *

As twilight settled over the Blow plantations, a strong and deeply spiritual slave woman, soon to be the inherited chattel of young master Peter Blow, paused in her picking and looked up at the retreating riders. She straightened to her full height and pregnant glory, then turned her gaze heavenward, caressed the tiny bulge from the kicking child in her womb, and returned to her soft humming.

"Go down Moses. Way down in Egypt land.
Tell ole Pharaoh, to let my people go."

Part IV

Him That Hath No Helper

"For while politicians contend, and men are swerved this way and that by conflicting tides of interest and passion, the great cause of human liberty is in the hands of One of whom it is said: '. . . He shall deliver the needy when he crieth, The poor, and him that hath no helper. He shall redeem their soul from deceit and violence: and precious shall their blood be in His sight.'"

- Harriet Beecher Stowe, Preface to <u>Uncle Tom's Cabin</u>, (quoting Psalms 72:12, 14)

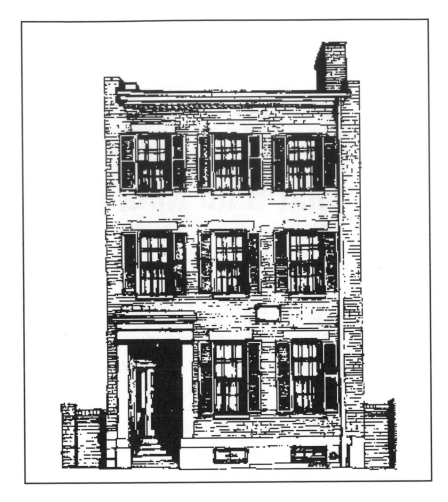

Walsh's Row
House of Rowsell Field

Chapter 7

All the World is Sad and Dreary

St. Louis, 1852

An early summer cloudburst pushed slanted rain against the front windows of the second-to-last unit on Walsh's Row, further dampening the spirits of the families, white and black, gathered inside. The humidity was like a wet wool blanket in the closed room, nearly suffocating those who awaited the return of the master of the house, Roswell Field. He was meeting at the courthouse just down Broadway with the judge and the lawyers for the other side. In March, Judge Hamilton had temporarily denied the Sanford's motion to hold the Scotts in jail or return them in chains to the slave quarters behind the Chouteau & Co. warehouses. Instead, they were to remain in the trust of the sheriff and the attorney, and the group's faith in young Roswell had grown considerably. Because of threats from b'hoys and ruffians, the Scott girls had been in hiding with abolitionist sympathizers well outside the city. Dred and Harriet were kept shut up indoors, cleaning house and doing laundry. Today was one of the first times they had all been together since that terrible night in the jail.

Despite the nearly suffocating heat, no one dared open the front windows, for just across the street, slave-traders had ushered several dozen pitiful souls into the infamous Broadway slave pen, some chained and the rest huddled together in the downpour. The Scotts had slipped into the Field's row house from the back, and Frances Field drew the drapes to prevent the Scott girls from seeing the horror out front. The reality of what might await the Scotts later that day was almost too terrible to consider, and the heavy drapes and closed quarters felt like a prison to the captive group. The yellow and white vertically striped walls of the dual parlors added to that impression. They could manage only small talk in subdued tones.

Nine-year-old Susan Blow sat on a corner chair near the back fireplace in the women's parlor. The dividing doors had been thrown open to accommodate the large group. The rain falling down the chimney plinked a rhythm that inspired her to pick up the Field's banjo and pluck out the tune of the popular Negro melody that, thanks to Stephen Foster, was on everybody's lips these days: "Old Folks at Home." Her perfect, sweet soprano drew attention away from her imperfect picking.

"Way down upon the Swanee River. Far, far away.
Dere's wha my heart is turning ever.
Dere's wha de old folks stay.

"All the world is sad and dreary, everywhere I roam.
Oh! darkies, how my heart grows weary.
Far from de old folks at home."

It was a sad and dreary scene. The innocence of childhood provided the only lift as Field's fourteen-year-old Mormon nanny Temperance played with the Blow and Field toddlers in the middle of the parlor.

"What do the sheep say?" she asked three-year-old Eugene Field, holding up a carved wooden lamb.

"Baaaaaaa!" blurted the blue-eyed lad.

"That's right, Genie!" encouraged Temperance, sneaking the toy cow under a handful of straw to her side. "Uh oh! Where the cow go?" she teased.

Peter, LaBeaume, and Eugene looked frantically about.

"Uh oh!" All three boys mimed, with eyes wide, tiny palms turned upward, shoulders hunched in genuine curiosity. Suddenly Eugene screeched, scurried forward, and pointed at Temperance's side.

"Der he is!" He snatched the cow from under the straw and began to dance about on tippy-toes, the rescued bovine held high. "Da cow in da corn! Da cow in da corn!"

A gust of wind scattered the "corn" as the front door opened and Roswell entered. It was warm, wet air, but it briefly ventilated the sauna. Frances took her husband's bowler and Chesterfield coat, shook them, and hung them in the entry while he stamped the rainwater from his trousers and brogans as he collected his thoughts and calmed his nerves.

"Temperance, can you please take the young 'uns up to my study?" Peter asked.

"Go with them, girls," Dred ordered his children as he wiped the sweat from his furrowed brow.

"Oh, Daddy, please can I stay?" protested the eldest. "I'ze big enough."

Before Dred could respond, Harriet patted his leg. "Let her stay, Dred. She sho' is big 'nuff to hear what the future holds."

Roswell entered the parlor, patting the tiny heads as they scurried past him into the hallway. His normally cheery face had the somber look he wore in the large oil painting hanging above the front fireplace. He took a deep breath, put on a smile, and announced, "Okay, folks, I had a good meeting this morning with Judge Hamilton. He wants us all down there this afternoon. Sheriff and Edmund LaBeaume will be there with their six-hundred-dollar bond, ledgers, and receipts for Harriet's wages." He pulled some papers from his leather case and handed them to Taylor. "You'll need to sign these and appear to swear to your signature on this bond you secured for Dred."

Dred couldn't wait any longer and rose abruptly from the serpentine-backed sofa.

"Wh-what he say 'bout us and the children?" he stammered, and then paused to find some spittle. Everyone waited while he worked his mouth around the dryness that had formed there, and found themselves swallowing with him. "The judge gonna give us over to Massa Sanford and his soul-drivers?"

Roswell had expected this question and prepared himself on the way back down to the row houses so his own fear wouldn't show.

"He didn't do it in March and I don't expect him to do it today, either. It's apparent he hasn't gotten over his disappointment that the Supreme Court overturned the jury decision rendered in his courtroom, and I can tell he wants to do right by you."

When the entire company breathed at once, Roswell realized they had all been collectively holding their breath. He held up his hand and plowed on.

"I do have to warn you, though, that there will be a lot of angry people there today. Word has spread, and it's well known that Pierre Chouteau has encouraged his son-in-law Sanford to fight hard to protect his property rights. The Chouteaus lost a number of their slaves over the years due to other freedom suits. Rumor has it they contributed financially to the '51 campaign of Justice Scott, who wrote the opinion that slavery was 'instituted by God,' and ignored decades of Missouri law to order you back into slavery. I tell you, Dred, your case has become a bellwether and rallying cry for pro-slavery sentiment, and those folks intend to see this through!"

"But Roswell," Peter interrupted. "They won. Today isn't about appealing this further. We know you want us to go to federal court, and it seems Dred and Harriet are set on that, but that's something we don't have to decide today. This is just about what happens in the meantime with Dred and his family, isn't it?"

"Well, Judge Hamilton did tell me in chambers today that he's going to ask Dred and Harriet what they intend to do, because it will weigh on his decision as to whether he hands the Scotts over to Sanford—who, by the way, arrived from New York last night and will be in the courtroom to demand rights to his and his sister's property."

Eliza had heard enough. She stomped her foot and and pivoted to face her parents. "Oh, no! Not Massa Sanford! He gonna take us away to New York for sho'!" she cried. "And we ain't never gonna see you no more in this life!"

"Hush, baby child," cooed Harriet as she took her eldest in her arms, muffling the sobs with her bodice. She looked at Roswell over the top of her daughter's curls. Her eyes were aflame with warning. "You was born free, my little gypsy, on the mightiest River Jordan in the whole world, and Mr. Roswell here, he ain't goin' let no man take that away from you!"

Roswell felt as though he was going to faint, but dared not break eye contact with the she-lion in her pride.

"Come on, child." She patted Eliza's back. "Let's let these men plan their battle." On the way out the entry, she turned her stare back on Roswell one last time. "You knows I'ze been callin' you 'Joshua?' Well, you best polish up yo' trumpet, 'cause the walls o' Jericho is right down that street!" And with that, she was gone.

Nervous laughter filled the room as the mens' confidence returned. Dred stuck out his chest and spoke first.

"Looky here. The way we sees it, we already lost, so we got nothin' to lose. Act'ly, we've got everythin' to lose and we can't take no risk on losin' our babies. My Harriet is right. We gotta fight the battle of Jericho! But you, Peter, and you, Taylor, and yo' sissies and the LaBeaumes and yo' children done fought 'nuff. It ain't yo' fight no more." He looked at Roswell. "I 'polegize, Mr. Roswell. Harriet don't have no right to put so much on you—callin' you 'Joshua' and all such stuff." He paused and rubbed the furrows in his forehead—furrows plowed by a half-century of slavery, grown deep and permanent in the past fifteen years with the weight of a wife and daughters to care for. "But we sho' does thank the Lord every day, and my tears wets my pilla every night in thankfulness for my friends, and we sho' needs yo' help. But I feel so 'shamed to ask you to put yo' own lives and fortunes in danger one mo' time."

The three white men went as one to Dred, strengthening him with their assurances and protestations of support. The sweet odor of frying venison filtered through the back door and filled the room, as a knock at the front door signaled the LaBeaumes' arrival for dinner, prior to the afternoon hearing.

"Come on in!" Roswell called to the men outside. "Smells like the women folk have about got the meal ready. I've got to get a few more signatures from these white boys. Dred, why don't you go make sure the food is seasoned enough. I know Charlotte, Sarah, and Minerva can cook Southern, but my Frances is a Yankee gal from Vermont, and it'll take four or more of you to keep the New England blandness out of her cooking."

"You got that right!" Dred chuckled and headed out back after greeting the LaBeaume boys, who were shaking rainwater off their clothes onto the hardwood floor in the hallway.

"Have ya'll seen that terrible sight across the road?" Sheriff Louis asked the others. "Dad-blame it, that makes me all wrathy inside! Ros, you just gotta prevail today."

"You missed Roswell's speech a few minutes ago," Peter said. "He had us praising Jesus and ready to row ol' Sam Hill hisself up Salt River!"

"That's right," laughed the sheriff, pounding Roswell on the back. "Ya'll give 'um Jesse today in court, Counselor!"

Although words were a lawyer's tools, Roswell looked at Louis cross-wise and shook his head. "I swear, Sheriff, I don't understand a word you're saying. Who's Jesse?"

The four Southerners broke out laughing at the counselor's confusion. Edmund stepped in to save him.

"My brother the lawman sometimes talks like the riff-raff he puts in his jail. 'Give 'um Jesse' is how we Missouri pukes politely say, 'Beat the hell out of 'um!'"

It was Roswell's turn to laugh. "All right, boys, we've got our work cut out for us, no doubt about it. But dinner is ready, so let's go get some grub, and then we do have to get serious because we face real danger. I've got to know now, because the judge will ask us in a few hours, if you are all prepared to go forward? Think about it while we eat, and then let's meet at my office—and I'll want your wives with you. Joseph told me he could break away from the bank and meet us there at one. Elizabeth and Frances can stay here with the Scotts, and then we can come back here and escort them over to the courthouse. Now, let's eat!"

Chapter 8
Times are Not Now as They Were

St. Louis, 1852

The rain had let up by the time Dred's white benefactors gathered at Field's law office next to the Bank of Missouri at the crossing of Market and Main Streets. Full bellies did not have the normal effect of lifting the spirits of the Blow family and their friends, but rather tended to simply add indigestion to the heartache they felt. Here were the Blows of Virginia, each one possessing his own first memory of the black man whom, as adults, they had worked so hard to defend. They were all there. The eldest, simpleminded but tender old maid Elizabeth; the one they called "matriarch" and her husband, Charlotte and Joseph Charless; Peter and Sarah; Taylor and Minerva; and the youngest, and still single, William. They had buried two brothers in Virginia, a sister in Alabama, their parents and most recently their dear sister, Martha

Ella, right there in St. Louis. But the many travels of the Blows had made them a tight-knit family that stuck together, and they made sure Martha Ella's widower, Charles Drake, had stayed close and was, by unanimous consent, the favorite uncle of the little ones. Charles had responded to their love and had been instrumental in securing funding and legal representation the past six years.

Those ties-that-bind had wrapped around Peter Blow's first in-laws, Louis and Edmund LaBeaume. The death of their sister and Peter's childless first wife, Eugenie, had not weakened the ties, as evidenced by the fact that the LaBeaume brothers had staked their names, reputations, and honor on this family by signing the bonds that had allowed Dred and Harriet to remain in St. Louis and in their employ—and therefore out of the hands of overseers and slave drivers.

The newcomer to this group, having emigrated from Vermont in 1839 but only brought into the case last year, was unrelated except in spirit. Roswell Field stood in awe of this tiny group. He was there because it was his job, albeit *pro-bono* at present, and when Edmund first contacted him, his interest had been in maintaining the rule of law and precedent that allowed a slave to gain his freedom in court. Ironically, his first case involving slavery was one in which he had represented a slave owner a decade earlier in trying to recover a fugitive slave.

Roswell had not been involved in any abolitionist organization in New England, but after coming face-to-face with the brutality of slavery, the only slave cases he had taken since then were on the side of the oppressed. He was a voracious reader and had secured one of the first copies of *Uncle Tom's Cabin* to arrive in St. Louis a few months ago. He literally burned the midnight oil and didn't put it down until he had finished it. It was not only his inspiration—it was his new abolitionist Bible.

He looked up at the only wall decoration he had, besides his portrait of George Washington. He had taken a popular abolitionist poster depicting a kneeling slave, feet shackled and attached to his chained hands, which were raised in supplication. Below it, a banner read:

AM I NOT A MAN AND A BROTHER?

In his best penmanship, Roswell had added a quote from Augustine St. Clare, the benevolent owner of Uncle Tom in Harriet Beecher Stowe's best-selling novel:

> *Talk of the abuses of slavery! Humbug!*
> *The thing itself is the essence of all abuse!*

To the soles of his feet, Roswell felt this case would be the most important of his legal career, and he meant to see it through. But he also knew he couldn't go it alone. He needed this Spartan band to stay together in the face of ridicule, ostracism, and even the violence he knew awaited them in this new chapter. He saw they had followed his gaze to the poster.

"I know I'm preaching to the choir," he began, pointing at the poster, "because I know you have all experienced enough of slavery that those could be your own words. But I want to make sure you all understood where this is going today, and what you can expect from here on."

Peter spoke first. "We know where yer goin' with this, Ros. Every one of us has taken our share of guff for feelin' the way we do." Everyone nodded in unison.

"I know, I know, but you realize, too, that times are changing. That's the only reason we lost this case, and the judges went against twenty-eight years of established law in this state. Do you mind a short history lesson?"

No one spoke, so he pushed on. "Missouri is literally at the crossroads, not only geographically as the gateway to the west, but figuratively as well when it comes to the issue that's dividing this nation. Congress created Missouri as a great compromise over the issue of slavery and the growth of our nation, and by that compromise, surrounded us on three sides by free states and territories. This one issue is tearing us apart. Look what's happened to Senator Benton. Thomas Hart Benton *was* Missouri! He was the first elected senator when Missouri became a state."

Joseph Charless spoke up. "I'll tell you what, 'Old Bullion' was the greatest senator of all time. Did you know he was the editor of the *Missouri Enquirer* at the same time my daddy was editor of the *Missouri Gazette?*" He chuckled. "Boy, did those two ever go at it. Anyway, it was all good-natured back then. Daddy even supported him for the United States Senate. Why, Missouri wouldn't be the gateway to nothing but for Benton's leadership on territorial expansion. His name is synonymous with Manifest Destiny! Five terms in the Senate, and then he came to town three years ago talking about how he had changed his mind about slavery. Had he been in office in '20 instead of '21, he would have been against allowing slavery here, or even in the United States."

"That's right, Joseph, and look what happened," Roswell continued. "First, that crazy loon of a senator from Mississippi tried to shoot him with a pepper-box on the floor of the United States Senate. And just last fall, he was voted out of office."

"Thas right," Sheriff LaBeaume broke in, "and folks say he co'nt be elected hogreeve!"

"His timing wasn't very good, but he always was an unusual politician—he had principles!" Roswell joked. "But about the time he was standing on principle, the people were motivated once again by the division over slavery and voted to change our state constitution so the people could popularly elect all judges. As a result, the Scotts' appeal was not heard by jurists with a long history of pro-freedom decisions like Chief Justice McGirk and Judge Tompkins, but by pro-slavery justices Scott, Ryland, and Gamble. And here we are today."

"Chief Justice Gamble owns slaves, but he voted with us," Charlotte broke in. "Why?"

"I know him well, and he is also a man of principle. He, like Benton, is what I've heard called 'a huckleberry above a persimmon.' But sadly, I suspect he'll suffer the same fate as Senator Benton. Justice Gamble feels very strongly that the role of the court is to make decisions based on established law and precedents, and not to get mired in politics and try to write policy. So here's where it gets scary. Until now, pro-slavery mob mentality has been kept out of the courts. Despite their strong sentiment on slavery, common folks still respected the rule of law and the role of the courts in preserving justice and defending individual rights."

"You know, thas right," Taylor broke in. "We was all shocked when Calvin Farris, Bill Syphert, John Morris, that Taylor boy, and the other slave-holders on Dred's jury voted to make him free."

"Yep, but I believe those durn . . ." Roswell paused at the sudden smiles on the faces of the Southerners and rubbed his hand through his thinning hair. "Did I just say 'durn'? Ya'll got me talking like . . ." Laughter cut him off. "See, there I go again with 'yu'll.' Anyway, those darn justices changed everything, not just by tossing nearly thirty years of precedent out the window, but by signaling it was worth doing it over slavery. And then they really stirred the viper's nest all to pieces by inserting words in their language that I swear could be charged criminally as inciting a riot! Listen to this."

Roswell rummaged around on his desk and pulled out a copy of the ruling. He ran his finger down the second page. "Here! Right here! Now listen to this extraordinary rationale:

73

"Times are not now as they were when the former decisions on this subject were made. Since then not only individuals but States have been possessed with a dark and fell spirit in relation to slavery . . .

"Did you hear that? A justice of the Supreme Court actually said that people opposed to the barbaric practice of slavery . . . 'the very essence of abuse' . . . that we are 'possessed with a dark and fell spirit!'"

"Dad-blame it!" hollered the sheriff, pounding his oak walking stick on the floor. "Why, I've a mind ta take this here rascal-beater of mine and learn that devil a thang or two 'bout who's possessed!"

Edmund tried to calm his brother. "Hold on there, Hoss. Let's let the counselor finish. I wanna know what we're facin' in that courtroom today. An' please remember, there's ladies present."

The big man suddenly turned docile, blushed, and begged pardon of the ladies.

"Thanks, Edmund," Roswell said. "I understand your feelings, and that's exactly why this is so upsetting. But it gets worse; Scott and Ryland go on to say that anyone who is against slavery is seeking gratification, and I quote, 'in the pursuit of measures, whose inevitable consequences must be the overthrow and destruction of our government!' These men of the law have told every pro-slavery Missourian that you and I are in open rebellion against the government and seek its overthrow!"

"Blast that cussed imp!" Louis hollered. "Let me go, brother, I'm for sure gonna give him the Jesse now!" He broke free of Louis and headed for the door. The Blow men blocked his path.

"This is not the way, Louis," Taylor calmed. "You know better. This is the way of the soaplocks and ruffians gatherin' outside the courtroom as we speak. We feel the same way you do, and we'll be damned if we ain't ready to lock arms and start knockin' heads. But

74

we got women folk and children to worry about, and I'm afeared right now what we're gonna face down the street."

"Taylor's right." Roswell stepped up and pulled a sodden yellow paper out of his pocket. He slowly unfolded it with half a mind to put it back in his pocket. *They have a right to know,* he reasoned to himself, and held up the flier. "These were posted for blocks around the courthouse, and they contain the very words from Justice Scott I just read to you."

SOUND THE ALARM!

Every Man Who Loves Missouri is Needed Today, June 28th

Our fair state, our laws and our rights is under attack! Those Blamed uppity-niggers Dred and Harriet Scott (and their two pickaninnies) and the no-account, nigger-lovin Blows will try today to stop our esteemed, law-abidin favorite sons John Sanford an his father-in-law, the Honorable Pierre Chouteau, Jr., from takin back their property. The highest court in the state of Missouri said this about the Blows and other nigger-lovers:

"They have been possessed with a dark and fell spirit in relation to slavery in the pursuit of measures, including the overthrow and destruction of our government!"

Our highest court has ordered the darkies turned over to their rightful owners, but the Blows and their snake-n-the-grass lawyer will try today to stop that.

MISSOURI NEEDS YOU! NOW! TODAY!
MEET AT THE COURTHOUSE BY NOON!
ARM YOURSELVES!

Charlotte screamed and Elizabeth swooned. William stepped up and pulled a long knife from his boot.

"I got my Arkansas toothpick!" he proclaimed. "I'm with Sher'f Louis. I ain't afeered of no puke!"

Roswell was once again amazed at the spunk in these Blows. "I hope that won't be necessary, Willie. I took one of these in to Judge Hamilton and he cussed a blue streak you would appreciate, Sheriff. He vowed he would not tolerate this while he was still a judge of the Circuit Court and promised to have the marshals and bailiffs both outside and inside the courtroom. If you all decide to go forward today, we cannot show any weapons that would give the mob an excuse. What do you think, Sheriff Louis?"

Louis had calmed somewhat and the lawman in him was returning. "I agree with Ros, folks. Thar may be a time when ol' Rascal Beater here will be necessary, but not today. I'm still a sheriff in this town," he declared, patting the star on his vest and then the six-shooter on his hip. "And I aim ta keep the peace and see this through. I best git on over to the jail for my dep'ties, then back over to fetch the Scotts. We can usher 'em in the side door. Do the girls have ta go, Ros?"

"Yes, I'm afraid so. However, the judge has asked all of you adults who wish to pursue this matter to be there as well. Of course, given the circumstances, he—and I—will fully understand if you don't show. I will emphasize one more time. Today might be a bit frightening, but if you decide to go forward, the judge wants a commitment you will see this thing through to the federal courts. Know that for the next months, and even years, you will not only be placing yourselves and your families at great physical risk, given the widening divide, but you will be openly taking on the most powerful family in Missouri, and you must all consider what that will mean to your business, financial, and property interests as well. Things are bound to get uglier with each passing day. Things are heating to a boiling point all across this state and ready to spill into Kansas. You've only got about thirty more minutes to decide how you want to proceed." He looked them each in the eye. "I need to leave and get to the court early, too. Folks don't know me yet as Dred and Harriet's lawyer, so I'll be fine. God bless! Whatever your choice is, I will always admire you for what you've done up 'til now. Let's go, Louis."

Roswell and Louis put on their overcoats, tipped their hats to the ladies, and closed the door behind them.

"I honestly don't know if I'll ever talk with them again, Louis."

"Oh, no, Ros." The sheriff smiled as he walked down the stairs. "You don't know the Blows like I knows the Blows." He opened the door onto sunshine and stepped after the lawyer into the heat of the afternoon.

St. Louis Courthouse

Chapter 9

The Pillars of Justice

St. Louis Courthouse, 1852

The clock in the bell tower struck two as Roswell Field, Esquire, stepped through the tall east doors that led from the majestic courthouse, and stood between the massive pillars that to him, were the very symbol of law and democracy. Between these pillars and through these doors passed the people who sought justice. He looked down at the courthouse steps where the weekly slave auction was held — a mockery of justice as people of color were sold like cattle to the highest bidder.

He'd always been proud of his chosen profession. He loved this mighty nation and its God-inspired Constitution. *How wise*, he thought, looking past the building toward the mighty waters, the setting sun behind him casting a golden sheen leading to the Illinois shore. *Our Founding Fathers declared that this new nation would be an empire of laws, and not of men.* For men were fallible—he smiled as the face of Justice Scott passed through his mind—but the law was meant to be supreme. He was here today because he believed that with all his soul. He prayed the Blows would believe the same.

Shouts from the street below brought him out of his reverie, and his heart skipped when he saw the mayhem stretched out before him. He reached back for the hard oak doors to knock wood for luck.

The size of the mob had surely grown, and so had the noise and courage of the dirty ruffians. The rabble filled Fourth Street and snaked around Market and Chestnut. It moved as a pulsating, hungry beast. The humid air was heavily perfumed with booze, tobacco, sweat, and hate. It was filled with every oath and cuss word ever invented, and some new ones, he was sure. Sticks, forks, rakes, and even some long guns waved and bounced up and down. Street peddlers weaved in and out, screeching out their ads, trying in vain to be heard above the crowd. Roswell felt some comfort, though not much, in seeing the uniformed marshals and bailiffs lining the walk in front of the courthouse. Right now, the anger and derision of the crowd was leveled at them.

"Hey, Tom!" a very rotund man in filthy pantaloons screamed into the face of one of the guards at the bottom of the steps. "What'n tarnation you doin'? Who's watchin' your slaves while you're here playin' high'n mighty in your natty grays? Why're you protectin' em cussed cuffies fer?"

"Now back away, Charlie," the guard warned, pushing him gently with his formidable long gun. "I got a job to do, and I 'spect you should be worrin' more about who's watchin' after yer wife than who's watchin' after my slaves!"

"Damn ya!" Charlie screeched, tobacco spittle flying from his mouth onto the uniform. But before the guard could react with a rifle butt to the scalawag's head, the crowd did his job for him.

"Ha ha!" they cried in unison, shoving the drunk back.

"Jim's right," a stick-thin man with no teeth called after him, his words barely distinguishable through his slur. "I jus' leff your wife, Charlie, an' there wath a line waitin' outthide."

Roswell leaned against the pillar and just shook his head. It was almost a quarter after, and it didn't look like the Blows were coming. The door swung open, and the bailiff called out.

"Mr. Field, the Scotts 're all safe inside the courtroom. Judge Hamilton is getting a li'l impatient." He waited a moment as Roswell leaned out and looked south and east toward his office.

"Thanks, Fergy. Tell him I'll be right in." He sighed as the door closed; he now felt very alone and unsure of himself. *They aren't coming. They've done enough*, he thought. *I was just asking too much, for anybody*. He turned toward the door and then stopped at the sudden uproar that was now focused only to the south. He whipped around, stepped to the edge of the stairs, and squinted into the dusty air. He didn't want to believe it, but the crowd seemed to be parting as something moved up the street. What appeared to be fruit and vegetables were tossed through the air as a huddled group rounded the corner off Market Street and onto the courthouse block.

"Could it be?" he asked himself as a laugh built in his chest. "Blessed Jesus, could it really be?"

The marshals and grays pushed the crowd back, and suddenly it was as if all time stood still. Years later, Roswell would swear a gust of wind flew in from the west and blew the sound all the way across the river to the Illinois shore. The cussing and hawking and barking were gone. Even the June bugs went mute at that moment. In years to come, he became fond of painting a verbal picture.

"And then the mob and the guards backed up as if on cue. It was like the parting of the Red Sea. Even the crudest scalawag let whatever weapon he'd been holding drop slowly to his side. No one moved; so noble, so majestic, was this procession. But the children of Israel passing through were none other than the Blow family of Virginia, late of Alabama and now Missouri. They moved together as one, followed by their kin. Five abreast strode the siblings: tall Peter, stately Charlotte, proud Taylor, sturdy Elizabeth, and brave young William. Arms locked in solidarity; backs straight and eyes fixed forward; never wavering, never hesitating. They pivoted as well as a regular-army militia on a parade ground and started up the steps. They smiled at me, and even though the sun was now behind the courthouse, their eyes glowed golden as if they'd captured its rays on their march up Market Street. The doors seemed to open by themselves, and the Blow family passed between the pillars of justice and crossed the threshold. The only sound I heard at that moment was the delighted squeal of little Lizzie echoing through the chamber and into my heart. In awe, all I could think was, 'Who are these saints—these Blows of Virginia?'"

Part V

The Blows of Virginia

The Far East has its Mecca, Palestine its Jerusalem, France its Lourdes, and Italy its Loretto, but America's only shrines are her altars of patriotism - the first and most potent being Jamestown; the sire of Virginia, and Virginia the mother of this great Republic.

From a 1907 Virginia guidebook

Example of a Cast Iron Fireback

Chapter 10

Saltire, Pomeis, and Crown

Southampton County, Virginia, 1799

Afrer a kingly feast of lamb stew, roast venison, pork chops, parsnips, turnips, carrots, sweet potatoes, succotash, and a variety of breads and puddings, the gentlemen retired to the study with their noble guests to savor the sweet, sharp aroma of Caribbean cigars, smoothed by apple brandy or chased by port. The room was warm from the fire glowing in the hearth and the new and renewed friendships glowing in the breast.

"A finer feast I had not in the Palace of Versailles, Colonel," Jefferson congratulated his host, fifty-four-year-old Richard Blow. He added, sniffing his apple brandy, ". . . although Madeira would put a nice cap on the evening."

To various mumbled "huzzahs," the vice president turned to the eldest Blow in the room and spoke loudly out of concern for the patriarch's advanced age. "Henry, I was telling Mr. Madison today that the genealogy of the Blows of Virginia is the very history of this nation. Would you relate to us the story of your fathers, which is likely the story of ours?"

The octogenarian had been nodding in the warmth, and with his fullness of belly, but perked up at the opportunity to educate two of the men who were already being referred to around the country as Founding Fathers. He slowly straightened, cleared his throat, and nodded in the direction of the fireplace.

"You honor me, sir, with your request. You may experience the history of my ancestors by looking there, in the flames."

Madison and Jefferson glanced sideways at each other, each with a slightly raised eyebrow expressing concern over the lucidity of the white-haired senior. But then Madison saw a glowing iron fireback through the flames.

"Is that the Blow family crest emblazoned there on the fireback?" Madison asked Henry.

"Most certainly it is, young man," softly replied the old man, "as well the initials of my great-grandfather, the first American Blow: George Blow."

Every family member in the room noticeably straightened as the two statesmen leaned forward to peer more carefully into the fire. There, indeed, on each side of the raised crest, were the initials **G** and **B**. Above the **G** stood out the number **16**, and above the **B**, number **72**. The cast-iron fireback itself was two feet wide and about the same height where it rose in a semi-circle to make room for what appeared to be a crown over the shield.

"Was that fireback truly cast in 1672?" marveled Jefferson, a true lover of the historical, amazed that this amber-glowing familial symbol had radiated light and warmth to six generations of Blows.

Jefferson and Madison waited quietly for a response as Henry stared into the fire, his weathered face absorbing the warmth.

Madison elbowed his companion and nodded toward the other Blows, who also seemed mesmerized by the fire. It was obvious that family history and tradition were of great import to this family.

The patriarch broke the silence. "Great-granda George understood that the hearth was the heart of the home. A few years before he died, he had that fireback cast in James City and started the long tradition of family storytelling. That old thing has warmed several Blow plantations and ended up here in the home of my brother Sam, who instructed in his will that it would remain here at the Olde Place, where his remains would lie until the morning of the great resurrection. Sam loved it, and was proud of Granda George's life and legacy so richly and permanently preserved in this family emblem. All of George Blow's descendents have sat facing this crest. In fact, several were born in front of it, including young Peter here," he added proudly, with upraised bushy white eyebrows. "And we're told the stories and the meaning of the 'Saltire, Pomeis and Crown.' Imagine all the family gatherings, birthdays, holidays, Bible readings, feasts, joyous birthings, as well as solemn wakes—all presided over by this fireback. It is who we are!" he concluded with great pride. "May I share our story?"

A hush had settled over the assembly. Jefferson glanced at James with an "I told you so" expression, but neither minded. Both had been drawn into the story and felt hypnotized by its spirit. It was not lost on either of them that even the darker faces of the Negro servants in the room beamed with pride and admiration as they, too, paused and waited to share in the family history.

Jamestown, Virginia

Chapter 11

Seven Years of Servitude

Atlantic Ocean, 1638

St. Andrew's ghost!" laughed the boy. Cold Atlantic saltwater sprayed his face and tickled his loins as the deck fell away from under his feet. He bent his knees and grabbed hold of the rail, waiting for the ship to rise up out of the trough, where it would hang momentarily at a great height and then rush down again. "Aye! This be the life I want, Georgie!" he shouted over the roar.

The greenish tinge about the neck and face of his slightly older shipmate indicated he did not share Jack's sentiment, and he punctuated his distaste for the seafaring life with an explosion of bile over the side.

"Blimey, mate!" yelled the youngster as he released his grip on the rail and slid away to avoid the fetid shower. "When we're done with our seven years of workin' land in Virginia, ye best keep yer hands in the soil. But it's His Majesty's Royal Navy for me."

As the vessel crested the next wave, the Bos'n Mate barked from above: "Land ho! Virginia Colony! Yer new home, lads! Land! Land hooooo!"

It was George's turn to praise the saints as he brightened at the knowledge that his two-month ordeal was nearly over. He would be happy to keep his hands in what he'd heard was the dark, rich soil of southern Virginia, and he prayed to St. Andrew he never again would have to feel the ground move under his feet unless he, himself, was in the process of turning it with a plow. His stomach clenched as the ship slipped sideways while it dropped again. *At least we know where we're headed,* he thought, pondering how truly awful it must have been for that first Virginia Company under Captain John Smith to have made the crossing, but then remain shipboard for months, exploring every inlet, cove, and river to find a suitable anchorage. They finally did on May 14th, 1607, some sixty miles from the mouth of the Chesapeake Bay on an island on the banks of a river, both of which would be named in honor of their sovereign and benefactor, King James I of England. He knew the stories well—John Smith, John Rolfe, Pocahontas, Powhatan— stories of adventure, exploration, famine, starvation, war, then peace, then war again with the Algonquian Indians. That was just thirty-one years ago, and now he would soon disembark and begin his own adventure in this exotic new land.

"Blessed be St. Andrew!" cried fifteen year-old George Blow of Lincolnshire. "Afore nightfall, I'll be plant'n me feet on the soil of America!"

George and Jack had signed on as indentured servants to Henry Catelyn as part of the headright system, which granted a wealthy man fifty acres of land for each servant he brought over from England. After early settlers realized there was no gold in Virginia, they quickly learned the land could nevertheless make them rich by producing tobacco. But tobacco wore out the land every four to seven years, so more and more land was cleared from the wilderness. Immigration of large numbers of workers was essential to the growth of the colony, and hence the headright system was developed. George would be going with his master and nine fellow servants to Upper New Norfolk County, several miles south and inland from Jamestown. There, they would repay their travel with seven years of servitude, after which each would be given his freedom, along with some clothing and equipment, and sent further into the wilderness where he could buy cheap land to clear. Thus would begin his own life and the raising of a family in this beautiful New World that held such promise.

Slave Ship

Chapter 12

The Slaver

Jamestown Landing, 1639

Up, ya lazy dogs!" growled Bates, the Catelyn overseer. "Off yer cots and at the trough a'fore day breaks, or by the devil, I'll tan yer skinny arses!"

The moment the hated voice broke into his sleep, George groaned and rolled out of his cot by reflex. Many times over the first two years on the plantation, Bates's hickory stick had made sharp contact when George rolled over and tried to hold onto his recurring dream. It rankled George that any man could take a stick to another man, particularly here in the land of freedom; what he despised even more was the heartless theft of his dreams.

George was blessed—some would say cursed—with vivid dreams that repeated near nightly, most of which involved running through virgin forests, hunting deer, fishing the many streams, and freely exploring—and subduing—the wild lands of southern Virginia. In his dreams, George was master, not of underfed and overworked boys fresh off the boats from England, but master of his own hands, working his own lands and inspiring others, including his future sons, to greatness in this New World. A hard poke in the back reminded him that his dream would only become a reality if he could endure, by his calculations, another six years and over two thousand more of Bates's bloody wake-ups.

He whirled and leaped to his feet at the second, harder poke, and looked down at his tormentor. At seventeen, George was already substantially taller than the overseer, whom he and the others privately called "short and squatty, all arse and no body."

"Oy, don' ye go puttin' on airs, Georgie!" Bates fumed, his breath reeking of something long dead. "You're a ninny an' I'll tan 'at skinny arse." He punctuated his point with the stick. George nearly guffawed at the "arse" comment, and could see over Bates's head the other boys doing all they could to control their laughter, with the overseer's own large backside in their faces.

"Al'right, put on yer canoes and let's get at it. We be goin' into Jamestown today." Bates nipped the "huzzahs" in the bud. "Don' get all excitable. We got two heavy barques to unload 'fore nightfall. You'll all be cryin' for yer mommies by mid-day, ya lot of ninnies! Out!"

The thought of being a beast of burden all day didn't flatten George's spirits. He loved working the land, but the new Jamestown was always a great diversion. The sights and sounds and smells were tantalizing, but not so much as the maidens in their finery. Ships arrived regularly, bringing as many as a hundred new, pink Chinese lassies straight from London and Liverpool and Lincolnshire. A boy would have to be dead not to get excited about a day in Jamestown, no matter how hard the work. But it was only one day, and it might be another six months before they went back.

George was turning sixteen in a month, and most young men his age would be thinking heavily about courtship by now.

But as an indentured servant he was not permitted those normal opportunities—another reason George despised a system that made a man less than a man and denied him all the natural rights a man was entitled to.

"Ah, merry!" he cussed with a wry smile as the wagon bumped along the rutted path. "He can't stop me from admiring the scenery, and I can likely sneak a wink or two."

By 1639, the original uniquely triangular fort at Jamestown had long since been destroyed and abandoned. In the mid 1620s, the colony had moved east, but retained the name, and was not only the capitol of Virginia Colony but the center and heartbeat of the entire Tobacco Coast. It was a thriving seaport and boomtown.

Bates granted the servants a short break between unloading the two ships. It was indeed backbreaking work, but George's long arms and legs were well-muscled and sinewy, and many a lass stared as the sweat glistened on his bare chest. It had been a great morning indeed. A bevy of giggling Brits had disembarked from a large ship just arrived from Liverpool, and George bore several angry welts from Bates's hickory for his lack of stealth in returning the attention to the beauties.

He nursed one mark that had broken the skin on his leg, cursed Bates for the thousandth time, and spoke to Jack, who was rubbing some mud onto a spreading welt over his knee.

"So, Jack, how many times have ye fallen in love today?"

"Not as many times as you, I see by the number of marks on yer back. But I did fall in love with the one I'll marry. I couldn't take my eyes off her, an' earned this knot on my knee. But oh, it was worth it, Georgie. In fact, I even know her name, and I intend to board her."

"Jack!" George howled and tossed a stick at his friend. "You can't talk so low about one of God's fair creations. I've a mind to knock yer block right off! An' ye can't possibly know her name."

"Hold on there, Sir Galahad, before you wipe the dock with me." Jack laughed, loving it when his teasing went so well. "Look down the dock a piece. She's right there." He pointed. "Oh, but she's a fair and stately woman, George!"

George couldn't see any such lass and stood to get a better look.

"I swear, George, yer as blind as a badger. There, see, her name is *Triumph*!"

"Oh, har-de-har-har!" George mocked, knowing he'd been had, for there floated a beautiful 32-gun Royal Navy frigate. She looked brand new. Her three masts towered into the pale blue Virginia sky, and a whitewashed figurehead of a beautiful and obviously female angel crowned her sleek lines. Young British sailors in their blue wool bellbottoms busily made ready their lines. George looked up and saw the mates in the riggings and along the spars. It appeared as if they were preparing to set sail. He glanced back at Jack, who truly looked in love. A shock of realization shot through him. "You really do mean to board her, don't you, Jack?"

"Shhh!" Jack cautioned, looking around slyly. "I'm rid of Bates and this place, George. I swear I'll never get the dirt out from under my nails, but a life at sea should do the trick. Today's the day, mate, and I'm going to sail with her, or"—he cast his eyes about again—"die trying!"

Before George could respond, he heard a shout from the *Triumph's* crow's nest, which signaled a defining moment in the young life of George Blow and made him forget all about his troubles and Jack's escape plan.

"Slaver-hoooo!" called a sailor with obvious distaste. "Bloody hell, I can smell her from here!"

Immediately an order barked from the helm. "Bos'n, muster an armed guard an' secure that dock! Not one scurvy, pox-infested swab is to leave that diseased crate!"

"Aye, aye, Cap'n!" replied a stout seaman, whose thick, windblown whiskers and hair stood out around his rugged face. George imagined some sweep had been using him as a human broom to clean gray soot from a hundred chimneys. The man rapped half a dozen sailors on the noggin with his jack-pin, and they scurried to the locker to retrieve their muskets.

The busy dock instantly stilled as all eyes turned to the filthy sloop edging into the dock opposite the *Triumph*. It was as decrepit as the man-of-war was polished. The sails were a patchwork of dirty linen, lines were tangled, brass was tarnished, and she obviously hadn't seen a fresh coat of paint in years. George was shocked when he made out his own first name on the bow: *George Menefie*.

The boat creaked and groaned like an old man, and the tell-tale sound of heavy metal chains clanked from the hundreds of manacles and cuffs dangling over the sides. Chains that had bound human flesh when the slaver left the Ivory Coast now hung chillingly empty. Handkerchiefs suddenly appeared along the dock and market to cover faces as the fetid scent of rot, vomit, and feces preceded the evil craft. It was the scent of death, and George's stomach churned in revulsion. But he could not look away. It wasn't just the shock that such a foul barque would carry his name, but the awful condition of its cargo. The two dozen chained waifs were more spectral than human, so close they seemed to death. Backs and legs were bent from many weeks of being confined in spaces George had heard were less than two feet high. Soiled rags could not hide the blistered, chaffed, and cracked skin; joints burst and oozing; stomachs distended; and the cruel brands still healing on arms and below breasts. Yet it was not so much the awful physical degradation but what George saw, or rather, did not see, in the eyes. They were full of despair and devoid of life. It was the terrible abandonment of hope, dreams turned to dust, that woke him from sleep for years to come.

What George experienced that day was seared into his memory and forever changed the way he viewed life. Never again would he curse God for his lot as an indentured servant, because, no matter how hard, he lived on the hope of freedom and the dream of being a man whose future would entirely rest in his own two strong arms, firm back, and solid determination to succeed. Thereafter he would bear with uncommon patience every poke, slander, and spittle hurled his way, because nothing he would ever endure would come close to the abject misery he witnessed as the *Menefie* disgorged her pathetic human refuse.

It was the crack of Bates's stick and his growl that brought George's attention back to his burden as the sad parade disappeared into the slave pens.

"Don' be gittin' uppity—yer a slave just like them!"

I ain't anything like them, George thought, but did not say. Instead, he glared at Bates with loathing and turned back to the load.

"By God! Where's that lazy son-of-a-whore Jack gone?" Bates screamed, looking around frantically.

George suppressed a smile. Jack was, indeed, nowhere in sight. "He was right here when the slaver pulled in," he replied. But Bates was already off, screeching oaths and epithets in an angry search for the boy. As he bent to lift a large crate, George caught a movement out of the corner of his eye. He paused, looked up to the bow of the *Triumph,* and nearly pitched headfirst into the bay, so surprised was he at the sight of Jack's arm furtively waving over the top, his jubilant face peering just over the bow rail. George looked around for Bates and was relieved to see his back was turned. He removed his cap, slapped it on his leg, and waved back at his lunatic friend—a friend, he now realized as the warship began to ease away from the dock, who was free.

"Huzzah!" George cried, waving his cap and bursting into laughter.

Emboldened, Jack leaped atop the railing, grasping a rope. He whistled and called out, "Ahoy, Bates, ye bloody bastard! You ever raise that stick at me again, and me Royal Navy mates will answer with a ball and shot!"

Bates ran like a madman toward the departing ship, screaming and tearing at his hair and cursing the laughing Jack. When it dawned on him that the ship was not stopping, and his charge was making a clean break, he gave one last guttural screech. In desperation, he hurled his hickory stick. Jack laughed even harder when it fell far short with a splash.

"Ha, ha, Bates, ye won't be beatin' any more boys with that damned hickory, but ye best be ready for the beatin' ye will get when Master Catelyn learns ye lost more than a stick!"

Knowing he would pay a bloody and painful price, but not caring, so happy he was for his best mate, George whooped and hollered, "Huzzah, Jackie-boy! Your dreams came true! Today your life and freedom begin! God bless ye, mate. As you see the world, don't forget your landlubber friend in Virginia, with soil in his veins!"

"Aye, Georgie!" Jack called, his voice suddenly caught in the flapping of unfurling sails. Both heard the unmistakable crack of wood on wood as the Bos'n struck his pike on the rail, just missing Jack's foot.

"Get down off'n there, pup," yelled the Bos'n. "This ain't a free ride. You're in the King's Navy now, and if you loaf, you'll swing from that yardarm afore nightfall!"

George gave a final wave and shook his head at the thought that Jack's freedom might not be what he expected after all.

Example of an Indenture Certificate

Chapter 13

Freedom Gifts

Upper New Norfolk, Virginia, 1645

George Blow sat in the Catelyn parlor, awaiting the document that would emancipate him from seven years of servitude. At twenty-three, he was not only strongly mature physically, but emotionally and intellectually. Bates was four years gone, and though George was still an indentured servant, Henry Catelyn recognized that his love of the soil, as well as the hard work, was contagious. He rewarded George's natural leadership and placed him over all the other headrights. George worked alongside his fellows during every daylight hour, and spent his evenings in conversation and study with Catelyn, from whom he learned soil types, drainage and water systems, fertilizers and crop rotations. He had gone further and been schooled by candlelight in business, economics, negotiations, markets, and finance.

George stood up somewhat impatiently and found himself admiring the large family crest Catelyn had elaborately carved in dark wood and hung behind the desk between the two large windows looking out onto the estate. Special curtains had been draped on either side, drawing honorable attention to the seal. It brought to mind the Blow family crest he had once seen in the home of a wealthy uncle just prior to the time he left for Virginia. He remembered how proud he was of the various components of the crest, and in particular, its emphasis on agriculture and the land.

Catelyn walked in as George committed to himself to someday research the Blow crest and incorporate it into his family heritage. Catelyn patted him familiarly on the shoulder, then shook the rough, strong hands of his one indentured servant who was the living model of what the headright system could do for this new land.

"Please, George, have a seat," Henry said, sitting behind his desk and unrolling a large parchment. "I know you are most anxious to get this Certificate of Redemption. It's well-earned, but if you will indulge me this one last time, I would like to impart something more."

George had heard many stories of landowners extracting additional years of service before freeing servants from their indentures, but he knew Henry Catelyn's reputation for fairness, and a glint in Henry's eyes told George he had nothing to fear. "Not at all, sir," George said, sitting in the chair in front of Catelyn's ornate oak desk. "I am always keen to hear good advice from you."

"Thank you, George. I am well-pleased with your growth and maturity. You are the epitome of the great potential of the headright system, and you, my young friend, are the future of our great commonwealth." Henry opened a top drawer in his desk and pulled out what appeared to be a rather new printing of the King James Bible. He opened it on top of the Redemption parchment and began thumbing through the Old Testament.

"As you know, most Virginia headrights receive little more than clothing and some farming equipment at the end of their indenture, but I think you know me to be God-fearing, and I believe strongly in the Good Book when it comes to my relations with my fellow man. Here," he said, adjusting his eyeglasses and pointing to a page. "Deuteronomy, chapter fifteen, beginning at verse twelve:

> *"And if thy brother, an Hebrew man, or an Hebrew woman, be sold unto thee, and serve thee six years; then in the seventh year thou shalt let him go free from thee. And when thou sendest him out free from thee, thou shalt not let him go away empty: Thou shalt furnish him liberally out of thy flock, and out of thy floor, and out of thy winepress: of that wherewith the LORD thy God hath blessed thee thou shalt give unto him. And thou shalt remember that thou wast a bondman in the land of Egypt, and the LORD thy God redeemed thee: therefore I command thee this thing to day.'"*

He closed the Bible and slid it across the desk toward George. "I came to this blessed land during the reign of our great sovereign King James the First, who gave us this literal translation from the original Hebrew as a guide to our daily lives. His appointed translators prefaced this version in this way." Catelyn locked eyes with George and continued from memory.

> *". . . the preaching of God's sacred Word among us; which is that inestimable treasure, which excelleth all the*

riches of the earth; because the fruit thereof extendeth itself, not only to the time spent in this transitory world, but directeth and disposeth men unto that eternal happiness which is above in heaven.'"

George had worked for, and learned from, this man for several years and had admired him as a teacher and mentor, but this was a side of Catelyn he had missed, and he was deeply moved by what he heard and felt. His parents were pious people who had taken him to church on holy days, but they did not own a Bible. His first experience with the direct word of God was in this office, being taught on an entirely new plane—and the words he heard spoke to his soul. He wanted to say something, but he felt choked up for only the second time in his life—the first when he bid goodbye to his mother in England.

Henry seemed to sense his discomfort and saved him from the embarrassing silence. "Son," he said, picking up the Bible, "God's eyes are on this land, and I believe He intends to prosper those who know His voice and acknowledge His hand in all things. Our sovereign king has made His word available to us. I want you to have this Bible as my first freedom gift to you."

George was even more speechless.

Henry reached down and pulled a leather satchel from behind the desk and then walked around to George, who stood up in awe. "This contains the rest of the freedom gifts I am providing you, pursuant to my God-given duty as set forth in Deuteronomy. This is more than I have ever given, but you have surely earned it. In here, you will find a new suit for your first visit to the bank. I have also provided you with one hundred dollars in cash, a secured line of credit at the implements shop in James City, and a deed for two hundred acres of virgin forest land south and west of here near the Blackwater River and swamp. Last, but not least . . ."

He turned, dipped his quill in a bottle of black ink, and affixed his signature on the Redemption Certificate. He then ceremoniously dropped hot red wax from a candle burning on the desk and stamped his signet ring next to his signature. He smiled warmly at George and gave him his freedom. "I look forward to doing business with you in the future, Master Blow!"

John Blow Family Crest

Chapter 14

Masters of the Land

Southampton, Virginia & London, England, 1645   1670

Georgc Blow took his Bible—which became the centerpiece not only of his home, but of his life—and his extraordinary freedom gifts, and did many years of honest and prosperous business with the likes of Henry Catelyn and other great Virginia pioneers of agriculture and industry. He and his sons and his indentured servants, black and white, drained swamps, cut hundreds of acres of timber, and began producing quality tobacco, cotton, and corn. His spirit of service and volunteerism was known throughout several parishes.

When war broke out with the Powhatan Confederation, he left his ax and plow, took up his tomahawk and squirrel rifle, and fought valiantly for the colony. He was there when Governor William Berkeley signed a treaty with Chief Necotowance, which set the southern boundary between Virginia and Indian lands at the Blackwater River.

The governor remembered George decades later and granted him six hundred acres on the south end of Surry County. The land slanted southwest through dense old-growth pine forests cut by the lengths of three navigable rivers—the Blackwater, the Nottoway, and the Meherrin—that would define the Blow family experience for seven generations. The following year, George claimed another six hundred and thirty-four acres on the east side of Blackwater Swamp, which formed the boundary with the Cheroenhaka Indian lands.

He was with Edward Bland in 1650 when the peaceful Algonquian guides told them the name of their age-old enemies who lived between the great rivers—the Na-da-wa, which in their language meant *vipers* or *adders*. Unfortunately, the name stuck with the Colonials and reverted to "Nottoway." The tribe lodged near the area where the Nottoway River forked with the Blackwater to form the Chowan River, which forked further south with the Meherrin and ran all the way to Albemarle Sound on the coast of North Carolina. George's children grew up exploring these forests and swamps threaded with Indian trails, filled with bears and deer, and dotted here and there with Indian villages.

George and his family developed their lands, raised cattle along with their cash crops, and invested wisely in dry goods and fabrics. He shared his innovations for draining swampland, and became known as a pious man who was quick with a handshake and a good deed. His name became well known in James City, Sussex, Surry, and Isle of Wight counties, and throughout the Commonwealth.

George was one of the last established landowners to buy slaves. For years he resisted all urgings of his business partners and children, so repulsed had he been by that first experience with the horrors of the slave trade on the dock at Jamestown. He hired Africans to work alongside his English indentured servants and treated them all with equal respect, and rewarded them as he had been rewarded by his mentor, Henry Catelyn. Several families of Virginia free Negroes owed their freedom to George Blow. However, as he aged and turned more of his dealings over to his sons and grandsons, they ultimately wore him down with the convincing argument that he could not continue to compete in business and clear, plant, and harvest sufficient lands to keep the business afloat without the life-long sustained labor of slaves.

Ultimately he relented, but he laid down the law as it pertained to Blow ownership of slaves, and set out five principles he considered inviolable in perpetuity:

1. *Blows would, whenever possible, buy whole slave families;*
2. *Blows would never break up slave families by selling members to different owners;*
3. *Blow slaves would be considered family members, and their births would be included alongside those of Blow children in the Blow family Bible;*
4. *Blow slaves would be given the Sabbath day off except under extraordinary circumstances, and only when Blow family members were required to work next to them;*
5. *Only such corporeal punishment as meted out to Blow children would be authorized for use on slaves.*

George Blow felt very strongly about the importance of family heritage and believed that all great British families, even in this new land, should live by a set of guiding principles of duty, honor, and virtue. As he grew older, he often thought of the great family crest in the home of Henry Catelyn, and yearned to reestablish his roots and leave a symbol of the Blow legacy for all those who would follow. In 1670, on his forty-seventh birthday, George and his wife Margery traveled back to England and Lincolnshire to visit relatives whom he had left behind. Many had been scattered and lands lost due to the loyal support the Blows had given King James and his son King Charles, but George learned much of the family heritage and was delighted when he was directed to London where he met his cousin, Dr. John M. Blow, who had risen to the position of organist at Westminster Abbey.

George knew his trip had been inspired when Dr. Blow invited him to his small study tucked behind the great organ. To his wonderment, on the wall was a parchment upon which was inked the Blow family coat of arms. He sat mesmerized, clutching Margery's hand, as his learned cousin detailed the meaning of the heraldic crest that was so tied to the land. He marveled as he saw confirmed in that ageless crest the love of the soil, and the spirit, drive, and almost innate ability to make it produce that had moved him throughout his life.

"As with most heraldic crests, our family coat of arms consists of a shield, the whole of which is occupied by a saltire—an x-shaped cross representing the form of the one upon which St. Andrew, patron saint of Scotland, was said to have been crucified. The use of that cross on a coat of arms was granted to one who was steadfast in defense of his beliefs. Our family has long been supporters, even to death, of King James I, who of course was a Scot, born in Edinburg Castle, the son of Mary, Queen of Scots."

John Blow placed his hand upon the large Bible that occupied most of his small desk. "I am particularly proud that our herald proclaims defense of the faith, and of the great gift of an exact and current translation of our Holy Bible under the direction of our most righteous sovereign King James."

George smiled as he pulled out the King James freedom Bible given him by Henry Catelyn.

"I see, Cousin, that we are indeed of the same cloth, though separated these many years by border and ocean," John said. "I feel perchance that ye are even more impressed by the fact that it was also our good King James who formed the Virginia Company and opened the way for you to make your future in the New World."

"That is so, John. I have long felt a special connection to King James and thought of him oft as I visited James City and sailed upon the James River. In fact, it was there I met my Margery. I will proudly proclaim my great respect and defense of the king and the faith of my fathers."

"Indeed," interrupted the younger man, standing taller. "Our family stood by the 'divine right of kings' and James' son Charles during the English Civil War. Though we lost life and lands, we stood fast, even after the execution of King Charles, and hailed the restoration of the Monarchy and the throne to his son Charles the Second near a decade ago." He paused, seeming somewhat embarrassed as he pulled a cloth from his jacket sleeve and dabbed at his eyes.

Likewise moved, but anxious to divine the rest of the meaning behind this wonderful crest, George tapped the St. Andrews' Cross. "Be there some meaning to the fact that the cross is black and the roundels in each quadrant are red?"

"Of course, my dear man," John continued, having regained his composure. "That is the beauty of the heraldic crest, with colors and shapes of distinct meaning. I must say this part of the crest has less meaning to me, but I suspect," he emphasized, looking at the weathered lines in his cousin's face and remembering the strength and roughness of his hands, "this will mean much more to you, a man who obviously has spent his life, like our ancestors, working the soil. The saltire is black, called 'sable' by some and 'Saturn' by those who emblazon by the planets. The Blow families for generations have been farmers and masters of the land. Hence, I suspect ye will be impressed that Saturn, the sower and Roman god of harvest or time of reaping, was also known as the god of fertility, especially of agriculture." John's smile mimicked that of his country cousin, and he enthusiastically continued. "He was believed to be the deity who introduced agriculture, and with it, civilization and government."

"Cousin John," George exclaimed. "If you only knew what this means to me."

John laughed outright. "Well, I've only just begun. The saltire sits between four red roundles, called in the French *Pomeis,* which are no doubt intended for apples. In ancient rolls, such roundles are called *tourteau,* which means a little tart or cake, and the figure is said to have been intended to represent the Sacred Host. In sum, my dear fellow," he said to the beaming Virginian, "our heraldic crest is all about making the land produce and blossom in service to our Heavenly King. You will note that a crown appears above the shield. When a crown appears on a crest of non-royal lineage, it is called a 'celestial crown' and signifies a heavenly reward. You have your Bible. Turn to the Book of James, the eighth verse of the second chapter, and I believe you will understand our purpose and what truly makes us all royalty."

Chapter 15

Love Thy Neighbor as Thyself

The Olde Place, Virginia, 1799

Mr. Vice President," Henry inquired, his voice grown whisper-thin from the telling of the tale, "would you honor us with reading from our beautiful Blow family Bible?" He indicated the heavy tome on the corner table. "You'll find it opens to the words of James. It's well-worn—I think you know why. It has been the crowning glory of our Blow family, lo, these many generations."

Thomas Jefferson rose and reverently grasped the thick Bible. He opened the dark brown leather cover, worn smooth by nearly a century of use. As he thumbed past the Episcopalian Book of Common Prayers and the Old Testament, he noticed that on the backs of title pages, births had been carefully recorded by a loving and graceful hand. He turned the title page bearing the King James coat of arms and the large inscription:

THE NEW
TESTAMENT
OF OUR
LORD AND SAVIOUR
JESUS CHRIST
Newly Translated out of the Original GREEK

The next turn indeed opened to the second chapter of the Book,

*If ye fulfill the royal law according to the scripture,
thou shalt love thy neighbour as thyself, ye do well.*

He grinned and looked at his traveling companion as he thought of the words he had spoken earlier that day to Madison. Jemmy's nod told him he remembered them as well. "I find it rather miraculous, friend Henry, that just this morning I said to Mr. Madison, 'To be born a Virginian in the Eighteenth Century is about as close as one could ever get to American royalty . . . to New World nobility.'"

"Thank you, honored guest." Henry broke the moment of comfortable silence that had settled upon the gathering. "Dr. Blow was so moved by the impact his copy of the Blow coat of arms had on his American cousin that he gifted him the parchment, which my great-great-grandfather George used to cast this fireback. Peter," he called, "be a good lad and fetch the family crest."

"Uncle," the tall young man complained as he rose and turned toward the library, "at twenty-three, I'm hardly a 'lad.'"

"I have to agree, Sir Henry." Jefferson laughed. "Your 'lad' appears even taller than his uncle Richard here, who I know to be over six feet like myself!"

Peter did not reply, but gave Jefferson a look of gratitude and a thankful nod.

"Bunkum!" the graybeard replied. "With all due respect, Mr. Vice President, to a man over eighty, anyone under fifty is a 'lad' and a 'pup,' though some pups be taller than others," he said with a playful wink at the five-foot-three Madison.

"Our noble forefather set the example for our family," Henry continued as Peter left the room. "From generation to generation, we have tried very hard to live up to our heritage and to be what we also believe makes us noble—how we serve our fellows and, indeed, how we treat others—even our slaves. I believe it is the same brotherly love that moved you two to be the earthly servants of our God and Heavenly King. I know it seems ironic that we own slaves," he went on, "but many Blows freed their servants, as evidenced by my brother Sam Blow in recording his history in that very Bible. Please, Thomas, if you will turn in the Lord's book and look at the back of the New Testament title page, where my brother began his family record."

Jefferson did as instructed and read the beautiful calligraphy beginning with a large cursive W. "William Blow was born the fifth day of November, Anno Dom 1738."

"Now turn to the back of the last page of the New Testament, and you'll see that my nephew Will was not the first birth recorded."

Jefferson did as instructed and smiled at Madison as he read, "Will, a Negro boy, son of Charity, born June 12th 1737."

He looked back at Henry, who smiled at the stooped, balding Negro near the parlor door, whom Jefferson recognized as the man who had served dinner. When the slave noticed all the attention in the room had turned his way, he straightened up but gazed, embarrassed, at his shoes.

"Will?" Madison questioned the servant.

"Yessir," Will, son of Charity, answered, but now with a hint of pride in his voice. "Massa Sam sho' 'nuff writ my name first in the Good Book."

"By the horn spoon!" Jefferson declared, slapping his leg and rising simultaneous with Madison. The great men shook Will's hand and sincerely congratulated him. Will was stunned, but clearly pleased by the attention. Jefferson noted that Henry Blow wore an even greater look of pride.

The evening was closing, and the other men in the room rose. Richard approached the guests.

"We have your rooms prepared. if you are ready to retire," he said.

Madison nodded with half-closed lids, but Jefferson dissembled. "If you're up to it, Captain, I'd like to take a stroll before bed."

"Certainly," Richard replied, delighted at the prospect of a few more moments with the great man.

A tall young slave in a brass-buttoned blue coat, whose skin was the color of the mahogany table he had been polishing, rushed to open the door for his master. "Will Massa Richard be needin' a coat?" he politely asked as they stepped outside.

"No, thank-e Limerick," replied Richard Blow. "It be a warm night, and I'm still sweating off our feast." He felt guilty as he said it, realizing his butler had likely not eaten yet that evening.

It was well past ten, but the full moon had courted the lightning bugs into a nocturnal dance.

"Remarkable," Jefferson said as they strolled down the lane. "I must remember to add this phenomenon to my botanizing journal." He smiled and turned to his companion. "Tell me, Colonel, was that your name I counted as the sixth entry in the family Bible?" Without waiting for a reply, he added, "From what I know of you, you have certainly added to the great Virginia Blow heritage. You would make your father and your great-grandfather very proud indeed!"

When Samuel Blow died in 1766 at the age of sixty-one, he left his twenty-year-old son Richard as his sole heir. He had dwelt at

The Quarters for several years and then purchased an additional plantation called Tower Hill in 1774. His prominence in Southampton County earned him a spot on the Committee of Safety and led to his involvement in the first major American victory at Great Bridge, Virginia.

They stopped outside the stable, and two magnificent equines whinnied as they sensed their masters. "I understand, sir, that six months before I penned the Declaration of Independence, you were involved in the immortal battle of Great Bridge that drove the British out of our beloved Commonwealth for the duration of the war."

Seeing his knowledge confirmed in Richard's downward gaze, he continued. "I can tell you, Richard, that victory, which we called the 'Second Battle of Bunker Hill,' with over a hundred redcoats killed and not one single American life lost, gave me and my fellow representatives the courage to sign that revolutionary decree by pledging our lives, our fortunes, and our sacred honor."

With the humility of a man who has served his country under arms, Blow interrupted the vice president before he could go on. "Please, sir, I was not yet commissioned at that early date. As a bearer of dispatches, the closest I came to combat was wearing out this filly's mama running an important missive to Colonel Woodford," he said, rubbing the black mare's muzzle, "and tried to impress a stout farm horse from an even stouter farmer." He laughed at the memory. "I had him by five inches, but he had me by fifty pounds, so I went for alarm as opposed to force of arms. I shouted, 'In the name of the republic,' leaped on the horse, and galloped off with my head tucked tightly to his neck."

"Huzzah!" Jefferson laughed, startling Richard and the horses. He patted his new friend on the back, then grasped him at the elbow. Looking directly in his eyes, Jefferson said something the Blow family would long remember. "You may defer my praise as a foot-soldier in the militia, but it is your service on the seas that has earned my eternal thanks, and that of a grateful nation."

After accepting a commission as a captain in the Fourth Virginia Regiment, Richard had felt he could better serve by using his considerable wealth to build ships that would aid the fledging nation in running British blockades and bringing critical supplies to armies and civilians alike. In 1779, he partnered under the name of Baker, Oldham, and Blow with a small fleet of eight schooners, several sloops, and packets. In 1781, having grown weary of always running, he committed his own resources to meet the enemy in combat on the seas and built a 10-gun frigate that was finished even as Lord Cornwallis surrendered at Yorktown. She was christened the *Count de Grasse* in honor of the great French naval commander who had played such a key role in America's victory.

"I heard you were actually captured by the British at some point. Is that true?"

"Indeed I was, though I'd hoped you had not been aware of that fact," responded a now-embarrassed Richard Blow. "I had the honor and the despair to witness both our finest victory at Great Bridge and our worst defeat at the siege of Charleston."

He stooped and picked up a stout branch lying in the road. The death or capture of over five thousand Americans by the hated British clearly still burned bright, nearly twenty years later. Richard's large hands tightened and turned red before he suddenly snapped the branch in two across an upraised knee. Jefferson waited for him to calm and continue the tale.

"I was aboard my swift little schooner *Venus* when we ran Clinton's blockade and delivered balls and powder to General Lincoln, but were trapped when the British warships entered the harbor and brought more than a hundred guns to bear. On the high seas, I would have tried to dodge and run, but in Charleston, I would have signed a death warrant for my crew."

He paused and tossed the broken stick into the night, silencing the cacophony of frogs. Jefferson needed no such silencing. He was fully awed by the tales of those who actually risked their lives and their fortunes in fighting for the freedom he and his colleagues had simply declared.

"I spent ten months below decks on a stinking, rotting barge at the mouth of Albemarle Sound. All I could think of during my captivity was that the river, where I floated in my prison and where I thought I would waste away and die, had its beginning just a few miles south of where you and I stand right now, where the three rivers that form the boundaries of this very county flow together. Imagine that, Mr. Vice President—the lapping water against my prison walls was the same water I had swam and fished as a boy!"

"I see why you named your first warship the *Count de Grasse*. I assume you were freed not long after he landed the three thousand French Troops and supplies that resulted in the defeat of Cornwallis at the Battle of Guilford Court House."

"You speak truth, Mr. Jefferson. Cornwallis abandoned the Carolinas so quickly to fight on in Delaware, we simply woke one morning to find our guards had slipped away."

"Let me guess," Jefferson interrupted, having fully taken the measure of this extraordinary Virginian. "You found a canoe and paddled your way home up the rivers of your childhood!"

Richard smiled. "Indeed I did. I paddled right up the Nottoway to the bridge you crossed at Jerusalem this morning. A few months later, after Cornwallis went scurrying back to Britain with his rather large tail between his legs, I made my way back to Charleston to find my lovely *Venus* tied up to the wharf, no worse for the wear, but I was never able afterward to rid her of the stink of kidney pie!'"

The hearty laughter that followed was a fine cap on the evening, and the two friends—one great in the eyes of his country and the other great in the eyes of the vice president of the United States—turned back toward the Olde Place.

"One final inquiry before we retire, if I may," Jefferson asked as they strolled back in the bright light of the full moon. "I am much preoccupied these days over our plight with the Barbary Pirates. When I was ambassador to France and resisted the order to pay ransom and tribute to the Dey of Algiers for release of the *Betsy* crew, I knew we were making a terrible mistake. It was my considered opinion that war was the only reasonable choice, and advocated the creation of a navy. To me, tribute paid to the pirates was money thrown away, and the only thing they understood was gunpowder and shot. This is actually the primary reason I asked to meet with you on this botanizing trip. My daughter Martha informs me she met you when your fleet had a run-in with the Musselmen off the coast of North Africa. If you recall, she was studying at a convent in France at the time, and was in transit."

Blow was a little surprised that Jefferson knew of his harrowing escape from Algerian corsairs twelve years earlier. "Yes, sir," he responded. "I was captaining one of the ships in a trade fleet that included several of my schooners when we were set upon by pirates. We used every skill with canvas and rope and rudder to elude capture."

He stopped at the foot of the porch steps and continued speaking with a distant look in his eyes. "When we were safely beyond Gibraltar, I had Martha to dinner on my sloop, and she told me of her fear. I forget her exact words, but I will never forget the look in her eyes."

Very serious now, Jefferson replied, "You might forget, but I cannot, for she wrote them down for me, and they have been seared into my conscience." He reached into the breast pocket of his vest and pulled out a worn and yellowed paper. He unfolded it gently and repeated as he handed it to Richard,

". . . only to return to a country that allowed slavery. Good God, have we not enough? It grieves my heart . . . that these, our fellow creatures, should be treated so terribly . . . by many of our countrymen."

As Richard looked at the note, Jefferson continued. "And so the topic turns again to slavery, which preoccupied much of my conversation with Mr. Madison on our way here earlier today. I fear our hypocrisy as a nation, and my own hypocrisy when it comes to slavery, might bring upon us the condemnation of God."

"I share your concern," Richard responded, returning the precious letter. "And I am taking steps to divest myself of my slaves and my plantations. I realize that my actions alone will make no difference on the large scale of things, but you never know what might come of individual action. I married the daughter of the mayor, and we have built a fine white house on the battery in Portsmouth. My shipping and other business interests there and in Norfolk will occupy all my time, and I will be handing over all my properties at The Quarter and Tower Hill to my only son, George. But I have also decided to do something for my young cousin Peter. His father, Richard III, was only five when his father died. My father took him in and, when I was born, named me after him. He was more like an older brother to me instead of the cousin he is. So when Richard III himself passed away in 1786, when Peter was just nine years old and I was yet unmarried, I asked my cousin John to become his guardian at Rose Hill."

He paused and turned to look directly at the vice president. "I can't explain it, but now I feel that something very special will happen if he's given an opportunity to make his own way, and so I intend to give this Olde Place plantation over to Peter, with its attached property and slaves, with the only condition that he care for the grave of his great-grandfather Sam and carry on the proud Blow tradition of expanding and improving these lands."

As if on cue, a young slave boy ran up to the pair, panting.

"Massa Richard, Hannah done giv' birth! He a tiny baby boy, and she say his name is Samuel!"

"Samuel, is it?" asked a smiling Jefferson. "If that's the Hannah in Sam Blow's family Bible, I'd call that an omen!"

"That's right, Mr. Vice President. Young Peter's property has just grown by one—and his name appears to be Sam Blow!"

"Huzzah!" Thomas Jefferson repeated, "Huzzah!"

* * *

On March 4th, 1861, Abraham Lincoln placed his left hand on a small Bible bound in burgundy velvet with gilt edges, raised his right hand to the square, looked Chief Justice Roger Brookes Taney squarely in the eyes, and took the oath of office as the sixteenth president of the United States of America.

Both men were accomplished lawyers, and it had been remarked how alike they were in physical appearance. They were tall, long-limbed, and boney, and that day wore similar ill-fitting black suits. But that is where the similarities ended. Lincoln stood ramrod straight. The Chief Justice stooped with his eighty-three years of age. Lincoln would be the seventh and last president to whom he administered the oath—more than any other chief justice in the history of the court. Taney was a sixth-generation American whose ancestors were aristocratic Maryland slave owners, and Lincoln a seventh-generation American whose forefathers were mostly successful New England businessmen, and of late, frontiersmen, who did not own slaves.

Surprisingly, it was a slave who, more than anyone else, brought these two powerful leaders together that blustery March day. They had been adversaries over Taney's ugly decision that kept Dred Scott and his African race in slavery. Lincoln had used his attacks on that unpopular decision to propel himself into a presidency that would lead to freedom. Their personal stories wove through the history of the nation and prepared them for immortality.

One year before the first George Blow came to Virginia, a humble weaver from Hingham, England, named Samuel Lincoln, made his way to the Massachusetts Bay Colony with other members of the Hingham Puritan congregation of the Reverend Peter Hobart. They built a new town outside Plymouth Colony and named it after their home in Britain. Samuel Lincoln became a successful businessman and a leader in the church, and with his Irish bride, Martha, raised eleven children in the promising new land. Many generations of Lincolns, including grandson Mordecai, were born in the Hingham home, but Mordecai later moved to New Jersey and his son John to Pennsylvania where he married. In 1774, John became the father of Abraham Lincoln, grandfather of the sixteenth president of the United States. As merchants, shopkeepers, and businessmen, the Lincolns never became slave owners.

In 1660, while George Blow was turning his indentured service into a great success as a Virginia planter, Michael Taney, a young Anglican from England, signed on to serve his own seven years as an indentured servant. By 1685, Michael had made a lot of money in tobacco and built a three-story white clapboard house on the crest of a hill above the Patuxent River in southern Maryland. His son, Michael II, and thereafter four more generations named Michael Taney, would be born in that home, including Michael V, the father of Roger Brookes Taney, who, as fifth Chief Justice of the United States Supreme Court, would render the terrible Dred Scott opinion. As plantation aristocrats, the Taneys were slave owners.

As Abraham Lincoln opened his own chapter in the life of this nation and Roger Taney closed his, one can only guess what was going through the minds of these political foes. While Taney recited and Lincoln echoed the oath to "preserve, protect and defend the Constitution of the United States," seven states had already succeeded from the Union and formed the Confederate States of America, and that very morning had raised their new flag, the Stars and Bars, above the capitol in Montgomery, Alabama. The nation was hurtling into a bloody civil war. One person was most likely on both their minds: an obscure but determined slave who had never stopped in his quest to be treated as a man, and to secure freedom and safety for the three women he loved more than life itself.

One hundred and forty eight years later, another thin man from Illinois would stand on that same spot on the south portico of the Capitol, place his hand on that self-same velvet bible, and take that identical oath as the first African-American president of the United States of America.

Part VI

Bloody Saline

"If I could only weep,
I think sweet help with my salt tears would come,
To ease the cruel pain that is so dumb,
And will not let me sleep."

- Ella Wheeler Wilcox (1850-1919)

Slave Trader

Chapter 16

We Sat Down and Wept

New London, Missouri, 1853

Poppy, tell us the name o' this river again," chirped seven-year-old Lizzie as she slipped into the brown, salty water.

"The Salt River," replied Dred matter-of-factly, knowing what was coming next as he waded toward her in the shallow bend of the river.

"No, Poppy, the Injun name." Her wry smile gave away that she knew exactly what the name was, but she wanted her father to say it again.

"Oh, that. Well, they jes' calls it the AUHA-HA-HA-HA-HAH!" The name turned into a belly laugh as he grabbed his youngest under the arms and tickled her into squeals of delight.

"Now, you say it, Lizzie!"

She barely got out "Auha . . ." before breaking into a giggle fit.

"Your turn, Gypsy." Dred turned toward Eliza, who had been born fifteen years ago that very day on the Mississippi steamship *Gypsy*. She sat in the water with only her cherubic face poking above the surface. Perhaps because she was brought forth into this life on the greatest of all rivers, Eliza loved the water as much as Dred.

"Auhaha—" She almost made it, but with her father and sister giggling, she couldn't help herself and broke out in a husky laugh that startled Dred a bit because of its maturity.

Dred caught his breath long enough to call to Harriet on the bank, emphasizing his request with a splash that caught her by surprise. "Your turn, Harriet! Say it!"

Always the serious one, Harriet wasn't about to join in the frivolity. "Dred! Jes' 'cause the Injuns calls it the 'Laughing Waters' doesn't mean we has to oblige them!"

"Aw, come on, Mammy, say it!" laughed Eliza.

"Yeah, say it! Say it!" chirped Lizzie, sounding like a myna bird.

"Fine!" Harriet replied, trying not to smile. "Au . . ." Her smile grew. "Auha . . ." She felt the dimples spontaneously suck in on her cheeks as her daughters watched her, wide-eyed and broad-grinned. "Au . . . heeheeheehee!" she erupted in a spray of girlish laughter that nearly bowled Dred over. Oh, how he loved that gal! She fell over backward and literally rolled around. The stunned silence of the three in the river at Harriet's wild abandonment lasted only a second, and then the whole family was laughing and splashing and loving life in this strange, salty river, far from the strife and fear and degradation of slavery and the notoriety of lawsuits.

Sadly, the magical spell of that beautiful moment was about to be shattered in a way that only the enslavement of one man by another could.

"Maaaaammy!" cried seven-year-old Lizzie as she clambered out of the Salt River and leaped into her mother's embrace. "'Liza done splashed water in my eyes and they's burnin'!"

Before her mother could scold her, Eliza dove under the surface, then came flying up like the dolphins Dred had once seen leaping in front of Richard Blow's ship when he sailed with him during the War of 1812.

"Thas not true!" she protested. "Lizzie's a baby and done splash herself! 'Sides, this water don' hurt—It makes my skin soft, an Sher'f LaBeaume say it kills chiggers! I'm never gittin' out!"

With that, her thick, curly locks again disappeared below the surface so she missed her little sister scream through her tears, "I'ze no baby!"

Lizzie calmed quickly in Harriet's arms, her gentle saline tears washing out the heavier salt of the river. Harriet had stopped laughing but still smiled, wondering why the natives had called this salty river "Laughing Water." But she startled when she saw the watery red tracks running down her baby's cheeks. For a moment she thought they were bloody tears. Dred, standing waist deep, saw them too and shuddered.

La Saline Ensanglantde. He whispered the French term for this part of the river. "Bloody Saline." His mirth disappeared and he wished he were out of the river. Dred had always been a superstitious man, and as he looked at the red autumn leaves falling into the water from the trees along the bank, he spontaneously uttered a curative oath and spit three times, then looked back at the river, suddenly fearful for Eliza. His heart stopped beating until he saw her on the dark brown bank where she had surfaced ten yards downstream. "Gypsy!" he called, surprised that the calm in his voice hid his panic. He had always felt his eldest daughter was magically blessed by water, having been born on the great Father of Waters. But now he urgently wanted her out of the river.

He knew its violent history, but he had brought his family here because of its more recent reputation for having healing properties. Still, the premonition he felt looking at what he thought were bloody tears on the cheeks of his youngest child had convinced him something truly wicked was about to happen.

In the spring of 1792, Maturin Bouvet, a Frenchman with LaClede's Colony at the site of what would become St. Louis, took an exploratory trip up the Mississippi and came to the wide opening of the river the Indians called "Auhaha." He followed the river several miles until he came upon several reddish springs that were heavily salted. He eventually built a salt works and established a homestead which he called Bouvet's Lick because of the deer and other animals that came to the shores at low tide to lick the salt deposits on the banks. Over the years, other settlers came along and established homesteads at springs along the river, including Trabue's Lick, Freemore's Lick, and Boone's Lick.

The Sauk Indians were angered that the white settlers were driving the buffalo, deer, and other wild game from their traditional hunting grounds, luring them with salt. After destroying the works several times, the Indians finally attacked and killed Bouvet, burning his body. They later massacred and scalped a large number of settlers working the de Lauriere Salt Works. The sorely misnamed "Laughing Waters" became *La Saline Ensanglantde.*

In 1816, Louis Auguste LaBeaume, father of the Scott's benefactors Charles Edmund and Sheriff Louis Tarteron LaBeaume, bought a farm next to the river. Both men later built homes in the city, but spent a lot of time at their farm in what became Ralls County, Missouri. It was from the LaBeaumes that Dred learned the bloody history of the river.

However, there had been peace along the river since the 1832 Black Hawk War. General Winfield Scott, thirteen hundred regular Army troops, and the help of Illinois militia—including a company from New Salem led by a young Captain Abraham Lincoln and commissioned by Lt. Jefferson Davis—defeated and signed a peace treaty with the Fox and Sauk Indians. Prosperous farms, salt works, and recreational bathing retreats for the city folk from St. Louis had sprung up along the river.

It had been a year since the Scotts appeared in front of the good judge Alexander Hamilton to declare their intent to file for their freedom in the federal courts. The mob scene at the courthouse had caused Dred and Harriet great fear for the safety of their girls, and they sent them to live well outside of St. Louis in relative isolation at the LaBeaume farm. The children flourished in the country, but Dred and Harriet had been kept so busy in their labors, they had only been able to see their girls a few times since then.

But it was October and Eliza's fifteenth birthday, and while birthday parties were generally unknown to slaves, the Blows, LaBeaumes, and Fields planned a large celebration. The parents wanted a few days alone with the girls before the weekend, when they would be joined by all their friends from the Rev. John Anderson's congregation and also their white friends and benefactors.

With the girls out of the water and being toweled off by their doting mother, Dred began to feel some comfort. But as the sun began to set, a chill wind abruptly changed what had been an unusually warm mid-October day. Dred shivered and pitched in to get his girls dressed and the family safely back to the LaBeaume's farmhouse. In their absence, their friends had been preparing the home for a wonderful surprise party for Eliza.

However, Dred's evil premonition was about to become a terrible reality.

Hurrying along the road, Dred heard the sound of a horse and buggy coming up the road behind them. He suppressed the irrational impulse to run with his family into the woods. They had never felt threatened here, over a hundred miles from the city, and it was likely friends arriving late for the surprise party. In an instant, the hack was upon them and nearly ran into Dred, who had pushed his wife and daughters to the outside.

Dred turned to confront the reckless man, his arms back behind him and surrounding his loved ones.

"Ho, horse," the driver screeched, cracking a whip over the horse's right ear. An icy shock coursed through Dred's body when he saw the crazed eyes of the man he hated most in this world: John F. A. Sanford, the brother of his absent missus Irene Emerson and therefore his surrogate master.

Not long after her husband John's death, Missus Irene moved to Massachusetts and remarried. She appointed her influential brother to handle her affairs and property in St. Louis. To the Scotts' relief, Sanford had moved to New York to handle American Fur Company's eastern interests. Although the Scotts knew he kept constant watch over them through his powerful pro-slavery in-laws, the Chouteaus, they hoped to never see him again. They hadn't heard he was back in town. Though physically absent, the cruel Sanford was never far from their minds. His agents and many ruffians from the Chouteau-owned American Fur Company checked on them and threatened them often.

Dred looked around quickly for anyone who might help him, but in vain.

"Into the barn, *now!*" barked Sanford. There was murder in his pale, glassy eyes, and Dred found himself looking for a weapon even as he instinctively obeyed the command, ushering his terrified family before him into the LaBeaume barn. To his dismay, he saw nothing within easy reach. An impromptu spasm arced across his back as he saw his master grab the ten-foot whip from the buggy.

"Oh, Dred, he's corned," whispered Harriet. Dred, too, could smell the strong odor of liquor on Sanford's breath. He knew this was going to be bad.

The family watched without another word as Sanford barred the barn door and turned to them, looking all crazy, the leather lash and cracker snaking a trail on the dusty floor behind him.

"You niggas have caused me and the Chouteaus more trouble'n you're worth! I heard your spawn was hidin' out here with the sheriff's kin, and lo an' behold, here's the entire Scott family! The good Lord must be smiling on me!"

Not surprisingly, it was Harriet who spat back, "The Lord's got nuffin' to do with what you has in mind, Massa John!"

"Silence!" bellowed Sanford. "Y'all are 'bout to be cow-hided!"

The whip cracked ominously just inches from Harriet's face. The girls screeched, and Dred scooted in front of his wife, glaring hatefully up at the much larger white man.

Sanford laughed at Dred's impertinent stare. "I'll learn you, you black cur. I can gouge out an eye with one flick o' this here popper."

Crack went the whip, and Harriet joined her daughters in a cry of fright. But Dred did not flinch.

"That's it!" hollered Sanford, spittle flying from his lips. "Dred and Harriet, disrobe . . . *now!"*

Dred didn't hear the pop, but felt his flesh tear along his left cheekbone. He was so startled he automatically started to remove his shirt. He suddenly realized that any opposition to this "Tom of Bedlam" might prove fatal to his family. He instantly reverted to the submissive slave, head bowed and eyes down, as he dropped his shirt to the floor.

"Please, Massa, not Harriet an' the girls, jes' me. It's all my fault."

The angry welt that instantly bloomed on Dred's bare chest was Sanford's only reply. Harriet quickly began unbuttoning her blouse.

"All your clothes," Sanford growled. "You think you's a man? You think you can walk into a white man's courthouse when you belongs on the steps? You think you can embarrass me and the entire Chouteau family by claiming you is free?" He cracked the tip of the whip on Dred's bony knuckles that fumbled with his britches. The pants dropped, and Dred cussed in agony, shaking the blood off his wounded hand.

"*Damn* you!" shouted Sanford. "You thinks you can cuss at a white man?" The strike on his shoulder whirled Dred around. The girls were crying, and Harriet sheltered them.

"Please, Massa Sanford, not in front a the girls." She turned and fell on her knees in front of him. "I begs you, please!"

But it was no use arguing with a lunatic.

"All your clothes, woman," he hissed. "OFF!"

Eliza and Lizzie huddled together in the corner, weeping and hiding their faces from the sight of their parents stripped naked, hands gripping the railing of the horse stall.

Thwack! Dred shuddered at the ungodly wet sound of flesh being flayed, but hearing his dear Harriet moan tore at his heart. He looked in her terrified eyes and then at Sanford. He wanted more than he ever had to kill another human being with his bare hands.

Thump! Dred felt his own tougher flesh raise but not break under the cruel cracker. He gripped the railing with all his might, not against the pain, for his rage blocked that out entirely, but with the sure knowledge that if he let go he would attack his tormentor and would not stop until he, or Sanford, was dead. If he did that, he knew that no one—not the Blows, the sheriff, or the bright young lawyer Field—could save his family.

Thawck! Harriet screamed this time, and Dred roared.

"Silence, dog!" Sanford shouted, and sped up Dred's beating.

Dred ground his teeth and tried to block out the sounds of combined suffering as the rawhide stitched terrible tracks across their backs. Each strike of the whip on his own weathered skin flashed like a white hot blaze, and he agonized to know that the violence on his wife's soft skin had to be terrible.

Schwack! Schwack! The strikes became wetter, and Dred prayed for strength. He feared that his submission and inaction would shame him in front of his wife. Her beautiful smooth back that had never been beaten was covered with gore. She had stopped crying out, and tears sprang from his eyes at her courage and his own lack thereof. She sensed his guilt and looked at him with love and compassion. Her "this too shall pass" nod told him to hold on.

And so he held on. Trembling with rage and the shameful submission of a dog, he stoically took his beating, though in his heart he was plotting his revenge. *Somehow, some day, Sanford will get his comeuppance,* he swore silently to God.

The blows stopped and Sanford doubled over, breathing deeply, sweat rolling off his brow. "That's more like it," he panted. "Let this be a lesson to y'all!" He dropped the whip and stood with his hands on his hips. Dred and Harriet quickly grabbed their clothes, and Sanford watched malevolently, his gaze settling on the two girls. He bent to pick up the whip. "Your turn," he growled.

"Mammyyyy! Poppyyyy!" they cried. Harriet spotted the pitchfork the same time Dred did, but she grabbed his arms in her strong hands. "No!" she whispered. "Let me try first!"

Harriet pulled her dress around her shoulders and threw herself onto the floor between Sanford and her girls. "Please, Massa John, we's learned our lesson. Please, not the children. Have mercy, sir. Please, I begs it. They's jes' babies!"

Sanford's hungry leer dashed Harriet's hope that there was any mercy or even humanity in the man. "Eliza sure don't look like no child," he mocked, licking his fevered lips. "And in fact, if that damned nigger-loving Judge Hamilton hadn't forbidden it, I would have sold her away to someone who knows how to treat nigger-bitches like her."

He stepped over Harriet and grabbed Eliza, pulling her to her feet. "Let's have a looky-see," he said and prepared to tear off her dress. Dred inched toward the fork in the hay, determined now to kill the man before he could defile his daughter. But just then, the sound of several distant voices stopped him and Sanford in their tracks, the former buoyed with hope of rescue, and the latter out of sheer cowardice.

"Train up a child in the ways they should go . . ." Sanford misquoted scripture. He grabbed little Lizzie in his other hand and pushed both girls to the feed trough.

"Bend over," he ordered the sobbing girls, "and take your lickin'."

The calls that were coming closer were all that stopped Dred from securing the weapon and impaling the beast before he laid a hand on his babies. Looking toward the door, Sanford grabbed the wooden handle of the buggy whip and beat the girls' behinds several times before sprinting for the door. He turned and spat out over the girls' caterwauling, "Y'all are gonna lose your federal case! And when you does, I'se gonna personally hunt you down and break you apart, and you won't ever find each other again!"

The barn door banged shut behind him, and the Scotts swept up their children in their arms, weeping in pain, embarrassment, and outrage. They all flinched as they heard the whip crack and the buggy squeak as it took off. They heard Roswell call to the fleeing villain, and Dred wished he could hide his family in their shame. But the door came back open, and the frame was filled with the sympathetic faces of their friends. In his humiliation and rage, Dred only saw *white* faces, and his anger grew as he watched it dawn on the crowd what had happened and that he, Dred, had been powerless to stop it.

"I shoulda kilt him, Mr. Field!" he cried. "I ain't no kinda man who lets a man beat his naked wife in front a his chillun!"

Roswell tried unsuccessfully to console him as the womenfolk enveloped Harriet and the children. "If you had killed him, it would have been the end of your family, Dred. You did right. That bad egg will get his comeuppance, mark my word!"

Dred was inconsolable. "I don' know 'bout that. Mebbe Nat Turner had it right. Maybe the only way to be a free man is to kill fo' it!"

Roswell looked taken aback by the level of his client's murderous mien.

"Dash it all, Dred!" Taylor Blow cut in. "You know that ain't the answer. We're gonna fix Sanford's flint in court!"

Dred looked in Taylor's eyes and almost believed him, but couldn't get his wife's torn flesh, and Nat Turner, out of his mind.

Sheriff LaBeaume called for a bucket of salt water from the river when he saw the bloody stripes soaking through Dred's and Harriet's blouses.

"That water's cursed," Dred complained. "They'll never be 'Laughing Waters' to me again."

"No, Dred, the man who did this to y'all is cursed. Them waters'll heal ya."

"It'll take mor'un salt water to heal these wounds," interjected Reverend Anderson, who had joined the crowd in the barn. "Only freedom can do it!" He raised his arms and eyes to heaven. "We are as the children of Israel, captives in a strange land, Oh Lord. Yes, we are as thy chosen people as it says in Psalms 137, 'by the rivers of Babylon, there we sat down, yea, we wept, when we remembered Zion. We hanged our harps upon the willows in the midst thereof. For there they that carried us away captive required of us a song; and they that wasted us required of us mirth, saying, Sing us one of the songs of Zion. How shall we sing the Lord's song in a strange land?' Please, Father God, let it be by the courts of this great land that we finally raise a song of freedom, and if not, then only through the Lord Jesus, as it says in the Good Book, 'and with His stripes we are healed.'"

* * *

Roswell looked his friend Dred in the eyes, and the sadness and anguish he saw there were almost unbearable. "Dred, you will have your day before the highest court in the land. That I promise you! And you won't be there just for yourself. Slaves all over this land are hoping and praying that your courage and your sacrifice and your unbending determination to seek justice will result in their own freedom some day."

Dred did not respond. He did not blink his blood-red eyes. There were no tears. He held Roswell's stare and moved his head ever so slightly to the right, then slowly to the left.

Feeling that his client was on cusp of a "fight or flight" decision, Roswell grasped Dred's upper arms in both hands. Dred's sinewy muscles tensed, and Roswell felt the flesh spasm under his touch and did not flinch as he felt the sticky wetness seeping through the cloth.

The words of an anonymous poet came to Roswell's mind. "Let there be such oneness between us, Dred, that 'when one cries, the other tastes salt.'" He witnessed Dred's visage soften ever so slightly, and so he stared right back and firmly but softly urged, "Trust me. Nat Turner was wrong, Dred. And all who follow his path will end up just like him—six feet under!"

Dred hesitated for a moment longer. Roswell could not read Dred's thoughts, but he did startle as he saw into Dred's tortured soul, the taste of bloody saline suddenly in his mouth.

* * *

True to his word, two weeks later, on November 2nd, 1853, Roswell Field filed *Scott v. Sanford* in the United States Circuit Court in Missouri, alleging diversity jurisdiction in that the Scotts were citizens of Missouri and John Sanford was a citizen of New York, thus beginning the final legal leg of Dred Scott's long journey for freedom—an odyssey which had begun at the turn of the century at The Olde Place, Southampton County, Virginia

Part VII

The Olde Place

"Civilization is a stream with banks. The stream is sometimes filled with blood from people killing, stealing, shouting and doing the things historians usually record, while on the banks, unnoticed, people build homes, make love, raise children, sing songs, write poetry, and even whittle statues. The story of civilization is the story of what happened on the banks. Historians . . . ignore the banks for the river."

- Will Durant (1885-1981)

Nottoway River Hanging Tree

Chapter 17

The New Jerusalem

Southampton County Seat, Virginia, 1805

The boys frolicked on the high bank above the Nottoway River while the adults kept one eye on the children and one on the celebration beginning at the Jerusalem courthouse just fifty feet behind them and continuing south along the river. This was the second grand July 4th festival in a row where the white folks from all over Southampton gathered at the county seat to celebrate what President Jefferson called "The Louisiana Purchase." Last year, the president had announced the treaty and purchase, and called for celebration that the United States of America would nearly double in size, and that the abundant resources of the great Mississippi River would enrich the country greatly. The transfer occurred in St. Louis in March of 1804, and the president had again called for special festivities to celebrate, not just the birth of the nation, but its grand rebirth, as in the words of treaty signer Robert Livingston, "The United States take rank this day among the first powers of the earth!"

The slaves who gathered along the east bank of the river felt no joy in the celebration. It seemed as though their masters were spitting in their faces as they crowed about their independence and freedom from the oppressive king of England, whilst denying their slaves the same grand opportunity. They wondered about celebrating a treaty that doubled the size of the United States. To them, it just meant more lands for more slaves to work. For most of their fellow slaves, this day was no different than the three hundred and sixty-four other days of the year. Those slaves in Jerusalem this July 4th were mostly drivers, valets, personal assistants, maids, and cooks, along with their smaller children who could not be left alone during the two days of merrymaking by the white Americans. The manual labor temporarily done, the Negroes were not expressly forbidden to participate, but none felt entirely welcome, either.

Red, white, and blue streamers, flags, and banners were draped on rustic booths scattered along the grassy area that ran between Main Street on the east, the river on the west, between the courthouse and Mahone's Tavern on the north, and St. Luke's Episcopal Church on the south. In the center was the stately white board home built in 1791 known as Seven Gables. It was festooned with bunting all along the wrap-around porch, and a flag hung on each of the gables facing Main Street. The booths offered fruits and cakes, blankets, quilts, and all sorts of homemade geegaws for sale. A small band on the Seven Gables porch filled the air with a brassy rendition of "Yankee Doodle Dandy."

Hannah's mouth watered as a slight breeze lifted the heavy humidity and brought with it the scent of roasting meat and vegetables. She looked unhappily at the stale pone o' bread and dried venison in her knapsack. She closed it, glancing toward her five-year-old son. The only similarity between what was going on a few hundred feet away in town and here along the bank was the children's laughter.

She brightened as she saw her tiny boy run with arms outstretched like a bird and leap off the bank into the air. He seemed to float momentarily, and then disappeared from sight. Her heart stopped for a moment until she heard the splash, then she smiled as all the other children along the bank cheered the brazen deed. She knew that as a mother she should be more worried, but Samuel had been like a fish in the water since he was barely old enough to walk. He swam in the Gum Branch of the Nottoway that ran through The Olde Place Plantation, and the several times each year when she and Samuel had traveled with Master Peter and Missus Elizabeth to town, she had watched him swim in the deep, though slow-moving, waters of the Nottoway where it made a bend north then south again right next to Jerusalem.

She laughed when she saw Samuel's little dark head poke above the edge of the bank, followed by his sinewy frame, the water slick on his ebony skin. The other children, big and small, gathered around him, laughing and praising and patting his back. "Sammy! Sammy! Sammy!" they cheered. She didn't approve of the pet names they used, and he'd told her not long ago that he wanted her to call him just "Sam." She couldn't do it. To her, he would only and always be Samuel.

Their eyes met, and she saw the pride in his wide eyes. He was very small for his age, which she knew already resulted in some teasing. But she repeated the same prayer of thanks she had said many times, grateful that his size meant he would likely avoid the terrible life of a field hand. That he was fearless, however, caused her some concern.

Hannah noticed Samuel, a slight frown on his face, looking past his admirers to another boy, whom she recognized as Nathaniel Turner from the Cross Keys plantation just south of The Olde Place. At four, and a year younger than Samuel, he was already the taller of the two. He sat solemnly by himself, seemingly disturbed by the adulation her boy was receiving. She knew instantly that Samuel noticed it, too. She watched apprehensively as Samuel broke away from the others and walked over to Nathaniel, whom the children called Nat, but relaxed when she saw Samuel's bright smile work its magic even on the strange Turner child. From here she could see the odd, warty bumps on Nat's forehead and naked chest, which either scared or amused the other children. Samuel sat down, and before long they were locked in some deep conversation.

Hannah noticed that Nat's "mother" also watched the two boys. Henrietta, an older woman like herself, was not the boy's real mother, but a house slave to whom the child was given to be raised. Nat's birth mother was said to be a young quashy named Nancy, who had been born in Africa, kidnapped, and brought to James City as a teen, then sold at auction to Ben Turner, who was the boy's father. Rumor had it the girl had tried to choke her newborn son to death, perhaps in anger and despair at the rape. But the child had survived, though many believed the assault made him "different."

When Henrietta started to turn her head, Hannah looked away. She did not want to listen to more stories about how "special" Nathaniel was, and how he could already read and saw visions and dreamed dreams and could sometimes tell the future, and that even the strange growths on his body were themselves a sign from God. From the moment of Samuel's "miraculous" birth, the night Mr. Jefferson and Mr. Madison had visited the Blows, she felt the Holy Spirit whisper that her own boy was destined for something special. But she had kept that to herself.

Samuel's father was a slave owned by one of the distant Blow cousins, and she never saw him again after the night Samuel was conceived. Hannah heard he'd been sold away to a man in North Carolina. She thought fondly of that man and that night. She found herself looking down the river she knew flowed together with the Blackwater and Meherrin rivers just south of the Virginia border, forming the Chowan River that flowed into Albemarle Sound on the northern coast of North Carolina. She couldn't help wondering if perhaps little Samuel was swimming the same waters in which his father might himself bathe later that day or fish the next morning.

Hannah considered herself a Christian and believed the teachings of the Bible she had been privileged to learn from a succession of kind mistresses. But she also maintained a strong attachment to the traditions, customs, and beliefs of her African ancestors. She held fast to the conviction that special events hallowed certain places, and that rocks—and especially rivers and streams—harbored benevolent spirits. She found herself praying that the spirits of the Nottoway would carry her love down to Samuel's father and let him know his son was doing fine. But Hannah quickly shook herself out of her meditation, for she had learned long ago it didn't help to dwell on such things, so she lost herself again in the joyful memory of her first hours with Samuel.

She knew his name from the moment she saw him. She had always wanted to name a child after the kind Blow patriarch who had put her name in the family Bible, just as he did his own children and grandchildren. The Blows were religious folk, and her various mistresses had read stories to her from that same Bible. As a girl growing up, she felt very special, knowing her name was written in the same Holy Book as the names of great prophets and heroes like Noah, Moses, David, and Samson. But she would never forget the night when Missus Martha, Sam Blow's wife, opened to the Book of Samuel and began reading, *"he had two wives; the name of the one was Hannah . . ."* She got a little shiver every time she thought of it. She remembered her missus' kind eyes and smile as she paused and nodded, then continued the wonderful story of the Bible Hannah's faith and prayers. As Hannah aged and yearned in vain for a child, the ancient story became more and more personal to her.

As the biblical account went, Hannah, too, could have no children, and her life was made unbearable by her husband's other wife, who had many children and so scorned and abused Hannah because she was barren. Hannah was sad and wept often and prayed at home and also at the temple. She promised God that if he would bless her with a son, she would give him to the Lord to be His servant.

One day she was praying at the temple, and the priest, Eli, heard her and was moved to promise that God would bless her because of her faith. Hannah believed Eli, and soon conceived, bringing forth a son. She called him Samuel, meaning "The Name of God." She remembered her promise, and after she weaned him, she loaned him to the Lord and sent him to live with Eli.

From that first day when Missus Martha read her the story of Hannah and Samuel, she always knew that she, Hannah Blow, would one day have her own son, and she would call him Samuel, and she would also loan him to the Lord for a very special purpose.

Although she had her share of sexual encounters, she never conceived, and as the years passed and she approached forty without having children, she worried, but did not despair. She continued to pray for her own miracle. At length, he had come.

"Hello, little miracle," she remembered saying as though it happened yesterday, the first time her Samuel opened his tiny dark eyes and looked into hers. And then, just like her biblical predecessor, she sang praises to the Lord as she nursed him to sleep;

not knowing how it could be possible, since she and her boy were slaves, but feeling nonetheless that someday her Samuel would grow up to be, perhaps, as great as the Samuel of the Old Testament. She often wanted to share her belief with others, including her son, but it was her experience with Nat Turner's "mother" that hot Fourth of July in Jerusalem, of all places, that kept her quiet until the day she died.

As the sun descended below the oak, cypress, and gum trees on the west side of the river, she felt the eighty-five degree heat and humidity dip appreciably. She stopped fanning herself and once again started thinking about choking down her dry meal, when she heard her missus, Elizabeth Blow, calling her name as she approached from the fair.

"Hannah," she said sweetly, "I thought you and Sam might like some hot food for dinner."

Hannah stood and whirled, trying not to drool as her master's kind wife handed her two steaming plates of roast meat, corn, and fresh, warm pone, with a heap of honey running down the side.

"Oh, thank you, Missus 'Lizbeth," she gushed as she curtsied and took the plates. "You din't haffa do that. I'se brung some stuff from home." She saw the skeptical look on her benefactor's face and added, "but I sho' 'nuff does 'preciate it!"

The friends smiled. Hannah had been present on the day just before Christmas four years ago when Peter Blow had married the beautiful twenty-five-year-old Elizabeth Ethelred Taylor. She had such a kind face that Hannah felt some hope her new missus would be benevolent to her husband's slaves. It wasn't long before her hopes were realized as Elizabeth asked Peter to bring Hannah out of the fields and into the Blow home as housekeeper, cook, and personal attendant. Hannah turned forty that March, and she didn't know how many more seasons she could have spent bent over in the cotton fields. It also brought her baby boy into the home, and his cheerful disposition made him a favorite of Massa Peter. Samuel was like a sweet big brother to the two little children, two-year-old Mary Ann and two-month-old Thomas Vaughn.

During the halcyon days of the young Blow couple's life together, their joy in each other and in their success showed in all their dealings with others. That included their slaves, who, in the Blow family tradition, were treated with kindness. Hannah and her boy were like family. Both Peter and Elizabeth lost their parents as children, but had been raised and mentored, in Peter's case, by an aunt and uncle, and in Elizabeth's by her grandparents. Although orphans, they were extremely fortunate to have inherited the ability to succeed as plantation owners, and they recognized and thanked God for their many blessings.

Elizabeth smiled at the children playing so carefree along the river's edge. She stood still, and though Hannah could not read her thoughts, for a moment she saw what seemed like sadness in Elizabeth's eyes. She shook herself out of her trance and looked toward Hannah. "Enjoy your picnic, Hannah; you certainly worked hard 'nuff to get our cotton yarn ready to sell. When you're done, I could sure use your help gittin' the babies ready for the evenin'."

"Samuel an' I'll be right there, Missus," Hannah replied energetically.

"Take your time, dear," her angelic mistress said, turning back to the party.

Hannah put a warm, juicy piece of venison in her mouth as she watched her mistress return to the celebration, then turned back to look for Samuel. This time what she saw did cause her some alarm. He hung about ten feet off the ground by his belly over a thick limb of a massive oak tree that clung to the edge of the bank, and had hold of both the Turner boy's outstretched arms. Samuel's legs provided a counter balance as Nat's feet kicked against the knobs on the craggy tree trunk. The limb ran parallel with the river and was thick enough to stand on. Hannah knew her boy, and knew instinctively that he was planning on the two jumping from the branch into the river twenty-five feet below.

Before she could intervene, however, Henrietta ran screaming at Samuel, which so startled both boys that their grip broke, and Nat fell eight feet onto his back just on the lip of the bank, knocking the wind out of him and rendering him unconscious.

"You kilt my chile—you devil boy!" She screamed at Samuel, grabbing a stick on the ground and striking up at him. Samuel had recovered from the shock and stood on the branch out of her reach. "Git down here, Sam Blow, an' I'll skin you fo' sure!"

Just as Samuel was about to cry, Hannah lit into Henrietta. "Now thas 'nuff, Henrietta! Ten' to yo' chile an' leave off'n mine!" She looked up at her son, knowing he was not at fault, so her voice was calm, but firm. "Samuel, git yo'self down outta that tree right now!"

Nat moaned softly in his mammy's arms. His eyes rolled back in his head, causing Hannah some alarm. She saw some of the white celebrants looking inquisitively in their direction and thought of running for help, but then she felt Samuel's arms lock around her leg,

"Did I kill Nat, Mammy?" he asked, genuinely frightened. Then in his naively practical manner he added, "Le's take him to a mas'r doct'r. I knows they can save Natty!"

Just then Nat started to cry and sat up. Several dozen blacks and a few whites started to gather.

"Mammy?" the boy stopped crying, his eyes focusing on Henrietta's concerned face. "I see'd snakes, and they was white—jes' like the eggs they was sniffin'."

There was a collective intake of breath from those who heard, and while some who did not understand looked for snakes in the

151

grass, most of the others stepped back and began making curative signs of crossing and spitting and turning in circles.

Henrietta soothed him. "Hush, ya'll, my boy done had another dream from the Lord. Jes' like Nathaniel in the Bible, this baby child is a 'Gift of God!' Hush now an' lissen to his vision! Tell them, Nathaniel, tell us what you seen."

The boy turned his glassy eyes on the others and when he looked at Hannah, she felt a chill run down her back. The lumpy growths on his body were dark, the color of blood. "There was red blood ever'where," he croaked. "An' the snakes was crawlin' in the blood, and there was fresh meat, an' then it turn bad, an' white maggots was pokin' outer it."

The crowd stood still in stunned silence. No one had ever heard of so many bad omens in a single dream. These Negroes were profoundly superstitious, and everyone present knew well the interpretations of dreams:

To dream of blood is a sign of trouble.
To dream of eggs is a sign of trouble.
To dream of snakes is a sign of enemies.
To dream of maggots or fresh meat is a sign of death.

Henrietta prompted him. "Did yo' break the eggs, Nathaniel? Did you kill the snakes?"

The boy paused, his eyes clear now, and Hannah was surprised at the intense, strangely mature and knowing look on his face. "Oh yes, Mammy, I smashed them white eggs, an' I kilt them white snakes—every one o' them!"

"What do he mean, Mammy?" Samuel asked innocently. Hannah knew exactly what the superstition said—"If you kill the snakes, you have conquered your enemies, and if the eggs are broken, your trouble is ended." She didn't like the way this was going or how ugly it made her feel inside. She found herself looking around quickly and was relieved to see that no white folks had heard what that odd child had just said.

"Never mind, son, le's jes' go." She took his hand and began to walk away toward the Fourth of July celebrations. She stiffened but did not stop as Henrietta saw her leaving and singled her out.

"Don' walk away from the 'Gift o' God,' Hannah Blow! This chile is special, and God have a pow'ful mission fo' him!" Henrietta seemed angered that Hannah paid her no mind, and she fairly screamed after her while preaching to her larger audience. "Mark my word! This dream is of God . . . an' God goin' make Nathaniel a mighty prophet to our people!"

Hannah heard the many "amens" and determined then and there, never to let her Samuel have anything to do with the strange boy. She would keep her own warm and comforting thoughts to herself, her commitment to God on the birth of Samuel, and her special feeling of her boy's holy purpose. She would wait until the right moment to tell him—and it wouldn't be in front of an audience.

As they approached the Seven Gable home, Hannah heard the familiar voice of her young master. "Sammy!" Peter called, the affection obvious in his cry and his face as he ran toward them. He scooped up the boy and tossed him giggling into the air. "You been havin' fun?" he asked as he caught him and held him on his hip.

Hannah saw Samuel glance briefly at her with a knowing expression of a secret between them, and then he looked in his master's eyes and rubbed his tiny hand on Peter's sparse beard. Peter was the only father figure and male mentor Samuel had, and the affection the two shared was obvious.

"Oh yes suh, Massa Peter! I'se the bes' swimmer in the whole county!" he bragged.

"That's right, Sammy!" Peter proclaimed, rubbing his hand back and forth through Samuel's thick nappy hair. "You shore is more of a fish than you is a boy! In fact," he said, continuing to tickle the boy's neck like he was looking for something, "I swear them gills is here somewhere!"

Samuel squirmed and squealed in delight. "I ain't no fish!" he protested, "but I sho' 'nuff can swim the biggest river un'er God's great heaven!"

Hannah smiled at his language, knowing at least part of her Bible lessons were getting through to him. Peter crouched and put the boy on the ground.

"The biggest river, you say? Well, guess what, Sammy? Did you know that today we's celebratin' the purchase of the biggest river on God's green earth?"

Samuel's eyes flew wide. Peter chuckled. "That's right, Sammy. It's called 'The Mighty Mississippi,' but the Injuns calls it 'The Father of All Water,' and you could fit a hundred Nottoway in it!"

Samuel didn't miss a beat. "Can us swim in the Mighty Miss-sip, please, Massa Peter?"

Peter thought a moment, and then patted his young protégé on the shoulder. "You never know, Sammy. If y'all keep practicin', maybe some day you and I will swim across it together."

* * *

Sammy followed his mother back toward the river as the golden twilight became violet dusk. Confusion settled over Sammy's young mind as the marshal music of the white masters faded and the soulful sound of the Negro spiritual grew. The nights had always belonged to the Negro slaves. Fireflies along the bank juba-jerked to the rhythm of the harmonic banjar, the beat of the bamboula drums, and the strangely melodic morimbabrett made of wire and different lengths of reed. Sammy found himself copying the movement of the glowing bugs with little slaps to his knees and thighs.

The boy wrestled with the irony of his situation. He loved Massa Peter and found himself yearning for attention and praise from his only father figure. But the music and the spirit of his Negro race struck a cord so deep inside, it always felt like he was truly coming home. He took one last look over his shoulder and scampered, clapping and slapping, to the lively gathering around the fire.

Several hours later, as the fire faded, the darkness deepened, and the fireflies went to bed, an ancient coal-black slave with a head of hair as thick and white as a yearling lamb began to sing one of the forbidden songs. Hannah gasped and looked back toward Jerusalem. Sammy felt her relax as she realized the white folk had retired to their tents and wagon beds on the opposite side of Main Street.

Sammy loved the seemingly bottomless, throaty bass of old Solomon. He scurried over to a spot on the same log so he could feel the rumble come through Solomon, move up through Sammy's bottom, and reverberate through his whole body until his palms tingled and his own bushy hair vibrated. Oh, how he hoped someday he could sing like that. His own childish squeak was embarrassing, and he tried to hold back on the echo verses. But he could no more keep from singing than he could stop his heart from beating.

"My Father, how long?" Solomon implored the heavens, his eyes and palms turned skyward.

"My Father, how long?" echoed Sammy and the others.

"My Father, how long," moaned Solomon, "poor sinners suffer here? And it won't be long," he answered.

"And it won't be long," the chorus copied.

"Poor sinners suffer here." The patriarch paused and looked toward town. Sammy thought about the cracker scars under Solomon's linen shirt and wondered if they hurt. Solomon looked back into the eyes of his brothers and sisters and finally down at Sammy sitting next to him. Sammy passed a hand over his own face and found tears on his cheeks. He suddenly realized he didn't care who might be listening.

"We'll soon be free!" Solomon musically declared and waited for the reply every slave knew.

"The Lord will call us home," the assembly chorused along with him, then waited for his solo.

"We'll walk the miry road." His profound vibrato witnessed to Sammy's body that the old man had walked many roads, and wondered at the irony of the response,

"Where pleasure never dies."

"We'll walk the golden streets," Solomon's voice rose along with his body as he stood and turned toward town.

". . . of the New Jerusalem!" they all chimed in. Sammy wondered at the mystery of their own anticipated journeys that would bring them to that town.

"We'll fight for liberty!" Solomon crescendoed alone, and then he swallowed up Sammy's tiny sapling hand in his own gnarled oak, while everyone joined together, hands, voices, and spirits in unison.

"When the Lord calls us home."

Chapter 18

People at the Fork of the Stream

Southampton, Virginia, 1808

Throughout the next several years, Sam reminisced on that night and wondered at Solomon's age and the strength of his hand. As a child, he thought Solomon must be at least as old as the giant oaks of Virginia. As time passed and he matured in his thoughts and understanding of things, it wasn't the physical age of the singer, but the immortality of that of which he had sung: Liberty.

It was a concept so foreign to him, and yet so much a part of man, he just knew it had to pre-date the gray-toothed ancient and stretched back before the Olde Place, before Virginia, across the sea, and even before Africa. He knew he was a slave, and that meant he had no liberty, but as a boy he felt free. So when he thought about that night in the new Jerusalem, and how he had felt deep down inside the collective sadness and yearning of his fellows, he would shake it off by running out into the woods, or swinging out freely over the gum branch on a hanging vine and plunging into the weightless freedom of the pond.

At such moments, he couldn't empathize with the older slaves. His life seemed to him to be idyllic. In a sense it was not unlike that of boys throughout the ages growing up amid forests, streams, and vast open spaces—at least, until he reached the age where he was considered strong enough to handle a hoe. Young slave children were generally considered "free" to run and play until they were "old enough" to become productive property. Because of his small size, Sammy got a few more years than other young slaves might have. Even then, because the Blows had brought him and his mother into their home, once he did some simple chores, he was free again to explore the lush wilderness of The Olde Place and its environs.

Active from sunup to sundown, there wasn't an ounce of fat on Sam's lean, muscular frame. No tree seemed too high for him to climb. He swung on vines and built forts. He swam every body of water he came across and even seemed unafraid of the many swampy areas. He could hold his breath for several minutes underwater.

Sam had become one with nature and all of God's creations and proved it by bringing home every creepy-crawly he could find; as he grew older, his "pets" grew larger and furrier. He and his mother lived in a twelve-by-twelve log hut behind the Blow's three-story plantation home. It had a dirt floor that Hannah kept neatly swept and a wooden chimney. Its sod roof was shadowed and protected by the limbs of Elizabeth Blow's fruit trees. The roof was high enough that there was room for the tiny loft where Sam slept and kept his "treasures."

In his many wanderings, Sam came across a few peaceful Indians who called themselves Cheroenhaka, or "People at the Fork of the Stream." With his naturally open and friendly way, he was soon accepted and spent much time with the Indians, learning how to hunt, trap, and fish. Peter Blow often bragged to his family and friends that the young slave was better than the Nottoway Indians at catching fish and trapping beavers, otters, muskrats, and mink.

On another muggy July day in 1808, Peter's cousins, William and Henry Blow, arrived. It was a joyous reunion—Peter had lived with them after his father died when he was nine. Since their home, Rose Hill, and the other Blow lands had been centered on the Nottoway reservation, the Virginia governor appointed them as tribal trustees and ordered them to take a special census of the Nottoway Indians. When they saw nine-year-old Sam run out from behind the house with nothing on but his britches cut off above the knees and a strip of deer hide wrapped around his forehead, they laughed.

"Aw, this must be the vast progger you've been telling us about, Peter," declared William.

"That's right," Peter beamed, patting the boy on the head. "Sammy, these are the cousins I grew up with at Rose Hill."

"You're the one we come to see, Sammy, not our adopted brother Peter," Henry chided, jabbing his cousin in the ribs.

Peter chuckled. "Sammy'd be glad to help, and he may let me come along," he said. "He's good friends with a couple of the braves—there ain't many of 'um around."

Henry smiled widely. "That's why we came here." Then continuing in a serious vein, he added, "None of us'll ever forget the night Thomas Jefferson visited The Olde Place."

"Thas the night I was birthed," Sam piped up, feeling proud.

All three men stopped and looked at him in astonishment, then broke into a leg-smacking good laugh.

"That's true," said Peter after he regained his composure and patted the stunned boy on his bare back. "Young Sam here thinks he's got a special connection to the president because of it, too!"

"Well, we're finding that Thomas Jefferson was pretty accurate way back in '84," William interjected, pulling a worn leather book out of his rucksack and turning to a page he had marked with a wildflower. "He wrote in this here *Notes on the State of Virginia*, and I quote: 'Of the Nottoway, not a male is left. A few women constitute the remains of that tribe.'"

"Thas not so," Sam interrupted, somewhat nonplussed. "I knows Tom Turner an' Littleton Scholar, an' some other boys that has the same name, Winoak!" He then feigned an aristocratic air and continued, "an' jes' so's you know, they don' like to be called 'Nottoway'—it means a snake. They prefers 'Char-en-hocka!'"

Most Virginia planters would have been put off by so much banter with a slave, even a child, but William and Henry had grown up with freed slaves who lived on the plantation and worked with their father; besides, the boy was so bright and spunky, they didn't mind at all.

"See, Billy," Henry chuckled to his brother, "we came to the right expert!" He turned back to Peter and Sam. "We're on our way up to Rose Hill, an' we want you to come along, Sam!"

Sam sucked in air and looked at his master with wide-eyed, wistful expectation.

"You can bring him too, Sammy," laughed William, nodding at Peter, "if he promises to behave hisself—you know, he lived at Rose Hill when he was about your age."

"That's right," Peter beamed. "Now run in the house and get my collection of Nottoway arrowheads and pottery shards while I hitch up the buckboard. Tell Missus they's in a mahogany box in the closet in my den. I spent many a long summer day exploring the remains of longhouses and digging for Nottoway treasures around Rose Hill, and along the bluff overlooking the Nottoway River."

"That's why we're headin' up there," William said. "Last week we asked Uncle John to spread the word all through the county for as many Nottoway as possible to gather at Rose Hill tomorrow."

Sammy did a gleeful cartwheel and sped up the front steps in search of the arrowheads. After they were gathered, Sammy, Peter, and his cousins were on their way to Rose Hill

* * *

Later that day as they came to the spot where Medicine Springs Road crossed over Indian Town Road, they spotted a half dozen Indians walking north.

"Hey there, Winoak! Howdy, Winoak!" Sam hollered at two natives who appeared to be in their teens. The group paused and waved as Peter pulled up the wagon. The Indians were dressed in tanned animal skins, and the one female stood out in her blue- and red dyed match coat. They all wore necklaces made of shells, and some of the men had streaks on their cheeks and foreheads of what appeared to be dry white clay.

"Can they have a ride with us?" Sam asked his mentor.

"Sure, we's all heading to the same place," Peter called down to the nervous Nottoway. "Climb on up, an' we'll save y'all a few steps on the way to the Cheroenhaka reunion."

The Indians would probably never have accepted a ride, but seemed stunned that this white man used the name they called themselves in their Iroquois dialect. When they saw their young black-skinned friend beaming at them from the bed of the wagon, they laughed, and playfully shoving each other, they tossed their deerskin bundles on the buckboard and hopped on.

Peter had a sweet wave of nostalgia pass over him as they drove up to the familiar large white two-story home with red brick chimneys at each end. He smiled as he thought of the many nights he and his cousins had slipped quietly out a second-floor window, onto the roof of the covered front porch, and down one of the four white pillars. He was Sam's age when he had moved here after his parents died, and he saw the same reckless spirit in his young slave, who, despite the color of his skin and his official status as his "property," was as much a son to him as he had been to his uncle John.

Peter's sons, Thomas Vaughn and Richard Benjamin, were four years old and one month old respectively. He loved them dearly, and looked forward to when they were older and he could teach them all the ways of the Virginia planter and outdoorsman he considered himself to be.

His thoughts of his uncle were rewarded as they drew closer and saw the old man in his rocking chair on the wide porch. Peter was surprised at how white his uncle's hair had become, but then realized John was well into his sixties. Peter was pleased to note that the old man's eyesight hadn't grown dim when his surrogate father raised his hand and called out, "Hallo, Peter! Welcome home, boy!"

That night, while Peter and his family reminisced up at the big house, Sam was invited to stay with the free Negro, Mathew, his wife Polly, and their two little girls in a small cabin out near the river. It wasn't much larger than Sam's little house, but it had a fine wooden floor and a solid rock fireplace. It was an awakening of sorts for the young man, who hadn't given a whole lot of thought to his status as a slave. He knew what it meant, and that he and his mammy and new baby brother, Dred, were the property of the Blows, but he explained to Mathew and Polly that he had always felt free to run and play and explore—even at nine—once he'd done his chores. He further explained that his Massa Peter and Mistress Elizabeth had never raised a hand to him in anger, and they treated him almost as if he were one of their own children.

Mathew listened with some amusement, and then decided it was his responsibility to school the boy somewhat in the ways of the white master and black slave worlds.

"Das all well an' good, Sam," he patronized the ideological youth, "but has you evah seen Peter strike his dogs in anger?" Mathew had also grown up with Peter at Rose Hill, being only a few years his junior, and knew of his kind disposition. When Sam shook his head back and forth, he continued.

"I was yo' Massa Peter's friend when he was about yo' age, and he always treated me like his equal. But jes' like his dog, Sam, yo' his property. Which mean, jes' like he wouldn't let his dogs wander off and choose thar own way, when yo' gets older, he ain't nevah gonna let yo' chose yer own path. Hell, he might even sell yo' to someone else who won't treat yo' so nice!"

Sam was so stunned he couldn't respond. He sat there with his mouth wide open for a moment. Then he closed it and swallowed hard, afraid he would cry if he tried to speak.

"Here now, Mathew—stop dat!" Polly ordered, slapping her husband on the shoulder. "You're scarin da boy! Go ahead an' finish yo' supper, Sammy, an' don't give no mind to Mathew!"

Sam did as he was told, but he did give Mathew's words some mind. He stayed awake most of the night, thinking about what had been said and trying to get his young mind around the whole issue of slavery and why some black folks were free like Mathew and his family, while so many others weren't. For the rest of his life, Sam looked back on that weekend at Rose Hill as an "awaking" of sorts, not only to the issue of freedom and slavery, but to a world where birth and race and heritage separated people into classes where some dominated and prospered, while others withered and died.

Sam put aside his own worries about what the future might hold for him and his family, and for two days listened with a growing sadness to the stories of a once-mighty people, whose hunting lands had extended from the Meherrin River all the way to the James where they intersected with the Powhatan Chiefdom, but were now reduced to a number he could count on his fingers and toes living nearly homeless around the Blow plantations. The 1808 census officially named seventeen members of the Cheroenhaka/Nottoway Tribe.

The Blows heard the full story as to why they hated to be called Nottoway, although they seemed to have given up on protesting that, too. The name did not come from the fact their traditional hunting lands extended up and down the Nottoway. A stooped old man who called himself Ouracoorass Jones, after the great chief who had once signed a treaty with the king of England, explained: When that great Chief Teerheer's grandfathers hunted these lands, the early white settlers near the James River asked the Powhatan and Algonquian speakers what tribe claimed the major lodging area between the two large rivers that joined together south of the great swamp, and which then ran to the ocean in the south. The Algonquian speakers, who had been Cheroenhaka enemies for many years, said they were the "Na-Da-Wa," which meant in their tongue "vipers" or "adders." The Colonials rendered that Nottoway—and the name stuck.

The treaty that Chief Teerheer signed created two small reservations in exchange for protection and payment by the British of an annual tribute. The one reservation was described as a circle with a radius of three miles, on the north side of the Nottoway River; the other as a diamond six miles on each side, south of the river. Sam felt some guilt when he learned that his master's roughly eight-hundred-acre Olde Place plantation filled much of the lower part of that diamond, and this two-thousand-acre Rose Hill plantation filled most of the northern half. He was angry that the white men had broken their treaty, and was stunned to learn that the Indians had asked the Commonwealth for permission to sell their lands. The Blows had been primary beneficiaries of that opportunity—but it still didn't sit right with Sam.

Sam had gained a great fondness for the customs and abilities of the Cheroenhaka. He loved how they painted and adorned themselves. They lived in the remnants of a few ancient longhouses, which seemed to Sam as palaces compared to his own shack, and he admired the light-colored clay pottery they produced and the weapons of rock they could still knap with both rock and steel tools. His participation in the census, however, left him with a great sadness for the Cheroenhaka and other native inhabitants of America. He felt they had been treated as badly as, or maybe even worse than, his own people. As he grew and began to experience the degradation and horrors of slavery, he could never fully deal with the fact that an entire people had been nearly wiped off the map. His experiences and sympathies would, in his later life, play an important role in dealing with other Native American tribes in the Midwest, which led to a friendship with the longtime Indian agent assigned to the Wisconsin Territory, Major Lawrence Taliaferro. That friendship would, in turn, lead to one of the greatest moments in his life—his marriage to Taliaferro's slave, his beloved Harriet Robinson.

But well before then—in fact, in just a few more years—Peter and Sam would find themselves in the middle of a war that would bring America's infantile experience in liberty and freedom to the brink of oblivion, and further exploit the terrible class distinctions of African enslavement and Indian reservations.

Drawing by Richard Blow

Chapter 19

The Applause of Their Country

Hampton Roads, Virginia, 1813

As the year 1812 drew to a close, a cry of panic swept through both Virginia and the rest of the country. On June 19th, Congress granted President James Madison's request and declared war on Great Britain. The country had grown sick of their old defeated enemy's escalating practice of "impressments," or the attacking of U.S. military and private commercial vessels and the kidnapping of sailors, forcing them to fight England's war against Napoleon Bonaparte. The president and Congress correctly deemed these to be acts of war and determined to put a stop to it. In the first six months of the war, most of the engagements were at sea or on the Canadian border. The country was riding high on the belief that they had beaten the redcoats once and would easily do so again. That belief was strengthened with the news of successful navel battles wherein principally the new U.S. Navy men-o-war, the *Constitution* and the *Hornet*, had performed admirably, sinking or capturing a number of British frigates.

Worry set in, however, when the country learned that American land forces had suffered a terrible loss in the battle of Queenstown Heights, where the British and their Indian allies killed or wounded about a thousand U.S. troops. Still, people in the Commonwealth were relatively unconcerned until the war came to Virginia the day after Christmas, when the sails of a hundred British warships entered the mouth of Chesapeake Bay and established an impassable blockade.

Virginia cotton and tobacco farmers and private commercial fleets knew the devastation a blockade could cause their financial interests, and hundreds of Virginians, including Peter Blow and many of his cousins, immediately formed into militia companies. An economic war was a significant concern, but greater alarm spread when it was learned from captured British sailors that a large army of infantry was housed on board many of the blockade ships. Lookouts from Hampton confirmed that scores of amphibious barges were tied up alongside sloops and frigates riding very low in the water. It was evident that a British attack was imminent, but not knowing where in the vast Chesapeake the British had set their sights, the orders spread throughout the Commonwealth for militia companies to assemble and begin training in earnest.

In March, four British line-of-battle ships with twelve low-riding frigates moved into Hampton Roads, where the James, Nansemond, and Elizabeth Rivers emptied into the salty waters of the Chesapeake. More intelligence was gathered that Admiral Sir George Cockburn, who commanded the British fleet blockading the Chesapeake Bay, and Admiral Sir John B. Warren planned to attack Norfolk and the Gosport Shipyard across the Elizabeth River in Portsmouth. Their goal was to destroy Virginia's shipbuilding capability and the dozens of small, but fast, U.S. gunboats that had been so successfully harassing the Royal Navy, and, most importantly, capture the greatest prize: the frigate *U.S.S. Constellation,* which had been in Portsmouth for repairs and provisioning since the declaration of war. She had been hemmed in when the British fleet had blockaded the bay. The *Constellation* was the sister ship to the *Constitution* and the *Hornet,* and was famous as the first warship of the new United States Navy to win a ship-to-ship battle when it defeated the French 36-gun frigate *Insurgente.* In 1800, this ship used her speed and agility in a five-hour nighttime battle to defeat the much larger 52-gun *Vengeance.* The one-hundred and sixty-four-foot long *Constellation* was not only a powerful frigate, with her thirty-eight 24-pound cannon, but of greater concern to her enemies, she was as fast as a Baltimore Clipper-ship, having earned the nickname "Yankee Racehorse."

During March, a number of northern Virginia militia companies had arrived to defend the birthplace of American democracy, but an unusually wet April and a hot May started the malaria season early, and a great number of northern volunteers became terribly sick and died. Brigadier General Robert Barraud Taylor, commander of the Virginia Militia in the Norfolk area, immediately ordered companies from the south, including those of the 65th Virginia Regiment, to march as quickly as possible to assist in building and manning defenses around Norfolk and Portsmouth.

After a final week of provisioning, Captain Peter Blow was prepared by the last week in May to lead his Southampton Company of the 65th on a forced march of forty miles to aid in the defense of Virginia and his homeland.

Truth be told, Elizabeth wasn't at all certain her husband was capable of leading his company. He had begun drinking heavily the past July when their firstborn son, Thomas Vaughn, had died of consumption, and Peter had only sobered up a few months ago when word of the invasion first arrived. She plucked a fluff of cotton off the single cape of his sky-blue militia uniform. She had sewn the red fringe on the thigh-length wrap-around hunting shirt with trepidation, knowing he might be going into battle. When she saw the pride and purpose in his eyes when he first tried it on, she prayed his new responsibilities would help move him past the pain of their terrible loss. She carefully sniffed his breath and was relieved there was no hint of liquor.

"You look mighty dashing, Captain Blow." She beamed up into his rugged face. At thirty-six, he had only a few flecks of gray in his short beard and thick hair. His gray eyes were clear, and the only wrinkles were the smile lines fanning from the corners of his eyes. As if on cue, the creases deepened as he smiled down at his bride.

"Thank you, ma'am." He winked and kissed her gently on the mouth. "You keep these young 'uns fed while I'm gone, and we'll be home after we send the lobster-backs swimmin' back to England!"

She hugged him close and whispered "I love you" into his ear, kissed his cheek, and turned to the teenaged Sam standing a little behind him.

"Sam, you look awful good in your uniform, too," she declared, wiping a tear from her cheek. He beamed back at his kind mistress. "Now y'all take care of my man an' make sure he comes home to me as handsome . . . and sober," she ordered, the last word said in a whisper so Peter wouldn't hear.

"Yes'm, Missus Liza," Sam spat out, his back ramrod straight, his narrow chin tucked into his chest like a soldier. As a slave, Sam wasn't mustered in as a formal member of the militia, but General Taylor had authorized Peter, as a company commander, to bring him along as his orderly. At barely five feet, Sam looked younger than his thirteen years, but Elizabeth knew he was an exceptionally talented and skilled youth. There had been enough material left over from her husband's uniform to make Sam a uniform coat, and she was so glad Peter had consented to the creation of it.

As an orderly, Sam would be responsible for maintaining all of Captain Blow's uniforms and equipment, including keeping the black round hat and black fan cockade stiff and unbent, the pair of shoes and half-gaiters shined, and Peter's U.S. model 1808 musket, cartridge box, tomahawk, knife, and bayonet clean, dry, and rust free, and the quart-sized tin canteen always full of fresh water. He would also keep the officer's tent clean and organized and run whatever orders and messages he was assigned.

Sam walked away from the crowd lined up in front of the courthouse on Main Street in Jerusalem while Peter said goodbye and hugged his four children: Mary Ann, eleven, a likely gal just starting to flower; Elizabeth, seven, and aptly named as she was the spitting image of her mother; tow-headed Richard, five, and the remaining son; and little Charlotte, three, in her golden ringlets and full skirt, looking the tiny Southern belle. Sam found his mother and little brother, Dred, with the other servants behind the families of the soldiers. Dred was ten years old, and Sam could tell he was going to be much bigger than he before long. Hannah never said who Dred's father was, but he didn't look like any of the eight other male Blow slaves. Sam shrugged it off. It didn't matter. He could see the pride and envy in his dear sibling's eyes, and the same—but flecked with concern—in his mother's. He hugged Dred, then turned to his mother.

"Don' worry none, Mammy, I'se too short fo' the redcoats to see. I'll make sho' Massa Peter come back safe, too. No telling what might happen to ya'll if he gets kilt."

"Hush, boy," his mama cautioned, spitting into the dust. She then pulled a little charm bag from a pocket and hung it around her son's neck. "I don' wanna hear no talkin' 'bout killin'. This here's a rabbit's foot—the left hind one—fo' sho' it'll keep you safe." She tucked it safely under his coat. "Jes' do yo' job, Samuel, an' take care a Massa so's he can take care of these other boys," she ordered, pointing at the rank and file of nervous young men. "You make us proud, Samuel! The Lord have a purpose in sendin' you ta war. Be careful an' learn all you can."

The drummers began to beat out muster, and Sam heard Peter call out an order to assemble in his commanding voice. It sounded so good to hear his master sober and in charge. Those were dark days after Thomas died, and he had seen a despondent and ornery side of Peter when "corned" that he hoped never to see again.

Two days later, a tired and sweat-drenched company of Southampton militia stumbled into Portsmouth. Their captain led them straight to the large Crawford street residence, offices, gardens, and shipyards of his great-uncle Richard who lived in a massive white home on the Battery next to the Elizabeth River. Peter ordered his corporals, Thomas Stanley and Jeremiah Gay, to follow his uncle's giant gardener, Hercules, down through the orchard and garden to the wharf and see that the company was bedded down properly in one of the warehouses.

Sam had never seen Hercules before and felt guilty that the thought which first entered his mind was that he must be a new . . . what . . . purchase? He couldn't help staring, mouth agape, at the sheer physical presence of the man.

He was dying to go down to the large warehouse where he had been a few times as a boy. The timbers, capstans, and figureheads of old wrecks and the massive rope coils and scattered barrels, trunks, and ballasts were a child's playground. But he reminded himself of the serious nature of the visit this time, and dutifully followed his master up the steps.

The tall and stately Richard Blow looked more like the merchant and bank president he was now than the Virginia planter he had once been. He greeted his nephew warmly, eyed Sam favorably, and invited them both into his home. Sam quickly forgot Hercules and now could not take his wide eyes off the stately old gentleman. He stood a full foot taller than Sam, with very broad shoulders and a trim waist. His iron gray hair was pulled back in a braided French queue tied with a black ribbon. He wore a white billowing shirt with a ruffled front, breeches to his knees, black silk stockings, and shoes with buckles set with brilliants.

"Limerick," he said to an ancient black butler wearing a long, dark blue coat with a dozen brass buttons, "please take Captain Blow and young Sam's jackets."

"How do, Uncle Limerick?" Sam smiled and winked at his old friend and handed him his new coat.

"Young Sam," Limerick croaked as he took it. "Don't ya'll be puttin on airs," he said stuffily. To Sam's surprise, he did not smile back. Sam shrugged and followed the two Blows through the large hall that ran the length of the house, past the parlor and dining room and to the door of the older Blow's study.

Richard turned to Peter. "George has been commissioned a Lieutenant in the 4th Virginia Regiment, and so will be joining you in this dastardly affair. I'm of a mind to grab a musket and march with you to teach those cussed lobsters another lesson! I don't know how long we'll be able to stand this blockade. Half my ships are at sea without the ability to return, and the rest sit idle at the wharf. I know you and George will do our country proud!"

Concerned he was failing in his duty as host, he nodded toward the door. "Sam, why don't you run out to the south kitchen and find Isabel. Ask her to feed you something, then set dinner for Captain Peter, Missus Frances, and me. Oh, and tell her we'll be joined tonight by our son George and Eliza."

173

As Sam turned to scurry off, Richard asked him to help Moses and Jim take vittles down to the regimental boys in the warehouse.

* * *

The Gosport Shipyard, where the *Constellation* was docked, was just north of Richard Blow's pier, and so it was that Captain Blow's company was tasked to board and work alongside U.S. Navy sailors to prepare several of the ship's cannon as it sailed a few miles up the Elizabeth to Norfolk, then to offload them to fortify batteries at Fort Norfolk and Lampert's Point. The men were never dry as they toiled nearly around the clock in the humid heat. They marveled at the American feat of creating a sea wall, from Lampert's Point across the Elizabeth River to Craney Island on the western shore, made up of a hundred schooners, sloops, and even Arabian feluccas captured in the Barbary wars, all locked together with heavy iron chains and thick ropes.

The feluccas, with their lateen sails, looked sorely out of place in America, but they served their purpose. Any British warship that approached would have to come to a stop, grapple the American ships, and disembark men to try to sever the chains, all while under a withering crossfire of heavy cannon from the island and the point, and small-arms' fire from the ships and boats.

On June 20th, the English frigate *Junon* approached the chain and was turned away, exactly as planned. Word then arrived that scores of flat-bottomed barges were being brought alongside the heavy ships stationed just north of Craney Island. On the 21st, with it clear that an attack on the island was imminent, General Taylor ordered additional soldiers and sailors to cross the river. Lt. George Blow asked Captain Peter Blow's men to join a group of volunteers from Isle of Wight County to reinforce the island. By morning, there were approximately six hundred regular and militia soldiers—

including infantry and artillery, although ten percent of them were too sick to fight—and one hundred and fifty sailors and marines off the *Constellation*.

At dawn on June 22nd, Sam stood nervously next to his master on the high northern battery of Craney Island as the fog cleared off Hampton Roads and its tributary rivers. He trembled as he watched the landing on the western mainland of well over two thousand Royal British Marines and soldiers of the seasoned 102nd Regiment in their terrifying red uniforms—the color of blood, he thought—the early morning sun glinting off bucklers, breast plates, and deadly bayonets. Other ships, with at least fifty attached barges laden with soldiers, were holding position just out of range to the north and east.

Sam found himself clutching the char bag and rabbit's foot his mother had given him as he looked on the much-smaller group of Americans scattered around this puny island. The ragtag organization, and even the proud new homespun uniforms of the Virginians, seemed to pale in comparison to the professional, seasoned soldiers who had formed into fighting phalanxes and marched crisply to fife and drum, flags and banners flapping smartly in the breeze. He shuddered and began to pray silently when he noticed that at low tide, the narrow passage between the island and the piney mainland referred to as the "Thoroughfare" was at most knee-deep and the terrible army was planning to march right across. He wasn't the only one to notice. He looked up at the grim faces around him, none of which showed the slightest fear, and Sam suddenly felt ashamed of himself—he so wanted to be a man like them.

Lieutenant Colonel Beatty, commander of the island garrison, lowered his field glasses and turned to infantry Major Wagner, artillery Major Faulkner, and the other company commanders assembled.

"Gentlemen," he began, "you may return to your men. You will please remind them that today the fate of Virginia, and possibly of these United States, hangs in the balance. If the British succeed in taking this island, they will then train our own guns on, and destroy, the western anchor of the sea-chain, which will allow their entire armada to sail past the island, outside the range of our guns on Lambert Point and at Fort Norfolk, and then move unimpeded right up to Norfolk, Portsmouth, and our shipyards. The destruction of our fine cities and Virginia's shipbuilding industry, not to mention the *Constellation*, would be a devastating blow to the fighting capabilities and morale of our country."

He looked back at the organized battle force approaching from the west, swallowed, and raised his voice so all the men on the battery could hear. "Yes, they look powerful, disciplined, and well-armed. But they are fighting far from their country, their homes, and their families—and for what? Revenge? The power to tax us once again? We, on the other hand, are fighting for our homes and our wives, our children and our lands, our religion and our liberties. We are fighting for the greatest cause of all—freedom!"

The gallant commander paused for emphasis, and Sam swore he glanced at him somewhat sheepishly for just an instant, then continued powerfully. "Today we will prove to these foreigners, who once were our brothers, and to the world, that this nation, founded on democracy and the rule of law, will not fail! Gentlemen," he said, raising his sword, "for the United States of America and for Virginia!"

"HUZZAH!" the redoubt erupted. "FOR AMERICA AND FOR VIRGINIA!" they cheered. "HUZZAH, HUZZAH!" the cheers spread, the sound raising spirits and the courage of them all as they moved down the hill to the nervous defenders near the shores.

"The foot soldiers will be slowed by the mud as they wade across the leeward passage," Colonel Beatty called after them. "What say ya'll to a fine Virginia lobster bake?"

With laughter and more cheers, the men moved to their positions, each in turn rallying the men under them.

"Those Brits look smart, marching on solid ground," Peter buoyed up his men, "but wait until they begin to flounder in the rich Virginia mud—we'll cut them to ribbons, boys!" He could feel these good Southampton volunteers relax. He put Sam in front of them, his hands on his shoulders. "The night Sam here was born, President Madison himself slept in my bed at The Olde Place! He's our good luck charm. Let's give 'em Jesse and end 'Mr. Madison's War' today!"

Sam's fear suddenly left him, replaced by pride and enthusiasm as the men crowded around. Johnny Vick, Tommy Harrison, and James Gay patted and jostled him. Anthony Wells from Cross Keys rubbed his head—"for good luck," he said, laughing.

The fife and drums stopped all at once, the silence almost more terrifying than the martial music. All heads snapped back to look across the two hundred yards of shallow water as bodies crouched and muskets were raised. They faced a seemingly endless line of men in tall red hats that made them look like giants.

Strangely, a loud voice called out across the shallow water, amplified by some mechanism that made it sound hollow. "Before we send you bloody Yanks to hell . . ." the voice paused while angry boos and vulgar threats flew back across the void. "By order of this Royal Majesty, George the Third, King of England and Great Britain . . ."

"Oh, git on wid it, ye bloody lobster," a Virginian cried out in a mock English accent.

The voice continued. "By order of the King, any Negro in your ranks who desires to be free"—a hush went through the American

177

ranks, and all eyes near Sam turned to stare at him—"and wants to be truly equal and not just some silly rot on a piece of paper . . ." The vulgar epithets erupted and continued unabated over the shouting from the British lines. "That man, who steps forward, shall be granted asylum by His Majesty and his freedom from slavery and the tyranny of the American hypocrisy!"

Sam was astonished and grieved by what he heard, but never in a hundred years would he think of stepping forward. His impulse right now was to shrink as far as he could into the ground, and he wondered if the soldiers from Southampton now regretted touching him for luck. He didn't have time to do anything anyway, for several shots rang out, and the voice was gone, replaced by a strange creaking sound from somewhere behind the line of red, check-marked by the white straps crossing the chests of each soldier.

"X marks the spot!" called out one volunteer to laughter as all recognized the joke, while also noting the bright target made by the straps.

"Ya needs to give them redcoats points fer courage," another man remarked. "I sure as Hades wouldn't want to wade across that open space directly into our . . ."

Almost on cue, the ranks parted and several cannon were wheeled into position. Curses and oaths erupted along the line as men pressed themselves into the logs and the ground.

"Here it comes, boys," shouted Captain Blow as the U.S. batteries immediately opened up from the redoubts before the British cannon could open fire. "Stay down, and do *not* fire your weapons until given the order! Sam," he said, pushing the teen down behind the sturdy logs. "Forget what that Brit said. Stay well below the log barricades! You can reload my muskets from there."

Sam didn't need to be told. He lay prostrate on the ground, tight against the barricade, and squeezed his eyes shut and his hands over his ears to try, to no avail, to shut out the terrible cacophony of death erupting all around him. Shot and ball were whistling overhead and exploding against the hill, the concussive force lifting his body off the ground and slamming it back down. Some rounds fell short, hitting the shallow water just off shore and showering the troops with wetness warmer than their own cold sweat. Sam felt dirt and sticks and rocks pelt him as the British cannon began to find their range. Sam heard horrible human screams above the din and waited for the Grim Reaper to wield his awful scythe at him.

Then suddenly the cannonade stopped as the much larger naval guns, placed in their redoubts earlier in the week by the men from Southampton, knocked out the enemy guns. The roar and shock of exploding shells were replaced by a different, human sound, and Sam realized it was the yelling of the redcoats as they splashed through the tide pools. He looked over the barricade and was astonished to see the line of grimly determined men already nearly halfway across, their muskets at low ready.

He pushed himself up to see better and felt a sharp pain in his left hand. He was shocked to see a five-inch splinter of wood impaled through his left palm and actually wondered how it got there. Blood oozed dark and slick around the ragged shaft, and his first thought was to look to his master for succor.

"Hold your fire, boys!" Peter was shouting next to him, his attention frozen on the red line slogging across the Thoroughfare. "Hold! Hold!"

Sam forgot his wound when a massive cheer erupted along the defensive line as a cannon ball exploded in a tremendous spray of water and bodies and blood. Again and again the awful effect of powder and iron on the human body was repeated in gut-wrenching gore. They slowed, but still the screaming masses came.

"Ready your guns," commanded Captain Blow, the order repeated along the line, muskets and rifles steadied on logs. He looked to see if Sam had the spare muskets ready and paused only for a moment as his eyes narrowed on the bloody mess that was Sam's hand. His brow furrowed, and he looked Sam in the eyes. "Are you okay?" he mouthed and Sam nodded. A few guns started popping off further down shore, and Peter turned instantly back to the fray.

"Steady, men! Wait for them . . . hold . . . NOW! FIRE!" he bellowed.

With a near-simultaneous explosion of smoke and sound, hundreds of Minié balls slammed into the line of humanity less than a hundred feet away. The advance was halted instantly as men screamed and fell and died. Those remaining fired off a few wild shots but then turned in unison and began their frantic splashing back to the opposite shore.

A cheer went up among the Americans, and Peter saw the company of riflemen from Winchester leap their barricade and run forward into the water, firing at the backs of the retreating enemy. He felt his men looking at him, anxious for the order to follow, but instead he told them to stay put.

"By my estimation, they only sent a fourth of their ranks into the water. There's still a couple thousand waiting for us on the opposite shore. Well done, men! You held your ground, and this first round goes to the good side!"

The cheering continued as the Winchester riflemen returned, and the realization that they had escaped death swept over the ranks.

But there were moans and screams from injured comrades, and the cheering stopped as they turned their attention to saving those who had shed their blood on that tiny island that, until today, had only known the calls of wild cranes.

Peter put down his musket and turned to Sam, who sat in a daze, tugging sheepishly at the splinter turned black with his own congealing blood.

"Sam, no," Peter cautioned, pulling Sam's right hand away. "You need a doctor. Corpsman!" he shouted, looking around, then back at Sam. The bleeding had nearly stopped, but he nonetheless tore a strip off his shirttail and started to gently wrap it around the hand and the wood. He knew that infection killed more men than enemy shot in any battle, and he wasn't about to let his loyal little friend suffer that fate.

"Does it hurt much?" he asked.

Sam worked up a smile. "Not as much as that time old Bullah done kicked me in the britches!" A chuckle broke through his pale lips, but a tear dripped off his cheek. "I couldn't sit fo' a fortnight!" He laughed, and Peter joined him, knowing that this friend was one tough piece of hickory who would surely long outlive him.

The shaft was smoother than they thought, as the bark had been blown clean off before it pierced his palm, but it left an angry scar that Sam forever after admired as a sign of manhood. In later years it would ache whenever the weather turned damp, and he would rub it and remember how free he felt, knowing he bled for his country in a winning cause.

The Americans had indeed won a great victory that summer morning—and it would be the only victorious land battle in Virginia during the entire course of the war. It prevented the enemy from establishing a central and secure operating base in the Americas from which to continue to prosecute their second war against their old nemesis.

At the moment the British infantry began the deadly crossing of the Thoroughfare, fifty large barges packed with infantry deployed from the ships and headed toward the northern and eastern shores. Captain Blow ordered his teams manning the two

24-pounders and four 6-pounders to ignore the covering navel fire from British warships, and to focus their aim on the approaching barges. His gunners did not flinch in the face of incoming death and trained their own cannon with fatal accuracy, sinking five barges and sending nearly a hundred men to their deaths in the turbulent waters of Hampton Roads. The other barges turned back, and Colonel Beatty sent orders to cease fire and to deploy men to try to rescue some of the injured Englishmen still in the water.

The British were done for the day. They retreated back to their ships and sailed away. They had suffered over two hundred dead and at least that many injured. Some sixty were captured, including twenty-two aboard Admiral Warren's own fifty-foot-long barge, the *Centipede*. Amazingly, despite many grievous wounds, not a single American lost his life that day. In forwarding Colonel Beatty's report of the defense of Craney Island to the American Secretary of War, General Taylor added his own remarks lauding the gallantry of his Virginians, writing:

> *The courage and constancy with which this inferior force, in the face of a formidable naval armament, not only sustained a position in which nothing was complete, but repelled the enemy with considerable loss, can not fail to command the approbation of the government and the applause of their country.*

Of course, the war was not over. The following year, the British would take "Madison's War" directly to his home, defeating a disorganized lot at Bladensburg, Maryland, then marching unimpeded into the new American seat of government, the District of Columbia, sacking and burning the president's home and the unfinished U.S. Capitol Building and many other government and commercial buildings. The demoralization of the country feared by Colonel Beatty set in and could have led to the end of the great American experience in democracy had it not been for the courage of another small group of brave men manning another tiny fort blocking the entrance to a major industrial port.

The Americans manning Ft. McHenry in Baltimore Harbor withstood an entire night of endless naval bombardment of exploding bombs from mortar ships and the new Congreve rockets that happily weren't very accurate, but struck terror in the hearts of all who saw their red glare, heard their awful whine, and waited for the explosion of shrapnel above their heads. The fort held, and the star-spangled banner yet waved over its broken, but still-standing, walls. The British again withdrew, and the war ended the following year in a mighty victory in New Orleans by Andrew Jackson and his Tennessee Volunteers.

America's strength as a world power was solidified, and it would be nearly two hundred years before major U.S. commercial buildings and government edifices in Washington D.C. would be targeted, attacked, and burned by a foreign enemy.

With the exception of the small town of Hampton, which the British raided, sacked, and pillaged in retaliation for their humiliating loss at Craney Island, Virginia would escape, at least for nearly fifty years, other battles of that war and death on her soil. Nevertheless, two years of blockade had a devastating effect on her economy, and few suffered more than the Blows. Losses due to the inability to market their crops were followed by several years of drought. The already-depleted soil from nearly two hundred years of continuous farming hit The Olde Place particularly hard, and as Peter's family grew and his resources dwindled, the unmatched feeling of facing and surviving a deadly foe faded quickly, hastened by his return to the bottle.

The Olde Place lost its luster, and the rivers, trees, and rugged beauty of Old Southampton—not to mention two centuries of Blow family heritage—were not enough to hold Peter to the land. He listened to tales of the fertile, rolling hills of the brand new state of Alabama, and he began many trips to the courthouse in Jerusalem to sign deeds of sale on portions of his nearly one thousand acres. He also entered into lawsuits against perceived enemies and neighbors alike, all for the purpose of amassing the money necessary to move his large family south and start over.

Peter took his valued servant Sam with him whenever he traveled to court, and while he had never considered teaching his young friend and assistant to read, Sam himself paid careful attention. He listened and he watched and asked questions and gained a rudimentary but valuable understanding of the purpose and power of the legal system. He saw that within the columned porticos of courthouses, white men could seek justice for harms, real or imagined. He kept his own thoughts deeply buried, but brought them out late at night as he sometimes stared up at the brilliant sky over Southampton and wondered to himself if there might be justice some day for the Negro within a white man's court of law.

The British had offered it to him that June day in 1813, but at what price? He had heard that tens of thousands of slaves had taken the British up on their offer or had simply used the chaos of war to finally succeed at running away. Many Negroes had even tried to find "justice" and freedom through shedding the blood of their masters. But Sam Blow waited. His life had been as good as any man who was owned by another. Better, in fact, than most. He still had his mother and brother. He felt loved by the Blows, and he dearly loved the Blow children growing up all around him. He would wait and he would learn, and for now, as the second decade of the nineteenth century came to a close, he would hope that Massa Peter could rediscover his zest for life and his own self-respect. Maybe he would find it in Alabama, and the spirit of another great river—this time the wild Tennessee—would speak to his soul, and two families—the Blows and his own—would grow and increase and perhaps even flourish somewhere along its banks.

* * *

On St. Patrick's Day 1777, just a few months after Peter Blow was born at The Olde Place in Virginia, Roger Brooke Taney was born into the aristocratic Taney family at their family plantation in Calvert County, Maryland. He was educated in private boarding schools and then at Dickinson College in Carlisle, Pennsylvania, where he was the valedictorian of his graduating class. His older brother, Michael VI, would inherit the family plantation, so Roger chose the law as his profession. He was an odd-looking man with blond hair, a long, almost bird-like, face, sharp, long nose, and even at a young age he had bags under his pale blue eyes. He definitely stood out in a crowd, and after apprenticing under Judge Townley twelve hours a day for three years, he made a name for himself as a highly intelligent and skilled practitioner of the law.

Less than a year after Roger Taney was born, Abraham Lincoln's father Thomas was born in the Shenandoah Valley, Virginia. When he was three, his family migrated west and homesteaded near Hughes's Station in Kentucky. About the time the United States was fighting the Barbary Pirates in the Mediterranean, eight-year-old Thomas experienced firsthand the brutality of the frontier. While clearing land in 1786, his father was shot and mortally wounded by Indians. His older brothers fled for help. Thomas stayed with his dying father and would not leave him even as an Indian in war paint approached and prepared to scalp them. His brother

Mordecai saved Thomas's life by taking careful aim from the cabin with his father's Revolutionary War rifle and shot the attacker dead.

In 1799, the year Dred Scott—then Sam Blow—was born at The Olde Place, the man who would one day officially declare Dred's race to be forever the property of white men, Roger Taney, was admitted to the Maryland Bar and won his first case defending a man for assault and battery in a fist fight. In 1808, while Robert Fulton was piloting his first steamboat *Claremont* from New York to Albany, Thomas Lincoln married Nancy Hanks in Hardin County, Kentucky, and Roger Taney married Anne, little sister to his fellow lawyer and best friend, Francis Scott Key.

As Captain Peter Blow and his slave marched with the 65th Virginia militia to the defense of Norfolk, Roger Taney made the decision to break with his Federalist party over its opposition to the war and publicly supported President Madison. He was attacked by his former political allies, but he silenced them by arguing that they had perversely put their politics and their property ahead of the good of the nation.

A year later, having been unsuccessful in Virginia, the British armada prepared to land an army to sack the nation's capitol city. Taney urged a former classmate who was commanding the Washington military district to call out all Marylanders to come together and stop the march on Washington. His brother-in-law, Francis Scott Key, responded to the call. The ragtag Maryland defenders were no match for the mighty British at the Battle of Bladensburg in August 1814, and the redcoats moved to burn the undefended city. As a lawyer, Key was ordered to go to the British to negotiate the release of Dr. William Beanes, a civilian non-combatant taken prisoner at Bladensburg, so he asked Taney to rescue his wife and children in Georgetown. As Taney delivered them safely to Fredericksburg, Francis Scott Key boarded the prisoner exchange ship and watched from the deck the terrible bombardment of Fort McHenry. All night long the sky was lit with the exploding of five-hundred-pound bombs and the terrifying new rockets. The next morning, fear filled the anxious American prisoners below decks who couldn't imagine the defenders of the fort had survived that brutal cannonade. They called desperately up to Key, "Oh, say, can you see? Is the flag still there? Is there still hope for our beloved nation?"

As the smoke and the mists cleared, Key was so moved to see that the large "star-spangled banner" yet waved over the fort so bravely held that he penned the poem that would become the national anthem. Unable now to attack Baltimore by sea, the British landed the same army that burned Washington, but the delay by the courageous defenders of Fort McHenry allowed the U.S. Army and Maryland militia to regroup, fortify, and turn back the land attack. The defeated army re-boarded their ships and sailed away to attack New Orleans the following year, where they would be met and decimated by Andrew Jackson and his Tennessee volunteers.

So moved was Roger Taney by how close the British had come to ending this great American experiment in democracy, and with hope for the future of freedom materialized in the birth of his only son, he freed his slaves and, with Francis Key, led a colonization society to return free blacks to Africa.

Part VIII

Running to Paradise

"The wind is old and still at play
While I must hurry upon my way,
For I am running to Paradise;
Yet never have I lit on a friend
To take my fancy like the wind
That nobody can buy or bind . . ."
- William Butler Yeats

"And when this transient life shall end,
Oh, may some kind eternal friend,
Bid me from servitude ascend,
Forever!"
- "Slave's Complaint" on marker stone at
slave cemetery on site of Peter Blow Plantation,
Oakwood College, Huntsville, AL

Riverboat and Flatboat

Chapter 20

The Great War Path

Tennessee Valley, 1819

Sam and Peter sat smoking on the bank of the Little Pigeon River, Tennessee, as the sun rose up over the Little Smokey Mountains. The dark orange glow of the fires through the windows of Isaac Love's new iron forge faded into the bright yellow rays of the new day. A large covey of passenger pigeons shattered the peace of the dawn as they exploded *en masse* from the beech trees lining the river. Sam blew smoke slowly out of his nostrils as he watched the birds dip and soar, some dropping beechnuts from their beaks into the river as they winged down the narrow valley toward the Great Tennessee River Valley, and beyond that, the Cumberland Range of the Appalachian Plateau, barely visible through the morning haze. The chill in the air and the scattered patches of color evidenced that autumn had arrived. Sam felt envious of the pigeons' freedom until several shots rang out downstream and what seemed like thousands of birds veered up and away in perfect unison. He threw his glowing cigar butt into the stream and turned to his master.

"So what's it gonna be, Massa Peter? Does you want me to head south with my brother Dred and try to parley with the Cherokee to let us pass unmolested down the Great Warrior Path? Or does we return to the boatyard, buy our own flatboat, and follow the route of that Colonel Davenport down the Tennessee River?"

Peter also tossed the stub of his larger cheroot into the river and pulled out his flask. It irked him that Sam spoke so bluntly, almost familiarly, with him. His first thought was to backhand Sam, but he tipped the flask to his lips and sucked down a long burning flow of the amber liquid of which he had become so fond and shuddered. He took a long, deep breath of the fresh morning air and let the itching in his right hand to smack Sam subside. He turned his head and looked into Sam's dark and blood-shot eyes. Sam looked right back without blinking or averting his gaze. Peter smiled and took another swig from the flask of brandy. Any other white man would take the look as impudence, but Peter realized it was simply a look of the trust and confidence that had grown between them since the war, during all the long trips to court, and working side-by-side preparing The Olde Place for sale and the family for this journey. He burped and handed the bottle to his friend, who waved it off.

"I know that if anyone could talk our way past the Cherokee, it would be you, Sammy-boy," Peter complimented and then realized, looking at his twenty-one-year-old companion, that though small, he was far from being a boy. "Sam, you're a gifted negotiator when it comes to talking with the savages. I know this because you grew up spending so much time with the Nottoway. But from what I hear, the Cherokee, though once as peaceful as the Injuns of Virginia, grew tired of the white man stealing their hunting grounds and began fighting back. Mr. Love says there's been peace for over a decade, but rumblings over past injustices as of late. There were terrible massacres by both sides in our lifetimes, and rumor is, the Cherokee have again allied with the Chickamauga, who helped them rebuild their five towns down at the Narrows, and they aren't in the mood for no powwow right now."

Sam nodded in agreement, and Peter continued.

"So until the U.S. Army or the militia decide whether, once again, to clear the Great Warrior Path by force, we have only two real choices: stop right here in Pigeon Forge, build a cabin and wait a year or more, or we go back to Kingsport, sell our wagons, and buy us a sturdy flatboat and try our luck at bypassing the Chickamauga towns on the Tennessee."

"You knows I love the rivers, Massa, but you also knows that the worst part of the entire Tennessee River lies right down that valley." Sam pointed toward the spot where the narrow Pigeon River canyon opened into the larger Tennessee Valley. "In the Narrows Gorge, the Suck and the Pot and the Skillet and the Pan have been known to carry many a boat and man down into the depths only to spit 'em back out miles downstream! It's a risky and dangerous trip for the young'uns, but it sho' 'nuff will get us to 'Bama afore the snow flies!"

Sam watched as his master thought about his options. He winced when Peter took another long draught of the spirits. *You won't find courage in that,* he thought but couldn't voice. They were friends, but Peter had grown more quick with a backhand during the past year as he drank more and disposed of lands that had been in the Blow family for centuries. Sam felt some sorrow for the man who had abandoned the place of his inheritance and took his young and growing family into the wilderness in search of new opportunities.

For many years after the war, Peter had been talking of uprooting his family from their soil-depleted lands, and when the U.S. Congress passed the Missouri Compromise earlier that year, it signaled that, indeed, the growth of this nation trended westward. Peter took it as a signal that his and his family's future lay to the west. He had originally spoken of going out to St. Louis and the lands around the Mississippi River, but then came news of the rich fertile lands along the Tennessee River in the northern part of the newly created state of Alabama, in what they called The Great Bend of the Tennessee. Though the Compromise inspired Peter to move west, it inspired Sam to greater dreams of freedom.

The Speaker of the U.S. House of Representatives, Henry Clay, had sponsored a compromise that was already splitting the new country into north and south over the issue of slavery. The compromise agreed that the new states of Missouri and Maine would enter the Union as slave and free state, respectively, and, to forestall future problems, it was agreed that no territories above 36° 30' N. latitude—roughly the southern border of Missouri—could enter as slave states.

Sam could not read, but Peter spoke with him often on their trips to Jerusalem and sometimes in the evenings while Elizabeth put the children to bed. Peter found Sam to be very intelligent and possessed with a rare interest, for a Negro slave. They often discussed the law, government, and politics.

Peter had become very litigious in the past several years. Southampton County court records were full of appearances by Peter in numerous legal disputes. As such, he had alienated himself somewhat from his neighbors, and when he began speaking of selling his lands to strangers, his Blow cousins stopped coming around. As a result, Peter sought out Sam more and more for manly conversation. Peter's three oldest children were girls: eighteen-year-old Mary Ann, fourteen-year-old Elizabeth, and nine-year-old Charlotte. Having lost ten-year-old Richard the prior year to a farming accident, when Peter wanted to discuss subjects only spoken of by men, he turned to Sam.

Of course, Sam felt great pride in being the object of his master's interest and actually felt as though Peter respected his views. It was a very rare and strange relationship, but Sam reveled in it and used it to learn all he could about the ways of the white man's world. He therefore understood fully the import and impact of what they were calling the Missouri Compromise, and he found great hope in the fact that a white Congress had made it impossible for slavery to exist in states north of the compromise line.

Sam thought of the two remaining Blow boys, five-year-old Peter and the toddler Taylor, and felt a great sadness for his master's terrible loss. He thought about his own fifteen-year-old brother Dred and could not imagine what it would be like to lose him, though knowing that as slaves, they could be separated at any time, should Massa Peter feel the need for more money. Peter Blow had sold everything and invested all he had in this new adventure in Alabama. Sam was determined to do whatever he could to make sure the Blows were successful in starting their new lives on the Great Bend of the Tennessee, as it would keep his own mother and brother close to him.

Out of a sense of gratitude for the way he was treated by Peter, and to a certain extent a need for familial preservation, Sam once again committed to be a mentor, friend and, most importantly, a protector of these two Blow boys. Taking the six Blow children, which also included chubby little four-year-old Martha Ella, through "the Suck" caused Sam a great deal of concern.

Peter rose and removed his hat, scratching his head in thought. He took another swig from his flask and looked into Sam's eyes as he slammed the cork home with the heel of his hand. He saw the loyalty and the confidence he had always known, and on which he had come to rely and appreciate of late. He knew Sam was brave and would undertake any task asked of him. Peter didn't have many close friends, and some of those he once trusted and called friends had sued him over property. He chuckled slightly to himself at the thought that his little slave was probably his best friend in the world.

He gazed over at the tents flapping in the early morning breeze where his young family slept, and then at the carriages, wagons, horses, oxen, cows, and goats that made up all he physically possessed in this world. As if on cue, a strong gust of wind struck his back, and Peter had to step one foot forward to keep from falling. The wind propelled him south where he believed lay paradise, the El Dorado of the West, in the rich, unturned soil of the Tennessee River Valley. He had been brought up in the Episcopal Church, and while he wasn't a Sunday-go-to-meeting kind of man, he considered himself a God-fearing man, and that gentle push was all he needed to move forward with his dream.

"Sam," he declared, turning to his friend with renewed confidence, "we've come two hundred miles, and I feel compelled to move forward without undue delay. Take your brother and return with haste to the boatyard at Kingsport. Buy us a sturdy flatboat and hire an experienced Tennessee River pilot and crew. I know it's a dangerous trip for two Negroes to be making alone, but I must stay here to look after Elizabeth and the children."

He handed Sam a considerable amount of cash and written instruction that Sam and Dred were owned slaves on an errand for their master, Peter Blow, of the Virginia Blows. For just the slightest moment, he hesitated at the thought of giving so much money and independence to an illiterate slave, and wondered if he would ever see the brothers again. But there was an unmistakable look of honesty, integrity, and a hint of pride in Sam's wide brown eyes which drove Peter's doubt away.

"We'll meet you in Knoxville in two months' time," he said, reaching out and shaking Sam's hand. Peter had considered sending his two field slaves, Luke and Will, along, but he didn't trust them like he did Sam. He also knew Sam wouldn't be able to stop them, should they decide to make a run for it. Sam and his brother would have to go it alone. Peter now found himself just fine with that.

"Yessuh," Sam declared, pulling on his master's hand and leaping to his feet. "See you in Knoxville!"

* * *

The December snow was flying when Sam returned with the large flatboat he had hired. Peter had to admit that Sam was, indeed, a talented and trusted servant. The boat was Broadhorn-style and looked sturdy enough to handle any of the treacherous rapids Peter had heard so much about. It measured twenty by one hundred feet and was built of heavy timber with a hull of squared-off logs. The sides were well-buttressed against potential gunfire, should the Cherokee indeed be in a war-like mood. A solid cabin structure ran two thirds the length of the boat, and Peter was pleased to see a rock chimney rising out of the rounded roof of the cabin near the stern. Sam popped out of the door in the front of the cabin, and his face lit up when he spied Peter on the dock.

"Ahoy, Cap'n Blow!" he hollered. "Say howdy to yo' new boat. We'ze callin' her the *Adventure Two,* after the famous Donelson flatboat that first made the trip down the entire length of this river." A rough-looking frontiersman, whose head and face were covered with an explosion of white hair, exited the cabin behind Sam and leaped up onto the oak gunwale. The deep crevices in the boatman's bronzed face led Peter to believe the man must be in his seventies, but he moved like a man half his age.

"And this here pilot is Edmond Jennings, the son of Jonathan Jennings who made that trip with the Colonel. Best not let Missus Elizabeth hear his stories of that dangerous voyage, but thar ain't nobody who knows this river better!"

197

The Blow family of eight, along with their eight slaves, set out three days before Christmas, 1820, on a flatboat large enough for thirty passengers, which provided plenty of room for all. "All" included the pilot, Jennings, and the three crew members needed to man the rudder mounted on a long tiller that rose to the roof, and the two sweeps, or long oars, on each side.

Hammocks had been rigged along the interior walls, and there were tables and chairs for meals. Peter sold the larger stock animals, but kept numerous goats, pigs, and chickens, secured in the bow. With the exception of sixty-year-old Solomon and Sam's forty-five-year-old mother, Hannah, who were allowed to sleep on mats inside the cabin, the rest of the slaves made their beds wherever they could find space on the deck, which was crowded with animals and all Elizabeth's furniture from the Olde Place Homestead that Peter would allow.

The river's edge was crusted in ice, and the air was bitterly cold, but Sam and the teenaged Dred were delighted to be back on the river and moving. Sam taught his little brother everything he had learned over the years about ropes, knots, steering, propulsion, sounding, and the peculiar colors in the water, indicating shallows, rocks, or a submerged log or other threat that could cause a disaster. Sam was proud to see that his brother was a quick study, and he felt a great love for the boy as he rose to every opportunity for growth and knowledge. At fifteen, Dred was already taller than Sam and had a smile that could disarm almost any foe. The rough boatsmen—Indian fighters in a previous life—treated the other slaves on board with disdain, but easily took to the lad and were soon joking and laughing with him. At night, much to Sam's disapproval, they shared their whiskey with him.

Since the river was at its highest in the winter, they had no problems during the first few days of travel. They floated smoothly down the middle between hills and mountains of bare hardwood forests, sprinkled with patches of evergreens and dark cedars on the lower slopes. Thorny briers and brambles lined the shores. Thousands of pointed tree stumps and rough dams gave evidence of beavers in abundance, and an hour seldom passed without sighting deer, elk, and bear along the shores. This was truly a bountiful land that held so much promise. Sam marveled at how depleted of game Virginia had become after two hundred years of human occupancy, and he urged Peter to order the boat to shore so they could hunt. But Peter appeared anxious to keep moving, and Sam could tell he was worried about the dangers they would face in the coming days when they entered the Narrows.

In two days they passed the junction of the Little Tennessee that first gave the larger river its name, and on Christmas Eve Day they came to the place where the Clinch River joined, nearly doubling the size of the Tennessee. They steered the large craft to the north shore, and a few miles downriver, docked at the small pier of the frontier settlement of Kingston. With pressure from Elizabeth, Peter reluctantly agreed to spend that evening and all of Christmas Day at Kingston. With a whoop and a holler, Sam and Dred set off with Peter's model 1808 musket from the war and the newer double-barreled shotgun to bring home some Christmas dinner.

Before nightfall, the boat was filled with the wonderful aroma of roast goose and broiled venison. After dinner, Jennings and his two rough sailors, well-lubricated with Christmas cheer of the type that comes from a flask, produced a banjo, fiddle, and Jew's harp from seemingly nowhere and began to entertain the stuffed family with rowdy songs of the frontier. At first, Elizabeth was concerned about whether the entertainment was consistent with her Episcopalian restraint, but the children were laughing and having more fun than they'd enjoyed since leaving Virginia six months ago.

Old Edward Jennings sensed Elizabeth's discomfort. He led his rough oarsman into an Americanized version of the delightfully entertaining English song of the wedding of a frog and a mouse, "Froggy Went A-Courtin'." As Jennings sang, Sam jumped right in to act out the part of the frog, hopping and dancing and strutting as he went about courting and marrying Miss Mousie. The children joined in the favorite tune and were soon clapping and laughing, then little Peter popped up and began mimicking Sam. He improvised his own gay dance, cleverly pantomiming the various critters that came to the wedding ball. Two-year-old Taylor couldn't sit still and, getting out of Mary Ann's lap, excitedly bobbed and stamped to the happy tune. The innocence and purity of the lads softened every heart, and a sweet Christmas spirit filled the entire cabin:

> *"Froggy went a courtin' and he did ride, uh-huh*
> *Froggy went a courtin' and he did ride, uh-huh*
> *Froggy went a courtin' and he did ride*
> *With a sword and a pistol by his side,*
> *Uh-huh, uh-huh, oh yeah.*
>
> *"He rode right up to Miss Mousie's door, uh-huh*
> *He rode right up to Miss Mousie's door, uh-huh*
> *He rode right up to Miss Mousie's door*
> *Gave three loud raps, and a very big roar,*
> *Uh-huh, uh-huh, oh yeah."*

Later that night as the children drifted off to sleep, the music turned to traditional frontier airs of "Leather Breaches," "Old Joe Clark," "Tennessee," and the favored fiddler dance tune "Old Zip Coon." That Christmas Eve of 1820, on the shores of the wild Tennessee, a family of adventurers shared a rare moment of unity and togetherness. White and black, bond and free, ancient and infant, irreverent frontiersmen and Episcopalians sang, clapped, danced, and laughed together. In the coming days they would share excitement and grave danger and, as one, they would arrive in a new land that held endless possibilities. Sixty years later Charlotte would write to her grandchildren that as a nine-year-old she dreamed of "money growing upon trees, and good old apple brandy flowing from their trunks;" but then added a sad footnote: "From this period commenced our misfortunes."

Carrying passengers with full bellies and happy hearts, the boat, rechristened on Christmas Day as the *Richard Benjamin,* in honor of the recently deceased Blow child, set out on the most dangerous leg of the voyage. For two days they traveled in nearly a straight line and watched in awe as the towering promontory known as Lookout Mountain grew toward the south. After passing the small Indian village of Chattanooga, the mountain loomed over them and the steep slopes came nearly to the water's edge. They pulled over to the north shore to secure all their property for the treacherous narrows that lay around the next bend in the river. They also prepared their muskets, shotguns, and pistols as they observed scores of Cherokee, Creek, and Chickamauga Indians coming out of their huts across the wide expanse in the rebuilt capitol of the Cherokee nation, Settico. The natives in their colorful dress hailed them as brothers in a friendly manner and motioned them to cross to their side of the river. But the family had listened to too many of Edmond's stories of slaughter by Indians lining the high banks along The Narrows and so ignored the entreaties, bending their backs to battening down everything for the coming rapids.

They pushed off in the afternoon with the children and animals secure inside the cabin. Every adult was positioned along the sides and the roof with long poles to push the craft away from the many rocks that awaited them in the Suck. Guns were kept nearby in case of an attack from above.

They rounded a sharp bend that took the river unnaturally due north. As it narrowed into a gorge, the boat sped up and began to dip and rock and dance with a life that didn't seem possible for the otherwise stodgy craft. As soon as they passed Williams, they were seized by the white waves of Tumbling Shoals and pulled violently into the Suck, where many a craft had been pulled under by the powerful eddies and crosscurrents where the Sulpher Branch and Suck Creek came roaring down a gorge with thousand-foot cliffs and crashed into the already violent rapids.

The girls screamed as the bottom of the flatboat crashed upon the rocks and heaved and tumbled and began to spin. Sam thought of the Indian legends the boatmen had told him of vessels being sucked down through the bottom of the river and forever trapped among an ancient supernatural race called the Nunnehi, who dwelled in the underworld. Sam didn't feel much like meeting them today and wedged himself tighter between the wall of the cabin and the stout log sides of the boat. He almost screamed as he saw his brother nearly topple over the gunwale near the stern. The boat continued to spin out of control as they neared the point where the river curved around Raccoon Mountain before plunging south again, and it seemed the puny arms of the gallant crew could do little to keep the boat from crashing into the rocky shores.

Thankfully, the good boat *Richard Benjamin* was adequately constructed to handle the violent assault. It emerged safely from the Suck and hurtled headlong south toward a wider expanse with fewer surface rocks, but whose many whirlpools and subsurface eddies had produced names like the Boiling Pot and the Skillet. Despite the great efforts of the experienced pilot on the rudder and the strong boatmen on the sweeps, the river was in charge and took the boat around and around.

Sam remembered the funny story Mr. Jennings had told him of a keelboat that had floated this stretch of river at night. The passengers had marveled that they had passed nine small cabins along the shore where drunken boatmen were dancing and clapping to the same fiddled rendition of 'Old Zip Coon.' When they finally pulled into the all-night party at old Jack Cogles's house, they realized they had been "bilin'" around and around in the Boiling Pot all night and had simply passed the same house nine times.

Sam didn't laugh now as, sure enough, the boat kept swirling around, now heading downstream, now up. As the entire crew fought the power of the current with seemingly useless sweeps and oars, the heavy boat suddenly leaped from the Pot and into the final dangerous rapids known as the Frying Pan. The boat began to buck and tremble. Before long, Sam thought he knew what a strip of bacon felt like a-sizzlin' on a hot skillet. At the same moment the boat rounded a bend and plunged to the west, Sam noticed a new danger, and it was of the human kind.

"Cherokee!" he cried out, and pointed to the long line of armed and feathered men trotting along the ridge to the south. All eyes on board shifted up to where Sam pointed.

"That worries me," Edmond called out. "They must've crossed over from Settico along the war path while we were being pulled north around Raccoon Mountain. They would've had to sprint the entire way, which can't be for a peaceful reason."

As if on cue, a puff of smoke appeared on the ridge, followed by a sharp crack that was clearly audible above the still-roaring rapids. The stern of the *Richard Benjamin* lurched violently, toppling the distracted Jennings from the roof and into the brown churning water.

"He's been shot," Peter yelled. "Take cover and grab your weapons!"

More puffs of smoke and the sounds of muskets, and Sam heard and felt the deadly buzz of shells zipping around him. He couldn't believe these natives, whom he did not know, but with whom he felt he shared a unique sense of bias and misuse at the hands of the white man, were trying to kill him, and for no good reason, as far as he could tell. He didn't want to shoot back, not feeling antipathy toward those men whose lands and people had been attacked, stolen, and wasted for centuries. But his motive changed the instant his young brother propelled himself onto the top of the cabin to grab the violently shaking tiller, left out of control when the captain fell overboard. Sam raised his musket and returned fire as sharp slivers of wood splintered off the roof around Dred, who leaned with all his strength on the rudder handle held under his armpit. Sam watched his brother with great pride, all the while reloading and shooting at the Indians lining the ridge. The lanky muscles on Dred's back and down his legs flexed and rippled as he slowly walked the tiller back to turn the boat around and point it downriver. As soon as it was no longer perpendicular to the current, the craft picked up speed, and soon the bullets were falling harmlessly into the water.

"Huzzah!" the boatmen cried on seeing they were out of danger both from nature and man, for they had emerged from the deadliest part of the Narrows. The river still flowed fast and changed course north and south over the next hour, but they had made it past the eddies, crosscurrents, and submerged rocks and timber.

"Cap'n Jennings!" cried Elizabeth, who had gallantly stood at her husband's side throughout the deadly ordeal. Sure enough, the unsinkable old man was bobbing along just ahead of them, his white hair now plastered to his skull but still sharply contrasting with the brown water. He was spitting and sputtering and cursing a blue streak as young Dred expertly steered the large flatboat to the side, so as not to run over the top of him. The filthy crewmember known as Skunk stretched a sweep out to his boss, who caught the oar and held on for dear life, skimming backward over the surface as Sam joined the other men in pulling their pilot back on board.

"Dad-gummed Injuns!" the waterlogged Jennings swore as they tore off his wet clothes, looking for a gunshot wound. Finding none, Jennings turned his cursing back toward the river. Realizing the pilot would live, Sam looked around to see if everyone else was safe. His heart leaped when he saw his brother slumped unconscious over the tiller still gripped tightly in his embrace. A large stain darker than the wet of the river bloomed over his thigh and down his leg, soaking dark red into the timbered roof of the cabin.

"Dred!" he cried, scrambling up the wall. "Miz 'Lizbeth, Mammy, come quick, my brother's been shot through the leg!"

Later that evening, as the *Richard Benjamin* crossed into the state of Tennessee and entered the long calm course where the river widened and slowed, Sam sat by his sleeping brother, whose wound had been cleaned and bandaged by the womenfolk, feeling a love he hadn't known he possessed for another human being. He marveled that the young man hadn't hesitated in that instant of dire need to leap into the fray and take charge of the situation. Though he had been shot through the thigh by an angry Cherokee's ball, he had not uttered a single whimper, but continued to guide their vessel out of danger until he passed out from loss of blood.

"I hopes to be more like you, brother," Sam whispered as he caressed the soft curls on Dred's head. "God, save my brother's life, and I promise to be more like him," he prayed.

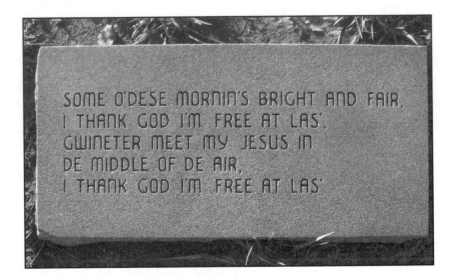

Huntsville Slave Cemetery Grave Marker

Chapter 21

The El Dorado of the West

Huntsville, Alabama, 1820

There was neither money growing on trees nor apple brandy flowing from their trunks, as young Charlotte Blow had imagined from all her father's hopes for Alabama. But the soil was indeed rich and dark with natural nutrients. After landing at Triana on the river, the family moved ten miles north to Huntsville, where thousands of other Americans were flocking. On January 5th, 1821, Peter, with his slave companion by his side, entered the new Madison County courthouse and filed a U.S. land grant for a quarter section of land in western Huntsville. With the ongoing migration, prices had increased dramatically since Peter had made the decision a year ago to uproot his family and move to a new land.

He knew there was no going back, so he spent all his remaining cash buying sufficient acreage to establish a thriving new cotton plantation to provide for his growing family.

His land would have to be cleared, and he would need farm equipment, draft animals, and building materials for quarters, so on February 3rd, he borrowed two thousand dollars from John N. Jones of Madison County and listed his eight slaves as collateral: "Solomon (60), Hanna (45), Luke, Will, Sam (20s), Dred (Sam's 16 yr old brother), Phyllis (also about 16) and Isaac (13)." Peter believed that putting up his slaves, and hence, his greatest income-producing capital, was a risk well-worth taking, given the apparently limitless potential of northern Alabama soil.

Almost overnight, Huntsville had become a thriving center in the U.S. realm of "King Cotton." The area, then part of Mississippi Territory, had been first homesteaded in 1805 by John Hunt, who built his cabin at Big Spring, which provided fresh water to the city. Three years later, there were five thousand new residents, enough for the governor of the territory to create Madison County and name it after the president. To raise money for the development of both county and town, the government offered tens of thousands of acres for sale at bargain prices. A wealthy Georgia businessman, LeRoy Pope, invested heavily in the area and earned the right to change the name of the new county seat to Twickenham, after the English birthplace of his famous ancestor Alexander "as the twig is bent, the tree's inclined" Pope. But after the War of 1812, British names fell out of favor, and the town was renamed after the Revolutionary War veteran and town founder, John Hunt.

By 1816, fourteen thousand settlers had spread out geometrically from the Big Spring center of town. In 1818, a large two-story brick courthouse was completed, establishing Huntsville as a true frontier metropolis. The next year, when Alabama became the 22nd state in the Union, Huntsville became the temporary capitol. It was there that the new state constitution was drafted and its first legislature convened. It was to this thriving city and land of hope that the Blow family arrived just as the new decade was dawning. Later that same year, Congress would take the extraordinary action known as the Missouri Compromise. This singularly historic act of Congress, that attempted to finish what the Founding Fathers had left unresolved in the Constitution regarding the institution of slavery, would be tested in the highest court some thirty-seven years later. No one in their wildest imaginings would have thought this little slave, newly arrived from Virginia, soon to begin clearing his master's land in Alabama, would be the impetus for that historic test.

* * *

Elizabeth gasped and put her hands to her mouth to stop from crying out as the carriage reached the top of a small rise, and she gazed down for the first time at their new homestead. The grass was green and oak trees were prevalent. The property sat in a large natural bowl with a babbling brook running west to east through the middle of the land.

"Oh, Peter, it's beautiful," she exclaimed. Tears sprang to her eyes as she looked at the man who had risked everything for his young family.

"Oh, yes, Daddy, it is beautiful," cooed young Charlotte from the rear of the hack. A spontaneous cheer of gratitude and excitement went up among the family at the recognition that their long trip had come to an end. Old Solomon and Hannah joined in, but Sam and the rest of the slaves could only see the trees and think of how much back-breaking labor of clearing the land for planting lay immediately ahead. Sam, driving the animal stock, dropped into the grass, correctly surmising it would be the last rest he would have for many months to come. Two weeks later, Sam would face the realization that, although he had a uniquely close and trusting personal relationship with his master, in the end he was still a slave and the property of that man.

* * *

Despite the late January chill, sweat rolled off the backs of Sam, Dred, and the other field hands. Sam, unaccustomed to and physically unprepared for the extreme physical labor, was near exhaustion. The life cycle of the cotton bowl was about twenty-five weeks, and the land had to be cleared and plowed for planting by April in order for the Blows to have cotton to sell in the late fall. Every slave was needed, and twenty-two-year-old Sam quickly gained an appreciation and growing sorrow for the terrible life suffered by the vast majority of his brother slaves.

The oak tree, being one of the hardest of hardwoods, seemed to be winning the battle for the Blow's Huntsville plantation. Axes and saws wore out quickly, and the stumps resisted all human effort to remove them. Seeing the evident lack of progress after two weeks of eighteen-hour days, Peter became increasingly frustrated. And this, combined with his drinking, turned him mean. Nothing could have prepared Sam for the afternoon in late January that changed his life forever.

Will, Luke, Sam, Dred, and even fourteen-year-old Isaac were struggling mightily with a stubborn oak stump. It had taken them nearly the entire day to cut down the largest tree on the property, and in doing so they broke the last saw Peter owned. Sam had urged his master the day before to buy a new double-bladed saw, as the one they were using was old and rusty to begin with. The suggestion had earned him a violent open-hand slap. More than the sting, the humiliation cowed Sam to silence. When the saw broke, an obviously drunk Peter picked up a stout oak branch lying near the leaning tree and struck Will and Luke, who had been manning the saw, on their legs, driving them to the ground in agony. Without a saw, the four slaves took turns with axes until the oak crashed to the ground. Despite bloodied palms and aching backs and shoulders, Peter would not let the crew rest. He wanted the stump out before nightfall.

While Will and Luke dug around the huge stump and hacked away at the roots, Sam and Dred harnessed up Old Trumpet, the largest horse the Blows owned, and tied the heavy iron hooks to the thickest rope in their inventory.

"This old mare ain't sturdy 'nuff for that stump," argued the teenaged Dred to his brother. "And even if it was, this rope sho"nuff ain't! You has to talk with Massa, Sam, and get him to understand."

Sam knew his brother was right, but his ego still stung from the physical rebuke earlier that day, and he wasn't in the mood for another, or greater, assault.

"We has to try, Dred. Massa Peter is worried that we won't get the land cleared in time for spring plantin'. And if that don't happen, he'll have to sell us downriver. The first to go will be our mammy, and then you and I will never see each other again. I couldn't go on livin' without you, brother." Sam hugged the young man he loved more than his own life. "No, we has to keep workin' and tryin'. We has to get this damned stump out tonight. If we does, Massa Peter will feel better and tomorrow will see reason. Then I can ask him to find a way to buy better saws and chains, and maybe even a strong work horse."

"But this is dangerous, Sam," Dred said, holding up the rope. "Mark my word, someone's gonna get hurt if we try this!"

"We all gonna be hurt if we don't, boy." Sam ended the conversation and began leading Trumpet to the stubborn trunk that refused to give up its century-old hold on that good Alabama soil.

"Eyaaah!" screamed Sam and switched the struggling beast. Trumpet glistened black as the others bent to their impossible task. Four taut lengths of thick hemp rope quivered between the horse and the hooks sunk into the stump, which was finally tilting out of the hole Luke and Will had dug. They chopped feverishly at the exposed roots. Peter removed his shirt and dug at the sides, trying to unearth more of the sunken tendrils. Dred was doing the same opposite, while keeping an eye on the rope he did not trust.

The men cursed and hollered as they pushed their tired bodies to the limit, and Trumpet snorted and whinnied and grunted as she did the same. Dred saw that his smaller, older brother was about to lose control of the frenzied equine as she dug in her back legs and reared up with her front. Seizing the moment, as he did that day in the Boiling Pot, Dred left his task and ran to Sam. He grabbed the reins, pulled with all his might, and brought the horse back down.

"I got this, Brother," he said with a strained smile and a wink.

Sam saw no criticism in the look, and he felt the boy's strength and confidence. He unquestioningly released his grip on the reins and stepped aside in awe of his brother's resolve.

Peter looked up and screamed at Sam to get back to work.

Dred drowned him out with his own deep cursing, and with a renewed vigor under the new control, Trumpet bellowed and lunged.

What happened in the split-second that followed would remain with Sam the rest of his life and would haunt his dreams and interrupt his meditations. As if in slow motion, Sam saw the inadequate rope splinter along two lengths and come apart in a spray of fiber. Before he could even turn and cry out a warning, Trumpet, suddenly free on her left side, violently twisted and fell directly on top of Dred. While Sam sprinted in horror toward his brother, the stunned horse bucked on the ground and, still attached to the ropes on her right, began pawing and thumping and finally stomped to her feet, unaware in her fright of the twisted and broken body of the boy beneath her.

"Drrred!" Sam wailed as he fell to his little brother's side. Bloody spittle bubbled from the boy's mouth, and Sam thought for sure his hero winked at him one last time before the dark eyes closed forever.

They buried Dred in a clearing on a small hill at the south end of the plantation.

From that day forward, Sam insisted on being called Dred.

* * *

One hundred and eighty years later, that same spot, which had become a slave cemetery, was discovered and restored by the prestigious Black Seventh Day Adventist Oakwood College, which today sits on the same land cleared by Dred and his fellow slaves on the Peter Blow Plantation.

Market place in New Orleans

Chapter 22

The Natchez Trace

Mississippi, 1821

The bond between Peter and Sam—now known as Dred—was broken, along with the slave's heart. He could no longer look at the man as a father and a mentor whom he had tried so hard to please. He didn't care anymore. He felt his own guilt about not listening to his brother's premonitions about the rope and for being too much the coward to bring it up with Master Blow, not to mention his belief that it should have been his body mangled under Trumpet's bulk. His body had been spared, but his free spirit was forever crushed. For the first time, he woke each day and thought of life as a chore. He was property. Peter Blow was his owner. And that was that.

In addition to taking his brother's name, Sam honored his brother's life and memory by committing within himself to be

Dred Blow in his actions and deeds, to step up to any challenge without hesitation and see it through even if it meant giving his own life, if necessary. He had experienced a freedom and accompanying self-respect that was very rare for a slave, but now he felt the chains of bondage and self-loathing. His only consolation was that his dear brother had crossed over Jordan and was at last free. He had met Jesus somewhere in the air and was now resting in the only true paradise. With each dawn from the day they laid his brother's broken body to rest, Dred awoke with a hunger for freedom in his mouth. He didn't know when or how, but he would be free in this life!

Finally realizing the job could not get done without new saws, axes, chains, and stronger animals, Peter made the decision to sell the teenaged Phyllis and Isaac. He nearly sold Dred as well, but unable to bear the loss of another son, Hannah intervened with Elizabeth, who enlisted the children who loved Dred. Their pleas softened Peter's heart, and he relented. Peter knew the special bond between himself and Dred had been broken, and in each quiet moment just before drifting off to sleep, he felt a pang of loss and regret for the man he had become. He justified his actions and salved his conscience, telling himself he had to provide for his large and growing family and that required the utilization of all his property, however he saw fit. Elizabeth and the older girls noted the change in him and yearned for happier times, but the work of building a plantation from scratch occupied all their time, and the days passed quickly in joint labor for the common good.

The timeless oak trees began to yield to the committed brawn of man and beast, and by May, two hundred acres had been cleared, plowed, and planted with cotton seed. A stout log cabin went up on a slight rise on the west of the cleared bowl, with less sturdy slave quarters built behind. Peter was filled with renewed hope as they tended the growing plants each day, and it became evident that this earth truly was gold. The plants grew with a speed and robustness Peter thought impossible, and he started planning that, with the money from a bounteous harvest, he would clear several hundred more acres and build his wife a large plantation home like the others that had sprung up around Huntsville.

And so that fall, it was with great anticipation that Peter oversaw the loading of four-hundred-pound bales of beautiful white cotton onto the *Richard Benjamin,* which he had kept docked near Ditto's Landing in Triana. The hiring of wagons for the ten-mile trip south from the plantation had been an extreme and unexpected cost, and Peter found himself wondering if it had been wise to build Huntsville so far from the river. He mentioned his concerns to several men at the warehouses along the river, and was pleased to hear that Thomas Fern, LeRoy Pope, and other planters had already put together the financing to canalize Indian Creek to make a navigable waterway from the river to Huntsville. Digging would begin in the spring, and Peter immediately offered his slaves to join in the public works project that would save him a lot of money in transportation costs.

The heavily loaded *Richard Benjamin* set out in early November for the long trip to New Orleans, where they would sell the cotton and the flatboat, then make their way back north. The flatboat was not built for traveling upstream, while the newer keelboats were better designed for that purpose. Some keelboats had made the long trip up river from New Orleans by use of warping (men pulling the boat ropes as they toiled along the banks) and bushwhacking (men on the boat pulling it along the banks by grabbing grasses, bushes, and trees and pulling the boat upstream) but it was terrible, backbreaking work, and the wages were high for those men willing to sign on for a journey that could take months. As a result, the common practice was for people to sell their products and their boats in New Orleans, sew their money into hidden linings in their coats and pants, and trek back north along the famous path known as the Natchez Trace. Of course, bandits also knew the practice and hid in wait for a different sort of bushwhack.

Dred had become one of the few men who could boast of having traveled the entire length of the Tennessee from its headwaters on the Holston River in Virginia down the Great Valley and through the Great Bend. This last length of the river made the Tennessee a geographical oddity, in that it ran for over a hundred miles due north. Dred had spent his life on rivers and joined in singing of the Jordan River leading to freedom. But as the river current pulled the boat unnaturally up, and the cold wind blew into his face, Dred's hopes rose as never before, and he felt a powerful premonition that freedom someday awaited him in the north.

It was nearly a spiritual experience for Dred as the sun rose at his back on a clear, cold day in late November, ten days after leaving Triana. He manned the tiller and steered the *Richard Benjamin* into the great confluence of two mighty rivers at the promontory where sat the town of Cairo, Illinois. Cairo made him think of stories he'd heard of the Nile, but as he felt the power and incredible majesty where the two currents merged, he knew there could be nothing greater than this Mighty Mississippi, the Father of Waters.

"We come a long way from the Nottoway," he whispered to the brother whose spirit he often felt nearby. He looked back over his shoulder at the rapidly diminishing sandy point that was his first sight of a land where slavery was prohibited. Chills caused by something greater than the weather ran down his back as a powerful impression seized him. This was his own River Jordan that he would cross in this lifetime, and it would somehow play a major role in his freedom from the yoke of bondage.

"Hallelujah!" he cried out. Luke and Will turned from their sweeps to look at their small companion and, feeling his spirit, joined in his jubilee.

"Roll Jordan roll," Dred sang out the popular spiritual in a low, prayerful bass.

His companions answered, "Roll Jordan."

"Roll Jordan roll," he repeated an octave higher.

"Roll Jordan," Luke and Will echoed, joined now by three roustabouts who had been lounging on the large cotton bales staked along the deck next to the cabin.

"I want to go to heaven when I die."

"To hear Jordan roll," they sang in unison.

Dred's voice caught as he began the second verse, "O brother, you ought to have been there."

"Yes, my Lord!" sang the slaves.

"A sittin' in the kingdom," Dred sang out to the heavens.

"To hear Jordan roll!"

Peter came out on deck and listened until well past sunset as the men who had never known freedom sang out their sorrows and their faith. A deep pang of regret passed through his heart, and he quietly slipped back inside to his hammock and fell asleep to the rocking of the boat and the soulful cadence from above.

New Orleans was by far the most exotic city he had ever seen. With a population of about thirty thousand people made up of French dandies, rough frontiersman, blacks, Spaniards, and beautiful Creoles, it was fast becoming the second busiest port in America. After the difficult task of unloading ten thousand pounds of cotton, Peter and the other planters had their pick of scores of drinking establishments, but left the tired slaves under guard on the boat. Peter knew how upset Dred still was with him, and he didn't trust any of the other slaves not to run off. He was confident that if they did, he could easily hire any number of slave hunters to track them down, but he wasn't entirely certain his property would be returned alive, and he needed them for next years' clearing and planting.

Two days later, the group of travelers, including white plantation owners, overseers, and slaves, had sold their goods. The sale of the *Richard Benjamin* had brought Peter an additional profit, and he had several thousand dollars sewn into his garments for the long walk home along the Trace—a well-worn foot path that passed five hundred miles through swamp and dense thickets in the south, then across prairies and up and into the hills and along the ridgelines of northern Mississippi, crossing into Alabama and Tennessee. It was a rough and narrow trail that could be walked as fast as it could be ridden, so no money was wasted on horses. The only equipment the men carried were bedrolls and packs with food stores—mostly what was known as an Indian ration of parched corn, jerked venison, and some cornmeal. Most importantly, they armed themselves with an assortment of guns, knives, and tomahawks for the dangerous trip on what had become known as the "Bloody Path."

Many were the stories of notorious robbers and murderers along the Trace through the decades. It had been fifteen years since the infamous Samuel Mason had been killed by his own men seeking a reward, and the brothers Big and Little Harpe had been done in. The big one, Micajah, was decapitated by vigilantes in retribution for murdering one of their wives, and his head nailed to a tree as a warning. The little one, Wiley, was hung by authorities. Some said that Mason's old murder site posters, "Done by Mason of the Woods," could still be seen along on the trail. Of course, as soon as one demon was brought to justice, another stepped in to take his place, so lucrative was the bandit trade on the Trace.

The trip north was uneventful, and at the insistence of the older sons of a fellow Huntsville plantation owner, they stopped at the trading store at Old Pontotoc just for a chance to gaze upon the renowned beauty of Peggy Allen, the daughter of Indian agent James Allen and Chickasaw princess Susie Colbert. Learning that the young woman, called by many "the most beautiful girl in the world," was betrothed to a Natchez planter, the men sated their disappointment with jars of juicy peaches put up that fall from the orchards surrounding the store.

Knowing Colbert's Ferry on the Tennessee was just forty miles away, the men hurried on, excited to be safely home. Unfortunately, they let their guard down. The first night out of Pontotoc, camped in a clearing a day's journey from the ferry, they were awakened in the night by a motley group of some thirty bushwhackers led by a tall, blue-eyed young dandy of about Dred's age, wearing a fine beaver hat, Bolivar coat, and a brace with one silver pistol across his chest. The other pistol was pointed directly at Peter's heart. An ugly, swollen brand was burned into the back of his hand: HT—meaning "horse thief."

Having failed to post lookouts, the group was surprised, and before they could reach their weapons, they had thirty guns pointed at them by men who were looking for the slightest reason to kill the whole lot.

"My name is John Albert Murrell," declared the bandit chief, removing his hat from his head of long black hair. "And I'm feelin' gen'rous tonight."

* * *

Back at Oakwood Plantation two weeks later, Peter was a broken man. He had left home with a bounteous harvest and great hope for the future, and returned penniless. Murrell knew where travelers hid their money. He had stripped Peter and his companions and made away with their entire fortune. His generosity was in letting them live, though Peter still wore a long purple welt on his left check from the barrel of the bushwhacker's pistol. He had hesitated too long in responding to the order to undress. He was lucky to be alive, for Murrell would go down in history as one of the bloodiest highwaymen on the Trace.

At least he still had his human property, Peter mused in a rare moment of positive reflection. Murrell, who fancied himself an abolitionist, but was really nothing more than a Negro-stealer, had offered the slaves their freedom in exchange for becoming part of his gang. Several of the other slaves instantly joined up, giving their former masters a good licking before they left. Peter was surprised that Dred, Will, and Luke didn't accept the offer, and was particularly baffled that Dred stayed with him, knowing how angry he was at Peter's role in the death of his brother, and the fact that after years of close familial relationship, Peter had begun to beat and abuse him.

In truth, Dred had considered the opportunity for freedom but for a moment. He had a powerful hankering to be a free man, but not at just any cost. He had promised his mammy, Hannah, years ago that his would not be a path of violence, but that he would learn and gain every experience and opportunity he could in life and trust in the Lord to be a light to his path. That light would grow in brightness and intensity until the perfect day.

Peter's neighbors at the Turn Key plantation offered to loan him the seed for planting in the spring, but Peter had lost heart for plantation life. That December he sold all his land and animals for five thousand dollars and moved his family and slaves overland due west along the northern banks of the river to the flourishing city of Florence. After nearly two hundred years and many generations of Blow planters, Peter would no longer make a living off the soil.

Chapter 23

The Practical Lessons of Industry

Florence, Alabama, 1821 - 1830

It was a beautiful spring day in 1821. Dred lay on his stomach atop an ancient Indian ceremonial mound. It was forty feet high, and the flat top measured one hundred feet wide and one hundred fifty feet long. It amazed Dred that at about the time Jesus Christ was born in the Old World, Indians of the Woodland culture lived here in this New World and were motivated by some spiritual drive to scoop enough dirt and rocks together to construct this mound. It was rumored to have been a place for either a temple or the chief's house. Dred thought it made a great lookout tower, and that was how he was using it that day.

Peter had sent him straight down Pine Street to the mound to await the arrival of the first steamboat to make it this far up the Tennessee. The Florence dock below him and to the west was crowded with people in their Sunday best gathered for the historic arrival of the new 149-ton steamboat *Osage,* with a cargo of dignitaries as well as groceries and hardware from New Orleans. The wharf and the shops and warehouses fronting the river were festooned with red, white, and blue bunting, and a band played the popular new hit, *Hail to the Chief,* from Sir Walter Scott's play *The Lady of the Lake.*

Despite their differences, Dred still found himself hoping that his master would finally find success in his new hotel business. Today was a big day for the family, for steamboats would now be disgorging passengers who needed a place to stay before making their trek to Athens and Huntsville, or even north to Nashville along the brand-new Military Road built by the great hero of the War of 1812, Andrew Jackson.

After today, the Blow family was sure to have a never-ending stream of guests. Dred now worked as a porter to bring the passengers' baggage and trunks on a horse-drawn wagon up the long slope of the hill to the new Peter Blow Inn on the northwest corner of Pine and Tennessee streets. When he wasn't doing that, he worked as a hostler, caring for the guests' horses. The property was large enough to house a small stable, and Dred loved working with the animals. Cleaning and mucking out stalls was laborious, but he found a lot of pleasure in grooming and tending to the powerful beasts. More than that, he enjoyed the time he spent with the two growing Blow boys. At five and three years of age when they arrived in Florence, Peter and Taylor spent much of their time outside for their lessons with Dred. He put them to work in the stables, and they often accompanied him to the river to meet the steamers.

The afternoon sunlight played beautifully on the blue-green river as the clear peal of the steam whistle rolled up the river and bounced off the cliffs. Dred jumped to his feet and peered downriver. His eyesight was very good, and he could plainly see the stacks and hurricane deck of the paddle-wheeler as she exited Bee Tree Shoals and rounded the bend in the river.

"Boys!" he cried to the kids frolicking nearby. "The steamer's a comin'!" He ran and scooped up Taylor to his shoulders and with Peter right behind, bounded off the edge of the sloping mound.

Hoooot. Hoooot, sounded the whistle.

"Hoot, hoot!" the two boys answered.

The crowd cheered below, the band played louder, and Dred and his young charges slid down the ancient hillock and ran toward the future.

* * *

The Peter Blow Inn did indeed become a very profitable enterprise for the Blow family. Master Blow in particular took to the role of genteel host. Charlotte Blow later wrote of her father, describing him as "honest, frank, social, communicative, and confiding [with] an unbounded confidence in his species, believing every man a gentleman who seemed to be one, or was by others esteemed as such, and, in transactions with them, considered their word as good as their bond." With financial success, Peter Blow drank less, and the time between his periods of depression increased. Dred began to see the goodness he once knew so well shine forth out of darkness.

The circle of life and death, so common in early American families, went on for the Blows. In 1822, they celebrated the birth of the tenth child, William Thomas, but lost their oldest, Mary Anne, to consumption. She had married John Key not long after the family had begun clearing land, and she had stayed behind to make her new home. Charlotte later wrote of the loss of her oldest sister, who in Huntsville had joined the Presbyterian faith, saying that her sister "like a pioneer, went before to show us the 'straight and narrow path' through the rugged scenes of this sinful world."

Elizabeth knew how important education was for her children, and not having much formal education herself, she left the schooling to the teachers in town, but in all other ways taught them the values and principles of a prosperous and happy life. In the words of Charlotte, "faithful she was in teaching [us] the practical lessons of industry and economy, faithful in dealing with [our] faults. The only one never checked was pride. This she appealed to as a stimulant to every other virtue; for virtue she esteemed it— and virtue it is, in its proper place, and under proper control."

The boys' father was often away from home, conducting business and spending time with the new associates in the rapidly growing city. After Mary Anne's death in 1826, he spent much more time in the saloons and gambling parlors. Dred was the boys' older brother, mentor, and role model. Not having had the opportunity to meet a woman and begin his own family, he took to their education in the manly arts with a passion.

In their free time, Dred took the lads fishing and hunting, and regaled them with stories of Indians and frontiersman, war heroes and Natchez pirates. He taught them to seek out challenges and hard work, and to take pride in a job well done. When they fell from a tree he had challenged them to climb, he held them until the pain subsided and then bound up their wounds. Skin color and class made no difference to any of them, and an unbreakable bond of love and friendship blossomed and ripened over the years.

Life for the other Blow slaves went on. Old Solomon worked around the hotel, sweeping and polishing and greeting all visitors at the door with a tip of his hat and a gentle "how do." Hannah was busy with the laundry, cooking, and housekeeping, and most days worked right alongside the blossoming Blow girls. Will and

Luke were the carpenters, plumbers, and all-around handymen, and they kept the inn in top shape. Dred elected to spend most of his time away from Master Blow and volunteered for the arduous tasks of offloading the baggage and heavy steamer trunks, hefting them on the wagon, and then unloading them and carrying them to guest rooms. It was hard physical labor, but Dred was wiry and strong, and the work kept him from the quiet moments when painful memories and regrets could become a consuming fire.

As the decade of the twenties drew to an end, and gambling and drinking reduced the ledger balance, Western fever struck again. Peter began talking of improving their income and their station in life by moving to the fastest growing city on the Mississippi—St. Louis, Missouri. There, he figured, he could pull in twice the number of customers coming and going, as commerce flowed both ways on the great artery of the nation.

And so it was on May 1st, 1830, as others danced around the Maypole in centuries-old celebrations of new life and rebirth, Captain Peter Blow, his wife, seven children, and five slaves boarded the *Atlantic*, the most elegant and expensive steamboat ever to have churned the great American waterways, and steamed toward the setting sun and to the Gateway of the West.

* * *

Nineteenth century frontier life was brutal. During the same period when Dred lost his brother and the Blows lost their daughter, Abraham Lincoln's mother took sick after drinking the milk of a cow that had eaten snakeroot, and died when Abraham was nine. Roger Taney's father, who a year earlier had stabbed a man to death in a knife fight over the honor of a woman, was killed after being thrown from a horse.

227

In 1819, Methodist Reverend Jacob Gruber preached a fiery abolitionist sermon at a camp meeting in Hagerstown, Maryland, calling for an end to the national sin of slavery.

"Is it not a reproach to a man," he queried, "to hold articles of liberty and independence in one hand and a bloody whip in the other, while a Negro stands and trembles before him with his back cut and bleeding?" Screaming in the throes of righteous indignation, he denounced slavery as immoral, condemned all slave owners, and asked, "Will not God be avenged on such a nation as this?"

A grand jury wasted no time in indicting Reverend Gruber for inciting slave insurrections, and Taney was hired to defend him. In successfully defending Gruber in court, Taney argued, "A hard necessity, indeed, compels us to endure the evil of slavery for a time. It cannot be easily or suddenly removed. Yet, while it continues, it is a blot on our nation's character, and every real lover of freedom confidently hopes that it will be . . . gradually, wiped away; . . . until the time shall come when we can point without a blush to the language held in the Declaration of Independence, every friend of humanity will seek to lighten the galling chain of slavery, and better, to the utmost of his power, the wretched condition of the slave."

A few years later, as the Blows were settling into the hotel business in Florence, Taney continued to solidify his personal views against slavery—although true to his heritage as a member of planter aristocracy, he never advocated for eliminating slavery by force. One day while waiting in a line with Negroes for the Catholic confessional, his priest, Father John McElroy, told him he didn't have to wait behind the Africans. "I'll wait my turn," the future jurist replied. "Thank God this is one place where all men are equal."

* * *

A year after that, as Taney prepared to defend his first appellate brief before the United States Supreme Court, sixteen-year-old Abraham Lincoln, with less than a year of formal education, left his first brief writings immortalized in a margin of his reader:

Abraham Lincoln,
His hand and pen.
He will be good,
But God knows when.

Abraham Lincoln is my name,
And with my pen I wrote the same.
I wrote in both hast and speed
and left it here for fools to read.

In April 1828, nineteen-year-old Abraham Lincoln signed up with his friend, Allen Gentry, to pilot a flatboat loaded with cargo to the New Orleans' markets for Gentry's father, and gained an education that cemented his lifelong antipathy to slavery. While in New Orleans, he witnessed a slave auction on the city's docks. He was horrified to see families split apart and mothers separated from their crying children. Of the experience he later said, "slavery ran an iron into me then and there," and he vowed to himself, "If ever I get a chance to hit that thing [slavery], I'll hit it hard!"

Part IX

Western Trade Winds

*"Twenty years from now, you will be more
disappointed by the things that you didn't do
than by the ones you did do.
So throw off the bowlines.
Sail away from the safe harbor.
Catch the trade winds in your sails.
Explore. Dream. Discover."*

\- Mark Twain

St. Louis Levee 1840

Chapter 24

The Gateway to the West

St. Louis, Missouri, 1830

Dred was on the upper hurricane deck polishing the brass knobs along the port side railings, his eyes constantly moving from his work on the orbs that gleamed brighter in the afternoon sun to the western shore of the muddy Mississippi. His river instincts were sharply attuned to the dangers of sandbars, trees, and sunken boats that might prove a danger to the vessel. He hummed in tune with the vibration that rhythmically beat from the rotation of the *Atlantic's* large stern paddle wheel as it pushed against the powerful flow.

The thrumming of the engines in the boiler room twenty feet below joined the cadence of the pistons and the slapping of each horizontal blade of the wheel against the water, ran through the ship like a pulse, and harmonized with the beating of Dred's own strong heart. His week on the Lower Mississippi nearly a decade earlier had given him a special reverence for the majesty of the river, but the last few days had taught him a new respect for man and his ability and ingenuity in taking her head on and devising a machine that could move a vessel loaded with passengers and commerce against her mighty current.

It had been one week to the day since the Blows had set sail from Florence with all their earthly possessions and dreams of new opportunity and an abundant life in the rapidly growing city with the odd religious name, St. Louis. Dred looked toward the pilothouse and could see Master Peter leaning in the door, speaking to the pilot and the captain with whom he had become quite friendly. Captain Stewart, a Virginian and fellow veteran of the War of 1812, had taken immediately to Peter and entertained the family at his dinner table during the voyage. He and Peter seemed to enjoy calling each other "Captain," and when Captain Stewart learned that Dred had fought beside Captain Blow at the Battle of Craney Island, he took to calling him "Private Blow." His respect for the wiry African grew as he saw how capable a sailor he was.

The skipper had grown so fond of the Blows, he invited the family to stay on board for a few days after they reached St. Louis while Peter finalized his lease of a boarding house just a block from the levee, which he planned to turn into a hotel.

Captain Stewart was patently proud of his beautiful new ship and confident it was the finest yet to dock at the city. He proposed to remain a few days, open her up for tours, and give to the good citizens of the growing western hub an on-board christening party, complete with music, dancing, and feasting, that they might fully appreciate its dimensions, comforts, and elegancies, and spread the word to potential future passengers. The fatherly captain had grown particularly fond of Peter's two eldest daughters, twenty-four-year old Elizabeth and twenty-year-old Charlotte, and decided the party would give them a grand coming-out to the eligible bachelors of the frontier town. They both celebrated May birthdays, and the goodly man had quietly schemed with their mother for a birthday cake the night of the gala. Of course to Dred, the other slaves, and the free Negro employees of the *Atlantic*, the party meant that, in addition to their regular duties as cooks, waiters, chambermaids, stewards, stevedores, and sailors, they were busy around-the-clock as they washed, swept, mopped, patched, painted, and polished the steamboat from stem to stern.

"Dred," Peter called from the pilothouse door, "git on up here. Captain Stewart sees the St. Louis waterfront and says he promised to let you blow the *Atlantic's* steam whistle to announce her arrival."

Dred dropped his rag and tin of polish, and winced as it quickly rolled toward the stern. He turned to see it curve to the right and sail through a gap in the railing. He hoped it would land on the passenger deck, but the look on Peter's face told him it had missed and was lost to the river. Peter raised a hand to box Dred's ear, and Dred was surprised when he saw the anger pass and the hand come down. There was a time when such a mistake would cost him dearly, but Peter had left his drinking as his hopes built for a successful future in this exciting new place, and the kinder, more forgiving fatherly figure had, to Dred's great relief, reappeared.

"Sorry, Massa Peter," Dred apologized as he stopped at the door to the pilothouse and looked in at the massive wheel. The bewhiskered pilot manning the helm turned and gave him a menacing look, but the portly captain smiled and invited him inside. Pointing north and west through the large windows, Captain Stewart showed Dred and Peter the outline of the city and the double black smokestacks of several other steamers tied up to a sloping levee that stretched out of sight north along the quay. It was by far the longest dock either of them had ever seen, and one with which Dred's feet and legs would become all too familiar over the years. He hoped this new place would bring his master some peace and the family the prosperity he felt it so deserved. He also couldn't help but wonder what possibilities lay ahead for him. He had turned thirty the past December, and while he had no illusions about his life as a slave, he found himself hoping that the large and growing city would provide an opportunity for romance.

Captain Stewart tapped Dred on the shoulder, breaking him from his sweet reverie, and pointed to the wooden handle dangling from a brass chain in the ceiling. "It's time, Dred," he prompted with a grin. "Go ahead and let them know you're coming."

* * *

The *Atlantic's* western christening-celebration-turned-Blow-birthday-and-coming-out party was a grand gala and instilled an enthusiasm and zest into the transient family that sadly would be short-lived. But the night was for the girls, and Elizabeth made sure her daughters were turned out in their finest street dresses with their hair perfectly coiffed for their introduction to St. Louis society. Nevertheless, their mother's ever-present sense of propriety would not let them dance with strangers, and so they spent their evening making the most use of their eyes in scanning the crowd for potential suitors and keeping time to the music in their hearts and feet in promenading around the large salon of the passenger deck.

As the night progressed, Charlotte kept noticing a handsome young man with dark hair, close-cut beard, fair skin, and striking gray eyes. He seemed at ease with life. Their eyes met once as he caught her staring while he danced with the belle of the evening. Charlotte's heart skipped a beat as he smiled at her, then waltzed his giggling partner away. Charlotte fell in love an hour later when the band struck up a Scottish tune and the dashing young man joined them, signing out in a melting Scottish lilt,

"Come over the heather, we'll trip t'gither
All in the morning early,
With heart and hand I'll by thee stand,
For in truth I lo'e thee dearly,

"There's mony a lass I lo'e fu' well,
And mony that lo'e me dearly,
But there's ne'er a lass beside thysel'
I e'er could lo'e sincerely."

Joseph Charless, Jr. stared smilingly into his future wife's eyes and repeated the chorus,

"Come over the heather, we'll trip t'gither,
All in the morning early;
With heart and hand I'll by thee stand,
For in truth I lo'e thee dearly."

The Blows made a splash that night and were welcomed with enthusiasm as fellow adventurers staking their futures on the unprecedented growth of the vibrant nation. Within days, Peter had concluded his transaction of renting a boarding house in need of repair located on Pine Street, just west of Main Street, two blocks from the heart of the St. Louis business and merchant district located at the cross-section of Main and Market Streets.

He had dared not dream of such a perfect location for his next business venture, and now the reality filled him with hope and a renewed love of life. The two-story wood frame building boasted a kitchen, sitting room, and ten guest rooms in addition to the family quarters. The rear yard held a washroom in a shed off the kitchen and a small shack for the slaves. There was a general store directly across Pine Street that could provide amenities for Peter's guests, and with a mercantile business and a law office next door, and the new St. Louis Theatre being built two blocks west, the immediate neighborhood was very respectable. So respectable, in fact, that just a block south on the corner of Main and Chestnut Streets lived Madame Marie Therese Chouteau, the recently widowed wife of the famed founder of St. Louis, Auguste Chouteau.

Auguste was only fifteen in 1764 when he left New Orleans with his stepfather, Pierre de Laclede, and landed at approximately the same spot where the Blow family had arrived aboard the *Atlantic.* He began clearing land along the river for a city, naming it after French king Louis IX. Despite his young age, Auguste became a full partner in a thriving trade with the Osage Indians. With his half-brother Pierre, the two began to make their fortunes primarily in furs, but they soon expanded into retail merchandising, real estate, and banking. They ultimately became one of the richest families in St. Louis, and even in America. The brothers Chouteau were the primary suppliers for Meriwether Lewis and William Clark and their Corps of Discovery in 1804, as they staged their extraordinary expedition across the vast western wilderness to the Pacific Ocean.

Little did the Blow children know that one day they would be locked in a desperate legal battle with the mighty Chouteaus.

As a businessman, Peter was particularly proud of the location of his hotel just two blocks up a gentle slope from the waterfront, which would attract lodgers tired after a long voyage on the river. Dred and the other Blow slaves were initially grateful for the proximity to the levee where they would be required to meet the hotel guests and as porters, move their baggage to the hotel. It wasn't long, however, before they found themselves missing Florence and the Peter Blow Inn, where they had used horses and wagons to transport the heavy chests. Peter insisted his human draft animals could transport the goods on a hand-drawn cart, saving him money on wagons, horses, and feed. The uneven yellow limestone cobblestones of the levee and streets were murder on ankles and knees.

While Peter tended to business, he put Dred in charge of the renovations. Dred soon had the men and teenaged Blow boys sawing, hammering, plastering, painting, and landscaping the large house. Little eight-year-old Willie followed Dred around and seemed eager to please the black man, who seemed so comfortable in command, and was always there . . . unlike his own father. Elizabeth took control of the women, and with the aging Hannah's help, sewed draperies, bed linens, and sofa covers, and cleaned and scrubbed and polished everything to a lustrous sheen.

Peter felt that guests at a hotel in this upscale part of town would expect fine furnishings, and so he spent a great deal of his money on Sheraton-style furniture. The beautiful cherry- and maple-veneered wood featured turned legs and lyre-shaped chair backs. Table pedestals and surfaces were ornamented with ears of wheat, sprays, and foliage, and the dresser drawer knobs were lions' heads with brass rings hanging from the jaws.

After two weeks of hard labor by the entire family and slaves, the family held a grand opening of St. Louis's newest hotel. Peter proudly named it "The Jefferson" after the former president who had opened the west, and this river in particular, with his brilliant

Louisiana Purchase, not to mention—although Peter always did mention as his guests checked in—had visited the Blow Plantation and supped with Peter when he was twenty-two.

Of course, Dred bragged to all his new acquaintances in the growing slave and free black population of the city that he had been born the night Thomas Jefferson had slept in the big house. Most responded with incredulity and derision, and condemned him for being "uppity."

The Jefferson Hotel was soon fully booked and stayed that way through the hot summer and fall. Things looked bright and rosy. Peter determined that, with a steady income, he could afford to hire on a slave girl from his neighbor Joseph Jennings to help old Hannah in the kitchen. One day a census worker from the United States government showed up and inquired how many lived at that address. In addition to the eight members of his family and six slaves, Peter listed nineteen guests of the hotel. The official 1830 record of the Middle Ward of St. Louis established the thirty-three members of the Peter Blow family as a force with which to be reckoned.

As winter approached and fewer passengers arrived at the levee looking for lodging, Dred found he had a little more time on his hands and determined that, notwithstanding the risks involved, he would finally go a-courtin'. It turned out he didn't have to look far.

* * *

On Christmas Day, 1830, a tranquil peace settled over the Jefferson Hotel. The family and guests enjoyed a feast of goose, duck, fish, turtle soup, and all manner of vegetables and fruits. After clearing dinner, the slaves were given time to celebrate and eat their favorite hog and hominy. With a full belly and his spirits bright, Dred finally got up the courage to ask the new hired slave,

Sarah, to walk with him and his mother to the Green Street Gathering Place. The not yet nineteen-year-old mulatto girl was taller and heavier than Dred, but was intimidated and a bit frightened by his ease with white men and his confident attitude. She was nervous about the invitation, easily divining the older man's intent, but she loved his mother Hannah, and on her account, accepted the offer.

Sarah had not known the kindness of a white family until she started working for the Blows, and she walked the earth with shoulders slumped and head turned down toward the ground like an abused puppy, always wondering when the next kick would come. It broke Dred's heart to see a woman so timid and meek and afraid of life. In limited conversation with her, he sensed a kindness and generosity that touched him. Hannah had informed him that when Sarah relaxed in private and finally opened up, as she often did to her, she was bright and engaging and full of wonder. Dred longed to see that side of this girl, and often found himself day-dreaming of seeing a spark in her big dark eyes and a smile on her beautiful lips. He thought he might be the man who could bring this girl to life.

The threesome stamped their wet feet and shook off their coats and shawls in the entry of the Green Street barn where Negroes—bond and free alike—were allowed to gather most Sunday afternoons to sing, dance, drink, and socialize. It wasn't Sunday, but being Christmas, there was a large gathering, and the music was already loud, and the singing and clapping was in earnest. Dred loved to dance and began tapping his leg immediately, then felt Sarah back into him and melt into his chest. He suspected it was her timidity and fear at the large and raucous crowd, but he imagined she did it out of familiarity and affection for him. He was amazed at how good it felt to sense a woman in obvious need of his manly protection.

He wanted to wrap his arms around Sarah in the worst way, but he noticed Hannah looking at him, smiling. Immediately, he read in her eyes a motherly caution to go slow. He put his hands gently on Sarah's upper arms, which flinched ever so slightly under his touch, then immediately relaxed as he guided her through the crowd to a place in the corner where they could find room to breathe. Dred was, by then, so overcome with emotion at having a beautiful woman in his care that he didn't know if he'd ever be able to breathe again.

He fetched his girls a drink and a slice of pone, found his breath, and before the nerve escaped him, invited Sarah to join him in a dance. He thought he heard a *squeak* before she turned to Hannah's protective shoulder. His mother shook her head, then nodded to the center of the room where a group of men were just starting into a rigorous Juba. She knew how athletic and light Dred was on his feet, and thought the girl would be impressed with his agility, despite his older age. She wasn't incorrect in that assessment. Dred scooted out to the hard-packed earthen floor and began the rhythm of patting his hands on his knees, then striking his hands back together, then the right shoulder with one hand followed by the left with the other, all the while, keeping time with his shuffling feet in the shifting sawdust.

The banjos plinked and the fiddles sang while the washboards thrummed and the jugs snorted. Dred's feet moved faster, and his body dipped and twirled without once losing the pattern of the Juba. He kept looking over at his mother and his girl, and found it funny how he already thought of Sarah as such. He was rewarded and emboldened when he saw her peeking at him from over Hannah's shoulder. How could one shy glance work such magic on a man, Dred did not know, but it did, and he found himself leading off the popular chantey of the Negro field hand.

"We raise the wheat," he sang out in his strong tenor voice.

"They giv' us de corn," chanted back the crowd of dancing men.

"We bake de bread," he called.

"They giv' us de crus'," the entire barn moaned.

"We sif' de meal," Dred lead the crowd while still performing his Juba.

"They giv' us de hus'," they groaned.

"We peal de meat." Dred watched in awe as Sarah straightened her shoulders and lifted her head as she joined in the clapping.

"They giv' us de skin," Sarah's voice rang out.

Dred paused in his singing and kept up the Juba while staring directly into Sarah's eyes, which now sparkled with a joy and a desire Dred found absolutely intoxicating. The music stopped as the large assembly waited for the final stanza and clapped, stamped and slapped in perfect unison, shaking the timbers of the barn and moving the earth beneath their feet.

"And that's de way," Dred sang in a plaintive *a cappella*, and the response could have lifted the roof off that barn.

"Dey takes us in!"

The Juba continued for several minutes with humming and moaning, and despite the depressing nature of the song and of the circumstance of the slave, Dred had never been happier as he made his way over to the swaying, clapping, smiling girl he was powerfully in love with.

Six months later, Dred and Sarah were married in that same barn surrounded by all their new St. Louis friends. Sarah wore a plain white cotton dress that was so bright and clean, it almost hurt Dred's eyes to look at it. The dress made a lovely contrast to her flawless caramel skin. Dred had never felt so tall as he stood proudly in top hat and loose-fitting tails loaned him by a friend. His black boots gleamed with a spit shine he had worked on for hours the night before, but the sheen off his boots was surpassed by the brightness of his smile, which nearly matched the color of

Sarah's dress. They both stood boldly straight, facing the colored preacher, Sarah's right arm linked in Dred's left.

"Do you want this woman?" the minister asked Dred.

"*Yes*, suh!" Dred nearly shouted, and giggles filtered through the crowd.

"Do you want this man?" he asked of Sarah.

Dred felt a tug of panic when she didn't immediately answer, but then he sensed her looking at him. He turned his head and read such love and respect on her face that he would have fallen over, had she not been holding on so tightly to his elbow. She winked, and his knees buckled.

"Oh yes, I does," Sarah answered without releasing her gaze.

"Bring the broom!" the preacher ordered. Frail old Solomon and aged, but solid, Hannah brought the broomstick, slowly bent over, and held it at ankle level right behind the couple.

"Now chillun," he ordered them. "Jump over the broom!"

Holding onto each other for balance and looking straight forward, they kicked up their heels and sailed backward over the broom.

Cheers and laughter spread through the barn.

"Thas yo' wife," the pastor said to Dred and walked away.

Dred stood dumb for a moment, and then Sarah grabbed him in an embrace. He grabbed her back, lifted her easily in his strong arms, and twirled her around and around.

"This here's my wife," he bragged over and over to the smiles and clapping of his friends. He stopped twirling when he came around and faced all the Blow children, who had stepped from behind the crowd. Each one, from Elizabeth down to young Willy, was clapping, their white faces beaming.

"This here's my wife," Dred introduced the familiar Sarah as his. The family immediately broke rank and huddled about their friends, hugging and congratulating them.

When Charlotte hugged Dred and Sarah together in her arms, she whispered, "Mother wanted to be here for you, but she has taken a turn." Her voice broke, and after a pause she continued, "She told me to give you her love and best wishes."

One month later, Elizabeth Blow, the matriarch and quiet strength of the Blows of Virginia by way of Alabama and now Missouri, was dead of the ague, and things went quickly from bad to worse.

With the death of his beloved wife and the disappearance of hotel guests as malaria spread through the city, Peter turned quickly back to the bottle and fell into a deep depression. The older children did the best they could to keep the business running, but what little money they brought in quickly disappeared into their father's old vices of alcohol and gambling. He fired Sarah and made an enemy of her master Jennings when he refused to pay three months' wages. When Dred protested, Peter struck him hard in the mouth. Dred spat out the blood and turned away more in pity than anger.

Charlotte's new fiancé, Joseph Charless, with whom she had fallen in love on board the *Atlantic* that first night in St. Louis, stepped in and became an anchor for the mourning and frightened family. He got the teenaged Peter a job as a store-boy in a dry-goods establishment, and knowing how much the family needed money, even employed the twelve-year-old Taylor at his drug emporium. Always the optimist, Dred thought perhaps the hotel could make it through the sickness and the terrible loss, and that Peter might yet bounce back. But then fate landed him a sucker-punch and this time knocked the breath clean out of him.

Dred had lost contact with Sarah after Peter released her. Jennings lived nearby, but apparently had sent her away to work elsewhere.

On an unbearably hot and muggy afternoon in August, as Dred went through town inquiring of other slaves and freedmen if they had heard of the whereabouts of his wife, he came across a group of men who had gathered around a poster on a fence near the newly expanded St. Louis courthouse. He stepped into the road to skirt around them, but as he passed, he overheard part of their conversation, and he stopped, frozen by what he heard.

"I'd take the horse," one of the men said, spitting a stream of tobacco juice onto the ground. "Don't know what I'd do with a mulatto."

"A lot different than what you'd do with a horse," another man jeered, and they all laughed.

"So, why's Jennings doin' this here raffle, anyway?" the first man asked.

Dred edged a little closer. He couldn't read the poster that held the men's attention, but he had to know what it said. He took a deep breath, working up his courage, and asked, in his most courteous manner, "Excuse me, I wonder—"

The men turned and looked him over. "You wonder what, boy?" one of them asked, stepping forward. "What right you got to wonder anything?"

Dred wanted to turn and run, but he had to know what they were talking about. He screwed up his courage again. "I wonder if you could read me what it say on that poster."

"Why would I wanna do that?"

"Maybe he wants to get hisself a horse," one of the men called out. "Or maybe that slave's his momma."

The men burst into laughter again, and Dred could tell they'd been drinking. "I jes' needs to know."

"You can't buy a ticket," the man said.

"I knows it," Dred replied, seeing some spark of humanity in the man.

The stranger let another long stream of tobacco juice into the dirt, then read aloud:

RAFFLE

Mr. Joseph Jennings respectfully informs his friends
and the public that, at the request of many
acquaintances, he has been induced to offer up his
celebrated

DARK BAY HORSE, "STAR,"

Aged five years, square trotter and warranted sound;
with a new light Trotting Buggy and Harness;
also, the dark, stout

MULATTO GIRL, "SARAH,"

Aged about twenty years, general house servant,
valued at nine hundred dollars, and guaranteed, and
both

Will be Raffled for

At 4 o'clock P.M., August ninth, at the selection hotel of
the subscribers. The whole is valued at its just worth,
fifteen hundred dollars; 1500

CHANCES AT ONE DOLLAR EACH.

Five nights will be allowed to complete the Raffle.

BOTH OF THE ABOVE DESCRIBED
CAN BE SEEN AT MY STORE,

No. 78 Olive St., at from 9 o'clock A.M. to 2 P.M.
Highest throw to take the first choice;
the lowest throw the remaining prize.

JOSEPH JENNINGS

Dred ripped the poster from the fence and stared at it, the words still not making sense, but at least he knew the secret behind them. "Thankee," he said to the man who had read it to him, and sprinted for all he was worth north toward Olive Street. He seldom kept track of the days, but something told him it was the ninth.

247

His insides felt like ice as he reached the Jennings store. Two large, shaggy white men in frontier leather hollered at him as he burst through the door and pounded on the counter.

"Where is Mista Jennings?" he cried, trying to speak while gasping for air. "I mus' speak to him now!"

The frightened clerk looked at the lunatic black man and up at the two approaching border ruffians. Dred followed the boy's wide-eyed gaze and turned just in time to see a hammy fist strike him full in the face. He collapsed to the floor like a slaughtered pig, blood spouting from his broken nose. He sensed being picked up off the floor and felt strangely weightless until his body crashed into the hard-packed dirt of Olive Street. He shook his head and looked up at the two men on the wooden walkway.

"Hand me that Arkansas Toothpick," one said to the other, who began to pull a long knife from inside his boot. Dred didn't need any more motivation. He immediately found his feet and scurried away crab-like on all fours. He heard the brutes' cursing and laughter fade away, but didn't stop, despite the derisive shouts and stares of a multitude of white people along the street.

He stood slowly and tried to wipe off the blood caked and congealed on his cheeks and chin, mixed with the dust of the street. His nose throbbed with intense pain, but it was not as exquisite as the pain in his heart at the thought of his Sarah being poked and prodded and assaulted for five days as white men judged whether to take her or the horse. The shame and horror his sweet, shy wife must have experienced was devastating, but it also made him angry and even reckless. He gambled on the possibility that his attackers might know where the raffle was being held, perhaps at this very moment. He had to risk another beating, and possibly death, in order to somehow save Sarah.

Running up and down the streets, he rounded a corner and nearly cried out when he spotted the long, matted hair on the shoulders of his attackers. He pulled up and followed them, keeping to the deepening shadows and praying he wasn't too late. He didn't know what he would do if he found her, but he had a rage churning inside him that he had never felt before, not even when he fought against the British. He knew he was prepared to kill, and die if necessary, to try to rescue his bride. As his animal nature took over his reason, he found that he felt more alive and more like a man than he ever had.

Dred followed the pair to the foot of Chestnut Street and watched in dismay as they turned into the Old Rock House, which Dred knew to be a warehouse built by the earlier Spanish trader Manuel Lisa to hold his beaver, badger, and buffalo pelts. The upper floors had been converted to a saloon, and he knew instantly that the two had not led him to the hotel hosting the raffle.

The sun was setting behind the city, and with it went his hope. The raffle would since be concluded and his love would have suffered her degradation, surrounded by fiends in abject and spirit-crushing solitude. He had promised many a night the past three months that he would always be there for her, and he had let her down.

His first impression was to run down the levee and drown himself in the muddy water, but he yet held out hope of finding her. He ran away and hid in Lucas Swamp by day, and every night he wandered the streets and the river's edge, inquiring of anyone who would speak with him what they knew of the bizarre Jennings raffle and the fate of the slave girl involved.

At week's end, the inevitable happened, and while speaking with a roustabout working a newly arrived steamer, Dred learned that, indeed, the "dark, stout Mulatto girl" known as Sarah had been the second prize that terrible day, the winner taking the horse and buggy, and the runner-up—a man known as a slave trader for plantations in the Deep South—taking Dred's wife, his joy, and his love forever down the great river of sorrow, never to return.

Dred returned to his hideaway in a massive hollow Cyprus suspended above the brackish surface of the water where it had tumbled and come to rest in some ancient hurricane. He'd heard the hounds trying to find him the first several days after he ran, but he was confident his lair would keep him safe. He spent the long, burning days of late August inside his sauna, and as he sweated what seemed like buckets of salty water, he slipped in and out of a tortured reverie. He found himself in deep spiritual turmoil, torn between his selfish desire to die, his chivalrous dream to attempt the impossible and head south and try to find and rescue his wife, and a strange, but compelling, drive to do something greater than himself and Sarah.

The warm days passed, replaced by the cooling temperatures of autumn, but Dred remained in hiding. No closer was he to a decision until one night in October. While carefully working the boats along the quay for information about Sarah, he heard the unbelievable news that a slave in his old home of Southampton had assembled and led an army of some sixty slaves in an uprising, and they had reportedly butchered at least fifty-five whites, the majority of which were helpless women and children. Still seething with hatred over what had happened to Sarah, he found himself sympathizing with the rebels and somewhat envious of the man who had led the rebellion. That was until he heard one stoker reverently whisper the name of that man.

"Nat Turner."

For the second time that month, Dred felt a physical shock course through his body as he tried to accept the reality of what he had just heard. Of course the rebel leader could not be the crazy lad from Cross Keys Plantation with whom he'd played so many summers ago on the banks of the Nottoway River.

But the more he learned, the more he became convinced that the murderer had to have been that strange boy who claimed visions and whose "mother" prophesied of his greatness.

As the days passed and the news of the massacre unfolded, Dred finally came to a decision as to the path he would take into the future, and it was the path that surprised him the most.

Nat Turner Massacre

Chapter 25

The Confession of Nat Turner

Southampton County, Virginia, 1828 - 1831

O f course, the "great" Nat Turner hadn't freed the slaves, but only succeeded in shedding the blood of innocents and leading his followers, and a hundred after them, to their deaths. Having been captured a week after the rebellion began, Turner dictated his confession and was ignominiously hanged. His name became a byword throughout Virginia and the country. His actions gave the excuse for mostly hateful, but some simply frightened, slave owners to brutally punish and even kill their slaves, to severely restrict movement and associations, and to break up families to try to subvert more conspiracies.

The boy whose odd facial growths matched his strange personality struggled through a tortured childhood, interspersed with spiritual mysticism and temporal magnetism. The bizarre vision the young boy claimed to have received after falling from the oak tree in Jerusalem nearly twenty years earlier had been but a foretaste of what was to come. At a young age, he had indeed demonstrated a superior intellect and learned to read, pondering much over the Bible—about the only book he could find. Taught and egged on by Henrietta, his fanatical surrogate mother, Nat read of God's people who had been enslaved for hundreds of years, but who were finally led by a great prophet. Moses spoke with God after killing an Egyptian overseer, and was then raised up by God in the wilderness to return to Egypt and lead his people out of bondage, and ultimately across the Jordan back to Jerusalem.

But what seemed to possess Nat most in his later teens were the stories in the New Testament from the birth of Christ in Bethlehem to His trial in Jerusalem, after which He was whipped bloody by the Roman masters and then nailed to a tree outside the city walls. The Jerusalem Nat Turner knew was the little village in Southampton where he and Dred played on that Independence Day so many years before. Nat believed it was no coincidence that he was born at Cross Keys, a name of religious significance, and that the place of his birth was not far from the little Virginia town of Bethlehem.

By the time he turned seventeen, Nat had come to the conclusion that he had assuredly been ordained of God for a heavenly mission here on earth. His revelations and visions during the next several years confirmed his belief in a divine calling. He was so extraordinary a young man that even his old master, Ben Turner, told Henrietta and other religious visitors that Nat was so intelligent and spiritual, the boy would never be of service to anyone as a slave.

Nat would later tell his executioners that Henrietta made Ben Turner promise he would free Nat at age twenty-one.

But Ben died before Nat's twenty-first birthday, and Samuel Turner, who inherited his father's slaves, was not impressed when Nat demanded that Samuel keep his father's promise and set him free. Instead, Samuel had Nat whipped and beaten for his arrogance and to remind him who was now master, and who was slave.

Nat spiraled into a spiritual crisis and ran away into the wilderness for forty days. He thought he saw in a vision the blood of Christ falling from heaven like dew and landing on leaves of corn. Another time, he saw what he believed to be sacred writings appear in the scarlet blood of Christ. He turned thirty in 1821, the same age at which Jesus Christ began His ministry, and Nat Turner knew the time of retribution was nigh at hand.

* * *

Nat Turner's capture ended his infamous insurrection, and he was jailed in Jerusalem. While awaiting trial, he gave his full confession to Thomas R. Gray of the District Court. After he dutifully recorded the full confession, Gray described the prisoner as follows:

> "He is below the ordinary stature, though strong and active, having the true Negro face, every feature of which is strongly marked. I shall not attempt to describe the effect of his narrative, as told and commented on by himself, in the condemned hole of the prison. The calm, deliberate composure with which he spoke of his late deeds and intentions, the expression of his fiend-like face when excited by enthusiasm, still bearing the stains of the blood of helpless innocence [sic] about him; clothed with rags and covered with chains; yet daring to raise his

255

manacled hands to heaven, with a spirit soaring above the attributes of man; I looked on him and my blood curdled in my veins."

This is the excerpted confession of the murderer, which, when later read to Dred by his master, firmed up in his mind the path he should tread.

I had the same revelation, which fully confirmed me in the impression that I was ordained for some great purpose in the hands of the Almighty. Several years rolled round, in which many events occurred to strengthen me in this my belief. . . . Now finding I had arrived to man's estate, and was a slave, and these revelations being made known to me, I began to direct my attention to this great object, to fulfill the purpose for which, by this time, I felt assured I was intended. Knowing the influence I had obtained over the minds of my fellow servants. . . . I now began to prepare them for my purpose, by telling them something was about to happen that would terminate in fulfilling the great promise that had been made to me.

. . .

And about this time I had a vision - and I saw white spirits and black spirits engaged in battle, and the sun was darkened - the thunder rolled in the Heavens, and blood flowed in streams and I heard a voice saying, "Such is your luck, such you are called to see, and let it come rough or smooth, you must surely bear it." And on the 12th of May, 1828, I heard a loud noise in the heavens, and the Spirit instantly appeared to me and said the Serpent was loosened, and Christ had laid down the yoke he had borne for the sins of men, and that I should take it on and fight against the Serpent, for the time was fast approaching when the first should be last and the last should be first.

. . .

And on the appearance of the sign, (the eclipse of the sun last February [1831]) I should arise and prepare myself, and slay my enemies with their own weapons. And immediately on the sign appearing in the heavens, the seal was removed from my lips, and I communicated the great work laid out for me to do, to four in whom I had the greatest confidence, (Henry, Hark, Nelson, and Sam) - It was intended by us to have begun the work of death on the 4th of July [but] the time passed without our coming to any determination how to commence - Still forming new schemes and rejecting them, when the sign appeared again, which determined me not to wait longer.

Since the commencement of 1830, I had been living with Mr. Joseph Travis [the stepfather of his young master, nine-year-old son Putnam Moore, who had inherited him in 1828 when his father Thomas died] who was to me a kind master, and placed the greatest confidence in me; in fact, I had no cause to complain of his treatment to me. On Saturday evening, the 20th of August, it was agreed between Henry, Hark, and myself, to prepare a dinner the next day for the men we expected, and then to concert a plan, as we had not yet determined on any. Hark, on the following morning, brought a pig, and Henry brandy, and being joined by Sam, Nelson, Will and Jack, they prepared in the woods a dinner, where, about three o'clock, I joined them.

. . .

I saluted them on coming up, and asked Will how came he there, he answered, his life was worth no more than others, and his liberty as dear to him. I asked him if he thought to obtain it? He said he would, or lose his life. This was enough to put him in full confidence. Jack, I knew, was only a tool in the hands of Hark, it was quickly agreed we should commence at home [Joseph Travis] on that night, and until we had armed and equipped ourselves, and gathered sufficient force, neither age nor sex was to be spared, (which was invariably adhered to). We remained at the feast, until about two hours in the night, when we went to the house [and] reflecting that it might create an alarm in the neighborhood, we determined to enter the house secretly, and murder them whilst sleeping. Hark got a ladder and set it against the chimney, on which I ascended, and hoisting a window, entered and came down stairs, unbarred the door, and removed the guns from their places. It was then observed that I must spill the first blood. On which, armed with a hatchet, and accompanied by Will, I entered my master's chamber, it being dark, I could not give a death blow, the hatchet glanced from his head, he sprang from the bed and called his wife, it was his last word, Will laid him dead, with a blow of his axe, and Mrs. Travis shared the same fate, as she lay in bed.

The murder of this family, five in number [including young Putnam], was the work of a moment, not one of them awoke; there was a little infant sleeping in a cradle, that was forgotten, until we had left the house and gone some distance, when Henry and Will returned and killed it; we got here, four guns that would shoot, and several old muskets, with a pound or two of powder. We remained some time at the barn, where we paraded; I formed them in a line as soldiers, and after carrying them through all the maneuvers I was master of, marched them off to Mr. Salathul Francis', about six hundred yards distant. Sam and Will went to the door and knocked. Mr. Francis asked who was there, Sam replied it was him, and he had a letter for him, on which he got up and came to the door; they immediately seized him, and dragging him out a little from the door, he was dispatched by repeated blows on the head; there was no other white person in the family.

We started from there for Mrs. Reese's, maintaining the most perfect silence on our march, where finding the door unlocked, we entered, and murdered Mrs. Reese in her bed, while sleeping; her son awoke, but it was only to sleep the sleep of death, he had only time to say who is that, and he was no more. From Mrs. Reese's we went to Mrs. Turner's, a mile distant, which we reached about sunrise, on Monday morning. Henry, Austin, and Sam, went to the still, where, finding Mr. Peeples, Austin shot him, and the rest of us went to the house; as we approached, the family discovered us, and shut the door. Vain hope! Will, with one stroke of his axe, opened it, and we entered and found Mrs. Turner and Mrs. Newsome in the middle of a room, almost frightened to death. Will immediately killed Mrs. Turner, with one blow of his axe. I took Mrs. Newsome by the hand, and with the sword I had when I was apprehended, I struck her several blows over the head, but not being able to kill her, as the sword was dull. Will turning around and discovering it, despatched [sic] her also.

259

A general destruction of property and search for money and ammunition always succeeded the murders. By this time my company amounted to fifteen, and nine men mounted, who started for Mrs. Whitehead's (the other six were to go through a by way to Mr. Bryant's and rejoin us at Mrs. Whitehead's,) as we approached the house we discovered Mr. Richard Whitehead standing in the cotton patch, near the lane fence; we called him over into the lane, and Will, the executioner, was near at hand, with his fatal axe, to send him to an untimely grave. [The terrible parade of death continued North until they came to the home of John T. Barow and they turned down the road that bore his and ran along the border of The Olde Place Plantationl.] I found the greater part mounted, and ready to start; the men now amounting to about forty, shouted and hurraed [sic] as I rode up, some were in the yard, loading their guns, others drinking. They said Captain Harris and his family had escaped, the property in the houses they destroyed, robbing him of money and other valuables. I ordered them to mount and march instantly, this was about nine or ten o'clock, Monday morning. I proceeded to Mr. Levi Waller's, two or three miles distant. I took my station in the rear, and as it was my object to carry terror and devastation wherever we went, I placed fifteen or twenty of the best armed and most relied on, in front, who generally approached the houses as fast as their horses could run; this was for two purposes, to prevent escape and strike terror to the inhabitants. [And this they did by cowardly preying mostly on defenseless women and children including a school house where they murdered the teacher, Mrs. Waller, and ten children!]

We started for Mr. William's- having killed him and two little boys that were there; while engaged in this, Mrs. Williams fled and got some distance from the house, but she was pursued, overtaken, and compelled to get up behind one of the company, who brought her back, and after showing her the mangled body of her lifeless husband, she was told to get down and lay by his side, where she was shot dead. . . . [W]e found a young man named Drury, who had come on business with Mr. Williams - he was pursued, overtaken and shot. Mrs. Vaughan was the next place we visited - and after murdering the family here, I determined on starting for Jerusalem - Our number amounted now to fifty or sixty, all mounted and armed with guns, axes, swords and clubs - On reaching Mr. James W. Parker's gate, immediately on the road leading to Jerusalem, . . . and my object was to reach there as soon as possible; [but] we were met by a party of white men, who had pursued our blood-stained track, and who had fired on those at the gate, and dispersed them, which I knew nothing of, not having been at that time rejoined by any of them - Immediately on discovering the whites. I ordered my men to halt and form, as they appeared to be alarmed - The white men, eighteen in number, approached us in about one hundred yards, when one of them fired.

. . .

I then ordered my men to fire and rush on them; the few remaining stood their ground until we approached within fifty yards, when they fired and retreated. We pursued and overtook some of them who we thought we left dead; [they were not killed] after pursuing them about two hundred yards, and rising a little hill, I

261

discovered they were met by another party, and had halted, and were re-loading their guns. Thinking that those who retreated first, and the party who fired on us at fifty or sixty yards distant, had all fallen back to meet others with ammunition. As I saw them reloading their guns, and more coming up than I saw at first, and several of my bravest men being wounded, the others became panick [sic] struck and squandered over the field; the white men pursued and fired on us several times.

Hark had his horse shot under him, and I caught another for him as it was running by me; five or six of my men were wounded, but none left on the field; finding myself defeated here I instantly determined to go through a private way, and cross the Nottoway river at the Cypress Bridge, three miles below Jerusalem, and attack that place in the rear, as I expected they would look for me on the other road, and I had a great desire to get there to procure arms and ammunition.

After going a short distance in this private way, accompanied by about twenty, I overtook two or three who told me the others were dispersed in every direction. After trying in vain to collect a sufficient force to proceed to Jerusalem, I determined to return, as I was sure they would make it back to their old neighborhood, where they would rejoin me, make new recruits, and come down again. On my way back, I called at Mrs. Thomas's, Mrs. Spencer's and several other places, the white families having fled, we found no more victims to gratify our thirst for blood, we stopped at Major Ridley's quarter for the night, and being joined by four of his men, with the recruits made since my defeat, we mustered now about forty strong.

After placing out sentinels, I laid down to sleep, but was quickly roused by a great racket; starting up, I found some mounted, and others in great confusion; one of the sentinels having given the alarm that we were about to be attacked, I ordered some to ride round and reconnoitre [sic], and on their return the others being more alarmed, not knowing who they were, fled in different ways, so that I was reduced to about twenty again; with this I determined to attempt to recruit, and proceed on to rally in the neighborhood, . . . we were immediately fired upon and retreated, leaving several of my men. I do not know what became of them, as I never saw them afterwards. Pursuing our course back and coming in sight of Captain Harris', where we had been the day before, we discovered a party of white men at the house, on which all deserted me but two, (Jacob and Nat), we concealed ourselves in the woods until near night, when I sent them in search of [the others. When they didn't return] I concluded Jacob and Nat had been taken, and compelled to betray me. On this I gave up all hope for the present; and on Thursday night after having supplied myself with provisions from Mr. Travis's, I scratched a hole under a pile of fence rails in a field, where I concealed myself for six weeks, never leaving my hiding place but for a few minutes in the dead of night to get water.

. . .

I know not how long I might have led this life, if accident had not betrayed me, a dog in the neighborhood passing by my hiding place one night while I was out, was attracted by some meat I had in my cave, and crawled in and stole it, and was coming out just as I returned. A few nights after, two Negroes having started to go hunting with the same dog, and passed that way, the dog came again to the place, and having just gone out to walk about, discovered me and barked, on which thinking myself discovered, I spoke to them to beg concealment. On making myself known they fled from me. Knowing then they would betray me, I immediately left my hiding place, and was pursued almost incessantly until I was taken a fortnight afterwards by Mr. Benjamin Phipps, in a little hole I had dug out with my sword, for the purpose of concealment, under the top of a fallen tree. On Mr. Phipps' discovering the place of my concealment, he cocked his gun and aimed at me. I requested him not to shoot and I would give up, upon which he demanded my sword. I delivered it to him, and he brought me to prison.

* * *

Ironically, Nat Turner finally made it to Jerusalem, where he was put on trial for murder.

The aforementioned confession was read before the Court of Southampton, with the certificate, under seal, of the court convened at Jerusalem, November 5th, 1831.

Twelve days after his capture, the court found him guilty and ordered him to hang for his crimes.

At noon on November 11th, 1831, Turner's jailers took him from his cell and past the Jerusalem courthouse to a massive oak tree on the bank of the Nottoway River. It was that same great oak upon which Dred and young Nathaniel had played on Independence Day a quarter of a century earlier.

The hangman's noose was tossed over the thick branch that paralleled the river, put around Nat's neck, and pulled until it lifted him off the ground, where he kicked and jerked until he was dead.

Nat hung from that tree for several days as a warning to other slaves who might reason that they could obtain freedom through a path of violence.

$200 Reward.

RANAWAY from the subscriber, on the night of Thursday, the 30th of Sepember,

FIVE NEGRO SLAVES,

To-wit: one Negro man, his wife, and three children.

The man is a black negro, full height, very erect, his face a little thin. He is about forty years of age, and calls himself *Washington Reed*, and is known by the name of Washington. He is probably well dressed, possibly takes with him an ivory headed cane, and is of good address. Several of his teeth are gone.

Mary, his wife, is about thirty years of age, a bright mulatto woman, and quite stout and strong.

The oldest of the children is a boy, of the name of FIELDING, twelve years of age, a dark mulatto, with heavy eyelids. He probably wore a new cloth cap.

MATILDA, the second child, is a girl, six years of age, rather a dark mulatto, but a bright and smart looking child.

MALCOLM, the youngest, is a boy, four years old, a lighter mulatto than the last, and about equally as bright. He probably also wore a cloth cap. If examined, he will be found to have a swelling at the navel.

Washington and Mary have lived at or near St. Louis, with the subscriber, for about 15 years.

It is supposed that they are making their way to Chicago, and that a white man accompanies them, that they will travel chiefly at night, and most probably in a covered wagon.

A reward of $150 will be paid for their apprehension, so that I can get them, if taken within one hundred miles of St. Louis, and $200 if taken beyond that, and secured so that I can get them, and other reasonable additional charges, if delivered to the subscriber, or to THOMAS ALLEN, Esq., at St. Louis, Mo. The above negroes, for the last few years, have been in possession of Thomas Allen, Esq., of St. Louis.

WM. RUSSELL.

ST. LOUIS, Oct. 1, 1847.

Runaway Slave Poster

Chapter 26

A Different Path

St. Louis, Missouri, 1832

By the time the first icy rain started falling, Dred had thought long and hard on what he should do. His anguish over the dreadful circumstances of the loss of his love, added to his brother's death and a lifetime of servitude, pushed him toward escape and revenge. But more and more the words of his mother came to his mind. While he never heard voices or saw visions as Nat Turner had claimed, Dred nevertheless felt somehow, in some miraculous and unforeseen way, he would find his way to freedom. But it would not be a path of violence. He had experienced the legal system in the distant and pleasant past when he accompanied Master Peter to the same courthouse that executed judgment on Nat Turner. Dred held onto a hope, which at that moment seemed impossible, that the white man's courts would give justice and mercy to the black race, just as assuredly as it had wielded the sword of justice against a black man in protection of the white race.

As the storm clouds parted and a brilliant orange harvest moon appeared to light his path home, Dred left the swamp and returned to the Jefferson Hotel. He crept quietly into the yard, hoping to enter the slave quarters without awakening his mother. As fate would have it, Peter Blow was sitting on the back kitchen stoop drinking and crying over his own losses, and about midnight saw the tiny ragged form he knew as well as that of his own children enter through the back gate.

"Sham!" he shouted, stumbling to his feet, his words slurred by the spirits. "Sham Blow! Ho there, boy! Where you been? You filthy, thieving nigger!"

Dred froze when he heard his old name called, then nearly bolted, his recent resolve dashed by his former mentor's insult. In all his life, through some very rough times, Dred had never heard Peter use that ugly word against him. But before he could move, Peter was upon him, and Dred saw in the ravaged face that friendship would never be possible with that man again.

"I gotcha now, you damned coon, and I'll make you wish you was never born." Peter dropped his bottle, grabbed Dred with both hands, and pulled him toward the tree in the center of the yard. Lights came on in the house, and the door of the slave house squeaked open.

Dred knew that, in his drunken state, Peter could not hold onto him if he wanted to escape again, but he had set his resolve. Though he had not imagined the hatred he now felt in Peter, nor what was about to happen, he was prepared nonetheless for whatever came.

"Papa!" the teenaged voice of Peter rang out as the door to the kitchen banged open. "Papa, what are you doing? That's our Sam! Leave him be!"

But Master Peter was unmoved and pushed Dred against the tree. "Shut up, boy, and bring me a stout rope!"

For a moment, only the sound of crickets could be heard in the yard, then Dred thought he heard a gasp and the door to the shack opened. Hannah strode forth.

"Please, Massa Peter." She rushed through the yard to beg for her son. "Please, don' kill my boy. He yo' friend! He been yo' faithful servant all these years!"

Her pleas were met with a mean backhand to her cheek, and she fell back, stunned, and landed with a splash in a puddle.

"Father!" several female voices cried out in unison as the whole Blow household emptied into the yard.

"That's Hannah, Father," Elizabeth cried, rushing to help Hannah up. "You've never struck her before!"

Peter stopped flailing for a moment, hearing the voice of his oldest daughter. She had been named after her mother, and in her twenties had taken on her likeness and mannerisms. For a moment, Peter thought that his dear companion was not dead, and he sobbed out, "Oh Elizabeth, why'd you leave me?"

"It's me, Father," Elizabeth soothed, coming to his side and putting her hand on his arm that still pinned Dred against the tree. She was shocked at how rock-hard were the muscles and sinews, and as the sour stench of corn mash reached her nostrils, she knew instantly that something terrible was about to happen.

Instead of being calmed by his own flesh and blood, Peter shook his head and, realizing his love was gone, his life was in shambles, and believing his kin had disrespected him, he became a man unmoved and incapable of reason or compassion.

"Get the girls inside, *now!*" he spat. "Or, by God, I'll hang him in front of you! Peter, where is that cussed rope?"

Elizabeth was so shocked at not being able to recognize this man before her, she rushed back to the house and forced her sisters inside.

Peter and Taylor tried arguing with their father and thought about trying to overpower him. But when they realized he wasn't going to hang their friend, but tie him to the tree, they relented and obeyed, hoping not to anger him further. They could hear their sisters weeping inside the hotel, and they looked up to see several tenants watching dispassionately from the open windows of their rooms. It broke their young hearts to see the father they still loved bind to a tree the man who had been their friend, mentor, and older brother.

As Peter stretched Dred's arms painfully backward around the tree and bound his wrists with the rope, Dred looked at the boys with eyes of sadness, not of anger or defiance.

"Don't look at them, Sam. Or Dred now, is it?" Peter hissed, then broke a stout branch from the tree and began pulling off the limbs and leaves. "Your dead brother was a bigger man than you. He would take his punishment without crying out. Will you?"

Dred stared into Peter's bloodshot eyes. It was then he noticed the ugly dark circles, and even in the moonlight, he could see the spider veins spreading across his master's sickly pale cheeks. Peter stared back as he raised the stick, and Dred was surprised that instead of anger or hatred for this man, he felt only pity and sorrow.

THUMP!

Peter brought the weapon down on Dred's chest and forced the air from his lungs. As he gasped for breath, Dred refused to break eye contact, and the blows continued to rain down on him.

THUMP!

With each assault on his body, Dred remembered a time when he and Peter had laughed; when they had conversed man-to-man on the way to court; when they had sweated side-by-side at some physical chore; when they had cried at the edge of an open hole in the ground while a small coffin was lowered; when they had cheered their victory against the redcoats.

CRACK!

Dred heard his ribs break, and a blinding pain shot through his core and out his back.

"Papa!" shouted Peter and Taylor in unison as they heard the unmistakable sound themselves. "Stop!" This time they did intervene, and young Peter grabbed the stick before it could swing again. "Enough, Father, you'll kill him."

A moment of hesitation and a look of recognition appeared on Peter's face. He was out of breath and his arm hurt, and he realized for the first time that his son had grown stronger than he. He looked at the bloody mess he had made on the arms and chest of a black man he had tied to a tree, and a wet sob escaped from his mouth as he realized it was Dred. He dropped the stick and began to weep as he looked around at the anguish in the faces of his loved ones in the yard and at the kitchen window. He looked at his boys and saw there anger and unmistakable shame. He looked again at his former friend whom he had just brutalized, and when he saw the pity in Dred's eyes, he sobbed louder and stumbled out of the yard, the gate crashing closed behind him.

Within six months, Peter would be dead, and Dred would be sold to a new master, thus opening a new chapter in his most amazing life.

* * *

In 1830, as the Peter Blow family was making its final move by steamboat to St. Louis, Missouri, the Thomas Lincoln family made its final move by ox-wagon to Macon County, Illinois, settling on a fifteen-acre tract overlooking the Sangamon River.

Abraham turned twenty-one after returning from his second flatboat journey down the Mississippi to New Orleans with a cousin and a brother-in-law. Under the law, he was now free to leave his father's house and make his own way in the world. He moved further along the Sangamon to the hamlet of New Salem and began working odd jobs. Word spread of his prodigious strength and work ethic, and so he had plenty of employment. He also gained a reputation as quite a storyteller, and folks were naturally drawn to him. On August 1st, having come of legal age, Abraham Lincoln took his first act as a full-fledged citizen of the United States and cast his vote.

By then Roger Taney had been serving in the public and private sector for thirty years, including stints in the Maryland House and Senate and as the state Attorney General. As an early supporter of Andrew Jackson's run for the presidency and with a reputation as a strong states-rights activist, he was appointed by President Jackson to serve as Attorney General of the United States. Despite his personal actions in freeing his slaves and treating blacks as his equals—at least in church—he issued a formal Attorney General Opinion that hinted at how he viewed the institution of slavery in the eyes of the law.

Taney sided with a South Carolina law that allowed the seizing and jailing of free Negroes serving on board foreign ships. The law also provided that if the ship's foreign captain refused to pay a ransom for the black sailor, the free man could be sold into slavery. He opined that any "privileges" granted to Negroes were a matter of kindness, not "right," and that members of the African race—free or slave—were not considered citizens protected under the United States Constitution.

Taney seemed to have no problem separating in his mind what was legal and what was, for him, moral. A year after stating his opinion that blacks had no legal rights, he quietly bought from a Major Hughes a slave boy named Cornelius for $450.00, then immediately freed him. He informally adopted the boy and cared for him almost like a son.

The national debate over what was legal and what was moral, when it came to slavery, continued to heat up across the country. That same year, William Lloyd Garrison started a militant anti-slavery newspaper, *The Liberator*, and incited the public with his fiery prose. He wrote in the first edition, "I will be as harsh as truth, and as uncompromising as justice. . . . I am in earnest—I will not equivocate—I will not excuse—I will not retreat a single inch—AND I WILL BE HEARD."

Many in positions of power struggled to be heard on the issue as well. Former president John Quincy Adams, having subsequently been elected to Congress, presented fifteen petitions from Pennsylvania calling for the abolition of slavery in the nation's capitol. Emboldened by the actions of the former president and son of the great John Adams, many more Congressmen followed suit and filed a multitude of petitions to abolish slavery outright. This enraged the representatives from the South, and they had enough votes to establish what they termed "gag rule," which required all petitions to be tabled without discussion.

From Washington D.C. to the Mississippi River, the country began to split apart over slavery. It would take a common enemy to stop the downward spiral, and Chief Black Hawk answered the call, if only for a small moment. As the old pattern of white confiscation of Indian lands continued toward its Manifest Destiny, the Sauk and Fox Indians were removed from their ancient lands east of the Mississippi and forced across the river into Iowa Territory.

During the War of 1812, the great Sauk chief sided with the British against the United States and defeated Major Zachary Taylor, stopping him from capturing the native's capitol of Saukenuk located where the Rock River flows into the Mississippi in northern Illinois. He declared that the cause of his making war was "known to all white men. They ought to be ashamed of it. The white men despise the Indians and drive them from their homes." Of course, he became a legend among the Mississippi tribes, and after a year of trying unsuccessfully to farm in Iowa, he determined to recapture the past glory of his people and once again war against the United States. On April 6th, 1832, he led some fifteen hundred of his people and those of the Fox tribes back across the river to regain their lost homeland, starting what became known as the Black Hawk War.

One of the largest islands on the entire length of the Mississippi was near where the Rock River entered and sat offshore from the ancient capital of Saukenuk. The United States strategically built Fort Armstrong on the southern tip of the island, near a set of rapids. Whoever controlled the rapids controlled the river. The Indians knew they did not have a chance of capturing the fort, so they began to cross on the north end of the island, which they claimed had been inhabited by their ancestors for a thousand years and had been a garden for Black Hawk's people, producing apples, plums, blackberries, strawberries, and gooseberries. The Sauk believed the island was watched over by a great white spirit with giant wings that resembled a swan, but ten times bigger. They called it the sacred swan, and were much distressed when the fort was built above its hiding place in a cave in the white cliffs, driving their protector away. The white man stole everything. Black Hawk wanted the island and the swan spirit back.

President Andrew Jackson would have none of it and dispatched his own famed veteran of the War of 1812, General Winfield "Great" Scott, to lead the U.S. Army up the Mississippi and put down the rebellion. With hostile warriors encamped in his state, Illinois Governor Reynolds determined he could not wait for the federal troops to arrive and called for thousands of recruits, including three hundred and fifty from Sangamon County. The men of New Salem, including a restless Abraham Lincoln, met at the farm of Dallas Scott and formed the 4th Illinois Militia Company, electing the confident and loquacious twenty-three-year-old Abe as their captain. Captain Lincoln led his band of volunteers on a forced march to the river, where he met up with federal detachments and was ordered to appear before a regular Army officer to be sworn in as a commissioned officer.

And so it was that, on the banks of the Mississippi River near Rock Island Fortress, the six foot four inch, one hundred and eighty pound future president of the United States raised his right arm, looked down, and repeated the oath of military office to the man who would one day be his arch enemy as the president of the Confederate States of America, Jefferson Davis.

Seeing the numbers of white soldiers gathering, Chief Black Hawk knew he could not meet them in a direct clash. In the dark of night, he moved his people off the island and headed north, opting for surprise attacks and battles on his terms. But after several bloody engagements at Kishwaukee River, Dixon Ferry, and Wisconsin Heights, he realized that, with many women and children to feed and protect, and only a few hundred warriors to face the nearly four thousand soldiers bearing down on them, retreat was the only option. He led his people north with the hope of finding sanctuary with the Winnebago. They made it all the way to Wisconsin Territory in the cold north, but his people moved slower than the white devils, many of whom were on horseback. He attempted to surrender three times, sending his scouts out with a white flag, but they were fired upon each time. Realizing all was lost, yet determined to save his people by crossing back over the Mississippi, he set them to the task of building the rafts to ferry them across.

On August 2nd, what became known as the Bad Axe Massacre began. Before all the rafts were completed, a thousand soldiers formed a half-circle around the camp. With the Indians' backs against the river, Black Hawk waved a flag of truce. When shots rang out, he ordered his people to board crude, unfinished rafts to cross the wide expanse to the western shore. Suddenly, the federal steamboat *Warrior* appeared, and soldiers began to rain down shot and ball on the helpless people. A bloody massacre of hundreds of Indians resulted. Those who made it across the river were met and slaughtered by Eastern Sioux who had allied themselves with the U.S. troops. Total Indian losses in the campaign were nearly seven hundred and fifty—more than the infamous massacres at Sand Creek or Wounded Knee.

His heart and noble spirit finally broken, Chief Black Hawk surrendered and was taken to General Scott. The chief asked if he could sign the truce on his favored Rock Island but was denied. He was forced to sign it in Iowa, in full view of the island and former nation upon which he would never again set foot. Afterward he was sent in chains to Washington, where he met President Jackson, then was imprisoned in Fort Monroe in Hampton Roads, not far from Craney Island.

As part of the treaty, the Sauk and Fox ceded all their land in Illinois and a fifty-mile strip of land along the west bank of the river, which became known as the Black Hawk Purchase.

In a few years, Dred Scott would be sent by his new master to swim across the river from Fort Armstrong to stake a claim on the Purchase.

Although not seeing much combat, Captain Lincoln returned home victorious from the Black Hawk War. He found that he quite liked the mantle of leadership and wore it well. He determined that, despite his age, lack of formal education, and newness to the area, he would nevertheless enter the crowded field running for the state legislature, representing the Macon County and Sangamon River area. He campaigned wearing a straw hat, coat made of denim, tow linen pantaloons, and boots. He stood before the crowds and, in an impossibly high voice for such a large man, described himself as "Humble Abe Lincoln." He declared that his politics were "short and sweet, like the old woman's dance." He narrowed his platform to support a national bank, spending on internal improvement projects more specific to the voters of that district, making the Sangamon River navigable, and a high protective tariff.

Although he lost the race, he made a very respectable showing and gained 277 of the 300 votes cast in his new hometown. Despite the loss, Humble Abe found he enjoyed politics and determined he would try again another day.

Part X

Journey to the North

"Though we travel the world over to find the beautiful, we must carry it with us or we find it not."
- Ralph Waldo Emerson

"It is good to have an end to journey toward, but it is the journey that matters in the end."
- Ralph Waldo Emerson

Fort Armstrong

Chapter 27

Give Me This Mountain

Fort Armstrong, Rock Island, Illinois, 1833 - 1836

Peter Blow's health deteriorated through the winter. In June, not quite one year after Elizabeth passed away, he was laid to rest next to her by his grieving children in the Bellefontaine Cemetery north of the city. Keenly aware of their father's personal travails and their mother's sorrows, the children had these words etched into the granite at the bottom of the joint headstone:

May They Rest In Peace

To their further dismay, the children found that their father had left the family in serious debt. The lease payments on the hotel had not been made for many months, and the landlord had them evicted. While the earth was still fresh over their father's body, other creditors came knocking.

Elizabeth had found employment as a seamstress, and the teenaged Peter and Taylor were store-boys. Charlotte had just given birth to a daughter, and her husband, Joseph Charless, Jr., was struggling to keep his own new business afloat. He kindly told his wife that her siblings were now his own, and he did what he could. But it became readily apparent that the only way to pay off the debts was to liquidate the only assets they had left: the slaves. They didn't bring much.

The Blow children could not bear to put their colored servants, who had been like family their entire lives and with whom they had passed through so much adventure, through the degradation of the auction block. The two strong slaves Will and Luke were bought by their former landlord at half what they were worth, but he claimed the debt satisfied, and so the transaction was complete—at least as to the Blow family. Only Dred knew the true end of his friends' human commerce. The two men were hauled away to Lynch's slave market on Locust Street, and Dred watched in anger from a dark alley as they were paraded out on the raised porch, chained to the railing, and auctioned off to a Mississippi trader for a thousand apiece. They were immediately marched down the street to the river, and Dred was able to catch their tear-filled eyes just before they were driven up the plank and onto a southbound steamer.

Had Dred been able to write, he might have expressed the same:

And here—oh! shame to freedom,
That boasts with tongue and pen!
We took on board a 'cargo' of miserable men;
A freight of human creatures, bartered, bought and sold
Like hogs, or sheep, or poultry—the living blood for gold.

Dred turned from the scene, for it was Sarah's own shameful parade he saw in his mind, and setting his jaw, he walked away.

Old Solomon was in his late seventies. Knowing he would bring them no real income, the Blow children set him free, but let him sweep up the Charless store in exchange for room and board in a small back room among the dry goods. Dred's mother Hannah was such a part of the family that her birth date of March 27th, 1761, had been entered in the old Blow family Bible. Charlotte could not bring herself to part from her second mother, especially one who had been with the family since before her own father was born, so she convinced her kind husband to allow Hannah to remain with them as a companion, cook, and nursemaid to tiny Elizabeth Blow Charless.

That left Dred. He was their favorite, but they simply could not afford to keep him. Besides, despite his many talents, slave traders would look on his diminutive size and cheat them on his real worth. They went to church and prayed for an answer, and it came in the six-foot, four-inch frame of an Irish Yankee doctor, John Emerson.

Emerson was born in Pennsylvania around the turn of the century and studied medicine for two years at the University of Pennsylvania, obtaining a degree in 1824. After moving from one job and one town to another, mostly throughout the South, he settled in St. Louis and soon found a position as a temporary civilian employee working for the U.S. Army at Jefferson Barracks, just down the river from St. Louis. His skills as a doctor were questionable—a gratuitous note in the Quartermaster's log next to the entry of Emerson's $100/month salary pointed out that "no competent physician could be obtained . . . at a lower rate." One skill it seems Dr. Emerson had in abundance was shameless self-promotion. He had a knack for making friends quickly, as well as a tendency, through what could only be described as a hypochondriacal nature, to cause those friends eventually to turn away.

Many of the soldiers returning from the Black Hawk War to their permanent base were still suffering the effects of the malaria that had killed more of their fellow soldiers than had the Indians, and they appreciated the attentions of the jovial redhead who spoke with a mixture of Yankee twang and Irish brogue. He soon made friends with the base commander, General Henry Atkinson, and rising star and future Confederate general, Lt. Albert Sidney Johnston. He found he quite enjoyed the camaraderie and *esprit de corps* of Army life and set upon a plan to obtain a regular commission as a medical officer. Knowing that the path to an appointment required benefactors, he threw himself into the St. Louis business and social community with the skill of a seasoned politician.

He immediately determined that he could quickly elevate his status in the Southern community by becoming a property owner. He did not have the finances to purchase real property, so he decided to do what he thought was the next best thing: he would buy a slave. As fate would have it, the opportunity soon presented itself for obtaining one at a bargain sale price through a new acquaintance, Joseph Charless.

For their part, the Blows were delighted that their friend and mentor would be going to work as a personal valet and assistant to a doctor whose height and zealous personality reminded them of their father in his earlier years. Dred marveled that he seemed always to be associated with tall men and saw it as a sign that God looked not upon the outward body, but what was inside in assessing character and stature. He bid a fond and tearful farewell to the boys and girls who had grown into adults by his side, and set off with a renewed enthusiasm.

Dred found he quite enjoyed the work as personal assistant to a doctor on an Army post, particularly in a location spread out so beautifully on a high bluff overlooking the great river. Removed several miles from the city, Dred found himself once again in the forests and meadows he loved as a child. Negroes were treated substantially better among soldiers than in the cities, and mostly were the brunt of jokes, those malicious in nature from the Southern troops and more "innocent" ones from the Northern soldiers. Dred had an easy laugh that caught the men off guard, and when they learned he had fought and been wounded in a battle against the British, the jokes stopped, and he began to be accepted as a comrade by Northerners and Southerners alike.

Within one year's time, Emerson's financial, social, and political investments paid dividends. With letters of recommendation from the barracks commander, thirteen members of the Missouri state legislature, and even the popular first U.S. Senator from Missouri, Thomas Hart Benton, Emerson was commissioned a captain in the U.S. Army Medical Corp and ordered to his first post, and one familiar from the many stories his patients had told, Fort Armstrong on Rock Island in the middle of the Mississippi River.

* * *

Despite the pelting sleet and choppy waves of an early winter storm, Dred stayed topside as the steamboat fought the current heading north. He wanted to breathe the air above free soil. He stood frozen at the railing, warmed with the embers of the freedom fire he thought had been dowsed. As the cold wind pounded his grinning face, he sensed a change as the boat passed over the boundary of slave ownership, and the glowing embers sparked into a furnace as if hit with the bellows of a smithy's forge. The boat yawed to starboard as the inflowing current struck the boat mid-river, nearly tossing him overboard. He held tightly to the iron rod of the railing, righted himself, and drew deeply through his nose. Oh, did it smell ever so sweet!

"Hallelujah!" he cried. "Hallelujah! Hallelujah! Oh sweet Jesus, Hallelujah." Only the captain and first mate in the pilothouse heard him above the storm, and looked out to see a crazy little black man doing a Juba on the hurricane deck, his sodden clothes clinging to his wiry frame, but emitting showers of spray with each slapping of his body. They looked at each other, shrugged, and turned back to the task of piloting the boat through Mississippi hazards, wondering what all the fuss was about.

Later that night, all the crew and passengers would be back on deck, some shouting "Hallelujah" and others crying out in fear that the apocalypse was upon them, for in the early morning hours of November 13th, 1833, an "awful, splendid" meteor show was witnessed all across America.

The next day, Dred had to laugh as a spunky little black girl, whom he knew to be the daughter of the ship's cook and chambermaid, found him on the fantail and described the night to him in wide-eyed childish wonderment.

"Did you see it? The stars was fallin' just like rain! Mammy was terrible skeered, but we chillun weren't a'feard, no suh! But Mammy, she say every time a star fall, somebody gonna die. Look like a lotta folks is gonna die from the looks of them stars. Everything was jes' as bright as day. You could've picked a pin up!"

Dred played along, making faces of great excitement and shock at her tale, and sent her laughing back to her play. He loved children, but worried his opportunity to be a father had passed him by.

Fort Armstrong was about as different from Jefferson Barracks as any Army post could be. It looked impressive, sitting on a thirty-foot bluff jutting into the river like the prow of a mighty warship. As they approached the island on December 1st, 1833, Dred could see a stout three-story log blockhouse extending into the sky above the earthworks at the top of the limestone cliffs. A large American flag flew atop the raised square cupola on the roof of the structure.

On closer inspection, the fort left a lot to be desired. The wood plank and log construction of its outbuildings had not weathered well the past twenty years.

As Dred carried his master's cases to their new home in a dilapidated and foul-smelling infirmary, he and Emerson stopped to look at a stone upon which a crude wooden sign had been placed. Frowning, the fort's newest doctor read out loud:

JOHN GALE

Surgeon United States Army,
Born in New Hampshire, 1790.
Died at Fort Armstrong, Rock Island, Illinois, July 27, 1830.

RICHARD M. COLEMAN

Assistant Surgeon United States Army.
Born in Kentucky,
Died at Fort Armstrong, Rock Island, Illinois, Sept. 2, 1832.

These men served with distinction at many frontier posts.

"Humprh!" Emerson grumbled, and then forced a cough. "I can tell you one thing, boy-o, my name won't be on that rock! Let's get a move on it." Dred scurried under his load to keep up with the long strides of John Emerson, Surgeon, United States Army.

Learning that both predecessors who lay buried beneath the stone had died of fever, Emerson set Dred to a furious cleaning and airing out of the commissary and small living quarters. The doctor took to calling Dred "striker," a common term for house servant, which Dred initially preferred to the derogatory "boy," rendered "boy-o" by the Irish accent. But after the first week, Dred found himself wishing for the charming sound of "boy-o."

"Striker, sweep up that rat crap!" "Striker, you missed that cobweb!" "Striker, get rid of that awful smell!" "*Striker*, get after that mold!"

The doctor was certain that germs from the diseased lungs of the hospital's former occupants had become imbedded in the very floors and walls. Dred scrubbed them until his knees and knuckles bled, and then he started over, with Emerson often breathing down his neck. Dred was certain he had never lived in a cleaner place, but Emerson's convenient cough persisted—and clearly worsened whenever any officers were in his presence. The doctor was not satisfied with Dred's skill as a housekeeper, and requisitioned two large canvas campaign tents. He also secured some land to the north of the fort in what appeared to be an ancient wild apple orchard. There, with the tents pitched strategically so the breezes off the river wafted consistently through the openings and with the scent of apple and huckleberry on the air, you would have thought the doctor satisfied. He wasn't, and started a letter-writing campaign to get himself reassigned.

The letters said much about the character of the man. He asked for a leave of absence for a "syphiloid disease" contracted during a visit to Philadelphia. Later he complained of a "slight disease" in his left foot, which made it so he couldn't wear a boot. Dred giggled to himself as he watched Emerson limp around with one stocking-clad foot for about a week after writing that letter. When illness didn't get results, Emerson alleged an argument with one of the commanders as a reason to leave. In truth, the argument was a reprimand when the War Department notified the post commander that it had been receiving letters of complaint from civilian friends of Dr. Emerson, and ordered that such improper communications cease and desist.

The year 1834 passed, and no transfer was in sight, but John Emerson was a schemer and never stopped looking for ways to advance his future. Notwithstanding what he considered his current miserable predicament, Emerson shifted his gaze to the lands of the Black Hawk Purchase directly across the river in what was called Iowa, but still officially a part of the Michigan Territory. He formally applied for a place in the upcoming auction.

However, one day while treating another officer, he learned that the wealthy American Fur Company trader, retired Illinois Militia Colonel George M. Davenport, had decided not to wait and take a chance on some future government auction. He had embarked on what could best be termed the "extra-legal" enterprise of "squatting." Squatting entailed taking physical possession of the land, and then for a fee of as little as $1.25 per acre, claiming a certain acreage, thereby establishing the principal right to the land. After all, "possession is nine-tenths of the law," it was argued. George also happened to be a distant cousin of Emerson's commanding officer, U.S. Army Lt. Colonel William Davenport, and had himself served as Quartermaster of the fort in the early years. That was all Emerson needed to know to spur him to action. The fact that someone as respected and well-connected as George Davenport was squatting made it seem hardly "extra-legal" at all.

A meticulous penny-pincher, Emerson had saved enough money to afford an entire section, and immediately ordered Dred to cross the river and squat on the choicest spot of land along the western shore, which, for his purposes, meant not the richest soil or the most aesthetic landscape, but the land abutting that of the rich and famous Davenport.

Emerson marched Dred down to the river's edge late one afternoon and presented him with a letter on official Fort Armstrong stationery authorizing the slave to act in all things as his "agent and power of attorney," put the letter in a water-tight pouch, and pointed to the spot he wanted to claim, more than three hundred yards across the mighty river.

"Go, striker!" he commanded. "Squat on that land, and do not let hell or high water move you. Do you understand?"

Dred looked at the turgid water boiling under his master's outstretched arm and back at his face, searching unsuccessfully for a sign that he was joking. During the days and nights spent on the river, Dred had heard stories of the dangers of the mighty river, from the freezing temperatures and deadly current, eddies and whirlpools flowing around the wrecked steamers ripe with ropes, lines, and snags just below the surface, to the snapping turtles, giant catfish, water moccasins, and cottonmouths. But what scared Dred the most were tales of the monstrous Alligator Gar lurking in the muck at the bottom of the river.

"Uh, can I take the ferry, Massa Emerson?" Dred begged. "I been swimmin' my whole life in dangerous rivers with poisonous critters, but I'se scared of the Gater Gar. He's a ten-foot-long water dragon with metal scales, poison spines, and razor teeth that could swallow me in one gulp!"

"That's hornswoggle!" Emerson laughed nervously and stepped back from the dark water lapping at his feet. "There ain't no such critter, and even if there was, he wouldn't be interested in a skinny little meal like you. Now stop wasting daylight and go find a stout log that will float!"

Dred did as he was ordered, but for the first time in his life he faced a challenge he wasn't at all sure he could meet.

The cold water caused Dred to suck in his breath as he waded in to his chest, towing a log with him. He looked miserably back at his master, who pointed at the descending sun and shooed him on. With a quick prayer, he pushed off with his feet, struggled until he was prone, and started paddling with all his might. As soon as he entered the current, he shot downstream as if fired from a cannon. He looked over his shoulder at the rapidly disappearing figure of Dr. Emerson, and his fear grew as he saw on his master's face a look of utter despair. Dred's wiry muscles worked against the current, but he hit an eddy, and the log began to spin across the surface like a water-skeeter. Realizing that he had no chance of propelling himself and the log across the wide expanse, he slipped off his buoy and plunged full body into the boiling current.

He was dragged immediately under the surface and was surprised at the loud crackling and popping from somewhere deep below. It was probably the movement of rocks and mud along the bottom, but he imagined the sound to be the clashing of the iron scales of the Gator Gar as it zigzagged its way toward him, snapping its massive jaws in anticipation of an afternoon snack. Grit from the river filled Dred's ears, eyes, and mouth and ground between his teeth as he kicked and stroked to the surface. Midway across the void, he felt the current smooth out and he gained hope, despite the numbness in his limbs. As he felt his muscles grow sluggish in the frigid water, he thought back on all the times he had looked across the river at freedom and thought of Moses crossing the Red Sea, and wondered if he could ever do the same.

"Go down Moses," he told himself, and felt courage flood his mind as he, too, trusted that God would deliver him. He doubled his kicks and felt almost as if he were lifting himself out of the water. He coughed as water rushed in his widening grin. He now completely understood why Moses had parted the sea as opposed to trying to swim it. But just as suddenly, his hope began to wane as his thoughts turned to the day when he and the Blow family, aboard the *Atlantic,* had entered the Mississippi at Cairo and turned north. He remembered holding his breath that day as they felt the power of the river strike the starboard side and push the riverboat sideways before she slowly turned upstream, her pistons pounding and the stern wheel struggling against the current. The captain's ominous words at that moment reverberated through Dred's mind—"Few of those who are received into its waters ever rise again." Fear and doubt gripped him, and his muscles began to freeze. The river seemed to be trying to crush the life out of him before dragging him down to the lair of the Gator Gar.

The sharp branches of a bobbing thorn bush tore across his face and brought him back to reality. Through his silt-glazed eyes he could see cottonwoods along the western bank. Hope returned, and he spat out a mouthful of sludge as he felt his arms brush against underwater branches. He put his feet down and felt the gravel of the shore. With a mighty leap, he caught the overhanging branch of a Cyprus tree and pulled himself out of the clutches of Old Man River.

That night as he sat shivering next to a small fire on the free soil of Michigan Territory, the official letter clutched to his scarred chest, Dred wondered which was the bigger surprise—that he had survived the river crossing or that he was officially empowered to act as the "attorney" for the crazy doctor across the river who had run up and down the bank of Rock Island, hopping and dancing when he saw Dred walking up the opposite shore an hour after he had disappeared in its current. That Emerson had kept watch that long had struck Dred quite favorably at first, but then he realized that the doctor's joy and enthusiasm had nothing to do with the fact that Dred had not drowned, but that Emerson was now, through the agency of his personal property, the proud owner of his first valuable tract of real property.

To work, squatting required that possession be continual and uninterrupted. Dred was not permitted to leave the claim for even a moment. From driftwood he collected, he cobbled together a rough lean-to and made his home for several months. He caught fish from time to time, and worked to improve his porous hut to keep him dry during the frequent rains. He tried to stay out of sight during the daylight hours, knowing that a lone Negro on the banks of the river would likely invite challenges from white men, and he particularly wanted to avoid the many cruel hunters who traveled the river looking for escaped slaves.

Dr. Emerson brought him provisions, including delicious apples and wild berries from the island. After six months, the claim was perfected, and Dr. Emerson became the proud owner of valuable riverside property. He worked side-by-side with Dred to construct a modest home and office, and he began seeing civilian patients as he supplemented his Army pay. Since the miraculous crossing of the river, Emerson had begun treating his servant with respect— even admiration—and they formed a mutual bond. They were two bachelors, not equals, but nevertheless companions in a frontier adventure.

Back at the fort on a warm spring afternoon, the two stepped out of the clinic for a breath of fresh air. They walked along the earthen ramparts, and Emerson climbed up and settled on a naval cannon. They watched a Great Blue Heron walking in the shallow water at the foot of the cliff. As the rapids came around the island, the water deposited sediment in a point of the tip of the island, and during most of the year that portion of land was a small wetland pocket alive with fish and wildlife, and also plenty of insects.

The doctor swatted at a couple of blue-green dragonflies.

"Oh no, Doctor, don't kill 'em! They eats the mosquitoes. In fact, the locals call them mosquito hawks."

"You know I hate bugs, Dred. Call them what you want— they're all pests to me!"

Emerson had dropped the "striker" label and had been calling Dred by his name. One day not long ago, Dred had politely asked if he could substitute "Doctor" for "Master," and Emerson insisted that he do so. Dred was relieved because it just didn't seem right to call a man "Master" while they were standing on free soil.

The doctor shied away from another shiny critter, but did not swat. "What's your last name, Dred?" he asked out of the blue. "I heard you dropped 'Blow' a long time ago."

"Jes' Dred, Dr. Emerson. I don't figure I needs no last name," Dred replied.

"Oh, but that's where you're wrong, my friend." The doctor turned on the charming bedside manner that had served him so well the last few years. "Take it from me, a man needs a last name if he is to be anything in this world. Why, even a slave needs a name he can pass on to his children."

Emerson gasped and turned bright red as he saw the cloud pass over Dred's countenance. He'd heard tell of the situation with Dred's wife, and he quickly tried to smooth things over. He slid off the cannon and put a large hand on Dred's shoulder.

"I know you have no children, Dred, but you're still young! Why, you're my age, and I intend to marry and have children just as soon as I establish a little savings for the future!"

Dred couldn't help being influenced by the man's charm, and he smiled back. "Well then, I'll take yo' good advice, Doctor, and start workin' on a name that fits me."

The tall man looked down, then over at the cannon and joked, "May I suggest 'Dred Bonaparte'?"

Dred got the joke, for he'd heard of the French emperor and general who was remembered more for his small size than he was for his extraordinary military conquests. He laughed with this man he was growing to like.

However, Dred wasn't a fool. He knew that, while officially they were living in free territory, he was still very much considered the property of John Emerson. On many a lone night in his makeshift shelter, he had thought of how easy it would be to start walking due west and never look back. It would be many days before Emerson would know he was even gone, and by then he could be . . . who knows where, maybe even the Rocky Mountains of which he'd heard tales.

He knew Lewis and Clark and the Corps of Discovery had found their way all across this grand country to the shores of the Pacific Ocean. He had seen William Clark and his wife many times in St. Louis. Wherever they went, people cheered them. He had even met their foster son Pomp, who was actually the son of the Lewis and Clark expedition's French guide and his famous Indian wife, Sacagawea. It impressed Dred that the great William Clark adopted the half-breed children of his former guides when they both died at an early age. It made him grateful for white men—especially the ones who were blessed with fame and fortune, but still had the human compassion to help others, even those of another race.

Dred had a good memory, and during his long and lonely nights he would often run through the things he had learned and stories he had heard from others. This practice kept his mind sharp, and more importantly, perhaps, kept him from painful thoughts of Sarah and the shame of being a slave. Meditating that night about the Rocky Mountains and William Clark, he remembered his mother's Biblical teachings as a youth, and the story of Caleb and Joshua came to mind.

After Moses led the Israelites out of slavery, but before he could bring them into the promised land, he sent twelve spies, one from every tribe, into that land to learn what they could about the enemies they might meet and to bring back a report on what their intended home was like.

The spies came back carrying honey and wonderful fruits—the grape clusters so large, they had to be borne suspended on a stick between two men. Egypt had been dry and desolate, and the people were always near starvation. When they saw the fruit, the people salivated and cheered, and called on Moses to lead them into the choice land of opportunity. But then Moses asked for a report on the inhabitants of Canaan. Suddenly the mood turned. The spies spoke of powerful armies, walled cities, and even giants. Ten of the twelve spies said they would be better off returning to Egypt and slavery than going into the land and their certain death.

But Joshua from the tribe of Ephraim and Caleb of Judah reminded the people that it was not the arm of flesh that had freed them from slavery, but the power of God. Certainly He would fight their battles for them and strengthen them to the task. But the people lacked faith, notwithstanding the mighty miracles they had witnessed, so God made them wander in the wilderness for forty years until a new generation of faithful were reared. They entered the land, and God fought on their side. Each tribe was assigned a portion of Israel as a place of their inheritance forever. The only two Israelites from forty years prior who were allowed to enter were Joshua, their new leader, and Caleb, who was then eighty years old. But Caleb was a man who liked a challenge, and when he was offered his first choice of any spot from Dan to Beersheba as a place for his family's inheritance, he chose not the lush river valley or the fruited plain, but a rocky prominence and declared, "Give me this mountain!"

Kind of like me diving into the Mighty Mississippi, Dred thought and chuckled to himself, then repeated the challenge, "Give me this mountain!"

"Give me this mountain," he repeated night after night by the lonely fire.

"I won't walk to them Rocky Mountains," he finally declared to the brilliant stars one night, "but I will face whatever challenge. I will climb whatever height. I will fight whatever fight, and I will never back down!"

On July 4th, 1835, General Winfield Scott, hero of the War of 1812 and hero of the Black Hawk War, returned to Fort

Armstrong. Slaves and soldiers alike were kept busy for a week, trying without much success to spruce up the rotting post for the visit of the man they were calling "Great Scott"—as much for his size as for his military genius. He was slightly taller even than Dr. Emerson and weighed well over three hundred pounds. He was primarily returning to the area for a celebration, as Michigan Territory, of which Iowa was a part, was to become Wisconsin Territory. At Colonel Davenport's solicitation, however, he agreed to review the troops still stationed at the crumbling fort.

General Scott rode out onto the parade ground upon a massive white horse. He was dressed in a magnificent blue uniform coat with two rows of brass buttons, a chest full of gold and silver medals hanging from brightly colored ribbons, and gold braid epaulets that extended at least a foot along the top of each shoulder. Upon his head he wore a peaked hat that added another foot to his height.

"Great Scott!" Dr. Emerson exclaimed when he saw the giant.

"Great Scott!" the crowd echoed along the viewing stands. The popular nickname had become a common euphemistic exclamation since the end of the Black Hawk War.

"Great Scott! Great Scott!" the troops joined in the chant.

"Scott!" Dred shouted at Dr. Emerson.

"That's right, Great Scott," Emerson replied.

"No, I said Scott, Dred Scott!" he shouted back. He stood upon his tippy toes, thrust out his chest, and bellowed, "Dred Scott! That's my name from this day on!"

"And so it is," Emerson laughed, extending his hand. "I'm pleased to make your acquaintance, Mr. Dred Scott!"

They both laughed and shook hands mightily.

Fort Snelling

Chapter 28

Let No Man Put Asunder

Fort Snelling, 1836 - 1838

General Scott reported to the War Department on the dilapidated condition of Fort Armstrong, and convinced them that the Sauk and Fox Indians posed no threat whatsoever to the United States. The order was quickly handed down to close the outpost and for Colonel Davenport to transport all his men and material three hundred miles north to the most distant frontier outpost of the United States of America, Fort Snelling, which was strategically situated high above the junction of the Minnesota and Mississippi Rivers.

In the spring of 1836, one hundred forty soldiers, plus slaves, servants, wives, and a few children, bid a very relieved farewell to the miserable island that had known so much pestilence and illness, and boarded the proud new addition to the Fulton Company steamboat fleet, the *Mississippi Fulton*. It would be her maiden voyage and would follow the path of Lt. Zebulon Pike who, at the direction of President Thomas Jefferson thirty years earlier, had explored the river to the source of the Mississippi. Colonel Davenport had been ordered to notify the Sioux, Chippewa, and all other tribes encountered along the way that the United States of America fully intended to exercise control over the entire Louisiana Purchase. He and his twenty men had to slowly pole and bushwhack their keelboat north along the shore for nine months from St. Louis to the Minnesota junction. The men and women on board the *Mississippi Fulton* ate, slept, and played inside the luxurious boat with no thought whatsoever of the hardships faced by their predecessors just a few decades earlier.

Dred Scott was kept busy as, at his request, Dr. Emerson had released him to the boat's captain. Learning of his past experience on some of the great waterways of America, including this one, the captain made good use of Dred's numerous nautical skills. Dred was becoming very familiar with the workings of a steamboat and lent a hand stoking the boilers, running the sounding leads, acting as lookout and messenger, and even mopping the deck and waxing the teak railings.

The familiar muddy waters of the Mississippi began to turn blue, and around noon on May 8th, the *Mississippi Fulton* rounded a bend and sounded her steam whistle. Passengers and crew alike poured out onto the decks and gasped at the beautiful citadel perched magnificently atop a one-hundred-foot bluff with sheer cliffs running nearly perpendicular down to the rivers.

Fort Snelling was built in 1819 on land purchased from the Sioux, along with another 155,000 acres of upper Mississippi land, by Lt. Pike for $200 worth of gifts, sixty gallons of whisky, and a promise of $2,000 more from the U.S. government. Fort Snelling was as regal as Fort Armstrong was pedestrian. The massive limestone walls with turrets at every corner rendered the fort impregnable, and not once had any of the numerous Indian nations of the great northwestern frontier tried to attack. Its mere presence was a testimonial to the might and grandeur of a country still in its youth.

Colonel William Davenport had been assigned as the new fort commander. Upon hearing the whistles of the approaching steamboat, the fort's cannon rang out a deafening 21-gun salute. The passengers on board cheered and covered their ears as the cannonade boomed and echoed down the walls of the ravine cut by the river millennia ago.

The boat docked at the foot of the bluff, and Dred got dizzy and nearly fell over as he looked straight up to see the happy faces of the fort's occupants peering over the edge of the wall more than a hundred feet above him. He wasn't alone—the boat's company appeared birdlike as they craned their necks upward and gawked at the impressive sight.

A band struck up somewhere along the parapets, and Colonel Davenport gave the order to disembark and march up the sloping ramp built along the southern wall of the fort. It ran several hundred feet, and to Dred it appeared to be at least at a forty-five degree angle. He was greatly relieved to see Indians with carts waiting for the parade to end so they could begin moving the passengers' luggage, and then thousands of pounds of equipment and supplies, up to the fort. After ensuring that his and Dr. Emerson's heavier trunks were safely stacked on a cart and properly labeled as belonging to an officer, Dred felt free to carry the smaller suitcases up the ramp.

It was slow-going, not so much due to the steepness of the ramp, but more to Dred's curiosity at the impressive engineering of the fort. Massive, round, thirty-foot-high batteries with two stories of cannon and gun slits dominated both land and river approaches. Cannon protruded from ports along the top of the four-hundred-foot-long wall. Where the rocky promontory dropped away, the architect of the fort, Josiah Snelling, had built a five-story warehouse comprising the commissary and Quartermaster's store directly into the wall. Food stuffs, furniture, equipment, and weapons were being hoisted up by winches and pulleys to the twelve freight doors on three levels. Dred later learned the fort could store enough provisions to last four years.

He shook his head in amazement and moved up the ramp. Near the top, he came to a hexagonal blockhouse with six loopholes for muskets on two levels and on a third level, a hole for cannon in each wall. He reached the top and saw a broad, undulating plain extending west, filled with tall prairie grasses and an abundance of wildflowers. Tepees, tents, and rough wooden shacks were gathered in tribal clusters around the fort, and hundreds of Indians in varied dress moved busily about. Rounding the corner, Dred approached the double-gated sally port opening onto a wide courtyard and parade ground where the full complement of five companies of soldiers were assembled for inspection by the new commander. As Dred entered the gate, he noticed the walls were nearly three feet thick, and he whistled in pity for any army that might try to challenge the might of the United States.

Dred walked past the guardhouse and found Dr. Emerson standing on the stoop of the first door of the large hospital building.

"Oh, there you are, Dred," Emerson greeted him and pointed at the crush of soldiers bumping and jostling into position. "Isn't it a magnificent sight?"

"Dress right!" shouted a drill sergeant. Hundreds of right arms flew out perpendicular to each body and pushed against the left arm of their neighbor. More shuffling ensued until the rows and columns became perfect. Each soldier carried a bayoneted musket over his left shoulder and was attired in a blue woolen coat, white trousers, and a leather bell-crowned cap. It was indeed a very impressive sight.

"Parade rest!" bellowed the sergeant, and all guns came down, right arms went behind the back, and feet spread slightly apart.

"Come on, Dred. Bring our things, and I'll show you where our quarters are, just down here," Emerson said, nodding to the right toward a very long stone building that ran more than half the length of the interior of the fort. "We just have enough time to unpack and freshen up before the parade and change-of-command ceremony begins."

Dred couldn't read, but he had been taught to count, and he quickly noted fourteen separate doors in the Officers' Quarters. He was sweating profusely under the hot summer sun and was grateful when Dr. Emerson stopped at the second door. Dred shook the sweat out of his eyes and looked over at the men on the parade ground, even more grateful he wasn't wearing a wool uniform.

"Come in and put the luggage in the bed chamber," Emerson instructed as he opened the door onto a nicely appointed parlor. "You'll be staying in the basement kitchen underneath me." Dred placed the bags where he was told and shrugged the pain out of his shoulders and neck. Coming into the parlor, he looked through an open door and saw his master standing on a porch out back.

Emerson leaned over the white wooden railing and pointed below as Dred joined him. "You'll have to go around and enter the kitchen from down there. See that cask of water? Go ahead and freshen up, and send me the bucket." He began lowering a bucket on a rope. "Be quick about it now; we haven't much time."

Several reviewing stands had been erected at the east end of the grounds near the front of the Commanding Officers' Quarters— a stately yellow limestone building with four red brick chimneys and large windows. One stand was nearly filled with what appeared to be Indian royalty from various tribes, so abundant were the feathers, beads, leather clothing dyed in a multitude of bright colors, and all manner of exciting cosmetics. The Sioux were the most impressive, with their entire faces painted vermillion, with white and green dots scattered about.

The other stand filled up with women gaily festooned in their finest prairie dresses, a number of children, and civilian men in their Sunday best. Although commissioned as officers, the doctors were not issued uniforms, but were invited to sit in the reviewing stand.

As Dr. Emerson and Dred approached the stands, Dred saw Colonel Davenport in dress uniform conversing with what appeared to be a civilian. The man was of average height, but carried himself very erect and seemed much taller. He wore a long blue coat of military design with a high, braided collar and cuffs, but no insignia of rank. A red sash was wrapped around his waist. He gave off the aristocratic air of a person of some consequence, and indeed he was.

"Dr. Emerson, please," Colonel Davenport called them over. "Let me introduce you to the most important official of the United States Government in all of Wisconsin and Michigan Territories, Major Lawrence Taliaferro. Major Taliaferro, Dr. John Emerson, our new assistant surgeon."

The two shook hands, and the colonel continued. "Major Taliaferro is the United States Indian Agent, and has been so for . . . what, Lawrence, seventeen years now? We had the pleasure of meeting and conversing several times on his visits to Rock Island. He is a talented man, beloved of the Indians, and one who has kept the peace among former enemy tribes," he nodded over at the packed Indian reviewing stand, "longer than any other Indian agent in the country."

"You are too kind, Colonel," Taliaferro demurred in what Dred noticed immediately was a Virginia accent. He continued to listen, now more interested, but found himself stealing glances at the regal woman by Mr. Taliaferro's side. She was perhaps the most beautiful white woman Dred had ever seen.

"We are delighted to welcome an officer of such renown as our new post commander," Taliaferro returned the compliment. "And welcome to you too, Sir Doctor. Despite the modernity and perfection of the frontier fort, this is indeed still the wild backcountry. Life here can be hazardous, so we are always pleased to have a skilled physician in our midst. I understand you'll be replacing a good friend of mine, Dr. Jarvis. I invite you to my home tomorrow night for dinner at the Agency Compound. Perhaps you'll have a chance to converse before Dr. Jarvis ships out. Now, I forget myself. Dr. Emerson, please meet my wife, Elizabeth."

Another Elizabeth, Dred mused as the woman took one step forward to shake Dr. Emerson's hand. But at that moment he forgot her and the familiar name. In moving forward, she revealed a comely young Negro woman of perhaps eighteen years old, standing behind two children whom Dred assumed belonged to the Taliaferros. She wore a simple pastel yellow prairie dress with puffed shoulders, and long sleeves covering her arms, which rested protectively on the little girl's shoulders. Dred raised his gaze to her face and was astonished that her lovely almond-shaped eyes were staring directly into his. It was customary for most women to look down upon meeting a man, and he had never known a Negress to look a man in the eyes. But this woman locked on his gaze with a confidence that stunned him. The corners of her mouth turned up slightly, and Dred lost his nerve and looked away. He was so rattled, he didn't hear his introduction.

"Mr. and Mrs. Taliaferro, may I introduce my assistant, Dred Scott. Dred fought alongside his former master, Captain

Peter Blow of the Virginia Militia, at the Battle of Craney Island in 1814."

Dred recovered quickly, smiled, and nodded. "Pleased to make yo' acquaintance," he said in his best Dr. Emerson impersonation.

"Well, it is my distinct pleasure, sir!" Major Taliaferro boomed, reaching out his hand. "I likewise served up north in the Virginia Militia during that engagement, although I never saw combat. God bless you, sir, for your service!"

Dred suffered another shock. Never had an unknown white man—and certainly not one as important as this one—addressed him as "sir" and offered a handshake. Lest he hesitate inappropriately, Emerson put his hand in the small of Dred's back and gave him a gentle push.

"Thank you, Massa Taliaferro," Dred instinctively responded and shook his hand.

"Oh please, Mr. Scott, I'm not your master, and you may address me as 'Major,' like everyone else." He looked over at the assembled army. "I miss my days in uniform and appreciate the title."

He noticed Dred was looking past him, and turned and smiled. "These are my children, and this beautiful woman is our servant and nanny, Harriet Robinson. Harriet has been with us since she was a child."

Harriet Robinson, Dred repeated in his mind, daring again to look at her directly. *Her name sounds like music,* he mused.

This time she gazed down. Her flawless skin was lighter than his, and he saw pink spread across her high cheekbones in a blush. She smiled and curtsied to the two men. "Good day, Doctor." She nodded to Emerson, then brought her gaze back up and met Dred's eyes. She shook a soft black curl out of her eyes, making the hoop earrings she wore jingle musically. "Mr. Scott," she said, her eyes now smiling.

Dred's heart stopped.

The next twelve months were the best of Dred Scott's life. Although the north was bitter cold, the time he was able to spend with Harriet Robinson was like a dream. He fell in love quickly—and hard. She was so different from Sarah in her attitude and self-confidence, and their love was the mature love of mutual respect and genuine friendship. After completing their chores, they spent all their spare time together, and they had a lot more time to do so in October when Dr. Emerson was transferred back to Jefferson Barracks, at his request. He had started sending written complaints as soon as it turned cold and he became "crippled by rheumatism." Dr. Emerson left Dred at the fort when he figured out that he could keep his military stipend for his "surgical assistant," rent him out while he was gone without notifying the Army, and save the cost of Dred's transportation to boot. He rented Dred to Major Taliaferro, who always had plenty of work maintaining the Indian Agency Compound and was said to have owned, over time, as many as twenty-one slaves.

The Indian Agent and his wife watched the blossoming romance with approval. Dred and Harriet seemed to work harder and complete tasks faster if it meant they would have more free time with each other. When assigned jobs together, they worked like a team and were pleasant and kind to all around them—to the five Taliaferro children in particular.

In the early fall, they held hands as they walked along the river banks below the fort and kissed under a colorful autumn canopy of oak, cottonwood, and willows. Throughout the long frozen winter, they tossed snowballs and made snow angels, then risked becoming actual angels by sliding down the treacherous ramp on deerskins, shooting across fifty feet of the frozen branch of the Minnesota, and crashing into a snow bank on Pike Island. They laughed so hard they cried, and then ran, slipping, arm-in-arm back up the slope for another run. Dred felt like a kid again and had not been this alive since running through the forests of Southampton. They huddled together under thick buffalo skins and kept each other warm during the long arctic nights, listening to the haunting sound of wolves outside the fort, howling their woes.

In the spring, they strolled through the prairie grasses and meadows and marveled at the endless carpet of color: big bluestem, Blazing Star, Prairie Cornflower and a thousand other varieties. After nearly six months of dreary white and brown, the painter's pallet moved Dred to things he didn't think he had in him. He picked Harriet a bouquet of wild lilies, minty roses and Sweet Williams, and pledged his eternal love in a whisper as they lay head-to-head among the shoulder-high grasses, the sound of the wind rustling the stalks which seemed to repeat his hushed endearments over and over again.

They talked endlessly of their lives and their hopes. Harriet had been born in Bedford, Pennsylvania, a slave of Mrs. Taliaferro's parents, who were innkeepers in that mountain community. When Elizabeth and Lawrence married, her parents gave Harriet to the major as a wedding present. Having belonged to the kind and benevolent Taliaferro, and his equally good in-laws before that, she was, therefore, mostly spared the horrors of slavery. She nevertheless spoke of freedom with a fervor to match Dred's and worried about ever having to raise children in slavery. Dred fretted over what Harriet would think of his brief marriage to Sarah, but when he spoke of the brevity of the romance and the endurance of the painful loss, she listened with great compassion and smoothed his hair as he wept against her chest.

She was even more tender and empathetic that day in the summer of 1837 when they sat on top of the east battery, their legs dangling into space, watching the two rivers merge, and Dred told her about Peter Blow and how his friend, hero, and mentor had turned into a monster. She ran her slender finger over the still-angry ligatures on his chest where his skin had burst under Peter's stick and cooed in his ear to soothe the pain that still burned just under that skin.

The one word that had been an unspoken taboo between them was "marriage." Their fear of an unknown future and the vicissitudes of slavery made it so they dared not even speak of taking that formal step. It would be hard enough to someday be separated—and they both realized that was likely—but to be married and formally pledged in unity, and then pulled apart, was too horrible to consider. They were both very spiritual people, and marriage, even one that only involved jumping the broom, was a religious rite and three-way commitment between each other and God. They could not imagine letting God "put them together," knowing that man could "pull them asunder."

But all that changed one night after dinner and a most interesting revelation.

In a rare exception to the unspoken social rule that slaves and Indians did not sit at supper with a white family, the Taliaferros invited Dred and Harriet to dinner with them and Captain Nathan Jarvis, the doctor whom Emerson had been sent north to replace. It was late summer when the two lovers sat down with their friends for what they assumed would be a casual evening. But before the night was over, they understood their lives would change forever.

Dred felt shy and embarrassed that his finest shirt and pants left him considerably underdressed for the occasion, but the easy manner of the Taliaferros and the steadying touch of Harriet's hand on his thigh made him relax as they moved through courses of fresh grouse, duck, deer, wild rice, asparagus, and corn. By the time they were offered a round of after-dinner coffee, Dred was full and comfortable enough to join in the conversation. The topic turned to slavery and the law, and it quickly became apparent that this was the motivation for the dinner. Dred shared the story of the night of his birth and the many discussions he and Peter Blow had enjoyed on their trips to various courthouses.

Captain Jarvis cleared his throat and put down his cup of coffee. "Ah, that's the main reason I agreed to come back, Lawrence," he began. "Your coffee is the finest blend I have tasted anywhere in my life of travel."

He took another long and somewhat dramatic sip and turned to Dred and Harriet. "May I share a most interesting story with you?" He went ahead without waiting for a reply. "During the wee morning hours of the very harsh winter of 1830, there was a knock upon the door of my residence, the self-same room where your Dr. Emerson resides," he said, pointing his biscuit toward Dred. "I was called to this very home for an emergency. Well, I demurred, not prone to midnight strolls through ice storms, and when I was told the emergency was the labored birth of a slave child, I bid the messenger a good evening."

He paused to gauge the reactions of his listeners. Seeing none of any consequence, he continued, nodding toward Major Taliaferro. "When the messenger told me the good major here had personally requested my assistance, given the fact that the girl in travail was the slave of Lawrence's Indian sub-agent, Elias Langham, and that she was bleeding and in great distress, I of course leaped from my toasty cocoon and made my way forthwith to this place."

Jarvis didn't seem to notice that Taliaferro had cleared his throat, as if to call bullocks on the doctor's recollection of his motivation for braving the storm that night.

"The gal's name was Rachael, and, indeed, the child was breech. But with care and exquisite skill . . ." This time he paused when he heard Taliaferro's louder "ahem." He smiled and continued, "I was able to turn the babe and safely deliver a chubby little urchin."

"Huzzah!" exclaimed a clapping Elizabeth, notwithstanding the fact she'd been present that night, holding Rachael's head and encouraging her through the difficult labor. "For some reason," she continued playfully, "Rachael named her son 'Jarvis.'"

"Simply out of gratitude, madam, I assure you!" he quickly retorted. "I had never even met the girl." He feigned offense, and then joined in the laughter around the table. Just as Dred wondered why the doctor was telling this story, Taliaferro interjected.

"You might be asking yourselves what this story has to do with you. Dred, you said you have a familiarity with our legal system. Have you heard of the case of *Rachael v. Walker*, filed in St. Louis?"

Dred admitted he had not. The major nodded to Dr. Jarvis, who reached into a satchel at his side and pulled out a small pamphlet. "*Rachael v. Walker*," he read, sliding it toward Dred and Harriet. "Supreme Court of the State of Missouri, 1836."

To Dred's quizzical look, Jarvis continued, "This is *our* Rachael, Dred, and she sued for her freedom. You see, before my cherubic namesake was yet one year old, Langham was reassigned and sold Rachael and Jarvis to a Lt. Thomas Stockton at the fort. He took her to Jefferson Barracks in St. Louis and then back up to Fort Crawford, just downstream here on the Wisconsin River. Ultimately, the scalawag took them back to St. Louis and sold mother and child in a filthy slave market to a man named Walker. Fortunately, with the kind *pro bono* assistance of legal counsel, our feisty Rachael sued to invalidate the transaction, since she was a free woman by the law of the State of Missouri at the time of the purported sale. That longstanding legal precedent is known as 'once free, always free.'"

Dred grabbed Harriet's hand under the table and squeezed tightly to keep himself from jumping up on his chair, so powerfully did that phrase enter his heart. "Once free, always free?" he asked, hoping he had indeed heard correctly.

"That's right, Dred," his host interjected. "It means that if a slave is voluntarily removed from a slave state to a free state or territory by his master, that slave is effectively manumitted."

"M . . . manumitted?" Dred repeated the unfamiliar, but exotic-sounding word.

"It means 'freed,' Dred," Elizabeth jumped in, "and once freed, he does not become a slave again if returned to a slave state."

This time Dred reflectively rose up from his chair, bumping his knees under the table, and knocking over his glass of water.

"Hold on there, jack rabbit," Jarvis laughed, as Harriet quickly toweled up the spill. "While the courts of most states, including Missouri, have upheld that law, they had never ruled on a case involving the slave of a military officer or other government official. Walker's attorneys argued that the 'once free, always free' law did not apply when a government official was ordered to a post in a free state or territory, and so that official could not have 'voluntarily' removed his slave, who naturally had to travel with him. Since the focus on effective manumission has been based on voluntary removal of slave property, the court might easily have ruled for Walker."

Jarvis paused for dramatic effect and noticed in the immovable expressions of the two slaves that he had been successful. He pulled the pamphlet back open to a dog-eared page. "Let me read the ruling. 'No authority of law or the government compelled him to keep the plaintiff there as a slave.' Ergo," he continued with raised finger, "freedom to the slave of an Army officer!"

"Huzzah!" shouted both Taliaferros in unison. Dred, overcome with emotion, still wondered at their excitement, since it seemed ironic to him that they owned Harriet and other slaves and had not freed them.

Apparently sensing their duplicity, Major Taliaferro continued. "Now let me give you our own happy news." Dred wasn't sure if he could take more surprises. He turned toward Harriet and held both her hands.

"I have been in correspondence with Dr. Emerson, and have offered to give to him, free of charge . . . you, Harriet Robinson." Before she could grasp what that meant, he proceeded. "That gift is on one condition, to which John has consented, and of course the two of you should, as well. The condition is that I, personally, as not just the highest civil authority in the territory, but also a sworn Justice of the Peace, perform an official marriage ceremony of Dred Scott to Harriet Robinson . . . Scott!"

Not even Harriet's strong hands could keep Dred down, and he actually leaped onto his chair. "Huzzah!" he cried.

The following month, in perhaps the finest private home north of St. Louis and west of Cincinnati, and perhaps for the first time in the history of the United States, two slaves—mere chattel in the eyes of the law—were feted to a grand white man's wedding. Dred Scott and Harriet Robinson exchanged vows and were pronounced a married couple by the highest civilian authority in the territory. Harriet Scott squeezed her new husband's hand as Major Taliaferro closed the ceremony with those words, "What God has brought together, let no man put asunder."

Later that night, after they'd made love for the first time as husband and wife, Dred sat and pulled Harriet up to face him. He cupped her head in both hands and ran his thumbs over her smooth skin and stared into her eyes. "Before God and His angels, I make a holy vow to you, Harriet Scott, that no man—be he master, slaver, or judge—will ever take you away from me!"

Of that, Harriet never doubted.

Mississippi Riverboats

Chapter 29

Gypsy Girl

Up and Down the Mississippi River, 1837 - 1840

Dred and Harriet weren't the only ones to marry that year. Emerson had been in St. Louis just a few months when he was transferred down to the Deep South to Fort Jessup in western Louisiana. He was only there two days when he realized Snelling was the best post in the entire country, and he started writing letters again, claiming the humidity had brought back a liver problem, and now the rheumatism was making it hard to breathe. Apparently the War Department had lost patience, and no transfer was in sight.

As John Emerson's pitiful requests fell on deaf ears, he was apparently healthy enough to court and marry Irene, the twenty-three-year-old daughter of another Virginia transplant to St. Louis, Alexander Sanford. As fate would have it, Eliza

Irene Sanford had come to Fort Jessop to visit her sister, who was the wife of Captain Henry Bainbridge, stationed at the same fort. Emerson and Irene were married on February 6th, 1838, in the post chapel.

Throughout the winter of 1837-38, Dred and Harriet were hired out, first to Lt. James Thompson and his wife Catherine, and later to the new Fort Commander Joseph Plympton. The couple did odd jobs about the fort and visited the Indian Agency as often as they could. Harriet missed the Taliaferro children desperately, and she and Dred had been hoping and praying to be blessed with a family of their own.

While Harriet tended the children, Dred made himself useful with the Indians. When Taliaferro learned that Dred had grown up with the Nottoway and had an uncanny ability to make the natives feel safe and comfortable, he began to employ him as a mediator of sorts to try to resolve differences before he would have to adjudicate an impasse. Dred didn't think anything could make Major Taliaferro any greater in his eyes until he witnessed the love and respect the various tribes had for him. They called him by a native honorific, *mah-sa-busca,* meaning "Four Hearts," for his ability to respect and act impartially with regard to each and every tribe.

One example of that ability was an extraordinary event Dred had witnessed for himself the prior July. The Sioux and Chippewa had been mortal enemies since the dawn of time, but when the Chippewa chiefs were summoned to a powwow with the representative of the Great White Father, Major Taliaferro, over one thousand men, women, and children arrived and set up camp on historic Sioux lands around the fort. At Taliaferro's urging and frequent intercession, no serious violence occurred. Dred found himself wishing for his own Indian nickname, but they just referred to him, and every other Negro, as "Black Frenchman."

When they weren't at the Agency or doing chores for their employers, the couple just tried to stay warm in the kitchen cellar where they had been permitted to remain. Although the cellar was a room beneath the Officers' Quarters and had a floor of hard-packed earth, because the building had been built on a slope, their home actually had a window and door that opened onto a wooden porch. Harriet obtained bearskin rugs from the Agency and decorated the walls with a variety of native wall hangings, and she made a pretty set of curtains from an old blue prairie dress. Except for the cold—there was no stove or fireplace—the room made a very nice home for the couple.

Perhaps wondering if he would ever be transferred again, and wanting to provide a servant for his bride, Emerson sent a dispatch to Fort Snelling instructing his slaves to travel south on their own and meet him in Louisiana.

So, in the spring of 1838, as soon as the ice began to break up on the rivers, Dred and Harriet bid tearful farewell to the Taliaferro family and boarded a steamboat for the long journey to Louisiana. Dred had never seen Harriet so emotional as she clung to Elizabeth and wept like a child. The steam whistle sounded crisp and clear in the frigid air, and Dred had to pry Harriet away so as not to miss their boat. She wouldn't eat, and she cried for days. When Dred saw her vomiting over the side one morning, he tried to summon the ship's doctor, but was rudely told that he was only there to serve white people. Major Taliaferro had known how roughly blacks could be treated onboard steamboats, and so he had tipped his friend, the boat captain, and asked him to separate the Scotts from the other passengers and keep an eye on them. He also provided Dred with a letter of safe passage on official United States stationery, which Dred kept folded in a pouch around his neck. He refused to let Harriet out of his sight, more so when she explained her strange behavior.

They stood near the bow one evening, watching the fireflies begin their dance along the shoreline and snapping turtles duck beneath the surface as the boat bore down on them. Dred thought there must have been a million frogs on the shore; he could hear them across the water and even over the hum of the boilers, squeal of the pistons, and splashing of the paddle wheel. Harriet had been crying earlier, but laughed when Dred started clapping and dancing to the rhythm of the boat, then suddenly hopped like a big old bullfrog and began singing,

> *"Froggy went a courtin' and he did ride, uh-huh*
> *Froggy went a courtin' and he did ride, uh-huh*
> *Frog went a courtin' and he did ride*
> *With a sword and a pistol by his side,*
> *Uh-huh uh-huh, oh yeah."*

Dred hopped right up to Harriet and lifted her, giggling, onto a crate. She wiped her eyes and started to clap along as he began the second verse.

> *"He rode right up to Miss Mousie's door, uh-huh*
> *He rode right up to Miss Mousie's door, uh-huh*
> *He rode right up to Miss Mousie's door*
> *Gave three loud raps, and a very big roar,*
> *Uh-huh uh-huh, oh yeah."*

Harriet squealed when Dred pounded on the wall next to her and roared like a lion.

"Shhh," she cautioned, looking quickly about, but no one else was on the breezy bow, so she tapped his lips with a finger. She coquettishly placed her hands on her hips and turned her head so he could whisper in her ear. And that he did.

"He said, 'Miss Mouse, will you marry me?' uh-huh
He said, 'Miss Mouse, will you marry me?' uh-huh
He said, 'Miss Mouse, will you marry me?
And oh so happy we will be,'
Uh-huh uh-huh, oh yeah."

She hugged him tight, then kissed him on the lips. "I will, and I did, Mr. Frog. Now let me sing the next verse." It was one with which Dred was unfamiliar, and he listened intently. He had never heard her sing before, and she had a lovely alto voice which she pitched as high as she could to sound like a mouse.

"Froggy and Mousey married in a tree, uh-huh
Then snuggled under blankets 'til quarter past three, uh-huh
She said, 'Right now it's just you and me,
But in nine months we will be three,'
Uh-huh, uh-huh, oh yeah!"

Dred looked at her playful face quizzically, not quite sure what just happened. So Harriet shook her head. "Stupid man." She lifted Dred's hand, put it on her tummy, and repeated very slowly, "In six months we will be three, uh-huh."

Dred's eyes flew open in sudden and delirious recognition. "Uh-huh?"

"Oh yeah!" she cried.

"Oh yeah!" Dred yelled, and Harriet was sure the entire ship's company heard him. He hugged her tight and patted her stomach several times, then started into a frantic celebratory Juba, chanting "uh-huh, uh-huh, oh yeah," over and over again.

The stars had come out and twinkled to the beat, and Harriet swore for the rest of her life that the fireflies blinked, the frogs croaked, the fish jumped, and the turtles dunked, all in magical rhythm with her dancing man, the father of her growing child.

* * *

Harriet was absolutely miserable as her abdomen grew in the oppressive heat and humidity of Louisiana, and she nearly jumped for joy in September when they received word that someone at the War Department had finally taken pity on the poor dying doctor and he was ordered to return to Fort Snelling.

"Why is it that with me, it is either feast or famine? One extreme to the other?" said Emerson, already complaining when he announced the news of the transfer.

More likely, the people in Washington jes' got sick of hearin' him whine, Harriet thought, then immediately chastised herself for being unkind. In fact, Master Emerson looked more gaunt and pale than she had remembered him at Fort Snelling, despite the southern sun. Her morning sickness had long since passed, but she wasn't entirely sure how well she'd endure the nine-hundred-mile journey up-stream against the current. She was excited that she would be with Miss Elizabeth when her baby was born, but she worried what would happen if the baby came a little early.

Harriet could see that Dred himself was as nervous as a child as he helped her waddle up the gangplank, but she appreciated his efforts to always comfort her and make light of a situation.

"We's sho' 'nuff livin' the gypsy life," he quipped as they stepped onto the deck of the Mississippi steamboat *Gypsy.*

The pilot had to navigate up river very slowly in order to spot and avoid all the sandbars and wrecks uncovered by the low water level. Depending on the amount of rainfall and the working of the tides, the river could be entirely different from one trip to the next. Dred volunteered, and the grateful captain accepted him as a spotter. He stood at the railing in front of the pilothouse and watched for changes in water color, eddies, or unusual waves, all of which could indicate a hazard just below the water's surface. Dred's eyesight was still sharp despite his nearly forty years, and by now he was a very experienced Mississippi deckhand. He was grateful for the job as it required his absolute attention, and that kept him from worrying about Harriet and the baby. At least he had some consolation that they were traveling with a doctor, but he wished that the new Mrs. Emerson were a more compassionate person. She was somewhat standoffish and complained nearly as much as her hypochondriac of a husband. But they were kind enough to rent a cabin next to theirs for the Scotts, despite the protestations of the other white passengers that coloreds were staying on the same deck.

Dred couldn't recall ever being on such a slow boat. He swore that the crude rafts he built and poled up the Nottoway moved faster than the *Gypsy*. She was a small boat to begin with, and since she had been hired by the U.S. Army for this trip, she was towing a barge heavily laden with supplies for the various forts along the route.

After putting off from Jefferson Barracks, Dred peered anxiously ahead to see how his old home of St. Louis was progressing. He was stunned to see that the city had more than doubled in size in the eight years he had been gone. The levee was completely buried in at least a hundred steamboats tethered two, and sometimes three deep, for a half-mile along the quay. He felt a strong current suddenly pushing the *Gypsy* toward the docked steamboats, and heard the pilot throttle up the engines as he turned the boat toward the Illinois shore.

"What was that, Captain?" he asked after rushing up the steps to the pilothouse. "I ain't ever felt that strange current before."

The captain pointed over to the far shore, and Dred could see that the strong current was caused by a dyke and revetment system on the Illinois side, extending out into the river.

"About five years ago, none of them boats you see now could tie up to the levee below Olive Street. Several years of high water formed sand bars and rocky shoals along that shore. If it had continued, it would have been a financial disaster for the city."

Dred remembered hauling heavy loads up and down Pine, which was right below Olive.

"But I hear tell of an engineering genius who saved St. Louis," the captain continued as they moved past the massive, man-made earthworks that had, for the first time, actually controlled the course of the Big Muddy. "Young officer from West Point name of Robert E. Lee. They say the city put up a monument on the levee in his honor. I'll bet you top monte that's a name that won't soon be forgot."

As the days dragged on, Dred did have to admit that the slow-going likely saved the boat, for he was convinced that had they been moving at normal speed, he would never have been able to spot the dangers that could easily have sunk them to a watery grave like hundreds of ships before. As it was, he called out obstacles several times an hour. Most nights, unless a bright moon was shining, the boat simply pulled over to the shore and tied up, then cast off again at dawn.

Most of the passengers on the *Gypsy* were military or government personnel and their families, so there was less violence than was customary on a Mississippi steamboat. On prior trips, Dred had been appalled at how roughly the black crew, regardless of whether they were slave or free, was treated by the guests and other shipmates. Porters had been kicked and beaten with sticks for accidentally bumping a white person with some luggage. Dred remembered one poor fireman who casually sat down to eat his lunch near the white employees and was nearly killed for his insolence. On his trip from St. Louis to Fort Armstrong, he remembered an ancient white matron with a cane who sat near the front of the starboard passage along the rail, and if a black person tried to walk past, she would lash out with a ferocity that belied her age and outward frailty. After his first encounter with the cane-wielding matriarch, he stuck to the port passage and nursed his bruised shins the remainder of the trip.

A harvest moon passed across the sky and lit the water as if it were daytime, turning the water orange and making nighttime travel possible. It was bright enough on the second night of the waning moon that Dred could clearly see—though he felt it first—the Missouri River emptying into the Mississippi as it had since God was a child.

It was on the fourth night of the harvest moon, October 1838, and Dred was peering intently down trying to see the anomalies on the surface of the darkening water when he heard the first mate's voice crying out his name. The entire crew had been awaiting the birth of a baby on board their ship, for it was well-known that such a miracle would charm the vessel, not to mention that a pool had been established and a considerable pot awaited the lucky crewman who had picked closest to the birth date.

"Dred! Come below! It's your wife," the mate bellowed. "The baby's coming!"

Dred sprinted past the pilothouse, the moon turning the teeth in his wide mouth a dull orange, and the pilot, having also heard the news, began sounding the whistle for his valued shipmate's celebration. By the time Dred reached the aft quarters, he heard the robust cries of a baby child.

"Oh, thank-e Lord!" he exclaimed as he ducked through into the passageway and into their cabin. Harriet was smiling and crying at the same time as Dr. Emerson finished swaddling the infant.

"It's a little girl, Dred," he said. "Here, why don't you hand your daughter to your wife."

Dred went to reach out, but pulled back his hands, and Emerson nearly dropped the baby. "Oh, no suh," Dred declined. "What if I breaks her?"

"Okay, boy-o," Emerson chuckled and handed the baby to Harriet. "Maybe you're right. You better go slowly. I've seen the way you carry luggage, and this is entirely different."

Dred sat on the edge of the bunk and watched in wonder as Harriet cooed at his daughter and tickled the pointy little chin. "Look Dred, she has yo' chin."

Dred looked closely in the dim light of the oil lamp and didn't quite know what she meant. "I don't see no whiskers, so I don't know whose chin that is."

"Oh Dred," Harriet laughed, and Dred realized she thought he had been joking. She tickled the cherubic cheek. The little thing opened her mouth, turned her head toward her mama, and began to root around.

"Well, looky here, Dred," she said. "Now I knows this is yo' chile. She has yo' appetite!" She pulled down the top of her nightshirt and brought out her breast for the baby.

Dred first looked away, a little embarrassed, but then couldn't take his eyes off the sight as his daughter quickly latched on and began sucking for all she was worth. Harriet peered over at him, and he saw the stress of labor melt away before his eyes. He stared at mother and child. It was positively the most beautiful sight he had ever seen.

"What's her name?" Dred asked.

"Don't you want a say in the matter?" Harriet replied and winked. "After all, you had somethin' to do with makin' her."

This time Dred blushed. "Oh, I dunno. I was thinkin' . . . maybe . . . Gypsy."

"Oh, don't be silly, Pappy," Harriet gently scolded, using a new nickname Dred kind of liked. "The other chillun'll tease her. I was thinkin' we should name her Eliza; you know, after yo' kind missus Elizabeth Blow and my Elizabeth Taliaferro."

"But won't that new pouty Missus Emerson think we named our chile after her?"

"She might," Harriet responded somewhat conspiratorially. "An' maybe it will soften her up, but since she go by her second name, Irene, nobody else will make the connection."

"Eliza it is, then," Dred agreed, liking the way his wife schemed and sensing that any argument would be futile, anyway. "Hello, little Eliza Scott," he soothed, touching the fine black curls that felt like silk. His chest filled with pride, and gooseflesh popped up all over his body.

Welcome to our family, my little 'Gypsy girl', he thought to himself.

✦ ✦ ✦

It was truly feast or famine, for there was heavy snow on the ground already when they disembarked the *Gypsy* at the place of their romance. It was October 21st, and when Harriet thought of their cold cellar, she held Eliza tighter under her winter robes. Emerson told Dred to go ahead and help his womenfolk up the dangerous slope and return later for their baggage. As they neared the top of the rise, Harriet saw Elizabeth smiling gaily and ran ahead to meet her.

"Oh, Harriet, welcome home," her kind former mistress called, and they embraced. Dred watched as Harriet pulled the little one from beneath the robes and uncovered just her face so Elizabeth could get a peek at her namesake. Dred laughed when a squawk erupted from the folds and carried down the hill on the frigid air.

The women hurried away, no doubt to the Agency, so Dred shrugged and turned back down the ramp for the luggage.

In the warmth of the Agency that evening, the family gathered once again for a feast of welcome and celebration. The Taliaferro girls were excused from the table and went to the parlor to take turns holding and making a fuss over the brand-new baby. Elizabeth and Lawrence watched them go and shared a smile at what they had put together. The major tried to put the clearly uncomfortable Irene at ease and asked after her family. When she told him her father was Alexander Sanford, he pounded the table.

"A small world indeed, Mrs. Emerson," he declared. "Then your brother would be Mr. John F.A. Sanford of Chouteau and Company! Didn't he marry Pierre Chouteau's daughter?"

"Yes, that's right—Emily Chouteau is my sister-in-law," she responded, furrowing her brow in surprise. "How is it that you know my father and brother?"

"Oh, don't be surprised, dear," Elizabeth interjected, laughing. "Lawrence knows everybody."

"Well, not everybody," Taliaferro feigned humility, "but my journeys on the river have brought me into contact with a number of people. I have known Pierre Jr. for over a decade, as his fur business has brought him here many times. He's quite wealthy, you know."

"Indeed!" Irene interrupted somewhat haughtily, and Dred was sure he noticed a clever smile on her husband's face.

"You can say that again, Mrs. Emerson! I'm sure you're aware that he even owns his own steamboat, the *Yellowstone*."

Emerson's eyes went full wide, and Dred realized that was news to him, anyway.

"And when he purchased John Jacob Astor's American Fur Company earlier this year, I'm certain he became one of the richest men in America!"

Dr. Emerson knocked over his glassful of wine.

"Oh, for heaven's sake, John," the cultivated Irene scolded. The red stain spread across the white linen as a lighter shade of red spread across her cheeks.

"Never mind, Mrs. Emerson," Taliaferro comforted, always the diplomat. "It seems we have one short leg on this table, Elizabeth. You'll recall the last time we sat here with Dred, he had a similar accident." Then wanting to get back to the discussion, he remarked, "In fact, when Mr. Chouteau was here, he sat in the very chair in which you're sitting, Dred."

Dred took no mind of the comment, but did notice a quick disapproving glance from Mrs. Emerson.

Major Taliaferro turned to Irene, who was still dabbing at the stain with her napkin. "Mrs. Emerson, I've known your brother John even longer than Chouteau. Before he married Emily, he was the Mandan Indian Agent, and we spent many days together working with the Indians. He knows his subjects well, and I'm sure he is of valuable service to the Chouteau Company indeed."

"Why yes, my brother is beloved of his father-in-law," Irene said, casually glancing at Dred and Harriet, "and he will do absolutely anything to please Pierre Chouteau."

The diners sat uncomfortably silent, not sure if Irene's words were meant as a compliment. Her husband scooted back in his seat while wiping his lips with his napkin. "Thank you, Madam Taliaferro—Major—for your hospitality." He slowly rose. "The two of you are the only bright lights in this otherwise dreary place."

Chairs scooted back as everyone stood. "Our pleasure, Doctor," Elizabeth acknowledged. "Would it be possible for Dred and Harriet to stay for a moment?"

Emerson gave a wave of indifference and escorted Irene to the door. Major Taliaferro saw them out while the rest quietly watched the strange couple depart.

"Please sit," Elizabeth invited, with some emotion in her voice. Dred immediately noticed and began to worry, and his fear grew as the major came and stood behind Dred's chair.

As if she'd read his thoughts, Elizabeth continued, pulling a crumpled letter from the side pocket of her dress. "I'm sorry I am the bearer of bad news."

Harriet reached for Dred's hand in his lap.

"I have a letter from Charlotte Charless, informing us of the death of your mother, Hannah."

Harriet gasped, but Dred sat in stony silence. He didn't even flinch when the kind Taliaferro placed a comforting hand on his shoulder.

Elizabeth waited a moment. "Shall I read it to you?" she asked, pulling a single sheet from the envelope.

Dred nodded.

"This is the part of the letter Charlotte wrote just for you." She cleared her throat, daubed at her eyes with a napkin, and continued.

> *"My dear friend Sam,*
> *I know you now call yourself after your beloved deceased brother, but you'll always be Sam to me and your mother. It is with a heavy heart I must inform you that Hannah has gone to join your brother in the presence of our Savior in the Great Beyond. Since her name was added to the Blow family Bible in 1761, she had been a member of, and devoted servant to, the Blow family for nearly eighty years. She was like a mother to my siblings and me, just as you were our older brother, and I want you to know how deeply we feel her loss. The entire family prays for you in your bereavement."*

Elizabeth's voice broke, and she paused to regain her composure. Harriet was softly crying, but Dred still sat numb.

Elizabeth continued reading Charlotte's words,

> *"I also pray God will forgive us for our grave sin of omission in allowing your mother to die a slave. We did not see her, nor treat her, as a slave, but a slave she was in the eyes of the law, and we stand guilty before the Lord. We will spend the rest of our lives doing whatever we can for you. Please forgive us. I hope you will find some comfort in the following words that sweet Hannah asked me to write you just hours before she drew her last breath."*

Dred leaned forward and placed his head in his hands, resting them on the table. Harriet rubbed his back, and Lawrence had taken a seat next to him.

"Are you all right, Dred? Shall I continue?" Elizabeth asked.

He didn't move or respond, but Harriet urged her to go on.

> *"My boy Samuel, I will soon pass over Jordan to meet my Jesus and your dear brother where I will be free at last."*

Dred sobbed, and Elizabeth looked at her husband, tears streaming down her cheeks. Dred raised his head and stared at the white woman, the color of her skin representing his and his family's bondage. But there was no hate in his eyes, only a profound sadness and resignation that changed to determination by the end of the letter.

> *"But you is still alive, my son, and while you live, I know you'll fulfill God's plan for you and our people.*

Hannah in the Bible told the Lord that she would raise her long-awaited son Samuel to love and serve Him, and because he listened when the Lord called him, he became a great prophet and leader to the Israelites. Through a long life of patience, sacrifice, and faith, he restored law, order, and justice to his people. I go to my grave believing you have that same purpose. I thank God you have chosen a path different from that terrible Turner boy who killed women and babies. That is not the way of Jesus. I imagine at times that you can free our people like a Mississippi Moses, but don't know how a small child from The Olde Place—a slave—can do that by himself. There is a lot of white folk who hate slavery, and maybe they will help you. The Blows have been good to me, and I ask them to be good to you if ever they get the chance."

Elizabeth looked at Dred again before finishing. He now sat upright, his back straight and his chin up, and Harriet mimicked his proud posture.

"I got to go now, Dred. I will call you by your new name that honors your brother. I gave you life. Keep living it as God would have you do. Never give up hope. I will visit you in your dreams. Hug your bride and that sweet baby chile that I will never hold in this life. Tell them that I love them. I'm passing over now, and will meet you all on the other side. I love you.   Hannah"

Elizabeth folded up the letter, put it back into the envelope, and handed it to Dred, who rose to accept it. He smoothed it against his chest.

"Thank you for a fine dinner and for being so kind to us, Major and Missus Taliaferro." He took his wife by the hand as she stood. "Come, Harriet. We gots work to do."

* * *

Dred watched Emerson carefully during that winter and noticed the weather really did seem to affect him. Dark circles appeared under his eyes, and he walked gingerly, as if every step caused him pain. One evening while cleaning surgical instruments at the hospital, Dred saw his master drink something out of a small bottle from the medicinal stores. It was either his pain or his medicine that turned Emerson's disposition increasingly sour. As December became January 1839, he began to snap angrily at his patients and even other officers. As January became February, he was prone to outbursts, and one day threw a scalpel into the wall. Remembering how Peter Blow had changed, Dred found himself praying for his master. Perhaps God heard his prayers, Dred considered, for it seemed the doctor's kindness toward Dred, Harriet, and the baby he had delivered seemed unconditional. On Valentine's Day, the two emotions collided in a nearly fatal confrontation.

Throughout the winter, Dr. Emerson had been demanding a wood stove from the Quartermaster to warm his slaves' frozen basement abode. He had been in their home and didn't know how they survived. When the Quartermaster was slow in filling the requisition, Emerson took it as an affront to him personally. He determined he would get the stove for Dred, so he could give it to Harriet as a Valentine's Day present. Dred could see his master was in distress that morning, and he urged him not to bother. But Emerson was determined, and off they marched to the commissary.

Banging the door open and bringing in a flurry of snow and wind behind him, as if he were Jack Frost himself, Emerson shouted in the stunned Quartermaster's face, "Mr. McMillan, I am here to pick up my stove. Bring it forthwith!"

The stocky Irish lieutenant looked up at the taller doctor and squared his feet.

Uh oh, Dred thought, watching the two Irishmen turn red.

"Are ye deaf, man, or just plain stupid? I told ye already, *no stove* for your niggers!"

Emerson leaned down into the fleshy face and started to curse, spittle flying from his lips. Suddenly the man, who unbeknownst to the two was the fort's champion pugilist, threw a quick right jab, hitting Emerson right between the eyes and breaking his glasses. Emerson was so stunned by the blow that he took one step backward, touched his nose, and rubbed the blood between his fingers. Lieutenant McMillan stood behind the counter, feet planted, and both fists up. Dred didn't know what to do, other than stay out of their way. Emerson looked up from rubbing his bloody hands, stared at his attacker, then turned on his heels and ran.

"Strike a superior officer?" he cried as he went out. "I'll give *ye* Jesse, you cussed little clerk!"

As Emerson ran to his quarters, Dred sprinted to the equidistant guardhouse, worried at just what kind of "Jesse" Emerson had in mind. Dred came out with two soldiers and saw his master, with pistols drawn and murder in his eyes, rounding the rock building, heading back toward the commissary. The soldiers saw him too, readied their muskets, and hurried, slipping and sliding on the icy ground as they tried to intercept him.

"Fetch Commander Plympton," they ordered Dred, and then shouted at the crazed doctor, "*Hold!* Put down your weapons, sir!"

Emerson appeared not to hear them, but the Quartermaster apparently did. The door opened, and he came speeding out. He set off down the length of the fort like a champion sprinter, not a fighter. Dred watched in horror as Emerson raised a pistol and aimed at the fleeing back.

"*Stop!* Drop your weapons *now!*" the guards screamed, raising their own muskets.

For years afterward, Dred wondered if it had been in answer to his prayers or the shouts of the soldiers, but Emerson slowly lowered his pistol, turned, and offered up both guns, handles first.

Commander Plympton had both officers tossed in the brig and began his own earnest letter-writing campaign to the War Department. A year later, John Emerson received new orders to Florida, and the two families left in May, 1840, for their last trip down the Upper Mississippi.

Interestingly, one day in late 1839, as the first snow began to fly, Dred entered his basement home and stood, stunned, to see a shiny black stove. He never asked, and Emerson never volunteered, but many a night during that winter, spent comfortably by their stove, Dred and Harriet talked in amazement about how it was that a white man had fought so hard for their benefit.

He wouldn't be the last.

* * *

In 1833, Great Britain made slavery illegal in all her colonies, thereby freeing some 700,000 slaves. But slavery remained entrenched in America, where people were proudly singing the words of Samuel Francis Smith's popular new song, *My Country 'Tis of Thee*, "From every mountain side, let freedom ring!"

In March, Abraham Lincoln and his new partner, William Barry, paid seven dollars for a license to keep a tavern in New Salem. Two months later, Abraham began his first job as a civil servant with an appointment by President Andrew Jackson to serve as postmaster. When asked how it was that a Whig and open supporter of Henry Clay could receive an appointment from the Democratic administration, the man who ran, and was obviously running again, as "Humble Abe" quipped that the office of postmaster is "too insignificant to make [my] politics an objection."

In September, President Jackson appointed Roger Taney to a substantially more significant office, Acting Treasury Secretary, for the express purpose of fighting the Bank War. Taney further solidified his political "states rights" reputation by immediately ordering that all future government deposits would be made only in state banks, and then started withdrawing all money from the Bank of the United States.

In 1834, Humble Abe succeeded in winning his first election and a four-year term as Illinois State Representative. As he was taking his seat in the assembly chambers in the Illinois Statehouse in Springfield, Acting Secretary Taney came under siege by the most powerful men in Congress: Daniel Webster, Henry Clay, and John Calhoun, who tried to block his official report criticizing the U.S. Bank. Missouri Senator Thomas Hart Benton came to his defense and got the report read and published in the Senate Journal. In retaliation, the others successfully blocked Taney's appointment to be permanent Secretary of the Treasury.

The following year, State Representative Lincoln voted in support of the Bank of the United States and against a motion to support the President's and Acting Secretary Taney's actions against the national bank. In Washington, on the last day of the 1835 general session as the retaliation continued, Senator "Black Dan" Webster made a motion to postpone Roger Taney's opportunity to be confirmed as an Associate Chief Justice of the United States Supreme Court. The motion passed. A few months later, the longest-serving Chief Justice of the Supreme Court, John Marshall, died after thirty-five years on the highest bench in the land.

Despite continued opposition from Webster, Clay, and Calhoun, this time arguing that, as a Roman Catholic, Taney would take orders from a foreign power, President Andrew Jackson finally succeeded in his efforts to elevate his staunch supporter and loyal servant. And what a position it was! On March 28th, 1836, Roger Taney replaced the great John Marshall and became the fifth Chief Justice of the Supreme Court.

In 1837, at the urging of the new Chief Justice, Congress added two more justices to the Supreme Court, bringing the number up to nine. Back in Illinois, Springfield's newest attorney, who began signing his name "A. Lincoln," set up a law practice with John T. Stuart. Later that year, Assemblyman Lincoln stood before the state legislature and publicly declared his opposition to slavery for the first time. He moved the passions of his fellow public servants, concluding his remarks with his conviction that slavery was "founded on both injustice and bad policy." The following year, his colleagues elected him Speaker of the House.

Now that he held the highest leadership position in the legislative branch of the State of Illinois, people all across the state started to listen and pay attention to the tall, gangly orator. After learning of the brutal murder of abolitionist newspaperman Elijah Lovejoy in nearby Alton, Lincoln chose the occasion of a January speech to the Young Men's Lyceum in Springfield to further solidify his position as a leading opponent of slavery and a fearless defender of the rule of law. To a packed house he declared, "All the armies of Europe, Asia and Africa combined, with all the treasure of the earth (our own excepted) in their military chest; with a Buonaparte [sic] for a commander, could not by force take one drink from the Ohio, or make a track on the Blue Ridge, in a trial of a thousand years."

As the crowd cheered wildly to his assertion that no foreign power could ever defeat them, he warned them that the nation was, nonetheless, being torn apart from within by the "wild and furious passions of lawless mobs." He condemned the horrible 1836 burning death of the mulatto McIntosh in St. Louis, and did not equivocate in stating that, even though that scoundrel deserved severe punishment for killing a police officer, it should have been under the laws of the state. He further warned of the dangers of "this mobocratic spirit," and predicted that if lawless bands could "burn churches, ravage and rob provision stores, throw printing presses into rivers, shoot editors, and hang and burn obnoxious persons at pleasure, and with impunity . . . this Government cannot last!"

Having firmed up his position as a leading politician, Lincoln turned his attention to romance. In 1839, he met twenty-year-old Mary Todd at the Springfield mansion of her sister and brother-in-law, Elizabeth and Ninian Edwards. Enchanted with her "delicate beauty and exuberant personality," he later wrote that he wanted to dance with her "in the worst way." Why he didn't is subject to debate, but he obviously filed the memory of that evening in a cubbyhole in his heart for future reference, and continued his public service by being re-elected the next year to serve a second term as Speaker of the Illinois Assembly.

Part XI

Once Free, Always Free

"Yes, thou art a man and brother,
Though thou long has groaned a slave,
Bound with cruel cords and tether
From the cradle to the grave!
Yet the Saviour, yet the Saviour,
Bled and died all souls to save."

- "Am I Not A Man And Brother? The Anti-Slavery Harp; A
Collection of Songs for Anti-Slavery Meetings," compiled by
William Wells Brown, a fugitive slave (Boston: 1848)

"Times now are not as they were, when the former
decisions on this subject were made."

- Missouri Supreme Court Opinion, (22 March, 1852)

AM I NOT A MAN AND BROTHER?

Words by A. C. L.   Air—"Bride's Farewell."

Am   I   not   a   man   and   broth-er?
Sell   me   not   one   to   an - oth - er,

Christ   our   Sa - viour, Christ   our   Sa-viour,

Fine.

Ought   I   not,   then,   to   be   free?
Take   not   thus   my   lib - - er - - ty.

Died   for   me   as   well   as   thee.

Christ   our   Sa - viour, Christ   our   Sa - viour.

D. C.

Died   for   me   as   well   as   thee.

5

Chapter 30

Red Rose around Green Briar

Missouri - Iowa - Texas, 1840 - 1846

Awarm July wind blew off the Missouri prairie and down the hill as the handsome black couple walked arm-in-arm up Market Street. It carried with it a faint hint of the wild grasses Dred and Harriet had grown to love during their courtship at Fort Snelling. The fragrant breeze brought relief from the musty rot of the St. Louis waterfront with which Harriet struggled after a life on the open frontier. Feeling suddenly alive, she squeezed Dred's arm, then skipped ahead of him, girlishly twirling in her new dress and laughing with an ease that made Dred's heart melt.

"Does you still love me like you did the day we married?" she cooed coquettishly as she danced back toward him.

"Nobody ever loved a woman the way I loves you," he promised as they turned the corner onto Third Street and saw the gas lamps ablaze in front of the National Hotel. "Not even Massa Taylor could be happier at this wedding than I feels right this moment with you!"

Dred's young friend Taylor Blow was marrying Minerva Grimsley, the daughter of popular state senator and the city's most famous saddler, Thornton Grimsley. It would be the social event of the summer, and the Blow children wanted Dred and Harriet there as friends, not as slaves. So they pooled their money and bought Dred and Harriet their first store-bought Sunday-go-to-meeting clothes. The Scotts slowed as they approached the hotel and saw the stylish young couples stepping out of carriages. But for the color of their skin, the Scotts looked like they might actually belong. Harriet wore a straight-bodice dress of pastel prints with fashionable leg-of-mutton sleeves and a broad white tucker collar, and she thought her man looked quite the dandy in his black "bang-up" jacket, gray waistcoat, and batswing bowtie.

Even with the new clothes, the Scotts felt wholly out of place as they waited in the shadows across the street from St. Louis's newest and finest hotel. They nearly turned and walked quickly away when they noticed a couple of obvious pattyrollers strutting down the middle of the road, wielding short whips. As if on cue from heaven, young Peter Blow emerged from the hotel entrance and paused. Looking around and seeing his friends, he shot down the stairs and saved them from their imminent confrontation with the cruel neighborhood patrollers.

"Dred, Harriet!" he cried, wrapping his long arms around the man who had been his close friend and childhood mentor. He stepped back and admired the pair. "You two are a sight for sore eyes," he beamed, and Harriet knew instantly why Dred so loved these Blows.

For his part, Dred was speechless. His former master's namesake, grown to manhood, so resembled his father.

At twenty-five, Peter was the same age as Harriet and only slightly older than his father had been when Dred was born. As Peter escorted them across the street and up the ornate steps of the hotel, anxious to introduce them to his wife of seven years, Dred couldn't help but think how proud his former master would have been to see his youngest son married at so grand a venue and his children welcomed into St. Louis society.

Charlotte, recent widow of successful businessman Joseph Charless, presided over the celebration with her delightful eight-year-old daughter Elizabeth at her elbow. Martha Ella introduced them to her attorney husband, Charles Drake, while Peter's pale-skinned, black-haired wife, Eugenie, presented her two large brothers Edmund and Louis LaBeaume, one of whom slapped Dred jovially on the back as if they were old friends. It was evident that all these new Blow family members had heard the stories of fun and adventure growing up in Virginia and Alabama with their "older brother" Dred.

Other than the many servants attending to the wedding guests in the National's grand ballroom, Dred and Harriet were the only Negroes in the company. But the Blow children, all of whom had married well, proudly escorted them around the room. Most of the wedding guests received the introduction with a polite indifference—that was, until Taylor's new father-in-law introduced the Scotts to St. Louis' wealthiest citizen, the arrogant Pierre Chouteau, Jr., to whom Thornton Grimsley had sold hundreds of his new frontier saddles used by American Fur Company trappers and executives alike.

Refusing to even look at Dred and Harriet, Chouteau turned to the father of the bride and huffed, "With all due respect, Grimsley, I do not consort with slaves!" He slammed down his crystal champagne glass and directed a hateful glare at Dred. "It is my understanding that this boy and his whore are the property of my son-in-law's sister. What they are doing here, putting on airs, is beyond me. But I'll be damned if I spend another minute in their company!" A terrible silence settled over the room as Chouteau shoved Dred aside and stomped out.

After an awkwardly long pause, Senator Grimsley noticed the horror on his daughter's face and the humiliation in the Scotts' bowed heads. He moved quickly to save the evening. "Never mind, folks," he reassured the wedding guests. "I've served with Pierre on many boards and councils over the years, and his hide's tougher than the leather with which I make the saddle for his rather prominent backside!"

An appreciative laugh swept the hall, and the orchestra struck up the tragic Scottish-Irish love song, "Barbara Allen."

Prodded by the three married Blow children, the Scotts joined the white couples in a romantic dance about the room. Dred could hear several people singing the words of the doomed lovers,

"They buried her in the old churchyard
They buried him in the choir
And from his grave grew a red red rose
From her grave a green briar.
They grew and grew to the steeple top
Till they could grow no higher.
And there they twined in a true love's knot,
Red rose around green briar."

Dred wrapped his left arm more tightly around his own dear bride's waist, but his trained smile hid the ugly premonition that the wealthy Chouteau would become the bane of their future existence, as it was entwined with that of the Blow's.

* * *

The Scotts paid the price for their reunion with the Blow family. For the next eighteen months they were required to live in a tiny shack on the property of John Sanford, Sr. They were ignored by Irene Emerson and treated with disdain by her father and brother. They had very little to eat and might have starved, had not the Blows found ways to sneak them food.

They were both worked very hard by the Sanfords and others to whom they were rented out. Perhaps out of spite, their masters refused the Blows' many offers to hire them, and sent goons to threaten them to stay away after the families combined their resources and offered to buy Dred, Harriet, and Eliza.

Dred's anger and resentment grew, and he blamed the Sanfords for Harriet's late-term miscarriages of two infant boys. He was sure it was due to her malnourishment and harsh work load. He let his animosity stew, and he again found himself daydreaming of escape, but worried that they couldn't care for little Eliza. He knew for sure that his family would be torn apart if they tried to run and were caught. He began to fear that if anything ever happened to Master Emerson, and the Sanfords got control, they would destroy his family just out of spite. He found himself praying mightily that the kind Dr. Emerson would return and save them.

The only peace they found was the half-day each Sunday when they were allowed to attend church. Although Dred was a man of deep religious faith in God and the Bible, he didn't much care for preachers.

For her part, Harriet loved a good sermon and searched for a preacher and spiritual advisor who spoke to her soul. She joined the Reverend John Berry Meachum's First African Baptist Church and wouldn't miss a Sunday service after hearing from the young associate pastor, John Richard Anderson.

Dred did not take to the wealthy Reverend Meachum, and it bothered him greatly that the freed man—a pastor—would himself own slaves, notwithstanding his argument that he bought them to care for them and would eventually free them. But Dred loved being with Harriett and was not able to spend much time with her during the week, so he went along with her to church each Sabbath.

Whenever Reverend Meachum got up to preach, Dred found he couldn't resist stepping outside, regardless of the weather, to smoke a cigarette. But when Anderson got up, Dred remained seated—primarily because Harriet would grab his hand and hold on tight. He soon found the humble young preacher to be full of faith, hope, charity, and always, of course, a fiery passion for freedom for his black brothers and sisters. Harriet didn't have to hold his hand for long.

Like the senior pastor, Anderson had been born a slave, but had purchased his freedom and worked as a typesetter for the abolitionist newspaper editor Elijah Lovejoy, who had been murdered by a mob a few years earlier just up the river in Alton. He spoke often of that terrible day when men full of hatred and evil had destroyed the press and brutally murdered the kind white man for the "sin" of publishing his personal opposition to slavery. Anderson had been sure he would also be killed, but he believed God had preserved his life for a purpose. Through the grace of Jesus Christ, his fear, anger, and hatred had been turned to pity and forgiveness as he gave his life over to the service of his fellow man. He preached against violence and urged his parishioners to put their trust in God, that He would deliver them in His time.

But Anderson confided to Dred and Harriet one Sunday after church that he also believed in the American court system. When they asked if he was aware of the several successful freedom suits filed in the Missouri courthouse, he excitedly told them he was, and wanted them to meet his friend. Francis Murdoch, the prosecutor in Alton, Illinois, had brought justice to Elijah Lovejoy and his family by convicting his murderers.

They made plans to meet Murdoch the following Sunday, but the next day Dred's year-long prayer was answered. Dr. Emerson arrived from Louisiana with the news that he had been discharged from the Army and they would be moving immediately back up river to his property in Iowa Territory, where Dred had crossed the river and squatted eight years earlier.

Dred was mightily pleased to have Dr. Emerson back, but he worried about the future more than ever as he watched his formerly tall and straight master moving slowly about the steamboat, bent at the middle with his shoulders stooped, as if he were in great pain somewhere deep inside. He frequently had to grab hold of railings and chair backs when Missus Irene's arm was not near enough for stability.

"I don't think Massa Emerson is long for this world, Dred," Harriet confided a few hours after they had embarked once again on a north-bound steamer. They sat on the floor of the balcony of the hurricane deck as they ate a meager supper. She wiped the grease from little Eliza's chin, put her into Dred's lap, then pulled out a length of raw cotton string and began to tie nine elaborate knots along its length. "If you can get him to wear this charm around his gut, it will cure those cramps that have him all tied up inside."

Dred smiled at his wife's fervent trust in superstition. She was a faithful Christian, but she also clung to the tribal rituals and simple beliefs handed down through generations of African forbearers. At least she was trying to do something for the man in whom they trusted to keep their young family together. Dred fretted that he didn't know what he could do.

He patted Harriet's knee in gratitude and looked down through the railing and into the parlor on the lower deck where Emerson sat hunched in a chair next to Irene. He pushed his food around his plate and stared with empty eyes at nothing in particular. Dred noticed the worry on Irene Emerson's face and said a silent prayer that Harriet's knotted string would bring relief to the man who had treated them so well—*except the time he tried to drown me,* Dred thought humorlessly as the steamboat chugged slowly north to their new home in Iowa Territory near where Dred had swum the river.

Dred wandered the top deck late that night after Harriet and Eliza had bedded down amidst the barrels, hogsheads, crates, and luggage. He was surprised at the number of large Atlantic steamer trunks on board and wondered at the people with heavy English accents who made up the largest part of the ship's passenger manifest. "Mormons," Emerson had called them, with a hint of derision in his voice. Dred was a very observant man, and he noticed that the ship's captain, pilot, and crew treated these white passengers with almost the same disdain they usually reserved for Negroes.

Not all of these Mormons spoke with words and accents alien to this country. There were several among the group who were dressed in Missouri homespun, but spoke with a Yankee twang. He found his spirits lifted as he moved along the periphery of their many smaller gatherings and listened to their lively and happy conversation about their destination up river—a place they referred to as "Nauvoo." His curiosity was further piqued when he heard them all, foreigner and Yankee alike, refer to each other as "brother" and "sister" and speak in reverential tones of a man they called a "prophet."

Around midnight, Dred spied a very large young Negro who had to weigh over two hundred pounds and was dressed the same as the American Mormons. Dred moved closer and was shocked that the white men were collegially chatting and joking with the black man, whom they called "Brother Green." When the young man roared out a hearty laugh and slapped the back of one of his white companions, Dred flinched at the expectation of fisticuffs. When instead the man patted Green in a brotherly way, Dred determined he would not sleep until he had investigated further. There had been moments over the years when Dred felt close to Peter Blow and John Emerson, but never had he felt such ease and companionship among men of different races.

It must have been three in the morning when the group finally broke up. Dred followed the large man called Brother Green through the light of the half-moon and up to the fo'c'sle. He cleared his throat to announce his presence as he moved forward along the rail. The man turned to him cautiously, and Dred knew instantly from light shining off his smooth, unlined face that he was probably not yet even in his twenties.

"Excuse me for intrudin' on yo' solitude," Dred politely began, removing his cotton cap. "My name is Dred Scott, and I wondered if we might have a word."

The stranger peered through the dark into Dred's eyes, then smiled broadly and stuck out a beefy hand. "Pleased to meet you, Mr. Scott," he introduced himself in a deep voice sugared with a Mississippi drawl. "My name is Green Flake, and I'se pleased to make yo' acquaintance."

Dred's hand disappeared into Green's paw, and he was nearly lifted off the deck as the unabashed stranger shook his arm up and down. Despite his recognition of the raw physical power of his fellow passenger, Dred immediately felt at ease, and they conversed like brothers until the pink light of a new day grew above the starboard shore.

Dred learned a great deal that night about the new Mormon religion and was most surprised to learn that, although still a slave and the property of a man among the ship's company named James Madison Flake, Green was a member of his master's church and claimed to be treated as an equal by the Mormons—an irony that seemed lost on the enthusiastic youth. Green told how he had joined the Church a year earlier when missionaries had come to his master's home in Mississippi, and he himself had been baptized in this very river. The missionary had almost lost his grip when he dunked Green in about four feet of water near the bank. As Green felt the current tug at him, he worried briefly that the Gator Gar would snatch him down to the river bottom. They laughed together at the thought of the large boy leaping out of the water praising Jesus. The Mormons along the shore were moved by his enthusiasm at being saved, not knowing how literally Green felt his redemption.

He told Dred the story of the new church founded just thirteen years earlier in New York by one Joseph Smith, who spoke with angels, translated a book from ancient golden plates, and, like Moses himself, had even conversed face-to-face with God. Dred was a great fan of the prophets of the Old Testament and listened with rapt attention to the stories of the rapid growth of the Church, despite many travails and mighty persecutions.

A bond of friendship was forged as Brother Flake listened to Dred's own story of swimming across the river, the sound of the Gator Gar's iron platting rubbing together and massive jaws snapping in his ears. Green reached out his hand, this time in respect, and felt awesome strength in the small man's grasp.

All the Mormons on board, including the members coming from England, were headed to the new city of Nauvoo, which lay north of Quincy on a large horseshoe bend in the river. Dred remembered the last time they had passed that bend coming south and saw a group of industrious people working in the mid-summer heat and humidity to drain the swampland along the shore of what he was told was a place called Commerce. Green confirmed that the town had been bought by the Mormons a few years earlier after they had been attacked, murdered, and driven out of Missouri under an order of extermination from Governor Lilburn Boggs, and it was fast becoming one of Illinois' largest and most beautiful cities.

The boat steered toward the eastern shore to go around a string of islands and sandbars in the river. The two men moved to the starboard gunnel and listened to the meadowlarks, warblers, and sparrows singing to the morning in the bulrushes along the bank. An odor of wood fire and roasted meat rose on the air as isolated homesteaders prepared for the new day.

"Um-um," the big man muttered, rubbing his stomach. "I'se still a growin' lad and swear I could eat five slabs of bacon right now."

Dred's jaw dropped as he stared at his mammoth companion. "If you was any bigger, you'd tip this boat right over!" They shared a friendly laugh, then Dred again turned serious as he thought how people's lives entwined in this journey of life and wondered how some could so easily love their neighbor, while others so equally hated.

"I can tell you'se a good man, Green," Dred continued more soberly. "And I can see that yo' white Mormon friends like you and treat you kindly. 'Cept for the chillun of my first massa, most white men has hated me just 'cuz of the color of my skin. I seen whites hate the Injuns, too; but I ain't so much seen pure hatred against their own kind. Why you think the Missouri pukes hates the Mormons so?"

Flake thought for a moment. "I don't rightly know, 'cept Brother Joseph been talkin' about doin' away with slavery by

1850, and says the U.S. gov'ment should pay the slave owners the value of their slaves so's they don't take up arms and shed more blood."

Dred was astonished at such a bold idea. He had heard the abolitionist call for freeing the slaves, but never had he heard someone say that they should be paid to keep peace in the country. He couldn't help thinking talk like that could get a white man killed lickity-click.

Flake could see that Dred was thinking about what he said, and so plowed ahead. "When I was bein' taught by the missionaries, they told me bad trouble started 'bout eight years ago, when thousands of Mormons from the north started to settle in Jackson County. They wrote a tract called *Free People of Color*, or some such thing, an' the pukes didn't like it too much. They attacked the Mormons, destroyed their printin' house, broke into homes and even burned some down, and then whipped and poured hot tar and feathers on their leaders, and finally drove 'em right out of Jackson County altogether like they wasn't even white folks! For ten years, they been driven from one place to 'nother and finally crossed the river to Illinois and built them a city right up yonder." Flake pointed ahead, and Dred was amazed at what he saw.

Gone were the swamp and marshlands, and in place of the couple dozen small homes he'd seen the last time he passed this spot, the rising sun illuminated a large city of uncommon beauty and tranquility. Over a thousand stately red brick and white board homes, stores, and various public houses spread along straight square blocks upon the flat alluvial delta next to the river. Behind them rose a hill that gently sloped up to the plain upon which a magnificent white limestone edifice was being erected. Dred assumed the structure would be the courthouse, and saw that even in its incomplete state, it would rival, if not surpass, the one in St. Louis.

"Glory, hallelujah!" Green Flake declared as he turned to face the city. "I understands why the Prophet named it 'Nauvoo,' which he said meant 'beautiful' in the ancient Hebrew tongue."

Dred found himself very curious about Green's Mormon prophet who spoke Hebrew and could create a magnificent city out of a swamp in just a few short years. The steam whistle blew, and suddenly the railings along all the decks were filled with Mormon immigrants cheering and celebrating as if they were approaching the Pearly Gates themselves. A large welcoming party assembled along a broad main street that ended at a wharf next to what appeared to be a large two-story hotel. Dred started to look for a man with white hair and flowing robes and wondered if the prophet himself would welcome the new arrivals to his promised land.

"I gots to go," Green said anxiously, turning back to Dred. "Brother Madison will need help with all his truck, and I wants to be one of the first to meet Brother Joseph, the Prophet."

"Did you see him?" Dred asked, looking back at the crowd near the dock. "I don' see no prophet out there. I was 'spectin' a man who looks like Moses."

"Oh, no," the friendly giant laughed again. "Brother Joseph is just a man like you and me, but he do talk with God, and I hopes to be his friend. Lots of folks have threatened to kill him, and I'm goin' to offer my services as a bodyguard!"

"Well, I sho' 'nuff wouldn't try to harm him if you was standin' at his back!" Dred shook the young man's hand one more time. There was so much he wanted to ask about the Mormons, and how it was Green could still be a slave, but called a brother and a man. He also had a strong hankering to meet a prophet of God and see for himself what all the fuss was about.

Dred watched as passengers poured out of the boat, and he smiled as a local band began to play a lively tune of welcome. He waved a final farewell to the large black man down below, whose size and ebony face made him look like a fish out of water. He found himself somewhat envious of Green, and determined that the next time he passed back down this river, he would stop and seek an audience with "Brother Joseph."

Thirty minutes later, having disgorged most of her passengers and taken on a couple dozen cords of firewood, the boat set out north around the bend, and by evening pulled alongside the levee on the Iowa side of the river across from the old post at Fort Armstrong. Dred wondered how many more times in his life he would travel up and down this river, and if he would ever do so of his own accord as a free man.

Throughout the summer Dred toiled nearly around the clock to build a home for the Emersons, not far from the rugged lean-to he'd built as a squatter. Despite his growing weakness, Dr. Emerson was present every day to supervise Dred's work and that of a small crew of hired hands, spending most of his time sitting on a stack of wood under a parasol, calling out orders. He only left for an hour or so each day to slowly canvass the new neighborhood, soliciting patients for his medical practice. Dred fretted that one would have to be mighty sick to seek the services of a doctor who himself looked to be at death's door. His compassion grew when Harriet pointed out that Mrs. Emerson was expecting a child, and Dred prayed the harder that his kind master would find a cure to heal himself.

But that was not to be. Four days after Christmas in 1843, Dr. John Emerson called his grieving wife to his bedside in their beautiful new two-story home, above the clinic he would never use. With Dred and Harriet as his only witnesses, he wrote out a will giving all his property to Irene, and upon her death, to his new baby girl Henrietta. He drew his last breath before the sun rose the next morning over the Mississippi.

Dred wept as he dug his master's grave in the frozen earth of LeClaire, Iowa Territory, the tears leaving an icy trail down his cheeks. He chastised himself for feeling sorrow at the loss of a man who had owned him and who once had clearly coveted this soil more than he had the life of the man who dug his grave. But he also realized that Dr. Emerson had, for the most part, treated him fairly, and but for him, Dred never would have met his love and joy, Harriet.

And so Dred dug and struggled again with the irony of caring for another human being who was kind and good, but who did not return the same recognition. In the end, as he tossed the final shovelful of cold earth out of the hole, his own body kept warm only by his solitary exertion as a final demonstration of a mixture of devotion and duty, Dred convinced himself that his grief was more for the uncertain future his family now faced at the hands of Irene Emerson, her brother, and his in-laws.

Once again, as if by divine intervention, Dred's fears were not immediately realized. Irene indicated that she wanted Harriet to stay with her in Iowa to help care for the infant, and Dred would embark on yet another experience with the Army. Irene's sister, Mary, and her husband, Captain Henry Bainbridge, arrived from Jefferson Barracks just in time for the funeral on New Year's Day, and when Captain Bainbridge learned of Dred's faithful service in both the War of 1812 and to his deceased Army surgeon brother-in-law, he offered to hire Dred from Irene as soon as he obtained approval from the War Department.

In July of 1844, Dred received news of the approval of his hiring as the captain's slave, or "striker," in the U.S. Army's vernacular. Harriet and Eliza clung to him at the quay and wailed, despite his promises that they would be reunited. He could never lie to his soul mate, and she sensed his own uncertainty at the veracity of that promise. He felt again the terrible rip in his soul as he held his prized possessions and recognized that his fate, and that of his family, was completely out of their control. He summoned up all the courage he had gained from a lifetime of trials, tests, and challenges, and finally spoke calmly and with assurance.

"Come along with me, Gypsy girl," he whispered, taking his five-year-old treasure by the hand and leading her down to where the river lapped against the rocky shore. He crouched next to her and scooped up a palm full of the dark water. He held it to his nose and breathed in deeply. "Um-um," he muttered and smacked his lips, "that do smell mighty fine!" He held the tiny puddle in front of his girl's face. "Can you smell it, Gypsy? What do it smell like to you?"

She bent close and made a loud snorting sound. "Eww, Papa," she grimaced and wrinkled up her nose. "It smells like dead fish." Dred laughed and watched the water slosh from his grasp.

"No, ma'am!" he protested and scooped up another handful. "That smells like life! The Injuns calls this river 'Mee-zee-see-bee.' Do you know what that means?"

Eliza giggled. "That sounds funny. Say it again, Papa."

Dred winked at Harriet, who was already smiling. The fear and uncertainty fled in the tender moment. "I will if you say it with me. Mee-zee-see-bee."

"Mee-see-zee-bee," Eliza tried.

"Close enough!" Dred proclaimed. "I want you to remember what it means. It means 'Father of Waters.' You can remember that 'cuz you was birthed by yo' mammy on this here river, and so it's also the 'Father of Eliza!'"

"You's my father," she laughed again and spanked his hand, splashing the water into his face. He snatched his girl up into his arms and looked into her deep brown eyes. "That's right, Gypsy. And I believe this river done give me life when I swam across it right yonder. I was buried under the waves and thought I was goin' to meet my Jesus when I heard the Gator Gar snapping his jaws." He snapped at Eliza's button nose, and she squealed in mock horror. "But I came out of the water like I was reborn, and now you knows that nothing can never stop me from coming back to my two gals," he promised, now as serious as he had ever been. With the fervent faith that only a child can muster, Eliza stopped playing and cupped her tiny hands about her father's whiskered cheeks.

"Will you even swim all the way back up this river to us if you has to, Papa?" she asked.

"Yes, I will, Eliza." Dred did not hesitate. He looked past his child to his wife. "Yes, I will!"

Dred didn't have to swim the Mississippi to get back to his family, but he did eventually swim in the stagnant Nueces River, more than a thousand miles to the south, where it emptied into Corpus Christi, Texas. After a short time at Jefferson Barracks, Captain Bainbridge received orders to take his Third Infantry Regiment to Fort Jessop, Louisiana, as tensions mounted along the Texas border with Mexico. The Texans had scheduled July 4th, 1845, to vote on whether to join the Union as the 28th state. The Mexicans had threatened war if Texas did so, and if the United States then tried to establish the border anywhere south of the Nueces. The U.S. had every intent to claim that the border was 150 miles south at the Rio Grande River, and war seemed imminent.

While the Army made final preparations to ship out to Corpus Christi, Captain Bainbridge escorted his wife, Mary, back up to St. Louis. He learned that his sister-in-law, Irene Emerson, had moved home to live with her ill father, and Mary wanted to stay there as well while her husband was off fighting the Mexicans.

Knowing Dred's wife and daughter would be there also, he invited his loyal servant to travel back north with him. His kindness was perhaps eclipsed by the fact he had become quite accustomed to his attendant's services.

Hoping the good captain might be an ally and an advocate in his plan to buy his freedom from Irene Emerson, Dred spent the year in the employ of the West Point captain as the best orderly in the Third Infantry Regiment. No brass buttons and bucklers ever shone as bright as those worn by Captain Bainbridge, and his boots were the envy of every officer and enlisted man in the regiment. Bainbridge bragged that he could look into his boots to shave.

Truth be told, Dred had become quite skilled with a straight razor as well. So perfect was the captain's uniform that his close friend, Lt. Ulysses S. Grant, was ashamed to stand anywhere near Bainbridge during inspection—that is, until Dred offered to put a spit shine on Grant's boots and buttons as well.

Dred became very busy, but was rewarded by quiet "huzzahs" as the regiment's inspection gigs became nearly obsolete. It wasn't long before even General Zachary Taylor himself was commenting on the "squared away" nature of Bainbridge's regiment, and when the time came to sail to Texas, he chose to accompany the Third.

Dred's reunion with Harriet and Eliza was short but sweet. As so often happens when men are home on leave, Harriet became pregnant, but asked Mary not to share that fact with her husband, lest word get back to Dred. She feared another miscarriage or stillbirth, and didn't want Dred to worry about her health.

Before they left St. Louis at the end of June, Dred added one more cog in his clever scheme to gain a permanent friend in Captain Bainbridge. He asked Peter if he might get his father-in-law to build a personalized Grimsley Military saddle as a gift to Bainbridge. He did, and they allowed Dred to surprise a very pleased and deeply touched officer with the hand-crafted rawhide saddle, complete with horse-hair padded seat, high brass pommel, and matching cantle, branded

Capt. Henry Bainbridge

on one side, and

Third Infantry

on the opposite. As his master-at-hire heaped thanks and praise upon a humble slave, Dred peeked out from under his down-turned brow and made eye contact with Peter Blow, who grinned and winked at him. *Thas one more debt I owes those chillun,* he thought, with every intent—but no idea how—to repay them.

On Independence Day, the citizens of the Republic of Texas voted to join the United States. Three days later, Dred and Captain Bainbridge boarded the new side-wheel steamship *USS Alabama* in New Orleans, along with the entire Third Infantry Regiment and General Taylor's command company under "Rules and Articles of War." The ship entered Aransas Bay, ten miles outside Corpus Christi, a week later. What would be a most miserable year awaiting further orders was preceded by a sweltering three weeks aboard the *Alabama* as she crawled her way through the shoals between the mainland and San Jose and Mustang Islands.

They finally arrived at the beach at Corpus Christi on August 3rd and began building a camp which grew to 3,500 infantry and cavalry soldiers by the end of the year. The land was barren, and the humidity hovered near 100%, but there was a lot of game, and Dred soon became a camp favorite, due to his tracking abilities learned as a boy from the Nottoway Indians of Virginia.

The Nueces River was filled with bacteria, and as there was little wood with which to build fires to boil water or properly cook meat, with the arrival of winter, sickness swept the camp. The regimental surgeon wrote to the War Department that "the whole army might be considered a vast hospital" and joined General Taylor in urging the federal government to allow them to march west and south to the Rio Grande, before his army was decimated by disease and unable to confront the enemy.

Finally, on February 4th, 1846, General Taylor received the long-anticipated order to "advance and occupy, with the troops under your command, positions on or near the East side of the Rio del Norte (the Rio Grande.)" Lt. Ulysses S. Grant, upon learning of the orders, expressed the sentiment of the entire army in a letter to his fiancée. "Fight or no fight," he wrote, "every one rejoices at the idea of leaving Corpus Christi."

Either out of simple human kindness or gratitude for the services of his striker, or perhaps having learned that Dred's wife was pregnant, Bainbridge ordered him to return home to St. Louis. On March 11th, Dred waved goodbye as Captain Henry Bainbridge rode out of camp at the head of his regiment, proudly erect in his Grimsley saddle, and into the annals of heroism as a decorated officer in the Mexican-American War. As he prepared to return to St. Louis, Dred knew not that his own heroic war was soon to begin.

Chapter 31

Bound to Aid Each Other

St. Louis, Missouri, 1846

Poppy's home!" cried Eliza as she ran into her startled father's legs, nearly bowling him over.

Dred dropped his bags and pulled her up into his arms. Hugging her tightly, he looked at his smiling and very pregnant wife rocking in a chair by the open window of the officers' slave quarters at Jefferson Barracks.

"I didn't know you was going to be here at the barracks. This is a mighty surprise, Gypsy girl!" He kissed her, then set her down and walked over to Harriet as she struggled to rise.

"No, no, Harriet, don't get up," Dred cautioned, easing her back into the chair and placing his hand on her large abdomen. "You might tip right over onto yo' lovely face." Eliza's laughter mixed with his.

"Oh, Dred, you is such a tease." Harriet slapped his hand. "Now you better make up by kissin' me right now!"

"Let's see if I can reach across this here mountain," he continued to joke, and squelched her playful screech with a long and tender kiss. "It's good to be home, Harriet. I loves you so," he whispered into her ear, then asked loudly, "Now when is this bun gonna be cooked?"

Dred was feeling powerfully happy at the prospect of adding another child to his family, but equally fearful that Harriet would lose this one, too. And if the child did survive, he was very worried about what the future held for them as slaves of Irene Emerson and her brother. He was relieved to learn from Harriet that, at least for the time being, they would be hired out to Samuel and Adeline Russell, owners of the Russell & Bennett grocery store on Water Street right in the middle of the bustling St. Louis quay.

Two weeks later, Sunday, March 22nd, 1846, Dred and Harriet strode proudly with their two healthy daughters into Liberty Hall next to the Liberty Fire Engine House at the corner of Third and Cherry Streets. It was a grand day for the newly formed Second African Baptist Church of St. Louis. It would be the first worship service of the new congregation, and the infant Scott would be dedicated into the Baptist faith as part of the larger dedication of the rented hall as their temporary place of worship. Some fifty parishioners—mostly slaves—were there that day to celebrate the dedications, accompanied on this occasion by the dozen white faces of the Blow family surrounding the Scotts. Peter and Eugenie were honored to be godparents to the child.

Dred proudly led his three girls, dressed in matching white calico dresses and linen head rags, to the front of the makeshift church while a quartet sang Isaac Watts' *Cradle Hymn*—the rich southern accents blending in a soulful rendition of the traditional Scottish tune.

"Hush! my dear, lie still and slumber,
Holy angels guard thy bed!
Heavenly blessings without number
Gently falling on thy head."

Dred nodded to Peter Blow and his wife, and they rose to join them as the congregation began to lend their voices to the popular lullaby, reaching a crescendo on the last two verses.

"Lo, He slumbers in His manger,
Where the hornèd oxen fed:
Peace, my darling: here's no danger,
Here's no ox anear thy bed.

"May'st thou live to know and fear Him,
Trust and love Him all thy days:
Then go dwell for ever near Him,
See His face, and sing His praise!"

"Glory, hallelujah!" proclaimed the Reverend John Richard Anderson, raising both arms above the Scotts, his round face encircled by his closely trimmed black hair and chin beard. "In praise to the Babe of Bethlehem, we assemble here today, my brothers and sisters, to welcome the glorious birth of this child of God and dedicate her to a life of love and service in His kingdom."

He gently lifted the sleeping bundle from Harriet's arms and positioned himself in the center, the Scotts on his right and the Blows on his left. Being careful not to wake her, he tenderly kissed the newborn on her forehead, eliciting a grunt, squirm, and a pucker of the tiny lips. The congregation verbalized its pleasure with a mixture of ohs, ahs, and gentle laughter.

361

Reverend Anderson turned to the Scotts. "By what name shall this child be known?"

"Lizzie Scott!" Dred proclaimed with a pride that only a father knows.

Someone in the back shouted "amen," and applause broke out along the makeshift pews. Lizzie startled, but did not wake.

"Jesus loved and welcomed children. One day as He was walking through a town in Judea, many parents came to Him with their little ones and begged of Him a blessing on their heads. The disciples rudely pushed them away, but when our Lord saw it, He rebuked them and said unto them, 'Suffer the little children to come unto me, and forbid them not: for of such is the kingdom of God . . . And he took them up in his arms, put his hands upon them, and blessed them.' Dred and Harriet, please place your hands on your child. Who has agreed to be this infant's godparents, to at all times look out for her and to care for her as one of their own, and to make her yours, should something ever happen to her parents?"

"We do," Peter and Eugenie said in unison, and crowded in closer.

"Then place your hands upon Lizzie Scott as well." As two sets of white hands joined three sets of black, he continued, "Let us pray . . . Almighty God!"

"Yes, Jesus," murmured Harriet as a tear dropped to the floor.

"In humility, we present Miss Lizzie Scott to thee and pronounce a blessing upon her. We bless this child, oh Lord, that she will grow strong and healthy and filled with a spirit of peace and love that will bless the lives of all those who cross her path during a long and fruitful life."

Multiple exclamations of "amen," "hallelujah," and "glory" filled the room.

"Lord, God," continued the pastor, while his family of faith verbally urged him on. "Beyond these walls, there are those who claim that this child, created in Thy image, is nothing but property, to be bought and sold and treated with disdain and disrespect simply because of the color of her skin."

Dred and Peter locked eyes as the preacher's voice rose.

"But we knows that in Thy sight, oh Father, she is free. The light of Jesus fills her soul, and the Holy Spirit dwells in her heart."

Lizzie's eyes fluttered open, and her dark orbs glistened as she stared heavenward. Harriet followed her baby's gaze and muttered a sound of joy and adoration.

"Bless her, Father in Heaven, to know Thee and to grow up and grow old and marry a fine man who will love her, and together they will produce a fine posterity that throughout all generations will bring honor and praise to her parents who have given her to Thee this day, Dred and Harriet Scott."

As a chorus of premature "amens" rose to the rafters, the Reverend Anderson waited. Slowly, the members of the brand-new Second African Baptist Church of St. Louis realized their pastor was not yet done. They quieted and watched him as he stared into Heaven, seemingly in a trance. Years later, some of those there that day swore a halo of light glowed in an aura around the young preacher, and a fire burned in their bosom as they listened to his next inspired utterance.

"And, oh, beloved and merciful God," he finally continued, his head now bowed and his eyes shut tight. "We bless our Lizzie Scott that she will, in her childhood, pass over the River Jordan to freedom."

Harriet gasped.

"Not in death," he quickly continued, "but in her mortal life." He opened his eyes and looked at Dred and Harriet, who were both in the attitude of humble supplication, then watched as seven-year old Eliza moved close, reached up, and took the tiny hand of her sister. There was not a sound in the borrowed chapel.

"I am moved by thy Holy Spirit, oh Father," he concluded, "to bless this beautiful family that they will all know freedom in this life! Amen."

"Amen," prayed Dred, his small voice sounding loud in a church hushed by the Spirit. His eyes met those of Reverend Anderson's white attorney friend, Francis Murdoch, standing on the front row. Murdoch nodded and mouthed the word, "amen!"

The dedication of the new meeting house continued for another hour, filled with prayers, an oration from a guest pastor, and congregational hymns sung in mostly "lining" fashion with the large, bald-headed co-pastor, Reverend Richard Sneethen, calling out a line of verse in his deep baritone, and the congregation repeating after him. Sneethen finally put on his oval spectacles and preached a long and fiery sermon from the Good Book.

The bell in the tower of the St. Louis Cathedral struck twelve, the metallic notes resonating down Third Street. Reverend Anderson rose to conclude the historic first meeting of his blossoming congregation.

"The Spirit of Almighty God has blessed us this day. It has burned in our hearts and opened our minds. We are inspired, my brothers and sisters, and our hopes, our tears, and our prayers go especially this day with the Scott family." He paused and looked at the white faces in his church, "and also with our friends of the Blow family and Mister and Missus Murdoch. They may not realize it right now, but they are about our Father's business. Remember them in your prayers. In closing now, will you all open your songbooks and sing with one accord in a voice to rattle the Pearly Gates, 'Am I Not a Man and Brother?'"

And so they did, to the familiar air known as *The Bride's Farewell*.

"Am I not a man and brother?
Ought I not, then, to be free?
Sell me not to one another,
Take not thus my liberty.
Christ our Saviour, Christ our Saviour,
Died for me as well as thee.

"Am I not a man and brother?
Have I not a soul to save?
Oh, do not my spirit smother,
Making me a wretched slave;
God of mercy, God of mercy,
Let me fill a freeman's grave!

"Yes, thou art a man and brother,
Though thou long has groaned a slave,
Bound with cruel cords and tether
From the cradle to the grave!
Yet the Saviour, yet the Saviour,
Bled and died all souls to save.

"Yes, thou art a man and brother,
Though we long have told thee nay;
And are bound to aid each other,
All along our pilgrim way
Come and welcome, come and welcome,
Join with us to praise and pray!"

Dred left church that day with the Murdochs and the Blows a
man inspired. He thought he understood how the disciples of his
Savior Jesus Christ must have felt on that glorious Day of
Pentecost, when the Holy Spirit was manifested as a tongue of

flame atop each believer's head. Dred's unquenchable resolve that he and his family would be free burned as an all-consuming fire in his soul. All the way home, he poured out thanks in his heart for the white pilgrims who surrounded him who would aid him along his path to freedom.

Dred and Harriet sat in stunned silence later that morning at the law office while Murdoch outlined to them his plan to petition the Missouri Circuit Court for a trial to prove that, under Missouri law and precedent of "once free, always free," Dred and Harriet were entitled to their freedom. The beginning to an end of a lifetime of slavery was within their grasp.

Dred did not understand the discussion about legal strategies, subpoenas, and deposition, but he was keenly cognizant of the fact that the process would be long and costly, and he dared not ask how he could ever possibly pay for it. Having Dred as part of his earliest boyhood memories, Taylor Blow easily discerned Dred's growing concern and moved quickly to put his mind at ease.

"Dred and Harriet," he said, pulling a thick envelope from a battered leather folder, "you don't need to worry about legal expenses. My brothers and sisters and I have been saving as much money as we could the last few years, hoping and praying this day would arrive." He smiled and handed the packet to Francis Murdoch. "Here is fifteen hundred dollars as a retainer for your legal services." He reached out and took Dred's hand in a warm, dry embrace. "Like that day you and your brother—God rest his soul—helped our father push our keelboat into the turbulent Tennessee, we are embarking on a frightening course filled with eddies, currents, and hidden dangers. As you know, the Chouteau family is wealthy, powerful, and for some reason, filled with a hatred for your skin color and will do anything and everything they can to keep you enslaved. But if our Blow ancestors taught us anything, it was that, despite our different skin color and legal status, we are family. Why, your own dear mother's birth was recorded right there in Great-grandpa Sam Blow's Bible, and we mean to be right there beside you, come hell or high Mississippi water!"

"Praise God!" Harriet sighed.

"Thankee, thankee!" Dred exclaimed.

"Come hell or high Mississippi water!" shouted Eliza, and everyone burst into joyous laughter.

But what to the Scotts was truly miraculous, kindness was not done. As soon as the impromptu celebration quieted down, Murdoch drummed his fingers on the envelope and spoke up.

"I hate to dampen your spirits, but as your attorney, I must tell you that the legal process is long and difficult. I cannot guarantee we will win, even though under the law, we should. We will have to fight a lot of legal motions and tricks by our opponents. Taylor is right about the Chouteaus. They will fully support Missus Emerson and her brother John, and will pay for attorneys who charge a lot more than I do. In addition, they will use all their political influence and commercial might against you, and all those who support you. We will need to act quickly to obtain a court order that prohibits your maltreatment, sale, or transport out of the jurisdiction of this court, and we will need to think of a strategy to ensure your safety and that of your little ones."

Harriet looked down at her slumbering child and instinctively pulled her tighter to her chest. Dred simultaneously reached for his Gypsy girl.

"Therefore," Murdoch said, picking up the money and handing it to Dred, "you must take this money and offer it to Missus Emerson to purchase your freedom."

Dred and Harriet sucked in air in disbelief.

"If she will accept it—and it is more than she would get if she tried to sell you—your freedom and safety could be secured immediately. I assume you don't mind?" he asked Taylor.

"Aye! Of course! By all means!" the Blows, Charlesses, Drakes, and LaBeaumes all chimed in at once.

Dred and Harriet were once again stunned to silence, but out of the mouth of little Eliza sprang an exultant "hallelujah!" and a hopeful celebration began.

* * *

Dred and Harriet walked tentatively down the long lane leading to Alexander Sanford's plantation, north of St. Louis in an area near the confluence of the Missouri and Mississippi Rivers called Spanish Lakes. Buds were just beginning to appear on the peach, quince, and cherry trees of the orchards lining the way. As if sensing something of significance afoot, many of Sanford's slaves stopped their pruning and stared at the well-dressed couple belonging to their master's daughter. Seeing them approach the front porch of the large home, an old man shook his frosted head and went back to his task of clearing grass from around the trees.

Dred pulled the money packet from inside his vest, smoothed his jacket, and knocked on the white double doors of the home. An icy bolt shot down his spine and he put a protective arm around his wife when he looked through the etched glass panes of the door and saw Missus Irene's brother John striding down the hall toward them.

John Sanford yanked open the door and screamed, "Ya'll get your uppity black carcasses to the back a'fore I have you horse-whipped!" All eight windows on the front of the house nearly exploded from their frames with the violence of the door slamming shut.

The terrified couple hurried off the porch, every fiber of their beings urging them to flee the property. After a brief, emotional argument, Dred convinced Harriet they had to try, and they moved cautiously around the house to the back stoop, where they found Irene and her brother waiting.

"We comes with a passel of money to buy our freedom," Dred forced himself to say while they were still some ten feet away. He pulled the bundle of bills from the packet and held them up as emphasis.

They were met with silent stares, Irene's indifferent, but her brother's afire.

"Fifteen hundred dollars," Harriet softly prodded. "Please, Missus Emerson, that's a lot of money. Please let us be free!"

"Who'd you steal that money from?" Sanford hissed and started down the steps. "I've half a mind to call the law."

"We didn't steal no money, Massa John," Dred countered and nudged Harriet behind him. "The Blows and their kin done give it to us so's we could pay Missus Irene for us and our chillun. It's mor'n she could get at the auction."

Dred thought of his last encounter with Peter Blow as the stench of alcohol and stale tobacco preceded the man who stopped a foot from him. He was breathing heavily and Dred changed his mind. There was a feral odor to the man that he had never smelled before. He looked down at Dred with a look of pure hatred, then violently slapped the money out of his hands, scattering the bills across the grass.

"My sister don't want no damn cuffee-lover money!" he screamed. "You and your pickaninnies are her property, and it's about time you learned that! Now get down in the fruit cellar!" He walked to the house and pulled up on the double doors, revealing dirt steps leading down into the darkness.

A wind gust kicked up several bills, and Dred dropped quickly to his knees to snatch them up before they blew away. Harriet also bent to scoop up their friends' money.

Sanford let the doors bang open and looked back, incredulous that his orders were not being followed. But instead of attacking the Scotts, he stomped back to his sister and grabbed a thick limb from a pile of firewood by the back door.

"We talked about this, Irene. Now take charge of your chattel!" he ordered his sister and handed her the stick.

Mrs. Emerson hesitated, and then jumped when her brother barked her name again. While she had never been friendly to them, Irene hadn't been physically abusive. Dred sensed that was about to change. It was apparent that John Sanford had been at his younger sibling.

"Leave the money and get in the cellar," she told them, and when they hesitated, she raised her voice and the weapon. "Now!"

"But we needs to first pick up the money so's we can return it to the folks who gave it to us," Dred reasoned and bent his head. He later marveled at how fast Irene Sanford was able to close the distance between them, for before he could pick up more than a couple of bills, his teeth cracked together as the branch crashed down on his neck. He heard Harriet scream out his name then shriek in pain simultaneous with a sickening thwack.

Dred pushed himself up, his body and mind in shock as much from the fact that Irene Sanford was beating them as he was from the physical blow. He threw his arms in front of his wife, who had crumpled to the ground, and heard his fingers crack before he felt the pain dart down his left hand and arm.

"Please, Missus," Dred pleaded, "we's going down the cellar. I'se sorry."

As Dred led a sobbing Harriet down under the house, he looked back over his shoulder and saw Irene drop the stick and put her head in her hands. John Sanford walked past her and picked up the branch. Dred hurried his wife into the gloom and flinched when the heavy doors slammed shut behind them, leaving them in inky darkness. The branch scraped across the wood, locking them into their stygian prison.

* * *

When the Scotts hadn't returned overnight, Peter and Taylor Blow went with attorney Murdoch and their brother-in-law, Sheriff Louis LaBeaume, to the Sanford plantation and talked Irene Emerson into releasing her slaves from beneath the house. Fortunately, her brother wasn't there, and her father, Alexander Sanford, was too ill to intervene.

The very next day, Monday, April 6th, 1846, Francis Murdoch strode purposely into the St. Louis courthouse and filed on behalf of his *pro bono* clients separate "Petitions for Leave to Sue for Freedom," which he had written out in his flowing cursive in indelible black ink. Dred's petition, to which he had personally added a firm + as his mark, was short and to the point, but set in motion a series of cases that could change the world.

> *To the Hon. John M. Krum, Judge of the St. Louis Circuit Court. Dred Scott, a man of color, respectfully states to your honor, that he is claimed as a slave by one Irene Emerson, of the County of St. Louis, State of Missouri, widow of the late Dr. John Emerson, who at the time of his death was a surgeon in the United States army. That the said Dr. John Emerson purchased your petitioner in the city of St. Louis, about nine years ago, he then being a slave, from one Peter Blow now deceased, and took petitioner with him to Rock Island in the State*

of Illinois, and then kept petitioner to labor and service, in attendance upon said Emerson, for about two years and six months, he the said Emerson being attached to the United States troops there stationed as surgeon. That after remaining at the place last named for about the period aforesaid, said Emerson was removed from the garrison at Rock Island aforesaid, to Fort Snelling on the St. Peters river in the territory of Iowa, and took petitioner with him, at which latter place the petitioner continued to remain in attendance upon Dr. John Emerson doing labor and service, for a period of about five years. That after the lapse of the period last named, said Emerson was ordered to Florida, and proceeding there left petitioner at Jefferson Barracks in the County of St. Louis aforesaid in charge of one Capt. Bainbridge, to whom said Emerson hired Petitioner-that said Emerson is now dead, and his widow the said Irene claims petitioners services as a slave, and as his owner, but believing that under this state of fact, that he is entitled to his freedom, he prays your honor to allow him to sue said Irene Emerson in said Court, in order to establish his right to freedom he will pray be.

Dred X Scott

Accompanying the petition was a statement of facts alleging:

On the fourth day of April in the year eighteen hundred and forty six, with force and arms etc., made an assault upon the said plaintiff, to wit at St. Louis in the County aforesaid, and then and there beat, bruised, and ill-treated him, the said plaintiff kept and detained him in prison there, without any reasonable or probable cause

whatsoever, for a long time to wit, for the space of twelve
hours, there next following, contrary to the laws of the
said state, and the will of said plaintiff.

Judge Krum signed the order drafted by Murdoch granting the
Scotts leave to sue, and of critical importance, mandating that Irene
Emerson was to give them reasonable liberty to meet with their
attorney to prepare for trial, prohibiting her from removing them
out of the jurisdiction of the court, and instructing her that they
would "be not subject to any severity on account of his application
for freedom."

And just like that, without bloodshed or force of arms, Dred
and Harriet Scott, slaves since birth, accessed the vaunted judicial
system of a "free" nation. The doors of the courthouse had been
opened, and a distant light appeared in the long dark tunnel of
oppression.

Alexander Pope Field

Chapter 32

Twelve Good and Lawful Men

St. Louis, Missouri, 1850

"May it please the court," Alexander Pope Field addressed Judge Alexander Hamilton as he raised his tall, raw-boned frame from the counsel table.

"Gentlemen of the jury," he nodded respectfully to the twelve white men huddled under blankets on the jury platform to the judge's left. They sat in three rows of four, each row slightly raised above the preceding one, giving all the jurors, regardless of their height, a clear view of the adversaries sitting at the counsel tables and of all proceedings within the well of the courtroom.

"Esteemed colleagues and good citizens of St. Louis," continued the barrister. The timbre of his baritone and precise elocution of the English language brought the entire courtroom to silence. This was going to be a show. "We are here today in this magnificent temple of justice," Field continued, sweeping his right arm outward and drawing all eyes to the white columns encircling the room every five feet, "presided over by a jurist who bears the name of one of our great Founding Fathers," he paused to let that fact sink in and noticed a proud smile on Judge Hamilton's face, "to determine whether Thomas Jefferson meant what he said when he penned those immortal words, 'We hold these truths to be self-evident, that all men are created equal!'"

It was evident that Field was already living up to his reputation as one of the best trial lawyers in the country. Dred, sitting with Harriet at the counsel table to the right, facing the raised dark mahogany judge's rostrum, was grateful once again for his kind benefactors, who didn't seem to know the word "surrender." The Scotts worried when Francis Murdoch had to leave the state for family reasons shortly after filing suit, but they soon learned that there seemed to be a never-ending supply of attorneys who were related by family or business to the Blows, and who agreed therefore to represent Dred and Harriet for free. Even though Martha Ella Blow had died in childbirth a decade earlier, her widower, Charles D. Drake, happily took over the case and conducted discovery. Because they were facing the Sanford and Chouteau families, the Scotts needed a lawyer of some renown to add viability, and got that in spades when Samuel Mansfield Bay, the former Attorney General of Missouri, joined the team. He was an officer of the Bank of Missouri and had served there with Charlotte Blow's husband, Joseph Charless.

From 1846 through 1849, the litigation had been plagued with court delays and a loss at the first trial based on a finding that the testimony of the Scotts' chief witness, store owner Samuel Russell, was based on hearsay. There followed appeals, petitions for writs of error, and a request for a new trial granted by Judge Hamilton.

The case was further delayed in May of 1849 by a terrible fire that started aboard the steamboat *White Cloud* while tied up at the levee. Before it could be pushed out into the river, the flames had spread to dozens of other boats, which then ignited the city. Before it could be put out, twenty square blocks of St. Louis lay in ashes. Nearly everything between the courthouse and river was a total loss. Even eight months later, the snow was black with soot, and a heavy odor of charred wood hung over the city.

But greater tragedy was on its way.

In the summer, a cholera epidemic swept the devastated city, and by the time the second trial rolled around, everyone in town had experienced personal loss. Taylor Blow moved his growing family to Carondelet, a French settlement five miles south of St. Louis. Drake and Bay had lost their office and homes in the fire. They fled with their families to avoid the plague and were no longer available. The Scotts worried where they would find lawyers to continue the fight, but their friends the Blows came to their rescue once again. Harriet counted it nothing short of miraculous that, despite their many setbacks and what appeared to be the wrath of God poured out upon their city, Alexander P. Field and his law partner David N. Hall stepped up to argue the case anew. Field and Hall shared office space with Peter Blow's brother-in-law Charles Edmund LaBeaume, just outside the zone of destruction. Harriet reminded her husband that they were indeed about God's business and testified to anyone who would listen that God had placed His protecting hand over them. Her "proof" was that neither their family nor the Blow's extended family lost any property in the fire, and notwithstanding the fact that fully one-tenth of the population of St. Louis died in the epidemic, not one of their family members was lost to cholera.

The large, domed chamber on the ground floor of the west side of the St. Louis courthouse was filled to capacity, despite the freezing temperatures and heavy snowfall. It was Friday, January 11th, 1850, and feelings were raw on both sides of the well-known case. A waist-high, semicircular mahogany railing separated the rostrum, clerk desks, jury, and counsel tables from the hundred pro- and anti-slavery advocates packed into the room. Judge Hamilton had sternly warned the audience that decorum would be maintained, and he positioned bailiffs around the hall to ensure that rabble-rousers would be hauled out immediately. With Alexander Field speaking, he needn't have worried.

The swarthy Kentuckian was a renowned orator, storyteller, poet, and singer who loved to quote verse to mesmerized juries. When he felt it would help turn them in his clients' favor, he would even sing. Born in Kentucky but reared in Illinois, Field had risen to political prominence and had served as the Illinois Secretary of State from 1829 to 1839. He had only lately relocated across the river to practice law in Missouri. With the exception of Irene Emerson, John Sanford, and their attorneys, everyone present that frosty morning was glad he did. They had expected theatre, and they were not disappointed.

Alexander Field had paused to let the names of Alexander Hamilton, Thomas Jefferson, and the words of the Declaration of Independence sink in. He walked to within a few feet of the jury platform and brought the steely glare of his gray eyes upon the jurors, then continued his opening argument.

"You men of the jury have just now sworn a solemn oath before God that you would 'well and truly try the matters in issue and a true verdict render according to the evidence and the law.'" He turned and pointed back to his clients. "This man and his wife have placed their trust in the Constitution and rule of law, and that trust extends to you men here today. John Adams proclaimed during that miracle at Philadelphia that this nation would be 'an empire of laws and not of men.' It is the law that is the bedrock of our republican form of government. And today, it is your sworn duty to put aside all your prior prejudices, personal experiences, and biases, and here fairly determine the facts, and to them apply the laws of this great nation and of the state of Missouri."

Field returned to the counsel table and stood behind his clients. "We are placing our trust today in a system of justice that is to the world a shining light upon a hill. That inspired process is embodied in you men." He placed both muscular hands on Dred's shoulders and continued, his voice rising for effect. "After hearing the evidence, we are confident that you will find, and have the courage to declare the self-evident truth, that this is a man within the meaning and intent of the Declaration of Independence to which Jefferson and fifty-five brave men mutually pledged 'our Lives, our Fortunes, and our sacred Honor.'"

No one in the courthouse stirred as all eyes were glued to the white puffs of air coming from Field's mouth. They could see how cold it was, but no one could deny the fire of his fervor. The great man strode up to the flags of the United States of America and State of Missouri.

"We are equally confident you will find that, although Dred and Harriet Scott were born in slavery under the laws of the states of their birth, under the laws of this nation and this great state of Missouri, they are now and forever free!"

A man in rough clothes leaped up and jeered, "Here in Missoura, them niggers is slaves!" Judge Hamilton rapped his gavel, and a beefy bailiff hauled the man out of the court. He continued to holler amidst jeers and cheers, "Them darkies is not people . . . they's animals . . . and y'all jury best not say different!"

A flurry of brown snow and icy wind blew in the courtroom as the bailiff pushed the man out into the street. Lawyers grabbed for papers, and the rest pulled on their coats and scarves.

"Order!" bellowed the judge. "Take your seats and remain quiet, or I will clear this courtroom! I want that man jailed for threatening the jury," he ordered Sheriff LaBeaume, who was exiting the door in pursuit.

The spell Field had cast over the room was gone, and he considered sitting down, but then noticed John Sanford lean back in his chair with a smug smile on his face, and his warrior spirit returned.

"If I may, Your Honor, I was not quite finished."

"Proceed," the judge huffed, staring out a warning to the crowd.

"Are we not grateful," Field stood squarely before the jury, "that we, among all nations of the earth, are not ruled by violence, threats, and fear? I thank God Almighty that we are a country of order! We are, I repeat, an empire of laws."

He moved quickly to the table as Attorney Hall handed him a thick legal tome. "The law is supreme." He held the book out and waved it toward the jury. "And the law of this nation, as set forth in the Northwest Ordinance and the Missouri Compromise, is that when a slave leaves a slave state and enters a free state or territory of the United States, he becomes free!" He slammed down the heavy volume, and several members of the jury flinched. Hall handed him three other fat leather books, which Field took in his large paws and hurried back to his audience. He waved them easily, as if they were mere pamphlets.

"This contains the laws as set forth and adjudicated over the years by the courts of the State of Missouri. And these cases have repeatedly, since before I was Illinois Secretary of State, and conclusively held—"

"Objection!" bellowed Irene Emerson's attorney, his chair legs screeching on the tiled floor as he rose. "Counsel is arguing."

"Yes, he is, Mr. Garland," Judge Hamilton replied, "and you shall have your turn. Continue, Mr. Field."

Dred and Harriet's advocate slapped the spines of the case reports in his hand several times while Hugh Garland, Esquire, sat and slowly and loudly dragged his chair back across the slate checkerboard floor.

"Since before you men were zipping up your own pantaloons," he continued to light laughter and smiles on the faces of the jurors, "the courts of this state have ruled that once a Negro goes to a state where he is free, and then returns to the slave state of Missouri, he is still free." Several abolitionists in the gallery applauded until a stern Judge Hamilton gaveled them to silence.

"That's the law, gentlemen. Once free, always free! And at the end of this trial, when you hear all the evidence and are instructed as to the law, you good and lawful men will find that Dred Scott is, and forever more shall remain, a free man."

He paused, pointed to Harriet, and repeated "At the end of this trial, you good and lawful men will rule that his wife, to whom he was legally married by the highest federal authority in Wisconsin Territory, is free! I am sure that at the end of this trial," he said in a smooth voice that exuded confidence as he moved to the railing and pointed at the Scott girls in the first row, "you good and lawful men will declare to the nation that Mr. and Mrs. Scott's two darling daughters, Eliza and Lizzie, are free."

He smiled at the two, and their wide grins confirmed that he was finally and forever on the Lord's side of this issue. He returned to the counsel table, then turned and pointed down at Irene Emerson, who slid lower in her seat under his withering gaze. Lastly," Field spoke firmly in a voice filled with condemnation, "I am confident that at the end of this trial, you good and lawful men will find that woman, Irene Sanford Emerson, guilty of beating, bruising, and unlawfully imprisoning these free citizens of Missouri!"

Emerson's lawyer, Hugh A. Garland, gave a brief, scholarly opening statement, claiming that the Northwest Ordinance disappeared with the ratification of the U.S. Constitution, and that the Missouri Compromise recognized the state's right to allow slavery within her borders. He then argued that the involuntary nature of Dr. Emerson's orders to frontier military posts in free states and territories made Missouri's "once free, always free" precedent inoperative.

It was clear that, while Garland's oral advocacy skills were eclipsed by those of Alexander Field, the Virginia transplant was his intellectual twin. Garland had served in the Virginia state assembly and was the Clerk of the U.S. House of Representatives during the Twenty-Sixth Congress. He was best known for his highly regarded, two-part biography of John Randolph of Virginia.

Alexander Field's co-counsel, David Hall, patted him on the back as Garland sat down and the judge ordered, "Mr. Field, call your first witness."

"This should be a walk in the park," Hall whispered. Field frowned slightly, not entirely sure if that was the case. He would soon learn that his colleague had sorely misjudged opposing counsel.

"Plaintiff calls Henry Taylor Blow."

Taylor entered from the hallway through the double doors, crossed the well, and walked up the three steps to the witness stand, which was between the judge's bench and the jury. After being sworn to tell the whole truth, he sat down in the comfortable leather chair, pivoted left in his seat, and nodded and smiled at the men of the jury as Field had instructed him to do.

"State your name for the record," the lawyer directed as he positioned himself so Taylor would be looking toward the jury as he responded to the direct examination.

"Henry Taylor Blow."

"Do you know the plaintiff, Dred Scott?"

"Yes, I do. He's sitting right over there with his wife, Harriet," Taylor responded, pointing at his friends.

"How long have you known Mr. Scott?"

"From my earliest recollection. When I was born in 1817 in Southampton County, Dred Scott was about seventeen years old, although back then he was called by the name of 'Sam.' He was a house slave owned by my father Peter Blow, but he was like a big brother to me, and sometimes even a father."

"Objection!" snarled Hugh Garland from his seat at the defendant's counsel table. "While I'm sure we are all deeply moved by the close personal relationship between the plaintiff and this witness, it is non-responsive to the question."

"Sustained," ruled the judge. "Mr. Blow, please limit your testimony to a direct response to the question. Oh, and Mr. Garland, please save your commentary for closing argument."

Taylor continued to reply to the easy direct examination, providing a chronology of the Blow family's life and travels, and ultimately testifying that his parents died shortly after moving to St. Louis. To pay debts, he told the jury, the family sold the plaintiff to Dr. John Emerson, who was an officer and surgeon in the United States Army, and was taken by him up north. Judge Hamilton sustained Garland's objection to any further answer as to where Emerson and Scott went, on the grounds of speculation and hearsay.

"Let me conclude this examination with a few questions about the defendant, Mrs. Emerson," Field prompted his witness. "Do you have any direct knowledge that Irene Emerson owned Dred after the passing of her late husband?"

"Objection, calls for speculation."

"You may answer if you have personal knowledge, Mr. Blow," the judge responded.

"I saw Mrs. Emerson treat Dred and Harriet as if they were her property. She would order them about, and on one occasion I personally offered to buy them from her, and she declined, saying—"

"Objection, Your Honor," thundered Garland. "Hearsay!"

"Yes, it is clearly hearsay, Your Honor," responded Field, "but Mr. Blow is about to testify to an admission by a party opponent and therefore covered by exceptions to hearsay rule."

"Overruled. The witness may proceed."

Dred had been to court many times with Peter Blow, and he had a substantial layman's understanding of the judicial system, but this was the first trial he had ever attended, and he found much of it exciting, notwithstanding the constant legal wrangling. He didn't understand most of the discussion surrounding the repeated objections by Missus Irene's lawyer, and he wasn't alone in that ignorance.

Most of the audience, including the jury, had no idea what the judges and lawyers were talking about, and they started to feel that, with all the objections, the defendant's lawyer was trying to hide something. This was a result the skilled trial lawyer, Field, was counting on.

Taylor continued. "I was about to say that when I offered to buy the Scotts from the defendant, she screamed that they were her property, that her husband had left them to her and their daughter in his will, and by darn, she was going to keep them and pass them on to her daughter as her property."

Field paused and turned to face the jury when he asked his last question. "Did Mrs. Emerson ever beat or abuse the Scotts?"

"Objection!" Both Emerson counsel jumped to their feet, shouting.

"Argumentative!" argued Norris.

"Speculation!" shouted Garland.

"Hearsay!" blustered both in unison.

"Dad-blame it," cursed someone from the gallery. "Shut up and let the man answer!"

"Bailiff, put that man in jail!" boomed Hamilton, drowning out the sound of his gavel. He stood up and leaned over the bench. "I have warned you all. He is in contempt of the court, and anyone else who speaks out will spend the night with him in the calaboose!"

The judge waited until the latest offender was escorted out. "Now, Mr. Fields, I trust your witness has personal knowledge to be able to answer your last question?"

"Yes, Your Honor," he replied, smiling at the bright red faces of his two adversaries across the room.

"Continue," the judge sighed.

"On the fourth day of April, 1846, my siblings and I gave $1500 to Dred and Harriet to buy their freedom. When they hadn't returned by mid-day of the fifth, we went to the plantation of Mrs. Emerson's father, Alexander Sanford, God rest his soul."

"You couldn't care less about my father's soul," hissed John Sanford from his seat next to his sister.

His lawyer grabbed him and whispered in his ear as Judge Hamilton gave one stark crack of the gavel. "My warning applies to the parties. Mr. Garland, control your client!"

"We went to the plantation and confronted Mrs. Emerson, who, after some heated argument, pulled our money from a drawer and shoved it into my hands. She repeated that she would not sell her darkies, and they would remain locked up in her fruit cellar until they learned their place. Sheriff LaBeaume and the attorney Murdoch eventually convinced her to release them, and when I opened the door to the cellar, Dred and Harriet came out. They had cuts and bruises on them, and Dred's fingers appeared broken."

"Thank you, no further questions," Field concluded.

Taylor began to rise, but the defendant's attorney beat him to his feet. "I have a few questions, Mr. Blow, if you don't mind." He signaled to the witness to sit back down, then launched into an aggressive cross-examination.

"So you owned the slave Dred Scott while living in the state of Missouri?"

"No, my father did."

"But after your father died, you and your family inherited him, is that not so?"

"Well, I guess you could say that," responded Taylor, scooting to the edge of his chair.

"I'm not on the witness stand, Mr. Blow. You are," replied the lawyer. "I'm asking if you could say that. Let me repeat. Did you inherit the slave Sam Blow, who later changed his name to Dred Scott?"

"Yes."

"And you didn't offer to free him, did you?"

"Um . . . no. We didn't."

"That's because he was valuable property, and your family was in debt, right?"

"Now, wait a minute. You're putting words in my mouth. I never considered Dred to be my property—he was my friend," Taylor responded defensively.

"Oh, so you're telling these jurors, then, that you sell your friends to pay off your debts?"

"Objection, argumentative!" Alexander Field interrupted to try to buy his witness time to recoup his composure. He caught Taylor Blow's eye and signaled him to relax.

"Sustained," the judge responded. "Please rephrase the question, Mr. Garland."

"Withdrawn. How much did Dr. Emerson pay your family for your slave Dred Scott?"

"I think it was about five hundred dollars," Taylor answered in a soft voice, feeling a deep shame pass over him. He looked at Dred, whose eyes were downcast. He looked at the jury and saw *hypocrite* written in the eyes of those who met his gaze.

"And did you use that money to pay debt, or did you use it to buy yourself a fine black horse?"

"Objection!"

"Overruled!"

"We used it to pay off my father's debts!" Taylor spat out without further prompting.

"But you would deny little fatherless Henrietta Emerson the same right by asking this court to forcibly deprive her of her property rights. Is that correct?"

Taylor paused and remembered his pre-trial preparation. "No, that's not correct. Her father deprived her of that right by taking Dred to free states and territories."

"Oh, how convenient for you, sir," Garland smirked, then added, "Withdrawn," as the Scotts' attorney began to rise. He sat back down.

"One more question," Garland casually remarked as Taylor began to slip out of a seat grown uncomfortably warm. "Were you present the night your father tied your slave Scott to a tree in your backyard a few blocks from this courthouse, and stripped his flesh from his writhing body with a horse-whip?"

"Objection!" shouted an obviously surprised Alexander Field as he sent his own chair screeching across the slate floor. But for the first time, he was unable to articulate a basis for the objection. He looked at Taylor Blow sunk in his chair, his head in his hands.

"Your grounds for objecting, counsel?" Hamilton inquired.

Field was in shock. He had not been told the senior Blow had whipped Dred. "Badgering the witness," he muttered.

"Denied. Answer the question, Mr. Blow."

Taylor cleared his throat and wiped his eyes, his heart breaking at the recollection of that night. The only sound in the courtroom was the wind rattling the large windows. "It wasn't a horse-whip," he finally croaked. "It was a tree branch, and I tried to stop him."

"So it was a tree branch that tore the flesh from his chest?" a triumphant Garland inquired. "Just like the one Mrs. Emerson allegedly used to spank the Scotts. And who, might I ask, fetched the rope?"

Taylor looked up at the stout inquisitor, wondering how he could possibly know the details of that night. He looked at his older brother Peter behind the bar. Peter's teary eyes met his gaze and then he looked away in shame. "I did," Taylor lied in a whisper.

"I'm sorry; I don't believe the court reporter heard your answer." The energized barrister couldn't help twisting the knife in the discredited witness.

"I did," Taylor repeated, looking straight ahead.

"No further questions for this witness, Your Honor."

"Fifteen minute recess," ordered the judge and rapped the gavel, the stark sound echoing around the hushed chamber.

For the next several hours, the Scotts' attorneys paraded witnesses to the stand who testified of their knowledge of the ownership of the Scotts by Dr. Emerson.

Miles Clark testified that he knew Emerson at Fort Armstrong on Rock Island, which was part of the free state of Illinois, and that Dred Scott was Emerson's slave. Under cross-examination, he admitted he was aware that Captain Emerson was stationed at the fort under orders from the War Department and that Scott was considered to be an official striker for the doctor, assisting him in his military and medical duties.

Catherine Anderson, the former wife of Lt. Thompson, and Major A.D. Stuart, who had been paymaster at Fort Snelling, both stated under oath that they knew Emerson and that Dred and Harriet were both slaves owned by him. At times when the doctor was away to other posts downriver, the Scotts were hired out as slaves to other officers at the fort. Mrs. Anderson initially denied that the Scotts, as free Negroes under territorial law, could have left the fort at any time, saying that they were always the hired servants of other officers when Emerson was away. She had to admit it seemed that the Scotts voluntarily remained in the employ of others.

Major Stuart acknowledged that Emerson was at the post in Wisconsin Territory under Army orders, which he was required to obey as an Army officer. He also revealed under Garland's relentless inquisition that the United States Army paid Captain Emerson a stipend for Dred Scott's services, despite the general knowledge and acknowledgment that he was a slave.

Army Captain Thomas Gray testified as an expert witness that Fort Armstrong was located within a free state and that Fort Snelling was within a free territory pursuant to the Northwest Ordinance and Missouri Compromise. He could not answer the question by Irene Emerson's lawyer as to how the U.S. government justified paying money to the owner of a slave for that slave's services while said slave was residing in a free state and a free territory.

John F. Carter testified that he was on the steamboat *Gypsy* north of the state of Missouri the night the child Eliza Scott was born, and Colonel Plympton from Jefferson Barracks told the jury that Dr. Emerson's widow hired Dred out to her brother-in-law Captain Bainbridge. He admitted under cross-examination that he had knowledge that the Scott's second daughter Lizzie was born at the barracks and was made to repeat the obvious—that said post was located within the slave state of Missouri.

At that answer, Harriet nearly fainted with worry that perhaps even if the law mandated that she, Dred, and Eliza were free, her precious baby Lizzie might by law be deemed a slave and subject to the whims of an agitated and vengeful master.

Her other attorney, Lyman Norris, calmed her fears as he whispered that, with this family, it was all or nothing, for if the jury found that the law kept them free when they returned to Missouri, Lizzie was born the child of free Negroes and inherited the status of her mother.

As the long day drew to a close, the judge ordered a recess for the lighting of more coal oil lamps. A dark haze filled the shallow dome as the last few witnesses took the stand.

Thomas O. Flaherty, who owned a boat and supply store in town, testified on direct examination that John Sanford, acting as an agent for his sister, had brought Dred and Harriet to his store and offered to hire them out at a very cheap price, saying that the two were lazy and shiftless slaves and were apt to cause trouble. Of course, he declined to hire them.

The two penultimate witnesses were the ones whose confusing testimony had resulted in the earlier verdict against the Scotts, Samuel and Adeline Russell, who owned the Russell and Bennett Store on Fourth Street. This time they got it right. Mrs. Russell explained that, as bookkeeper and store manager, she had dealt directly with Mrs. Emerson in hiring her slaves to work in the store. Samuel testified that he paid their rent directly to Irene Emerson or her brother John Sanford, acting as her agent.

On cross-examination, however, he stumbled again and admitted he wasn't exactly sure, when he handed payment to John

Sanford, if John was acting as agent of his sister or whether he was their owner.

It had been a long day that began dramatically, and Alexander Field strategically wanted it to end the same way before they recessed for the evening to prepare their final closing arguments, which would begin the following morning.

"The plaintiff's final witness will be Dr. Ernest Watts." An audible sigh of relief spread through the crowded room as the congregation thought appreciatively of the approaching opportunity to stretch their stiff muscles and warm their backsides before a fireplace.

"Please state your name and occupation."

"Doctor of Medicine Ernest Watts," began the witness with a backwoods accent. "I treat patients of all races and socio-economic status at my clinic on the north side of Green Street, below Third Avenue. I'm what some call a 'country doc,'" he finished proudly.

"Very good. Thank you, Doctor." Field continued signaling toward his clients. "Have you had occasion to care for the plaintiffs Dred and Harriet Scott?"

"Yes indeed," he replied, opening a black ledger book. He pulled a pair of reading spectacles from his vest pocket, balanced them precariously on his blunt nose, and thumbed through the pages. "Here," he declared, stabbing his finger into a page. "On the fifth of April, 1846, I examined and treated Dred and Harriett Scott for multiple contusions and abrasions, and it says I set two broken phalanges . . . er . . . fingers . . . on Mr. Scott's left hand." He snapped the book closed and looked up at the attorney, then over at the Scotts. "Yes, I remember, it was them two sitting over yonder at the table." He waved. "Howdy, sir . . . ma'am!"

Dred and Harriet smiled and waved back, and the tension seemed to finally leak out of the room at the genuineness of this man.

"Did you speak with them at the time of treatment?" inquired the lawyer.

"Oh yes, but of course. To best treat them, I needed to know the mechanism of their injury, and so I asked them."

"And what did they tell you?"

Hugh Garland began to rise to lodge another hearsay objection, but knew it would be overruled as statement necessary for medical treatment. He believed he already had enough for his closing arguments and plenty of grounds for an appeal, should the case go against his clients. He eased back into his chair.

"Mr. Scott told me their injuries were inflicted by his missus, who beat them with a tree branch." He paused and reopened up the book to the page he had marked. "Mr. Scott's injuries included a large abrasion with ecchymosis . . . bruising . . . across his neck and back, and the broken left phalanges I referenced earlier. Mrs. Scott was suffering from abrasion and ecchymosis, with possible rib fractures under her right arm. She had bled extensively from several wounds, but the blood had coagulated some hours earlier, and I recall having to carefully tear her blouse away, for it had become stuck to her side. Unfortunately that reopened her wounds." He paused and looked back at the counsel table, removing his glasses. "I'm sorry that I hurt you, Mrs. Scott," he tenderly apologized.

Harriet smiled back at the kind doctor, while the judge hesitated in admonishing the witness. He ultimately decided that the rules of decorum were sacrosanct in his courtroom, and so, in his friendliest tone stated, "Doctor, please direct your responses to counsel only."

He immediately regretted his decision when the doctor turned to him. "Oh, my dear, honorable judge. I am so sorry. I meant no disrespect."

"No further questions," Field declared as a happy chuckle spread around the room.

"Cross-examination?" asked Judge Hamilton, suggesting the answer he hoped for with his tone. He wasn't disappointed.

"None, your honor," replied Garland.

"Plaintiffs rest," concluded the Scotts' attorney.

Hamilton nearly employed his gavel when he heard a hushed "huzzah" from somewhere in the gallery. But he demurred, feeling much the same way.

"Mr. Garland, I will continue this trial for another hour to accommodate your first witness."

Both of the defendants' attorneys rose together. As lead counsel, Hugh Garland addressed the judge while looking deliberately at the jury. "We do not believe that the plaintiffs have come close to proving their case, and so we do not feel the need to call any witnesses in this matter, Your Honor."

Alexander Field made to object to this premature and clearly impermissible argument to the jury, but when he saw a couple of jurors sigh with relief, he held his tongue.

"Very well then, counsel will be in my chambers at eight of the morning to go over jury instructions. Doors to the gallery will be open at that time, and we will commence closing arguments promptly at nine. I will caution the jurors to refrain from discussing today's testimony with each other, or anyone else, for that matter, and direct you to inform me in the morning if anyone tries to talk with you about the case." He looked slowly about the room to make sure his instructions were overheard. "Anyone who attempts to speak with the jurors will be jailed! Hearing adjourned." He banged down the gavel, and loud huzzahs filled the chamber as people rushed to the doors.

Dred and Harriet didn't move. They were too worried about the course of events. They looked at their advocate, who was putting books and papers into his leather case. Their fate was in his hands—or better said, his voice—and they could tell he felt the full weight of that responsibility. As the Scotts' girls ran up to them, Alexander Pope Field buckled the strap on his valise and smiled down at his trusting clients.

"It went well today," he comforted them as he ran a hand through his thick hair, which had fallen onto his forehead during the day's battle, taking long enough to control his voice to hide his own uncertainty. "They tried to sully our witnesses, but none of the cross-examination left questions in the jurors' minds as to credibility. We got our facts out, and so did they. The case will be decided now on two things: the jury instructions we will argue over in the morning, and the strength of closing arguments. I hope I don't sound too haughty when I say that I love closing, and I'm actually pretty good at it." His laughter brought the comfort his words lacked.

The Scotts laughed too, and bundled up their two treasures. As they headed for the doors along the half-circle banister, Harriet stretched up on her toes to try to reach her tall lawyer's cheek. "May I?" she asked the man, who, in a prior life had advocated in support of slavery, had come completely around to the opposite view, but had never touched a black woman.

"By all means." He did not hesitate.

Harriet kissed his bony cheek, and then whispered in his ear. "Thank you, and don't worry, I will be prayin' all night and all day tomorrow that you will speak with the voice of an angel."

The rugged lawyer laughed heartily as he opened the door to the outside cold. In that prior life, he was also renowned for his prodigious drinking and carousing, and he was certain no one had ever imagined using the word "angel" to describe him.

He had to admit, as he crunched through the snow toward home, that he just might take a liking to the new and improved Alexander Pope Field.

But first he had to convince a white jury—consisting of six current slave owners and three who had slave owners in their families—that his two black clients were entitled to their freedom in the slave battleground state of Missouri.

Roger Taney

Chapter 33

But Not His Chain

St. Louis, Missouri, 1850

The snow stopped falling, and the sun shone brightly through the frigid air as a packed courtroom waited for the second day of *Scott v. Emerson* to begin. The spectator gallery was full by eight o'clock, and several hundred interested citizens milled about outside the west steps, bundled up in heavy winter clothes and blankets. This was just one in a series of freedom suits held for over a decade in the St. Louis courthouse, but the state of Missouri was of late being split open over the issue of slavery. This trial was at the crossroads of clear battle lines between the "old" pro-slavery elite of the city, represented by the Choteaus/Sanfords, and the "new" abolitionist progressives, exemplified by the extended Blow family. Adding to the excitement were the renowned legal gladiators doing battle for each side.

The city and county had provided extra police presence outside and inside the courtroom, which kept most of the brawling to heated verbal exchanges. With an officer or bailiff stationed between each of the pillars around the courtroom, conversation was hushed as the assembly waited for the trial to recommence. Dred and Harriet held hands at their table, and Irene Emerson and John Sanford at theirs. Sanford continually glared at the Scotts, who turned their backs and prayed. The muffled voices of the lawyers and Judge Hamilton could be heard coming from his private chambers. From time to time, the deep sound of Alexander Field's voice rumbled through the walls, and it was obvious the war had recommenced over the proposed jury instructions proffered by each side.

Nine o'clock came and went, and the sound of legal wrangling had muted, but no one appeared through the chamber doors. The level of conversation picked up within the courtroom as the masses grew impatient, and despite the glowering men in uniform, threats, epithets, and curses began to erupt between the different factions.

Suddenly a piercing call in a high-pitched voice came from somewhere outside. The room quieted as all ears tuned to the strange, repetitive sound of a loud salesman hawking his wares. People found themselves trying to guess what was being sold, so unique was the cry. It didn't sound like the newsies or blade sharpeners, not the milk vendor, calling "Milk, fresh milk!" It wasn't the fishmonger shouting, "Fresh fish fit for the pan!" or the common, "Oysters, oysters, fresh from the pot, oyster, oysters, get 'em while they're hot!"

Several people shushed those who were still talking.

The voice outside was sharp and filled with derision, and cheers and jeers punctuated the air after each loud cry, which had a sing-song cadence to it. Every few moments, the crack of a hammer shot through the thin air, and people looked to see if Judge Hamilton's gavel was still up on his bench.

A gust of cold wind suddenly burst through the entry leading into the rotunda as someone opened the doors to the east steps on the other side of the courthouse, carrying with it the clear cry, "Bid 'em in, get 'em in!"

Everyone instantly recognized the call of the auctioneer, and the next words sent a chill through the hearts of all but the most ardent pro-slavery advocates in the room.

"Give me a bid. What will you give me? She's young, and take a look at them hips—she'll make a dern good breeder!" Not a word was spoken as the auction echoed through the rotunda and shot like a bullets into the room with each rap of the hammer.

"I'm looking for four. Anyone give me four-fifty? That's a bargain, folks, a bargain. How about five?"

"Pappy, what's goin' on outside?" the sweet, pure voice of eleven-year-old Eliza Scott called out.

Dred left his chair to go to his daughter. Peter Blow jumped up and shoved his way through the crowd to try to get to the door.

The auctioneer was revved up, and his offer sped forward. "She's good in the field and has house skills, too. Strip her down and look her over. She's plenty full up front and has decent teeth. What am I bid? Come on, let me hear them bids."

CRACK!

Dred knelt and extended his arms through the bars of the railing to bring his fast-maturing child close. Peter reached the double doors, stretched wide, and pulled them shut—but not before the final, terrible words passed through.

"Wipe off those tears, girl. Don't pay her no mind, men. Just give her a good whippin' and she'll fall into place. Six! Six-fifty, you gotta be faster than that. Seven is the bid, gonna let her go. And we're goin', goin', gone! Now, let's see who else we got."

CRACK!

The door to the judge's chamber flew open and hit the wall as the Honorable Alexander Hamilton hurried in, the lawyers right behind his flowing black robes.

"All rise!" the chief bailiff commanded.

Judge Hamilton made himself comfortable in his high wing-back chair and looked out over the audience. Bright white flooded the room from the large windows on each side of the bench. He wondered why the crowd was so subdued, and thought he even saw a number of the womenfolk crying into their white handkerchiefs.

All present remained standing as the jury was led in, and Dred, back at the counsel table, wondered if they had heard the auction from wherever they had been sequestered. He dearly hoped they had.

"Ladies and gentlemen," Judge Hamilton began. "Let me repeat my admonitions on courtroom decorum, although I must congratulate you all on your demeanor thus far. Feelings are high on both sides of this issue, but this is a court of law where passion and prejudice are replaced with reason and fact. Now then, is counsel ready to proceed? Very well, Mr. Fields."

The Scotts' powerful advocate rose and strode to the jury platform. "As I promised you yesterday, we have presented more than sufficient eye-witness testimony to establish beyond any doubt that the facts are such that the law requires you to do your duty. That duty is to declare Irene Emerson guilty of vile acts that, while, sadly, would have been lawful had they been committed by her against her slaves, but were, in this instance, unlawful, for Dred and Harriet Scott were, by the laws of these United States and the State of Missouri, free!"

Fields articulated point by point the facts and testimony that established the Scotts were no longer slaves: they had been taken against their will by their masters to free states and territories where their legal status had become that of free Negroes; Eliza had been born on the Mississippi River outside any slave state and therefore born free; they were all three returned to Missouri and, because of the law of the land, their freedom followed them.

"Now you must understand, gentlemen," the skilled barrister continued, wanting to make sure that each man truly did understand his reasoning, "that the Scotts did not know they were free. And because they did not know, they could not, and they did not, voluntarily consent to reenter slavery. Which of you, I might ask, would knowingly and willing submit yourself to be the property of another man? "They did not know!" Fields reiterated. "They thought themselves the property of Dr. Emerson, and subsequently his wife, the defendant. So they did not run. They did not hide. They submitted themselves to the law as they understood it. They had a multitude of opportunities to flee to freedom. Their master left them in a free land. Canada was very close. The vast open plains and western wilderness rolled out in front of them as they walked hand in hand amongst the prairie wildflowers in Wisconsin Territory. They could have kept walking and never looked back. Wouldn't you?"

He saw one man nod ever so slightly and another man gulp. The adrenaline surged as he knew they were coming along. He continued to weave his story.

"Dred and Harriet traveled up and down the mighty Mississippi many times without their master to keep them in check. He trusted them. They rode upon the waters of a river that thousands, if not millions, of their people considered the powerful embodiment of their spiritual River Jordan. They were obedient to what they understood to be the law; notwithstanding it was a law that kept them in bondage and servitude; a law that drove their very humanness into the ground. Their baby was born in freedom, but they did not know."

Field looked at each of the men he knew from the jury selection process to be fathers, and continued his remarks directly to each of them.

"Remember back on the day your first child was born. Feel the joy and the pride and the hope you wished on your child for the future. Now try to imagine how that joy would be tarred by the thought that the only future your child would have was one of slavery, poverty, degradation, assault, and sorrow. Dred Scott felt the same way you did when Eliza was born." He turned and pointed to the bright-eyed youth, her soft black curls pulled into pig-tails on each side of her smiling face. "Dred hoped beyond hope that she had a future. He did not consider hurrying her away in the dark of night when the steamboat *Gypsy* docked on the shores of free Illinois, Iowa, or Wisconsin. But he did plan for that future. You see, he had heard of the case of a slave who had given birth to a daughter at Fort Snelling, and thereafter had returned to this state and this very courtroom and won her freedom. Oh, did he and Harriet ever plan. They talked and they planned during the long, cold northern nights, rocking their baby by the warmth of their tiny stove. They planned as they watched the stars pass overhead as they moved down the river. And on many a warm night under the southern sky near Mexico, alone and yearning to be with his pregnant wife as she approached childbirth, Dred pictured this courthouse and these great pillars of justice and this bar and this bench!" He caressed the polished corner of the judge's extended podium with his left hand. He continued, his voice rising in waves of passion. "Dred dreamed of justice, gentlemen. He thought of equal access to all the great blessings that freedom in America offered to everyone whose skin was white; a freedom that white men had fought and bled for; a freedom for which he had fought and bled at Craney Island during the War of 1812. Yes, kind sirs, he bled. And his blood was exactly the same shade of red as the blood of all the sons of Virginia who paid the ultimate sacrifice that day for freedom."

Everyone in the courtroom was mesmerized by the show, and it just kept getting better. Their entertainer pointed across the room to the American flag. "Dred's blood, which soaked into the sand that day, was the same shade of red as the stripes on that flag, the flag that still flew above Fort McHenry during that same war, and which inspired Francis Scott Key to write the words we all know so well, when he saw through the early morning light and the clearing smoke after a terrible long night of cannon and rocket fire. That star-spangled banner that still flew over . . . what?" he asked, and then watched as a few jurors' lips moved silently with his own, "over 'the land of the *free*, and the home of the brave!' Dred walked away from the battle and that war with a sure knowledge. He was a man! His contribution was equal to that of the other men who fought in the war. From that day forward, through danger and challenges, loss and horrible ill treatment at the hands of a man he loved and next to whom he had faced the redcoats, he never stopped dreaming and planning that, somehow, he would be free, and others would finally come to see and acknowledge what he knew—he was a man!"

Alexander Field walked backward until he stood directly in front of John Sanford and started to tap his right finger on the counsel table. He looked at Sanford's scornful scowl, then back at the jury. "Dred wanted to be free, and that desire became a burning passion when he became a husband and a father and had his girls to protect. But Dred refused to take the easier path of hatred, violence, and unlawfulness." He paused and looked back sternly at Sanford, and then at Irene Emerson. "No, he detested violence and mourned with all America when his former childhood playmate, Nat Turner, chose to follow the devil and murder innocents in his quest for freedom. In moments of fear and anger and despair, even as his flesh was being torn from his body, he closed his eyes and pictured not revenge, but rather, the pillars of justice he had passed through to enter many a courthouse."

The lawyer moved up near the railing enclosing the court clerks' desks and reached for the bronze statue on the judge's dais. "May I, Your Honor?" he asked. Hamilton nodded, and Field hefted the heavy figurine of a woman dressed in Greek robes with a sword in her right hand and scales in her left. He returned to the jury and held her out to them.

"When Dred thought of freedom for the women he loved, he thought of this woman."

"Objection," Emerson's counsel threw out. "Arguing facts not in evidence."

"If I may be afforded some literary license in my closing statement, Your Honor?"

Anxious to hear the rest of the story, the judge overruled the objection. Some of the women in the audience pictured the handsome attorney in the toga of a Roman senator as if speaking in the ancient Forum itself.

"Her name is Themis, the Greek goddess of law and justice. The sword, which represents the might of the law, is down, and she holds aloft the balanced scales, which signify 'equal justice under law.' Dred Scott waited and toiled and prayed for this day. He comes to you, not asking anything more than to be treated fairly and to have his claim of freedom adjudicated by you under the laws of this state and these United States."

He returned the statuette to the bench and walked over to his counsel table. "Now, how did we get to this sacred hall of justice, immortalized in marble and bronze for centuries? Dred and Harriet submitted unknowingly, blindly obedient to the woman they believed to own them, Irene Emerson. When she rented them to the Russells, they went where they were told and did the work they were ordered to do. They, of course, were not paid for their labors. Mrs. Emerson, their mistress, was. When she hired Dred out to her brother-in-law, Captain Bainbridge, and he took him away to the border of Mexico, Dred went along uncomplaining, even though his wife was great with child. But when Dred Scott returned and was handed his new squalling baby girl, and he looked at his growing beauty he affectionately called 'Gypsy,' he knew the time for action was at hand, but still wasn't sure how he could access the courts for his freedom. Despite the fact that he had labored his entire life, he had not one red cent to call his own. And lawyers are expensive. Well, at least the ones sitting at that table are," he chuckled, pointing at the defendants. A comfortable laughed filled the hall and the jury box.

Field strode over to the bar behind his own table and reached out to shake Taylor and Peter Blow's hands. He sat against the railing and continued in a loud voice so every juror could feel his words. "Then one day these good people came along, honorable citizens of this fair city, feeling perhaps some guilt at the past, but knowing only one thing: they loved Dred Scott. They loved him despite the color of his skin. They loved him and respected him despite his legal status. They wanted, perhaps, to atone for centuries of slave ownership by the Blows of Virginia, but they loved Dred and wanted him to be free precisely because of a family history of love, kindness, and acceptance of their colored servants. And so they pooled their resources, appealed to their relatives, friends, and associates in the legal profession, and thereby opened the doors of this courthouse to a man who could not open them by himself!"

He rose and returned to the middle of the well, and summed up his argument while grasping both lapels in his hands. "Like the great founding declaration that set this nation on the path of liberty, the self-evident truth that all men are created equal, freedom, to Dred and Harriet Scott, is right now still theoretical. It is up to you twelve good and lawful men to make equality, and their freedom, a self-evident reality. If you find—and find you must, as you consider the evidence we have presented—that the Scotts became free in the north, and by law were free when they returned, but nevertheless were treated as slaves, rented out like draft horses for money, and physically abused and imprisoned by Irene Scott, then you must find her guilty and declare Dred, Harriet, Eliza, and Lizzie Scott henceforth and forever, free!"

More than half the audience broke into cheers and applause until a rather somber Judge Hamilton gaveled them back to order.

It was Hugh Garland's turn, and he got right to business. He rose, clapping softly, and continued to clap as he strolled toward the jury, keeping a watchful eye on the judge. "I applaud my opponent's mesmerizing theatric performance. I would call for an encore, but I fear we would be here until the Sabbath." Only a few people chuckled at his joke. He shrugged and pushed ahead. Passion, brilliant elocution, and emotional plucking at one's heart-strings are well and good for the theatre, but this is a court of law, and when you strip away the rhetoric to the cold, bare bones of the facts, you see that the plaintiffs have not proven their case. Remember, the burden is on them to tip the scales of justice in their favor with the greatest weight of the evidence. They have failed to do so. Not only that, but the true facts force that scale firmly down on the side of the defendant, Mrs. Irene Emerson. I will be brief and to the point—I'm sure you will appreciate it.

"First, the oh-so-noble Blow family was fine with Dred Scott being their slave, and stood silently by while he was nearly murdered by their father after Scott did try to take matters in his own hands and became a runaway and a fugitive. They were happy he was their slave so they could sell him when they needed money. Tsk, tsk," he said, looking at the family stretched out behind the bar.

"Second, when they sold him to Dr. Emerson, Dred became his lawful property under the laws of the United States and the State of Illinois." The scholar was on a roll.

"Third, Captain John Emerson was ordered by the War Department of the United States of America to leave Missouri and take up a post at Fort Armstrong, and later Fort Snelling. He did not voluntarily remove his slave to a free state and territory. He had no choice but to follow orders and go wherever his country needed him most.

"Fourth, as a United States citizen, Captain Emerson had the Constitutional right to take his lawful property with him. That included his property Dred Scott.

"Fifth, as an Army officer, he was also entitled to have his orderly, or striker, accompany him. It was written in his orders.

"Sixth, the United States Army paid to Captain Emerson, as part of his regular salary, a stipend for the service of his slave, thereby proving that the United States government considered Dred Scott a slave, even while he lived and worked for them at federal outposts in states and territories declared free by that self-same government. They did not free Dred Scott. They paid his master." Garland paused again to let his reason sink in, and he thought it had when he saw the expressions of the jurors. He knew the slave owners on the jury wanted any excuse to rule against the Scotts, and he was giving them all that, and more.

"Let me give you a relevant illustration as to the absurdity of the plaintiffs' argument. Suppose Congress should pass a law declaring that the keeping of black horses, a species of property existing in Missouri and recognized by the constitution of the United States and of Missouri, 'shall be and the same is hereby prohibited in the territory of Utah.' The same government that passes the law through the executive department orders an officer, who unfortunately owns a black horse that he can neither sell, loose, nor give away, to the territory of Utah, and he takes with him his said horse—I admit that the horse, if there were horse abolitionists there, would get his freedom in Utah—but when he comes back here and asks you to give him up, would you do it? This is perhaps a strong and coarse illustration, but is it not a case in point? Finally, therefore, because neither Dred, nor Harriet, nor their offspring were ever recognized to be free while outside the state of Missouri, they most certainly cannot now come back to this state and thumb their noses at our laws and the national law embodied in the Missouri Compromise that admitted this state into the Union as a slave state. Your only possible verdict in this matter, gentlemen, is this: never free, always slaves!"

He returned to his table and stood behind his client. "Mrs. Emerson's actions in disciplining her slaves were not unreasonable and certainly not unlawful. The law allows a man to take a stick to an errant dog or a whip to an unruly horse. Doing so might offend the sensibilities of some, but I know many in this room who have taken a switch to their dear little ones' britches. Furthermore, it seems odd that the saintly Blows would look down their long noses at my client when they themselves were parties to much worse treatment of the same. Hell, Taylor Blow there even supplied the rope. Let's see, lock a person overnight in the fruit cellar—with plenty of preserves, I presume—versus tying him to a tree. You decide which is worse." Garland flashed a smug smile at a stoic Alexander Field.

"Furthermore, Irene Emerson lawfully utilized her property for the benefit of her fatherless daughter Henrietta. That is a right that is hers as a citizen of Missouri. It is a right many of you share. Do not deprive her of her rights. I can quote the Declaration of Independence too, Mr. Field, and it says there that God himself granted Mrs. Emerson the unalienable right to the 'pursuit of happiness,' which many, including the great John Randolph, of whom I am the biographer," he couldn't help adding before finishing, "historically interpreted as meaning the right to 'property.' Your only possible verdict, gentlemen, is 'not guilty!'"

The gifted and experienced barrister Alexander Pope Field recognized the brilliance of the underestimated Hugh Garland's legal strategy, and he was worried. He believed that if the jurors would listen to the judge's instructions they had hammered out that morning, and understood them, they would have to find for his clients. But jury instructions were notoriously complicated and too legalistic for most laymen, and right now, he didn't place a lot of faith in a positive outcome.

"Mr. Field, you are entitled to a final closing rebuttal. Do you wish to proceed?"

"One moment, Your Honor," he stalled, then leaned over in conversation with his colleague Lyman Norris, who would be the lead appellate attorney, regardless of who won at trial. He then whispered to his clients, and when they nodded, he rose to his feet.

"A few final words, thank you, Judge Hamilton." He then returned to his audience, his students. He'd had them once and had now lost them. He would need all his expertise to pull this off. He glanced back toward the counsel table and saw Harriet wink. And perhaps he would need a little help from Harriet's God, he acknowledged to himself.

"On behalf of my clients, the Dred Scott family, I want to thank you for your time and attention. As a man who chose the law as a profession and the courtroom as an office, I personally want to thank you for willingly doing your public duty in serving here today. You have heard all the facts on both sides of this issue and will soon retire to deliberate. As you do so, please remember that the only facts you need concern yourselves with are those which are relevant to the legal question which has brought us together. Those legal questions will become clear when Judge Hamilton shortly reads you a set of instructions in the law. I'm sure His Honor will do an admirable job of trying to make them sound interesting, but sadly, they are rather dry. But it is critically important to the interests of justice that you pay close attention and then apply the relevant facts you will receive from him to the law. Those facts are simply these: Dred Scott was a slave. He was taken to a free state, became free, and returned to a slave state where he was mistreated as a slave by Irene Emerson. That's it. Apply those facts to the law you will hear, and you will do the right thing. Thank you again, and may God bless you in fulfilling your sworn duty."

He turned and started to walk back to the table, but he paused when he felt a tingling sensation pass from the crown of his head through his body. Suddenly a thought popped into his head, and a still, small voice, as it were, whispered to his soul. He had often recited poetry from memory in his trials, and one about slavery came instantly back to mind; but how to employ it, he wondered. He did not know that earlier that day, these twelve men had been huddled in a room on the other side of the courthouse with a window facing east. They heard every awful word of the auctioneer merchandizing in slaves on the steps just outside the doors, and they had all peeked out the window as a fifteen-year-old girl was stripped, fondled, humiliated, and sold while they waited to be called by the judge to adjudicate the case of *Scott v. Emerson*. If he had known, he wouldn't have wondered nor hesitated.

"Mr. Field, please take your seat, if you are finished," the judge ordered.

"Wait," he spun around. "I'm not finished. I forgot something. I apologize, please bear with me." He returned to the jurors.

"I know half of you currently own slaves, and it must be very hard for you as you consider how you might have treated them, and how important they might be to your professions and livelihoods. The majority of you come from slave-owning families, and all have experiences. Please know that, whatever your decision today, we do not judge you. Look at my clients. Dred and Harriet Scott do not judge you. They trust you as human beings—even with the frailties and imperfections we all have—to do the best you can today. We have referenced repeatedly the greatness of our Founding Fathers. Remember that even they could not solve the issue of slavery if they were to create a full union of all states. They left it for men who would come later to right the wrong they had to live with. Perhaps you are among those men.

"So, if I might impose on you for just a moment longer, I would humbly request that each of you, at some point during your deliberations, consider for just a moment what it would be like to lose your freedom. What it would feel like to be a slave the chattel of another? What it would do to you to have the majority of those around you consider you as something less than a man? I believe that doing so, you will be at peace, and able to fully and fairly do justice for the man who placed fifty years of trust in the system—and you are that system. To help you in this difficult task, I want you to consider the words of the poet John Pierpont." He recited those words with passion and conviction.

"Is it his daily toil, that wrings
From the slave's bosom that deep sigh?
Is it his niggard fare, that brings
The tear into his down-cast eye?

"O no; by toil and humble fare,
Earth's sons their health and vigor gain;
It is because the slave must wear
His chain.

411

"Is it the sweat, from every pore
That starts, and glistens in the sun,
As, the young cotton bending o'er,
His naked back it shines upon?

"Is it the drops that, from his breast,
Into the thirsty furrow fall,
That scald his soul, deny him rest,
And turn his cup of life to gall?

"No; for, that man with sweating brow
Shall eat his bread, doth God ordain;
This the slave's spirit doth not bow;
It is his chain.

"Is it, that scorching sands and skies
Upon his velvet skin have set
A hue, admired in beauty's eyes,
In Genoa's silks, and polished jet?

"No; for this color was his pride,
When roaming o'er his native plain;
Even here, his hue can he abide,
But not his chain.

"Nor is it, that his back and limbs
Are scored with many a gory gash,
That his heart bleeds, and his brain swims,
And the MAN dies beneath the lash.

"For will and hope hath not the slave,
His bleeding spirit to sustain: —

No, he must drag on, to the grave,
His chain."

"Unchain Dred and Harriet Scott. The law allows it. Your soul demands it. Thank you, Your Honor. I am now done."

There wasn't a sound in the room. Even Pierre Chouteau, Jr., who had been watching from a corner of the room, while a couple of his large overseers stood guard, sat in stony silence.

"Okay, let's wrap this up and get you good men into the deliberation room. Let me add my thanks for your willingness to be here today and do your public duty. As Mr. Field explained, I will now read to you the instructions in the law, which you will be required to apply to the facts. They are, indeed, somewhat boring. Perhaps next time, Mr. Field, you can submit them for us in rhyming verse." Relieved laughter spread through the room. "I will send these written instructions in with you. The beauty of our legal system, I believe, is that you twelve laymen, not trained in the law, will now render a legal opinion. We don't expect you to know the law, which is why I will tell you what it is, with regard to this case." He then proceeded to read the instructions.

If they found that Irene Emerson herself, or through her brother, hired the Scotts out to the Russells or any of the others, then it was evidence she held them in slavery for purposes of the law on "once free, always free." He also told them her actions weren't excused if they found she was acting for someone else when she hired out the Scotts.

Having moved through the easy laws, both sets of attorneys waited anxiously for the final critical instruction, which could make or break the case. The judge withheld making a final ruling on that instruction that morning and only now revealed that decision. It immediately became clear that he had refused the defendant's instruction that would have required the jury to find for the defendant if they found that Captain Emerson had taken Dred to a military post pursuant to his orders from the federal government, and that Dred, and later Harriet, remained under the jurisdiction of the military. Field and Hall smiled at their major victory and finally relaxed as Judge Hamilton gave the final two instructions they had requested regarding the Northwest Ordinance and the Missouri Compromise. Garland and Norris folded their arms and scowled.

Hamilton read verbatim from the slips of paper he would send in with the jury.

"If the Jury believe from the evidence that the plaintiff was held in Slavery by the deceased Doctor Emerson at Fort Snelling situated in the Territory of the United States North West of the river Ohio, as defined by the act of Congress of July 12, 1787, entitled "An Ordinance for the Government of the Territory of the United States North West of the River, Ohio," at any time after said ordinance went into effect, and at the time was the property of Said Emerson, then Said Plaintiff is entitled to his freedom.

"If the Jury believe from the evidence that at any time after the 6th day of March 1820. the plaintiff was held in Slavery by the deceased Doctor Emerson, at Fort Snelling, or at any other place in the Territory ceded by France to the United States, under the name of Louisiana, which lies north of 36 degrees & 30 minutes North latitude, not included within the limits of the State of Missouri, and that at the time he was So held in Slavery he was the Property of Said Emerson, then Said Plaintiff is entitled to his freedom."

After two hours of deliberation, the jury came back into the courtroom. The chairs in the gallery had been removed, and folks were packed in tight. The judge had allowed inside the bar, and into the ample well of the courtroom, the Blows and their extended family, and the Chouteaus and other immediate family to support the defendant. After taking their seats, the jury foreman arose and delivered the written decision to the bailiff, who walked it up to the judge. He reviewed it and rapped the gavel.

"I find the verdict to be in the proper order. I would ask each of the jurors to stand when I read your name and acknowledge that you agree with the decision. I have made special accommodations to allow more people into my courtroom. I am well aware that sentiments on both sides of this issue are very strong, and obviously one side will disagree with the decision. I will caution you all once again in the strongest terms, there will be no verbal or physical violence in this building when I read the ruling. These members of the jury have done their civic duty, and they are to be treated with respect. Any word of retribution or harassment, and I will see the perpetrators serve a significant amount of time in jail. Is that understood?" A chorus of affirmation responded.

"Very well then, the parties and counsel will rise." He read the verdict, and each juror stood when his name was read and nodded his assent:

> *"This day come the parties by their attorneys and comes also a jury Court: Calvin Farris, C. H. Rosburg, William Syphert, H. S. Taylor, Robert Nest, John C. Morris, T. P. Grantham, L. Whyland, D. Welsh, C. W. Grantham, A. H. Foster, and N. W. Sterrchum, twelve good and lawful men who being duly elected tried and sworn the truth to speak upon the issue joined between the parties upon their oaths, do find and say that the*

defendant is guilty in manner and form as in the plaintiff's declaration alleged. It is therefore considered that the plaintiff recover his freedom against said defendant and all persons claiming under her by title derived since the commencement of this suit. It's further considered that the plaintiff recover of the defendant his costs in this behalf and have thereof execution."

The room erupted into absolute pandemonium which poured out the courthouse and into the street. But thinking back on the moment years later, Alexander Field recalled only two things: Harriet, standing with her arms upraised in a V and shouting over and over again, "Hallelujah, oh thank'e Jesus, we's free! Hallelujah!" and Dred Scott, as if in slow motion, dropping to one knee, his hands together in silent gratitude. He then stood with legs apart at shoulder-width, hands on hips and chest puffed out, chin up and dark eyes shining bright. "I am a man!" he said and repeated.

Nobody on God's earth could say otherwise.

* * *

In 1839, an incident occurred on the high seas that would propel the abolitionist movement and eventually involve a former U.S. president and a Supreme Court chief justice. A Spanish ship, *La Amistad,* left Cuba for Spain with a cargo of fifty African slaves who had been kidnapped earlier that year and sold in Cuba. Led by an African man named Cinque, the slaves broke free, killed the captain, took over the ship, and ordered the helmsman to take them back to Africa. He tricked them and instead headed north, where the ship was seized by a United States Navy vessel, sparking an international controversy. Spain demanded the slaves returned pursuant to treaty, but a group of Connecticut abolitionists formed to support the Africans. In 1841, the case came before the Supreme Court, and seventy-four-year-old former president John Quincy Adams argued for twelve hours over three days for the slaves. In a decision supported by Chief Justice Taney, the court held that the treaty with Spain only applied to legally held slaves and ordered them released on the grounds they had been kidnapped and enslaved contrary to the laws of humanity and justice.

On September 22nd, 1842, Abraham Lincoln rowed out to an island in the Mississippi just above St. Louis and nearly ended his career before it had really gotten started. Earlier in the year, Lincoln had written a series of anonymous letters to the editor of the local *Sangamon Journal,* severely criticizing a political nemesis, Illinois state auditor James Shields. The Democrat politician did not appreciate the satire, and when he learned the author was the Speaker of the Assembly, he demanded an apology. When Lincoln refused, Shields challenged him to a duel, notwithstanding the fact that dueling had been illegal in Illinois since it was made a territory. Not wanting to back down, Lincoln agreed to the duel and chose a weapon he was sure the much shorter Shields would refuse, and so he would come out on top: "Cavalry Broadswords of the largest size."

But Shields agreed, and the two men stood across from each other on aptly named Bloody Island, Missouri, swords in hand. Lincoln was distraught that this silly thing had gone so far, and worried that win, or lose, it would destroy his career. He reached the sword up and hacked off some high branches of a willow tree. When the future Brigadier General saw he could not possibly reach the same branches, he decided discretion was the better part of valor and withdrew his demand. The two made up, though were never friends, and of course both went on to unparalleled service. Shields became a hero in the War with Mexico, and later the only American to serve as a U.S. senator from three different states, where, coincidentally, Dred Scott himself had lived: Illinois, Minnesota, and Missouri.

Having survived his brush with the ridiculous, Lincoln decided it was time to settle down. On November 4th, 1842, he married Mary Todd, the daughter of an old Kentucky slave-owning family. On the two-month anniversary of their wedding, Mary was invited, along with some of the other prominent ladies of Springfield, to attend an extradition hearing for the Mormon prophet Joseph Smith, who had been building up the fast-growing city of Nauvoo on the Mississippi.

Earlier in the year, former Missouri Governor Lilburn Boggs had been shot. Although there was no direct evidence linking Smith to the crime, the fact that Boggs had ordered all Mormons exterminated or driven out of Missouri in 1838 was enough for Boggs' successor to list Joseph Smith as a suspect in the assassination attempt, and he asked the brand-new Illinois governor Thomas Ford to extradite him to stand trial in Missouri. Smith filed a writ of *habeas corpus*, and on January 4th, 1843, was brought before Judge Nathaniel Pope, accompanied by several of his apostles. Smith's clever attorney, the U.S. attorney for Illinois, Justin Butterfield, opened the hearing in a way that memorialized a rather routine proceeding.

"May it please the court," he began, "I appear before you today under circumstances most novel and peculiar. I am to address the 'Pope,'" he bowed to the judge, "surrounded by angels," he bowed still lower to Mrs. Lincoln and the other ladies, "in the presence of the holy Apostles, in behalf of the Prophet of the Lord."

The next day, Judge Pope denied Missouri's request and set Smith free. Smith and his brother were themselves murdered by a mob less than eighteen months later. A few months before his death, Joseph Smith announced his candidacy for president of the United States on an anti-slavery platform.

Mrs. Lincoln was already pregnant when she attended the hearing, and gave birth in August of 1843 to the couple's first child, Robert Todd Lincoln. Later that year, a repentant Henry Clay visited his old foe, Chief Justice Roger Taney, apologized for fighting for so long against his presidential appointments, and declared, "no man in the United States could have been selected more sufficiently able to wear the ermine which Chief Justice Marshall honored."

The next year Lincoln opened a new law firm with William Herndon, and when his Whig party hero, Henry Clay, lost to Democrat James Polk in his fourth campaign for U.S. president, Lincoln, the leader of the Illinois Whigs, brought prominent members to his home to discuss the future of the party. They determined to stay the course, and the "Great Compromiser," who had engineered the Missouri Compromise in 1820, was now, thirty years later, the chief architect of the Compromise of 1850 which attempted to resolve the sectional dispute over what to do with the vast western territories acquired after the War with Mexico. Under the agreement, California entered the Union as a free state, and New Mexico and Utah Territories were allowed the right to determine for themselves whether they would be slave or free. Utah had been settled in 1847 when the Mormons were driven out of Illinois after their prophet had been assassinated, and immigrated *en masse* to the west. In exchange for these concessions, the Northern members of Congress agreed to, and passed, the Fugitive Slave Act, which made it a crime to help a runaway slave. The compromise was viewed by the growing numbers of radicals on both sides of the slavery debate as a retreat from principle, and tensions continued to mount.

After the birth of his second son, Edward, in 1845, Lincoln's star continued to rise. In 1846, he was elected to the United States House of Representatives and headed off to Washington as the only

Whig congressman from Illinois. He worked hard, and did not try to stand out. But one day he looked out the window of the Capitol Building and spied nearly within its shadow, "a sort of negro livery-stable, where droves of negroes were collected, temporarily kept, and finally taken to Southern markets, precisely like droves of horses." The fact that slavery was legal at the seat of the government of the United States infuriated him, and he set out his second year in office to outlaw the evil practice in the District of Columbia. He lost his bid for re-election, but his Whig mentor, Clay, picked up the baton and ended slavery in the nation's capitol as part of the Compromise of 1850.

Great tragedy struck the Lincoln house when, in 1850, their darling Eddie died of consumption just shy of his fourth birthday. Overcome with grief, the couple, who throughout the tragedies of their lives took great comfort in poetry, sat down together and poured out their love and grief in a poem they titled, "Little Eddie." Printed in the Illinois State Journal, the words testify of the Lincoln's great love, tenderness, and abiding faith.

Those midnight stars are sadly dimmed,
That late so brilliantly shone,
And the crimson tinge from cheek and lip,
With the heart's warm life has flown -
The angel of Death was hovering nigh,
And the lovely boy was called to die.

The silken waves of his glossy hair
Lie still over his marble brow,
And the pallid lip and pearly cheek
The presence of Death avow.
Pure little bud in kindness given,
In mercy taken to bloom in heaven.

Happier far is the angel child
With the harp and the crown of gold,
Who warbles now at the Savior's feet
The glories to us untold.
Eddie, meet blossom of heavenly love,
Dwells in the spirit-world above.

Angel Boy - fare thee well, farewell
Sweet Eddie, We bid thee adieu!
Affection's wail cannot reach thee now
Deep though it be, and true.
Bright is the home to him now given
For "of such is the Kingdom of Heaven."

Part XII

Not a Man

"*That which is not just is not law. You can not possibly have a broader basis for government than that which includes all the people, with all their rights in their hands, and with an equal power to maintain their rights.*"

- William Lloyd Garrison, abolitionist and editor (1805-1879)

"*. . . beings of an inferior order, and altogether unfit to associate with the white race, either in social or political relations, and so far inferior that they had no rights which the white man was bound to respect.*"

- Opinion of the United States Supreme Court, by Chief Justice Roger B. Taney (March 6, 1857)

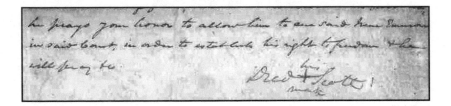

Chapter 34

That Which I Cannot Do for Myself

St. Louis, Missouri, 1850 - 1854

From the moment the glorious sunrise of freedom burst upon Dred's world that cold winter day in a St. Louis courtroom, the Scott family had enjoyed perpetual summer. The seasons changed, and two more winters came and went, but for Dred and his family, no outside weather could eclipse the warm internal peace of knowing they were their own masters. No man told them when to get up or what time to lie down at night. They came and went as they wanted, and didn't have to look back. They had no fear of the whip, the rope, or the auction block. They experienced for the first time the overwhelming satisfaction of excelling at something—not out of fear of punishment or a desire of reward from "Massa"— but just out of simple respect for themselves. Personal choice and accountability were virtues that had their own rewards, and those keys to his employer's store that Dred wore like a royal pendant around his neck were more valuable to him than keys to a bank vault, for all the money in the world could not buy the ennobling mantle of self-reliance.

And then came that terrible March day on the St. Louis levee in 1852 when Old Man Winter returned with his icy chains of slavery. He blew in from the west in a twist of irony that froze Dred's heart. The unjust ruling of the two newly elected Missouri Supreme Court justices was issued from their court in the capitol, Jefferson City, named for that American who had first declared in writing the equality of man and who had stayed at the Blow's Olde Place plantation the night Dred was born. It seemed that nothing could thaw the perpetual chill that encircled the Scott family. When Roswell Field had taken them in June through the gauntlet of hatred and into the courtroom to notify Judge Hamilton that they intended to challenge the ruling of the Missouri high court by filing a lawsuit in the federal system, he told Dred that his freedom wasn't gone—it was just in hibernation.

Dred had allowed himself a smile at that notion. 1852 passed, and 1853 was well-progressed, and no one had violated the judge's order that the Scotts were to be unmolested during the pendency of the appeal. The Scotts began to believe in their lawyer's hibernation metaphor.

Then came October's attack in the barn, and with it the lash and humiliation, and Dred chastised himself for being so wrong. It was slavery that had appeared to be hibernating, but the sleeping bear had awakened in the form of John Sanford.

* * *

It was the Fourth of July, 1854, and the Scott, Blow, and Roswell Field families were visiting at the Taylor Blow homestead in Carondelet near the river halfway between St. Louis and Jefferson Barracks. Taylor Blow had recommended the reunion away from the crowds, clamor, and stench of St. Louis to relax over barbequed fish and meats, pie, quince butter, and mint juleps in celebration of Independence Day, and to strategize the next steps in the federal lawsuit. The small settlement of mostly French and German immigrants had doubled in size after the 1849 St. Louis fire and cholera epidemic, and the town was now large enough for a formal celebration committee that had planned an evening flower parade. While the men conversed, the women prepared a barbeque, and the Field's nanny Temperance kept the children busy weaving bouquets and sewing fresh flowers onto their clothes. A light breeze rustled through the oak trees, bringing some relief to the sweltering summer heat. A few of the men had removed their shirts to cool off, but Dred would never remove his again. The long purple scars from the whipping he had taken from John Sanford the prior fall no longer hurt, but the shame and humiliation were raw and painful.

The long up-and-down struggle had worn Dred out, and he was physically and emotionally exhausted. In just the last five years, he had ricocheted between the unmatched heights of ecstasy to be declared a free man in the St. Louis courthouse, and the unfathomed depths of hell in the LaBeaume barn when he was powerless to stop Sanford from brutalizing his dear wife in front of his daughters. The joy of freedom was as exquisite as was the agony of slavery, and he yearned with all his soul to know that joy again.

But the recent setback delivered in a small backroom over a store on Main Street in St. Louis by Federal Circuit Court Judge Robert W. Wells had pushed Dred into a deep depression, and if he didn't fear for the fate of his wife and girls, he would tell these good white folk to just stop and go back to their lives.

After the heartbreaking 1852 reversal of the jury verdict that had freed the Scotts, the team of friends and advocates regrouped and filed suit in the federal courts, this time against John Sanford. Although Irene Emerson still owned the Scotts, she had delegated all of her business and legal affairs to her brother, acting as her agent. Since it was Sanford who had assaulted them, it was appropriate to charge him directly.

After experiencing years of political delay in the Missouri state court system, they were pleased and encouraged when a trial date was set less than six months from when they filed. They had also placed a lot of hope in Judge Wells. Although he had once owned slaves in Virginia, the judge and former Missouri Attorney General was not openly pro-slavery, and had of late expressed his concern that the nation would never progress until it did away with the practice.

The jury trial took place on May 15th, but no witnesses were called, and counsel from both sides had submitted an Agreed Statement of Fact. The Scott team's hopes were shattered, however, when the judge instructed the jury that Missouri law on slavery was controlling on the issue of whether John Sanford was guilty for restraining and beating the Scotts. And Missouri law was what the most recent Missouri high court said it was. Dred and Harriet were slaves.

The jury quickly found for the defendant. The United States Supreme Court was literally now the Scotts' court of last resort.

As the stomach-rumbling scent of roast pork and venison wafted on the breeze, Roswell Field laid out the challenges they faced, and it instantly became evident that the key to any chance of success was in finding a quality lawyer with Supreme Court experience. Field made it very clear that he was not qualified, that the unique oral and written advocacy of an appeal to the nation's highest court required the right man, and they could not proceed unless they found him, and he was willing to take the case for free.

As had been feared, the Chouteau family and friends had turned on the Blows and all their extended family. Business dried up as their customers received promises, threats, and bribes, and it became almost impossible for any of them to obtain credit. The only bright spot was that, by sheer force of personality, Taylor Blow had won a seat to represent southern St. Louis County in the Missouri State Senate. Unfortunately, the job didn't pay much, and he had only been in office a few months.

The bottom line was that the Blows had not only run out of money, but also family, friends, and business associates who could help. They could not afford the fees of an experienced appellate attorney, and so they used the occasion of an Independence Day reunion to brainstorm a solution.

Dred could tell by the increased saliva in his mouth that the meat was nearly done. He wanted to thank his friends for all their love and support, then tell them he was through fighting. But Field had made it clear that if they did not file a notice of appeal, Judge Hamilton back in the state court would have no choice but to end his involvement and turn the Scotts over to Sanford without any further protection of the court. He had kept his order in place that prohibited Emerson, Sanford, or anyone acting on their behalf from selling or separating the Scotts, and the sheriff continued to collect and hold the wages paid for their services.

Dred, Harriet, and the girls had been living in a small hut some six blocks west of the courthouse. Harriet took in washing, and Dred was hired out as a janitor, whitewasher, and gardener. They were kept busy eighteen hours a day and had little family time to speak of. This brief excursion to the country should have invigorated the unusually optimistic father, but he was filled with a sense of impending doom.

Dred shook himself to end the malaise and interrupted the tense discussion. "Mista LaBeaume, could you please read what that newspaper say about us?"

Louis picked up the copy of the *St. Louis Herald* and read, "'Dred is, of course, poor and without any powerful friends—'"

"Hey, what about me?" asked Senator Blow, feigning outrage. "I'm no picayune!"

Peter laughed at his politician brother and shoved him. "Yeah, and you ain't no Philadelphia lawyer, either!"

Everyone in the group laughed until they saw that their frightened friend wasn't.

"Sorry, Dred," Peter apologized. "Go on, Louis. We know that compared to the Sanford and the Chouteaus, we aren't what anyone would call 'some pumpkins'."

Louis folded and smoothed the paper and started over. "'Dred is, of course, poor and without any powerful friends, but no doubt he will find at the bar of the Supreme Court some able and generous advocate, who will do all he can to establish his right to go free.'"

The group sat silently and watched Dred think. Despite the fact that he had never learned to read or write, they knew there was a powerful intellect behind those dark eyes, and when his brow was furrowed, like it was now, the wheels were turning inside. Dred was thinking, and he found that the fresh air and heavenly odors were lifting his spirits and clearing out the cobwebs of depression. He looked at his supporters and fixed each one with a stare. He saw in their eyes that they weren't licked yet, and he knew at that moment he would move on. He slapped his leg and stood up.

"I agree with the paper, 'cept about you, Senator Blow," Dred interjected, looking at Taylor. "What we need, then, is an able and generous apricot!"

The men all looked at each other, not wanting to laugh at Dred's mistake, then broke out in guffaws when Dred winked at them and said, "I'se just fooling with you. Let's eat, and then we can find a . . . what ya call it . . . advocate!"

After dinner and the flower parade, the adults gathered in the parlor of the Taylor Blow home to continue their discussion. The women joined in as well, and as they were getting started, Charlotte spoke up, pulling a pamphlet from her apron pocket.

"This evening at the parade, some women from the Ladies' Anti-slavery Society handed me a pamphlet containing a speech given by the freed slave Frederick Douglass two years ago at their Fourth of July celebration. Can you imagine that? They asked a former slave to speak about Independence Day! They said every American concerned about our country should read it, and will be inspired to take action." She paused to collect her composure. "I read much of it, and it spoke to my heart and gave me an idea. I am so glad we have taken a stand for Dred, Harriet, and the girls, that perhaps we might ourselves atone for the sin of our father."

Cannons began firing down river, presumably from Jefferson Barracks, the rumble of the celebratory cannonade pealing along the river and over the hills. No one spoke, so Charlotte continued. "Let me read to you a few of Mr. Douglass's extraordinary remarks. He begins with the most articulate elocution of why we celebrate this day that I have heard from any man, let alone a black man who was born into slavery." Charlotte quoted from the pamphlet:

> "*The 4th of July is the first great fact in your nation's history . . . Pride and patriotism, not less than gratitude, prompt you to celebrate and to hold it in perpetual remembrance. I have said that the Declaration of*

Independence is the ring-bolt to the chain of your nation's destiny; so, indeed, I regard it. The principles contained in that instrument are saving principles. Stand by those principles, be true to them on all occasions, in all places, against all foes, and at whatever cost. Your fathers staked their lives, their fortunes, and their sacred honor, on the cause of their country. In their admiration of liberty, they lost sight of all other interests. They were peace men; but they preferred revolution to peaceful submission to bondage. . . . With them, justice, liberty and humanity were 'final;' not slavery and oppression."

Charlotte stopped reading and held up the pamphlet. "After going on for some time on the virtues of the Founding Fathers, Mr. Douglass then surprised his audience by asking them why he was asked to speak on that day, hence, the title of his speech, *What to the Slave is the Fourth of July?*" She turned a few pages and continued,

"What have I, or those I represent, to do with your national independence? . . . Are the great principles of political freedom and of natural justice, embodied in that Declaration of Independence, extended to us? Am I, therefore, called upon to bring our humble offering to the national altar, and to confess the benefits and express devout gratitude for the blessings resulting from your independence to us? I say it with a sad sense of the disparity between us. I am not included within the pale of this glorious anniversary! Your high independence only reveals the immeasurable distance between us."

The group of friends were as close as they had ever been, but at that moment the majority realized the heart-breaking truth that, though seated in their midst, an invisible gulf yet divided them from the Scotts. They looked in shame at the ground and prayed for twilight to hide the national guilt they shared as their oldest sister continued reading.

> *"The blessings in which you, this day, rejoice, are not enjoyed in common. The rich inheritance of justice, liberty, prosperity and independence, bequeathed by your fathers, is shared by you, not by me. The sunlight that brought life and healing to you, has brought stripes and death to me. This Fourth [of] July is yours, not mine. You may rejoice, I must mourn. To drag a man in fetters into the grand illuminated temple of liberty, and call upon him to join you in joyous anthems, were inhuman mockery and sacrilegious irony. Do you mean, citizens, to mock me, by asking me to speak to day?*
>
> *"Fellow-citizens; above your national, tumultuous joy, I hear the mournful wail of millions! whose chains, heavy and grievous yesterday, are, to-day, rendered more intolerable by the jubilee shouts that reach them. I do not hesitate to declare, with all my soul, that the character and conduct of this nation never looked blacker to me than on this 4th of July!"*

Charlotte began to cry and could not continue to read. She handed the tract to her oldest brother Peter and pointed to the spot where he should start. He made it through the first few lines, then had to pause to regain control of his own voice before spitting out the gut-wrenching scene painted by the words of Frederick Douglass:

"What, am I to argue that it is wrong to make men brutes, to rob them of their liberty, to work them without wages, to keep them ignorant of their relations to their fellow men, to beat them with sticks, . . . to flay their flesh with the lash, to load their limbs with irons, to hunt them with dogs, to sell them at auction, to sunder their families, to knock out their teeth, to burn their flesh, to starve them into obedience and submission to their masters? Must I argue that a system thus marked with blood, and stained with pollution, is wrong? What, to the American slave, is your 4th of July? I answer: a day that reveals to him, more than all other days in the year, the gross injustice and cruelty to which he is the constant victim. To him, your celebration is a sham; your boasted liberty, an unholy license; your national greatness, swelling vanity; your sounds of rejoicing are empty and heartless; your denunciations of tyrants, brass fronted impudence; your shouts of liberty and equality, hollow mockery; your prayers and hymns, your sermons and thanksgivings, with all your religious parade, and solemnity, are, to him, mere bombast, fraud, deception, impiety, and hypocrisy - a thin veil to cover up crimes which would disgrace a nation of savages. There is not a nation on the earth guilty of practices, more shocking and bloody, than are the people of these United States, at this very hour."

"Stop, Peter," Dred spoke up. He walked over with his hand out. "Please, stop! Mister Douglas ain't speaking 'bout you. He don't know what you done for a poor black man and his kin. Leave it be. We can still celebrate this day, and I for one sho' 'nuff ain't givin' up on the courts. We have a final battle to fight, and I knows that, with your help, we can win!"

As darkness began to creep around the bushes and the trunks of the trees, Dred took the pamphlet from Peter and examined it closely. He thumbed through the pages of characters he could not decipher, but an almost palpable power seemed to emanate from its crisp paper, and it inspired in Dred a thought. "The written word is powerful. It moves people to do things," Dred continued. "You knows I can't write, but maybe if one of you could write down my story for me, and we could make our own Dred Scott pamphlet, we might harvest a whole bushel of Supreme Court apricots."

Dred's joke and idea moved the group out of their melancholy, and Charlotte spoke up again. "You know, Dred, I once heard an African proverb that said, 'great men think alike.' Well, I'm not a man, but that is exactly what I was going to suggest!"

She reached for the tract. "May I read the final paragraph of Douglass's speech? It will inspire us at the close of this Independence Day. Next year may we all rejoice in freedom together!" The crickets sang, and the night birds began their frantic dance, chirping as they swooped down and around the assembly of imperfect Americans trying to be better. Charlotte opened to the back of the pamphlet and read,

> "Allow me to say, in conclusion, notwithstanding the dark picture I have this day presented of the state of the nation, I do not despair of this country. There are forces in operation, which must inevitably work the downfall of slavery. 'The arm of the Lord is not shortened,' and the doom of slavery is certain. I, therefore, leave off where I began, with hope. While drawing encouragement from the Declaration of Independence, the great principles it contains, and the genius of American Institutions, my

spirit is also cheered by the obvious tendencies of the age.
. . . In the fervent aspirations of William Lloyd Garrison,
I say, and let every heart join in saying it:

> *"'God speed the year of jubilee*
> *The wide world o'er*
> *When from their galling chains set free,*
> *Th' oppress'd shall vilely bend the knee,*
> *And wear the yoke of tyranny*
> *Like brutes no more.*
> *That year will come, and freedom's reign,*
> *To man his plundered fights again*
> *Restore.'"*

Roswell Field prepared a twelve-page pamphlet outlining the story of Dred and Harriet Scott and their fight for freedom. Edward LaBeaume scraped together enough money to pay for the printing, and by the end of the month, they had mailed several hundred copies to newspapers around the country and to a list of qualified Supreme Court attorneys. Inside the front cover under the heading, *An Appeal From Dred Scott In His Own Words,* it read:

> *I have no money to pay anybody at Washington to speak for me. My fellow-men, can any of you help me in my day of trial? Will nobody speak for me at Washington, even without hope of other reward than the blessings of a poor black man and his family? I do not know; I can only pray that some good heart will be moved by pity to do that for me which I cannot do for myself; and that if the right is on my side it may be so declared by the high court to which I have appealed.*
>
> *Dred* X *Scott*

Fall brought vibrant red, yellow, and orange colors splashed across the state, but not one answer to their solicitation.

Dred and Harriet went back to their menial day labor in the city but the girls remained in hiding, this time with Taylor Blow's family. With the onset of winter, the dark clouds of war hurtled from the east, sped over the rolling hills of Missouri, and billowed into a monstrous thunderhead above the new state of Kansas.

With abolitionist passions still seething over what they considered a grievous sin committed by Congress with the passage of the Fugitive Slave Act as part of the Compromise of 1850, Democratic Senator Stephen A. Douglas of Illinois inserted a stick into the angry hive and stirred it up. In January he introduced a bill to create the new territories of Kansas and Nebraska, to repeal the provision of the Missouri Compromise that had prohibited slavery in any new territories in land acquired by the Louisiana Purchase north of the thirty-sixth parallel, and to allow the citizens of the new territories to decide for themselves if they wanted to allow slavery. Kansas and Nebraska were both above the thirty-sixth parallel. Douglas argued for the popular sovereignty of the people of those territories, but opponents saw it as another gift to the slave-holding South.

Battle lines were drawn, and opposing political armies were formed.

Fifty-three "concerned citizens," made up mostly of Whigs and Free Soilers, met on March 20th in Ripon, Wisconsin, and started the Republican Party, with the abolition of slavery as the basis of its platform and opposition to the Kansas-Nebraska Act its first priority. The new political party quickly became a moving force in American politics. The Congressional battles raged in Washington for four months, and on a very close vote, the law passed and was signed into law the end of May by President Pierce.

Abraham Lincoln had jumped back into politics with enthusiasm over his opposition to the Act and was re-elected to the Illinois legislature, but when the Kansas-Nebraska Act passed, he decided against taking his seat in the State House so he could run for United States Senate against the hated Act's sponsor, Senator Stephen Douglas.

Almost immediately, pro-slavery Missourians crossed the western border into Kansas to stack the vote for a pro-slavery delegate to Congress. Calling them "Border Ruffians," *New York Tribune* editor and rabid abolitionist Horace Greely rallied the Republican Party to send abolitionist Northerners to Kansas in an attempt to counter the influx of ruffians.

As pro- and anti-slavery armies grew, Abraham Lincoln spoke in Springfield, Illinois, to what he called a "Gathering of Interested Citizens." He titled his speech, "An Appeal for All Good Men to Stand with Anyone Who Stands for the Right," and as a foretaste of the future Lincoln-Douglas debates, made his most scathing attack on slavery to date. He blasted Congress for their pro-slavery actions, saying, "this declared indifference for the spread of slavery I cannot but hate. I hate it because of the monstrous injustice of slavery itself. I hate it because it deprives our republican example of its just influence on the world; enables the enemies of free institutions with plausibility to taunt us as hypocrites; causes the real friends of freedom to doubt our sincerity; and especially because it forces so many good men among ourselves into an open conflict with the fundamental principles of civil liberties; criticizing the Declaration of Independence and insisting there is no right principle of action except self-interest."

Northern immigration into Kansas was totally dwarfed by that from Missouri and the South, and the pro-slavery candidate easily won the November election. A total of 6,000 votes were cast, notwithstanding that Kansas only had 1,500 registered voters. In a few months, the larger battle to influence the election of the new territorial legislature would result in what Greely termed "Bleeding Kansas."

Perhaps because the nation was so caught up in the larger fight against slavery, no one noticed, and no lawyers responded, to the desperate personal war that had been waged for nearly a decade by Dred Scott and his small group of friends christened the "Band of Brothers" by Roswell Field.

After much research, Roswell determined that the only man for the job of representing Dred Scott before the Supreme Court was a lawyer he had known in St. Louis by the name of Montgomery Blair, who had moved to Washington D.C. and was living in his father's home, the Blair House mansion across Pennsylvania Avenue from the White House.

The Blairs were Southern aristocrats who opposed the expansion of slavery, and Montgomery Blair had been very outspoken against it. He and his brother, Frank, were leaders in the Free Soil Movement that fought against the Compromise of 1850 and the Kansas-Nebraska Act. There, father Preston Blair was very close to the powerful Missouri Senator Thomas Hart Benton, who, after losing the seat he'd held for thirty years, was elected to Congress and was one of the leading voices against the Kansas-Nebraska Act. Montgomery Blair was a talented constitutional lawyer and an experienced Supreme Court attorney, but he had not responded to Field's direct personal appeal.

The families gathered again at Roswell Field's house on Walsh's Row for Christmas Eve, and after a peaceful dinner, held an exchange of gifts and an evening of laughter and games involving the expanding Blow families, the Field children, and the Scott girls, who played together as equals.

As the clock tolled ten, the men retired upstairs to Roswell's large office. Roswell read them his second letter to Montgomery Blair, wherein he articulated a powerful argument why Blair was the only man who had a chance of winning Dred's freedom in what he was sure would become one of the most famous cases in the history of the Supreme Court—one which law students would study for two hundred years—and his name would be forever linked with the abolition of slavery.

With the glow of the holiday upon them, Roswell admitted to his friends that he had felt inspired by God to pursue Blair, and the words he had written were not his own, but those of the angels, who on that night nearly two millennia ago, had declared the birth of the Savior to a tiny band of humble shepherds keeping watch over their flocks by night. He then raised his eggnog.

"You've heard me call you my 'Band of Brothers,' and that you are. Dred, Peter, Taylor, Louis, Edmond, and Charles, I toast you this night in the words of Shakespeare's King Henry the Fifth to his men before facing an overwhelming French army at the Battle of Agincourt: 'We few, we happy few, we band of brothers, For he today who sheds his blood with me shall be my brother, Be he ne'er so vile, this day shall gentle his condition, and gentlemen in England now abed shall think themselves accursed they were not here, and hold their manhood cheap whilst any speaks, that fought with us upon St. Crispin's day!' That small, happy band of brothers had a stunning victory that day, and so shall we."

"Here, here," the brothers replied.

On December 30th, 1854, Montgomery Blair responded to Field's Christmas Eve letter. Encouraged by his father and armed with a commitment from Gamaliel Bailey, the editor of the anti-slavery paper *National Era*, to find a way to underwrite the court costs, Blair wrote that he would appear *pro bono* as Dred Scott's "advocate before the Ultimate Tribunal."

Before the day was out, Blair walked into the basement of the United States Capitol Building and filed the petition.

An apparently near-sighted clerk misspelled the defendant's name when he entered the case title into the official court record: Case 3230, Docket G, p. 3388, *Dred Scott v. Sandford*.

It wouldn't be the last thing the court got wrong.

Roswell Field

Chapter 35

A Bird for the Sportsman's Gun

Washington D.C., 1855 - 1856

It was January, 1856, and Dred found himself back inside the courtroom where he had first tasted the sweet savor of freedom. The kind Judge Hamilton, knowing what the room had meant to him, allowed Dred and Roswell Field to use it as an office whenever it was available. The day wasn't nearly as cold as the day of his trial six years earlier, and sunbeams from the south windows moved slowly across the floor as Dred and his lawyer spoke about the case, which would finally be argued the next month in the Supreme Court of the United States.

At fifty-five, Dred was beginning to show the signs of the vicissitudes of his life. Although his hair was as thick and dark as it was as a child, the creases that ran from the corner of his nose and encircled his mouth were getting deeper, and wrinkles that used to appear on his forehead and between his eyes only when he was worried or deep in thought had become permanent. He kept a cotton cloth in his pocket to dab at his perpetually watery eyes. Dred glanced over at his eldest daughter, Eliza, who sat on the floor in a ray of golden sunlight that radiated off her smooth, unlined skin. She looked more like her father than her mother, and she had always been his shadow. She loved going with him to meet with the lawyers and join in the discussions of the case and other current events, while nine-year-old Lizzie, who took after Harriet, preferred to stay home and help with the laundry business.

Eliza turned the page of the newspaper she was reading, and looking up, caught her father staring at her and winked. Dred's aging heart nearly gave out at the sight of his pride and joy, reading. He had thanked God in his daily prayers that the Blows had disregarded the law that prohibited teaching slaves to read and had given a gift to his children that, second to freedom, was the greatest prize a person could attain.

"What ya reading there, Gypsy girl?" he asked with a smile.

"Actually, I'm reading about you, Poppy!" she replied. "This here *National Review* article from two weeks ago says Mr. Blair will finally be arguing our case before nine justices of the Supreme Court."

"'Bout time!" Dred shouted, smacking the table with the palm of his hand, sending dust flying toward where Eliza sat. "Read me what it says, Gypsy." Dred loved to hear his daughter read more than the finest sermon by the gifted preacher Reverend Anderson, more even than the song of the mockingbird or the music of a babbling brook.

Eliza folded the paper into a smaller square as the dust particles caught in the sunbeam surrounded her like an aura. "Okay, this was written by the editor, Mr. Bailey, hisself. I can't rightly figure his first name." She looked up at Field. "You knows him, don't you, Mr. Roswell? How do you say his given name?"

"I do know him," replied their lawyer, who was also now a close friend. "It's pronounced 'Gam-a-lee-al.' He's the man who promised Montgomery Blair that he would find a way to pay the court costs for bringing the case in the Supreme Court." He looked at Dred, whose deep forehead wrinkles had turned to crevasses, so deep in thought was his client. "What is it, Dred?" he asked.

"I was just thinking on that name. I believes that Gamaliel in the Bible was a lawyer and a leader of the Pharisees, and he even taught the law to Saul, who later became the apostle Paul."

Roswell Field shook his head in astonishment at the depth of knowledge his illiterate friend possessed.

"Oh, Poppy, you're so smart!" exclaimed his adoring daughter.

"I did not know that, Dred," Field admitted, then began to add, "You probably don't know—"

Dred cut him off. "That's 'cuz you don't go to church like you should."

The lawyer chuckled guiltily and continued. "You are probably right. What you don't know is that you have a lot of friends beyond this courthouse and this city, Dred. I didn't tell you, but last year Gamaliel went to every member of Congress who opposed the Kansas-Nebraska Act, told them your story, and asked each one to contribute two dollars to pay for your cost of filing in the courts! You won't believe it—heck, I hardly believe it," he said, laughing, "but he collected one hundred and fifty silver dollars from seventy-five Congressmen, and then pitched in four dollars and sixty-four cents himself to make up the total cost of the filing!"

"Oh, Poppy, isn't that wonderful?" Eliza asked, clapping her hands together and creating a glowing dust-devil above her head. "Who would've ever thought that so many high-n-mighty white politicians would notice, let alone give their own money to a poor slave from Missouri?"

What the three didn't know was that one of those seventy-five politicians was a new congressman from Massachusetts named Calvin C. Chafee, the new husband of the Scotts' mistress Irene Emerson Chafee. Apparently the fact that she owned four slaves back in Missouri was something she hadn't found a way to tell her abolitionist Republican husband.

"That sho' 'nuff is a miracle," Dred marveled. "What's our friend the Pharisee have to say?"

Eliza found her place and read, "'The case is a peculiar one. The plaintiff brought the suit to try his right to freedom. He claims to have been emancipated, his master having taken him to reside in Illinois, which act, according to the Constitution of that State, was sufficient to give him his freedom.'"

"He got that right," Dred said appreciatively, looking about the birthplace of his freedom.

Eliza nodded and continued, "'He subsequently returned to Missouri, in which state he had formerly resided; and it was decided by the Circuit Court that the master's right, dormant while in Illinois, had revived and the other states were not bound to respect the law of Illinois. The case will probably occupy the court several days, and the decision will be looked for with great interest.'"

"He can say that again," Dred exclaimed, feeling relieved that the additional delays were finally at an end. "Do you think Mr. Blair is prepared?"

"Montgomery Blair is one of the smartest lawyers I know, but I am going to send him my thoughts on one more important issue I hope he'll focus on when speaking to the justices. In fact, that's why I asked you to come down here today, Dred. Since we lost in the Circuit Court, like the article said, the normal thing to argue to the high court is the reason why the lower court was wrong, and why they should reverse that ruling. I'm sure Montgomery will do that very well. But what do you think if we encourage him not to just ask for reversal, but also to ask them to support the one good finding by Judge Wells, that a black man has a constitutional right to sue in federal courts?"

He could see that Dred wasn't following his reasoning. "You see, those seventy-five Congressmen and all the abolitionists in this country absolutely hate the Fugitive Slave Law, as rightly they should, and if we make it part of our case, it will bring vast public pressure on the judges to rule, not just in your favor on the Missouri Compromise, but on your right to sue in court as well. And if they sustain Judge Wells' ruling on the right to sue in court, it will deal a death blow to the Fugitive Slave Law."

"How so?" interrupted Eliza in a very lawyerly manner.

"Do you still have that copy of Frederick Douglass's Fourth of July speech Charlotte gave you?"

Eliza sprang to her feet and went for her satchel. "Yes, I always carry it with me."

"Good. Can you find the place where he criticized judges for not allowing a man accused of being a runaway to defend himself in court?"

While she thumbed through the worn pamphlet, Field explained. "If the highest court in the country agrees that an alleged slave has a right to challenge his status in court, every judge will have to allow it in every state, and the terrible injustices being done will be rectified."

"Here it is," the young apprentice said excitedly. "Should I read it?"

"Yes!" demanded Dred, even before his lawyer could.

She walked back into the bright sunbeam and read the powerful indictment of the law and the judicial system.

"By an act of the American Congress, not yet two years old, slavery has been nationalized in its most horrible and revolting form. By that act, Mason & Dixon's line has been obliterated; New York has become as Virginia; and the power to hold, hunt, and sell men, women, and children as slaves remains no longer a mere state institution, but is now an institution of the whole United States. The power is co-extensive with the Star-Spangled Banner and American Christianity. Where these go, may also go the merciless slave-hunter. Where these are, man is not sacred. He is a bird for the sportsman's gun. By that most foul and fiendish of all human decrees, the liberty and person of every man are put in peril. Your broad republican domain is hunting ground for men. Not for thieves and robbers, enemies of society, merely, but for men guilty of no crime. Your lawmakers have commanded all good citizens to engage in this hellish sport. . . . Not fewer than forty Americans have, within the past two years, been hunted down and, without a moment's warning, hurried away in chains, and consigned to slavery and excruciating torture."

"Now skip down to the part about where the judges are appropriately condemned," Field prompted her.

"Here it is," she said, hurrying on, excited that the words of her hero might impact the lawsuit brought in the name of the only man she admired more than Frederick Douglass—her father.

"The Fugitive Slave Law makes MERCY TO THEM, A CRIME; and bribes the judge who tries them. An American JUDGE GETS TEN DOLLARS

FOR EVERY VICTIM HE CONSIGNS to slavery, and five, when he fails to do so. The oath of any two villains is sufficient, under this hell-black enactment, to send the most pious and exemplary black man into the remorseless jaws of slavery! His own testimony is nothing. He can bring no witnesses for himself. The minister of American justice is bound by the law to hear but one side; and that side, is the side of the oppressor. Let this damning fact be perpetually told. Let it be thundered around the world, that, in tyrant-killing, king-hating, people-loving, democratic, Christian America, the seats of justice are filled with judges, who hold their offices under an open and palpable bribe, and are bound, in deciding in the case of a man's liberty, hear only his accusers!"

Eliza's powerful recitation echoed through the empty sanctuary of the law, and Roswell Field pondered that, in a free society, this young lady would make a fine trial lawyer.

"So what do you say, Dred? Should we encourage Mr. Blair to go beyond just getting a reversal of your case, and try to run a dagger through the diseased heart of the Fugitive Slave Law?"

"Yes!" Dred and Eliza said in unison.

* * *

Roswell Field had accurately read the growing national public sentiment in the Northern states throughout the year between the initial filing of *Scott v. Sandford* in December of 1854 and oral arguments set for February of 1856. Outrage grew to a fevered pitch over what was considered an immoral compromise of principle in the recent Acts of Congress. In the South, the determination to maintain sovereignty over the right to own slaves likewise swelled. The battleground continued to be centered in Kansas.

In March of that year, United States Senator David Atchison from Missouri left office and the state to lead a small army of border ruffians into Kansas, and founded a city on the west bank of the Missouri River. Southern squatters continued to multiply and easily elected a pro-slavery territorial legislature which convened on July 2nd and began to immediately pass laws to institutionalize slavery. Despite their own manipulation of the vote, the new government and its newspapers blasted the northern migration. In the July 4th edition of the *Squatter Sovereign*, the publisher, John Stringfellow, wrote of celebrating Independence Day with the "pleasant pastime" of hanging abolitionists.

Not willing to accept defeat by fraud at the polls, anti-slavery Kansans and Northern homesteaders met in August and drafted the Topeka Constitution and formed a "Free-State" shadow government, which they claimed was the legitimate government of the territory. In October John Brown arrived, bringing with him the first of twelve hundred modern Sharp's rifles, supplied by the anti-slavery New England preacher Henry Ward Beecher and nicknamed "Beecher's Bibles." Not only were many of them smuggled into Kansas in boxes marked "Bibles" and "books," but Reverend Beecher himself had sermonized that the "Sharp's Rifle was a truly moral agency, and that there was more moral power in one of those instruments, so far as the slaveholders of Kansas were concerned, than in a hundred Bibles. You might just as well . . . read the Bible to Buffaloes as to those fellows who follow Atchison and Stringfellow; but they have a supreme respect for the logic that is embodied in Sharp's rifle."

While the eyes of the nation were drawn to the Missouri-Kansas border during that long hot summer of 1855, the Scotts quietly went about their lives. Dred had gone back to work as a porter at the new Barnum Hotel, and in his spare time he delivered the laundry Harriet and the girls did at their small house in an alley off Carr Street. Far away on the east coast, unnoticed by a nation tearing itself apart, an intensely private tragedy occurred in the life of the man who within eight months time would listen to oral arguments by the Scotts' lawyers as the Chief Justice of the Supreme Court.

Roger Brooks Taney had been leading the court for nearly a quarter of a century. He loved his country and had tried to serve honorably and uphold justice and the rule of law. But as the court broke for the summer recess that year, Taney watched in sadness as that nation was being split along sectional lines, and he rightly feared that spilled blood in Kansas would lead to a terrible bloodbath that could easily destroy her well before she could celebrate her 100th birthday. He felt helpless, however, to do anything to stop it. He did not like that feeling, and saw the Dred Scott petition as a possible tool he might use to arrest the rush toward disunion. So, as he packed for his family's annual summer vacation at Old Point Comfort on the far southern tip of the York peninsula, the only reading material he took with him were copies of documents that had been filed in the federal circuit and Missouri state courts.

Although five generations of Taneys had lived in the border state of Maryland, they considered themselves to be Southern gentlemen—plantation aristocrats. Their financial success as tobacco planters came off the strong backs of their slaves. Roger Taney personally disliked the practice and had long since freed his workers. But the Chief Justice never lost the strong Taney sympathy with sovereign state rights against Northern and centralized government meddling. For twenty-four years on the bench, Taney had tried very hard to divorce passion and personal bias from his process of judicial reasoning. But he was nearing eighty years old, and his patience toward abolitionist aggression was growing very thin. So personally prejudiced had he become against Northern attitude that he went into a rage when his youngest daughter, twenty-eight-year-old Alice, told him she had decided to break with family tradition and would vacation that summer with her sister and brother-in-law in the more fashionable resort of Newport, Rhode Island.

"I have not the slightest confidence," he argued, "in [the] superior health of Newport over Old Point, and look upon it as nothing more than that unfortunate feeling of inferiority in the South, which believes everything in the North to be superior to what we have."

Not wanting to upset her aging father, Alice agreed to accompany him and her mother, Anne, to Virginia. Their summer cottage was near the old lighthouse, which had been used as a signal tower in the War of 1812, and whose light had shone across Hampton Roads Bay to Craney Island and illuminated Dred and Peter Blow's nights as they worked to fortify their redoubts before the battle with the British. Summer languished into September, and with it came a sudden outbreak of yellow fever across the bay in Norfolk. Fearful that the disease would spread and trap them on the peninsula, Anne and Alice tearfully begged Roger to catch a boat back to Baltimore. The worried husband and father decided the risk of infection was greater on a ship, where they would be packed in and isolated, and insisted they stay put. Within a few weeks, his dear child and his wife of nearly fifty years succumbed to the epidemic a few hours apart.

Roger Taney was devastated and blamed himself for his terrible judgment. So, laid low with grief, he told his relatives he would never again take the bench. He was not in the middle chair when the Supreme Court session started anew, but within a few weeks, he recovered his strength and turned his anger back to the sectional strife that had even infected him to the point that he lost all reason and was responsible for the death of those he loved more than his own life.

With the dawn of the new year, the chief of the executive branch of government, President Franklin Pierce, declared the Free-Staters to be in revolution and ordered the U.S. Army to prepare to intervene. Convinced the other branches of government had failed in their constitutional responsibilities and had done nothing but fuel the coming conflagration, Taney saw the upcoming oral arguments in *Scott v. Sandford* as the platform from which the judicial branch could douse the fire. His resolve returned, and he determined that he and his court would stop the strife and restore the Union with the might of legal reasoning and the power of the rule of law.

* * *

On February 11th, 1856, Montgomery Blair entered the east doors of the United States Capitol, walked down to the first floor courtroom, and stood before the nine justices of the country's supreme judicial tribunal. To his right were the imminently qualified attorneys for John Sanford—Reverdy Johnson and Henry S. Geyer. The Chief Justice gaveled the hearing to order in a nearly empty courtroom. Most notably absent were the parties to the decade-long litigation. John Sanford was reportedly ill and his sister apparently still had not told her congressman husband that the hearing on slavery, beginning just across the Rotunda and downstairs from his desk on the floor of the House of Representatives, involved her slaves.

For their part, Dred and Harriet had yearned to be in the courtroom that day to make the nine men who held the Scott family's fate in their hands look them in the eyes and feel their humanity. But the long years of litigation and financial hardship brought upon their white benefactors by the influential Chouteaus had made such a trip impossible. And so that February morning, the Scotts, the Band of Brothers, and their families gathered at a special service with the three hundred members of Reverend Johnson's Eighth Street Baptist Church, renamed in 1851 when they moved to a newly constructed chapel at the corner of Eighth and Green Streets. They spent the day in prayer, song, sermonizing, and more prayer, and waited for that first telegram, which would tell them how Montgomery Blair's arguments had gone.

Dred didn't understand the magic that made it possible for words to move along a wire faster than a champion racehorse could gallop, but he thanked God that someone had been inspired to create such a device that made it possible to know what had occurred seven hundred miles away. By the time lunch was laid out by the ladies of the Sunday School, Dred had his fill of praying and wanted to satiate his curiosity.

"How soon you think we's goin' to hear how the first day went?" he asked Roswell Field.

"Mr. Blair thought they would give him about three hours today. He expects that will be the longest the judges will sit each day, so it could take four days of argument."

"And how soon before we knows how it went?" Dred persisted in his examination of his lawyer.

"We should receive the first telegram within a few hours after he's done," replied Field.

Dred whistled. "That is a miracle, it sho' is. Who was it that built a machine that can talk over the wires?"

"You never stop asking questions, do you, Dred?" Taylor interjected. He wandered over with a fried chicken leg in one hand.

"You're going to find this very interesting, Dred, because the very first time Samuel Morse—that's the man who invented the machine called the telegraph—the first time he ever used it was from the very courtroom where they're hearing your case right now."

"Is you teasin' me, Taylor Blow?" Dred asked incredulously.

"No, he ain't . . . isn't . . . teasing, Dred," Roswell jumped back in. "It was in—what, Taylor—1844 or thereabouts, and Morse was trying to get money from the government to build his machines all over the country. So he strung up a wire between a railroad depot in Maryland and ran it to the Capitol Building and into the courtroom. He then sat down at the key and tapped out four words in a code he had developed earlier that replaced letters with dots and dashes."

"What you mean, dots and dashes?" Dred asked.

"A dot means you tap the key just once, and a dash means you hold down on the key a little longer," continued Roswell. "Hey, who knows Morse Code?" he called out to the other men.

Louis LaBeaume came over. "I learned it so I could get telegraphs from other law enforcement officers. Who wants to know? Is it Dred again?"

The men chuckled in unison. The former sheriff looked around and picked up a candle from a table. "Let me show you how to spell your name in this code. The letter 'D' is dash, dot, dot." He tapped the candle down slowly once, followed by two quick taps.

Dred's eyes grew wide. "I can't spell my name with letters, but I reckon I could with Morse Code!" he exclaimed.

Louis let out a loud belly laugh that caused the ladies to pause in their chatter and look over disapprovingly. "I reckon you could. Your name is pretty easy. 'R' is dot, dash, dot." He tapped it out with the candle. 'E' is one dot, and then you repeat the 'D,' dash, dot, dot."

"Thas it?" Dred asked. "Thas my name? Do it again . . . fast."

LaBeaume complied, tapping the candle rapidly on the desk. Dash, dot, dot . . . dot, dash, dot . . . dot . . . dash, dot, dot.

Dred grabbed the candle and repeated the pattern perfectly. "Hey, Harriet," he called, "I just spelled my name!"

Before she could respond, Dred's inquisitive mind returned to the topic. "What was the first four words Mr. Morse sent over his new machine?" he asked.

"'What hath God wrought,'" replied the attorney. When no one said anything, he continued, "I think it's something from the Bible. You know the Bible, Dred—what does it mean?"

"'What hath God wrought,'" repeated Dred. "I don't recognize that scripture. Reverend Anderson," he called out and waited for the minister to look over. "We gots a Bible question for you, if'n you don't mind leaving the ladies." A couple of Dred's companions cleared their throat in embarrassment.

Dred asked the question, and before long, Anderson had found the passage in the Book of Numbers. "It's from the story of when King Balak of Moab offered great riches to the Israelite prophet Balaam if he would curse his own massive army before they could destroy the much smaller Moabite army. Balaam wanted those riches something awful, so he kept pestering the Lord, hoping He would let him give just a little curse so he could then be a wealthy prophet. But God wouldn't let him, so he finally had to tell the king with great sorrow that God brought them out of slavery and protected them with mighty power against all their enemies so that for years the people of Canaan would marvel, shake their heads, and ask themselves, 'what hath God wrought?'"

Reverend Anderson's lecture was followed by silence, as his listeners still weren't sure what he meant.

Suddenly Dred grabbed his Benjamin travel coat and headed for the door. "Come on," he called to the startled men, "let's get over to the telegraph office. I wants to be there to hear my name and the rest come tapping out like Massa Juba in the Vaudeville."

"What's the rush?" called Peter Blow after him.

"Don't you want to know what God done wrought in that courtroom today?"

Dred was at the telegraph office every day and marveled at the speed with which the telegraph operator could write down the words coming from Washington. The messages were short, but from it all, the Band of Brothers was able to piece together the arguments that had been given. Newspaper accounts followed a few days later, and eventually Montgomery Blair himself returned to town and made a full report on the proceedings, which included twelve hours of oral argument.

Blair followed the plan and said that few questions were asked, so he had a hard time guessing which way the majority was leaning. He did express concern over the large number of Southern Democrats on the panel. Seven of the nine justices were Democrats, and five of those were from Southern slave states.

"We must hope and pray that they put aside their personal attitudes, politics, and biases, and rule on the law and precedent."

He then went over the testimony in some detail, but boiled down his argument to two main points. He first tried to persuade the Court that it must rule that Dred was free because, under the Northwest Ordinance, he became free when he resided in the state of Illinois. Dred and Harriet's freedom was further solidified pursuant to the law of the land set forth in the Missouri Compromise when they lived in free Wisconsin Territory. And under the doctrine of *res judicata*, long-standing Missouri law declared that they remained free after they returned to Missouri. Secondly, he argued that a man of African descent was a citizen and had the right to sue in court.

As expected, Sanford's attorneys took turns arguing that the federal government did not have the authority to dictate how the citizens of future territories should treat the issue of slavery, and therefore the Missouri Compromise and Northwest Ordinance were both unconstitutional. They didn't even argue against "once free, always free," but simply tried to show that Dred and Harriet were never free to begin with.

Blair seemed unconcerned with his opponents' presentation, but he was facing gifted and influential adversaries. Reverdy Johnson was a long-time constitutional lawyer from Maryland and had earned fame around the country. Henry Geyer was the current Senator from Missouri who had defeated Senator Thomas Hart Benton after thirty years on the bench. Geyer was rabidly pro-slavery and had represented many slave owners, including Pierre Chouteau, in freedom suits.

Spring came, and still there was no decision. Then in May, Field received a telegram from Blair saying that any hope of a resolution that year had been dashed when the court requested additional arguments in the next court term. The justices wanted more specific arguments on the issue that Roswell and Dred had urged upon Montgomery Blair a year ago—did Circuit Judge Wells properly rule on the plea in abatement as to whether a Negro had the right, as a citizen, to even sue in the federal courts in the first place?

Newspapers carried numerous stories, and the public attention and interest in the case began to grow. The highly respected *Washington Evening Star* reported that *Scott v. Sandford* was "one of the most important cases ever brought up for adjudication by the Supreme Court." Dred and Harriet went dejectedly back to their work, still wondering what God had wrought, but knowing that the courts had once again wrought delay.

The delay was occasioned by the fact that a majority of justices were not ready to take the dramatic judicial step of ruling, for the first time in the history of the court, that a major Act of Congress was unconstitutional. They knew they could, because of the famous 1803 case of *Marbury v. Madison* written by Chief Justice John Marshall, which had established the equality of the judicial branch with the other two branches of government in the power of the court to declare an act of the other branches of government to be "unconstitutional." But the Missouri Compromise was one of the grandest, most far-reaching legislative enactments in the history of the new republic. It had been in effect for nearly forty years, and states and territories had been created and governed pursuant to its mandates. It was clear to Blair that Chief Justice Taney didn't have the votes to so rule, and so he gave himself more time to persuade his rebellious Southern colleagues to go along with him. It was hoped that the additional argument would bring them more reasons to vote with the Chief.

If Taney had hoped to use the case to avert violent conflict, he learned very quickly how wrong he was. Within a few days of the decision to continue the case to December, blood was drawn in the most unlikely of places. On May 19th, Senator Charles Sumner rose on the floor of the Senate and vigorously denounced the Kansas-Nebraska Act, calling it a "crime," and those who voted for it, "criminals." He focused most of his anger on the Act's sponsors, Stephen Douglas and Andrew Butler of South Carolina. He compared the tall Butler to Don Quixote, the crazy Spaniard who tilted at windmills thinking they were giants, and scoffed at the nickname "Little Giant" that people used to describe Douglas. "More like the stupid sidekick, Sancho Panza!" he declared, eliciting cheers and jeers from the body.

Two days later, Representative Preston Brooks from South Carolina crossed the Capitol Rotunda and entered the Senate Chamber, looking to avenge the honor of his uncle Senator Butler. Finding Sumner at his desk, he quickly, and without warning, struck him on the head with the gold handle of a heavy cane made of gutta-percha wood imported from Asia. Tangled in his desk, the large Sumner was unable to defend himself from the blows, and an accomplice from the House kept help away by brandishing a pistol. Sumner's blood flew as the assailant rained down blows, and he might have killed the senator had not the cane broke. It took three years for Sumner to fully recover from the beating, and the incident was added to the abolitionist battle cry.

Once blood had been shed on the sacred floor of the Senate Chamber, nothing could stop it from flowing onto the soil of Kansas. A few days later, pro-slavery forces attacked the shadow government stronghold at Lawrence, burned several buildings, and destroyed the printing presses. At the end of May, the fanatical abolitionist preacher John Brown and his boys attacked a settlement of Missouri border ruffians at Pottawatomie Creek, and using cavalry swords, brutally hacked five men to death. Violence begat violence, and battles erupted across the eastern border of Kansas.

Abolitionists marched into battle singing *The Song of Freedom:*

"From the bloody plains of Kansas,
From the Senate's guilty floor,
From the smoking wreck of Lawrence,
From our Sumner's wounds and gore,
Comes our country's dying call
Rise for Freedom! or we fall!
Speak! ye Orators of Freedom,
Let your thunder shake these plains;
Write! ye Editors of Freedom,
Let your lightning rive their chains;
Up! ye Sons of Pilgrims, rise!
Strike! for Freedom, or she dies!"

By the end of the year, fifty more Americans would be struck down.

Abraham Lincoln, who many said resembled the lanky Brown, preferred the title "Orator of Freedom," and rather than take up arms, he pursued an aggressive political course to get in a position of authority so he could use his voice, his wit, and his leadership to make a real difference. Having organized the new Republican Party in his home state, he sought the Party's nomination for vice president at the first Republican National Convention held in Philadelphia. Although he was virtually unknown on the national stage, he nevertheless garnered one hundred and ten votes—the second highest out of fifteen candidates. He stumped the rest of the year for the Party's presidential nominee, John C. Fremont, and quietly resolved that he would find a way to further his renown before the next presidential election in 1860.

Snow was falling December 16th, 1856, and the muddy roads were icing over when again the justices and counsel for the petitioner Dred Scott and respondent John Sanford met in the Supreme Court for another round of arguments. This time the courtroom had packed to overflowing. Newspapers had spread word that the legal disputes underlying the turmoil in Bleeding Kansas were being heard by the court, and both sides of the great divide hoped their side would prevail.

There was another change in the courtroom this time. Montgomery Blair had been joined at the petitioner's large mahogany counsel table by George T. Curtis of Massachusetts. Surprisingly, Sanford's attorneys had not objected to the obvious conflict of interest the Scotts' new co-counsel presented. Benjamin R. Curtis, as the second-most junior justice, was seated at his mahogany desk at the far right of the dais directly across from his brother, George Curtis. Johnson figured that opposing counsel

461

must have known that, if they started bringing up ethical conflicts that might disqualify justices from hearing the case, he would lodge his own objection. On the respondent's side, Marylander Reverdy Johnson was a life-long close friend of the Chief Justice. While that fact alone would not require that the Chief Justice recuse himself, it would certainly inflame public sentiment and anger Taney, and Blair was still hopeful that he could convince the panel of justices to free his client.

The large clock hanging above the mantel at the back of the chambers was commissioned by Chief Justice Roger Taney specifically to keep his fellow justices on time. It was three and one-half feet in diameter and was kept running five minutes early to ensure they started promptly. When the hands clicked to ten o'clock, Taney once again brought the gavel down to commence oral arguments.

Back in St. Louis, Dred demurred from attending another prayer service at Eighth Street and insisted on being left alone to meditate and pray for his lawyers in the far-off capitol. He wandered the streets of his adopted city and made his way down toward the levee. The entire city had changed dramatically since he had first landed here with the Blow family thirty-six years ago this month. The population of the city had exploded ten times over to more than one hundred and sixty thousand souls. All of the mostly wooden buildings that had been destroyed in the St. Louis Fire of 1849 had been replaced by multi-story brick edifices, and the four blocks between the courthouse and the river were a teaming commercial center.

Dred walked down a crowded Walnut Street and looked up at a verdigris copper spire capped by a large gold cross towering over the St. Louis Cathedral—the only building to have survived the fire. He rubbed his thick mane and wondered again if God did indeed watch over His children here below. He plucked a black strand and examined it. Did a loving Father in Heaven, as Hannah had so often taught him from the Good Book, truly number every hair of the head of a poor, insignificant slave in a city of hundreds of thousands? He dropped the hair as he continued walking east and looked up one more time.

"Did you see that?" he asked the heavens, then chuckled and chastised himself for his irreverence and lack of faith. Of course God had saved a passel of poor slaves from the land of Egypt, and had blessed Dred with a taste of freedom. *Or maybe it was a curse,* he thought as he passed his place of employment, the Barnum Hotel. The manager had given him time off in light of the hearings that week. He waved to his friends, the bellmen and porters, all but one of them a free man, and they called out to him.

"Good luck!"

"We's praying for you, Brother Dred!"

He made his way between the tall warehouses on Commercial and Front Streets and took a deep breath of the cold air as the unchanged levee spread out before him. The sloping uneven cobblestone, leading down into the lapping water, was the same, but what once was a busy quay was now a chaotic mercantile anthill of humanity. Despite the chill in the winter air, commerce was in full swing. Hundreds of steamboats and barges were tied up four deep as far as the eye could see.

Dred wove around dock workers, porters, roustabouts, businessmen, steamboat passengers, and sailors. He dodged hogs and goats, horses and dogs as he threaded his way north through crates, barrels, and moldering bails of cotton, left too long in the elements. A thousand sounds filled his ears. Bleating and squealing of sheep and pigs competed with the calls of salesmen hawking hundreds of items. The rumble of boilers and whistle of steam pipes blended in chorus with the rhythmic splashing of giant paddle wheels and the chanting of a chain gang as they hoisted a heavy load to the hurricane deck of the large side-wheeler *Adriatic*.

> *"You hear dat whistle shoutin'*
> *You hear that little bell;*
> *Oh, swing around that derrick,*
> *We's got ter work a spell;*
>
> *"And dar's de mate a-comin',*
> *De captain's up on deck,*
> *Oh hurry up, you rousters,*
> *You'll cotch it in de neck!"*

Dred rubbed his own tired neck and moved on, stopping at a familiar spot. He stubbed the toe of his boot into the inverted iron rail that ran perpendicular to the river up the slopping brick levee. Dred had pushed his porter's cart up that same track more times than he could count during that year he brought the truck of lodgers from the river to the Jefferson Hotel. He looked up to Olive Street and didn't recognize a single landmark. He pivoted and gazed down at the river, where he saw familiar lines rubbed into the levee by the eternal motion of thick ropes and chains tethering boats to the shore. He could hardly see the river for the press of ships. He rose up on his toes and leaned left, then right, but could not see the free soil of Illinois across the river.

"How many times has I come down to the river to pray, oh Lawd?" Dred closed his eyes and murmured under his breath, "How long must I suffer? How many more years must my family and my people languish, weighted down with the chains of oppression, and beaten with the lash of hatred?" He looked around, and no one seemed to notice the nondescript black man as commerce hustled all about him.

He pulled the collar of his Benjamin up around his neck and repeated for the thousandth time, "Go down Moses. Way down in Egypt land. Tell ole Pharaoh, to let my people go!" He turned back toward the city and retraced his steps up the levee. The dots and dashes reporting the day's events from Washington should soon be dancing once again.

For four days, Dred repeated his circuit of the city and the quay, always ending up at the telegraph office, where he met Field and some of the Blows. The news was sparse and appeared positive. Montgomery Blair had argued for five hours, leaving only one hour for his new associate, the brother of the Justice, and Johnson and Geyer had shared their six hours. Before the end of the four days, newspapers had arrived by fast packet and reported in more detail the proceedings before the court. Dred wouldn't let anyone but Eliza, now eighteen years old, read them to him, and she did so several times over those tense days at the end of 1856.

Eliza opened the December 16th edition of the *New York Times* and read the lines she felt were the most relevant. "'Mr. Blair contended that the plaintiff is legally a free man of Missouri, within the elevation section of the act of 1789. It had been objected that he is not entitled to all the immunities of other citizens, but if that is a test of citizenship, three-fourths of the whites of the United States are not citizens, because the census shows that there is not more than one voter in every five inhabitants. Therefore, that hypothesis does not hold good.'"

"That's right!" Dred declared. "You tell 'em, Mr. Blair."

Eliza moved her finger down the column and stabbed one spot. "I like what he argued here when he started quoting a Judge Gaston of North Carolina." She began reading again. "'. . . there has been no law repealing the general principle of common law, and that birth makes citizenship induced. The act of the Missouri Legislature of 1845 expressly recognizes free Negroes as citizens, and declares that none shall come there who are not declared by other States as citizens.'"

Eliza paused and looked at her poppy. "Mr. Blair then tried again to convince the judges that they should support the Missouri Compromise by bringing up the Declaration of Independence." Dred perked up at that reference, and his daughter continued, "'The Declaration of Independence declares liberty to be one of those rights which are inalienable, and are we to be told that a Negro by any act of his own can abrogate this act?'"

"He's right, Gypsy," Dred interjected. "Thomas Jefferson wrote that liberty is given by God, and no man can take that away—not me and not Dr. Emerson."

"You're thinking just like a lawyer, Father," Eliza said to her beaming progenitor. "Listen to what Mr. Blair argued next about John Emerson: 'This man took his negro to Illinois under a knowledge that he thereby became free and could not be held; he intended to violate the law which prohibits Slavery or involuntary servitude.'"

Dred took great joy in the next three reading sessions with his daughter as *The Times* reported each day's proceedings. On Tuesday, Sanford's lawyer Henry Geyer took over and argued points quoted in the paper and highlighted to Dred by Eliza. Father and daughter worried as she read his points:

"An African is incapable of being made a citizen . . .

"At the time of the adoption of the Constitution, every State, except one of the Slaveholding States in the Convention . . . left open the African Slave-Trade for twenty years, and [therefore] it was not the intention of the framers of that instrument to make importation of material [eligible] for citizenship."

"Tarnation!" Eliza hollered, shocking Dred as she slapped the paper and continued to cuss. "I don't care if he is a United States senator—he's a gol-derned scalawag if he thinks we are nothing but 'material!' Material don't fight back, and we're fighting back, ain't we?"

Dred had to laugh. His daughter had been educated by various Blow family members, and he could tell that some of that education had come from the two boys, Peter and Taylor. But he didn't mind. He loved her gypsy spirit. Sometimes she reminded him of himself. "Easy there, darlin'." Dred patted her leg. "Jes' keep readin'."

> "The law of Missouri says if a negro comes to that State with the naturalization papers from another State he shall not be whipped, but it does not recognize him as a citizen.

> "If the master carries a slave into a State where Slavery does not exist, and the slave is not discharged by local law, and then he takes him back to a State where Slavery is established, the latter is not bound to enforce the law of the other State . . . It had been decided everywhere that the mere temporary residence of the master in a non-slaveholding State did not emancipate the slave."

"I'm not a lawyer, and I know that's a lie!" Eliza continued to editorialize. "Besides, didn't you and Momma live at Fort Snelling for four years? If that's 'temporary,' then I was just temporarily an adolescent."

Dred snorted at his daughter's sassy wit, and felt good. They were half-way through the proceedings, and he was sure they were winning. But his optimism was short-lived as Eliza began reading the report of day three and turned serious immediately.

> *"Mr. Reverdy Johnson made a powerful argument for defendant . . . he attempted to show that the Constitution of the United States was never designed to consider black men as citizens. It maintains throughout that man can have property in man; and so sacred is this description of property, that the Constitution pledges the force of the Union to protect it."*

It was Dred's turn to quarrel. "I'se been talking about the Constitution my whole life. Massa Peter told me all about it when we went to court together, and you knows that Brother Roswell and the other counselors would have told us if it said it was okay to own another man. I just don't believe it. You think the judges will make him prove it?"

"They will if they'll do their jobs," Eliza said bluntly, anxious to continue reading. It frightened her when the article turned to the issue of popular sovereignty.

> *"The State of Illinois cannot legislate on this or any other subject for the citizens of Missouri.*

> *"The people of the South do not stand in the relation of servants to the people of the North. They stand where the Constitution placed them, equal in the sight of God and man.*

> *"He concluded with a eulogium upon the high character and justice of the Court, and a tribute to the Union."*

"Oh, I hate that man!" Eliza growled and threw the paper on the floor. "He's a liar. I can just picture him prancing in front of the court, flattering the judges with praise, and wooing the newspaper reporters with fancy words. But I think he's like those Amanitas mushrooms that grow out by the swamp. They make your mouth water, they look so delicious. But there's a reason people here about call them 'Destroying Angels.' Even his name, Reverdy, sounds like a false prophet to me."

"I was thinking more Biblical," Dred replied. "He's just like them lawyers and Pharisees that Jesus cursed as 'whited sepulchres'—beautiful on the outside, but inside, full of dead men's bones. I hope Mr. Blair calls them what they are."

Their hopes were uplifted as they read quotes from the proceedings of the final day of arguments. Montgomery Blair returned to a well-supported defense of the Missouri Compromise and the authority of the Congress to enact it. He urged the justices to do their duty under the rule of precedent and the doctrine of *res judicata*, and wisely cited to them the words of the revered "Father of the Supreme Court," Taney's predecessor, Chief Justice John Marshall, who was as close to deity as one might ascend in the American judicial system.

> *"John Marshall laid down the law as it relates to power of Congress, which is, in his own words, 'unlimited, supreme, subject only to certain limitations imposed by the Constitution.' He made it very clear that the federal government possessed general sovereignty over the territories and had the right to control all rules and regulations governing them. In fine, Justice Marshall concluded that 'there are no limitations forbidding the prohibition of Slavery.' Mr. Blair urged the justices to stay the course charted by the court over the past seventy years."*

Dred was already feeling better when Eliza perked up even more, "Oh, listen to the words of our other attorney, who got to have the last word. And they are good ones, Poppy:

> *"Mr. George P. Curtis, of Boston, made a powerful argument in favor of the Constitutionality of the Missouri Compromise. The third section of the fourth article of the Constitution gives Congress authority to 'make all needful regulations for the government of territory.'*
>
> *"The great unoccupied lands within the boundaries of the older States were almost the only subject of contention in those states. No sooner had Virginia made a cession of land beyond the Ohio than the question arose, what disposition shall be made of it? By the deed of cession the United States were clothed with power to erect it into Republican States.*
>
> *"Congress shall have power to dispose of and make all needful rules and regulations respecting territory or other property belonging to the United States, and nothing in this Constitution shall be so construed as to prejudice any claims of the United States or any particular State.' . . . All undeniably rest in the judgment of Congress as to necessity."*

The Supreme Court adjourned after the fourth day and a full twenty-four hours of argument. The Chief Justice began feverishly to try to craft a majority opinion that could be announced prior to the following March 4th when he would swear in the newly elected President James Buchanan.

The Band of Brothers pulled together a Christmas celebration back at the enlarged Taylor Blow estate south of the city to try to take everyone's minds off the coming ruling, but it was a muted event. Eleven years of litigation, filled with ups and downs, magnificent triumphs and abject defeats, verbal and physical attacks, and economic hardship had worn everyone down.

But the heat of their trials had forged a bond among family, friends, and lawyers—black and white, slave and freeman—that had the strength of steel. Hearts, hopes, faith, fears, and prayers melded together into one unbreakable chain that, regardless of the ultimate ruling of the Supreme Court, would stand as a testament to the possibilities of the future and a lesson to all succeeding generations.

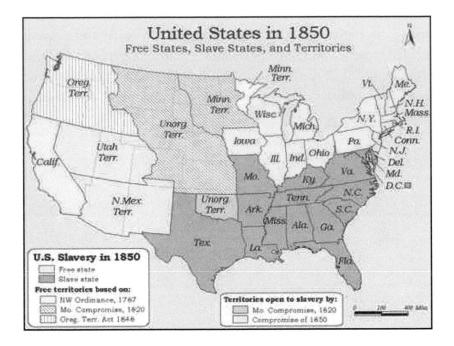

United States in 1850
Free States, Slave States, and Territories

U.S. Slavery in 1850
- Free state
- Slave state

Free territories based on:
- NW Ordinance, 1787
- Mo. Compromise, 1820
- Oreg. Terr. Act 1848

Territories open to slavery by:
- Mo. Compromise, 1820
- Compromise of 1850

Chapter 36

An Ordinary Article of Merchandise

Washington D.C. & St. Louis, Missouri, 1857

Despite the fact that the case had gained widespread national attention, a terrible tragedy occurred, which further delayed the court in getting together to discuss the case. On January 3rd, Justice Peter Daniel's wife accidentally brushed up against an open flame, her dress caught fire, and she died of her burns a few days later. Daniel, a Virginian, was perhaps the strongest defender of slavery on the panel, and the Chief Justice refused to call the court together until he could join them.

As January gave way to February, Taney came under intense pressure to render an opinion prior to the inauguration of the newly elected Democratic president James Buchanan.

A Pennsylvania Democrat, Buchanan had a long history of public service. He had served ten years in the U.S. House of

Representatives, ten in the Senate, and ten in the executive branch as ambassador and Secretary of State. His election was viewed as a compromise in the midst of the fractious dispute over territories and slavery. Buchanan was the one candidate with the rare combination of being a Northerner with a well-documented history of sympathy toward the Southern cause. The president-elect knew that the historic case of *Scott v. Sandford* would play a major role in his first one hundred days, and he knew he had to speak of it in his inaugural address.

Buchanan had his representatives contact the Democratic Chief Justice and pressure him to render a decision before he was sworn in on the steps of the Capitol on March 4th. So, despite his knowledge that his fellow justice was deeply mourning the loss of his wife, Taney convinced Daniel to join them in mid-February to begin deliberations of the issues in a case they all recognized would have far-reaching and long-lasting consequences for the nation. After first polling the panel of justices, Taney became very concerned at just how far they were from reaching any kind of majority consensus.

The justices were split four-two on whether the case was even properly before them, on the grounds that Circuit Court judge Wells had improperly granted Dred Scott the right to sue in the first place. They came down three-two against Negro citizenship and six-two that the Missouri Compromise was unconstitutional. But on the issue of the sovereignty of the State of Missouri to determine whether Dred Scott was free after he returned from freedom in Illinois and Wisconsin Territory, all seven Democrats on the court agreed that the law of Missouri ruled, and based on the Missouri Supreme Court ruling nearly seven years earlier, Dred Scott and his family would remain slaves.

At that point, Chief Justice Taney could have ended the case with a decision upholding the Circuit Court ruling and denying

Scott's petition. But he had long since determined that if he could get the necessary votes of his fellow justices, he would go well beyond the specific issue and use his position as the head of the Judicial Branch to do what the other branches had not done, and by judicial decree, resolve the issue of the expansion of slavery into new states and territories and the rights of all Negroes, bond or free, to citizenship in the United States. It didn't take him long.

Ignoring the Whig and Republican, both of whom believed Dred had become free, pursuant to the Missouri Compromise, he focused on pressuring three or four of his popular sovereignty brethren to join him in declaring that the Negro is not a citizen, and firming up the others to a consensus on the specific legal rationale as to why Congress did not have power under the Constitution to prohibit slavery in any state or territory. He believed, correctly, that a five-four decision on such a contentious issue would not be strong enough to cause the country's warring factions to accept the Supreme Court ruling as the final word.

As March approached, Buchanan grew anxious. In an extraordinary breach in the wall that separated the powers of the executive and judicial branches of government, he secretly wrote separate letters to his close friends on the court, fellow Pennsylvanian Robert Grier and Tennessean John Catron. At the request of President Andrew Jackson, Buchanan had been Catron's strongest Senate supporter in 1837 when Congress increased the Supreme Court to nine justices. Buchanan had been elected on his promise to be a peacemaker, but he had no specific plan to make that happen. He hoped the Supreme Court would provide that plan, and determined that if the president of the United States and the Supreme Court were in agreement, the rest of the nation would follow.

During a two-week period, as many as eight letters were exchanged between the president and the two justices.

Although Taney did not write or receive any letters, he was kept apprised of the communications by Justice Catron.

Catron, for his part, was unaware that Grier had also been corresponding with the president, and when he found out that his Northern colleague had decided to join New Yorker Samuel Nelson in bypassing the issue of the Missouri Compromise, he wrote two quick letters to the president on February 19th and 22nd, urging him to put pressure on his fellow Pennsylvanian Grier to go with the majority.

The president immediately wrote to Robert Grier, and the next day the justice responded in a shocking letter.

> *On conversation with the chief justice, I have agreed to concur with him. Brother Wayne and myself will also use our endeavors to get brothers Daniel and Campbell and Catron to do the same . . . But I fear some rather extreme views may be thrown out by some of our southern brethren. There will therefore be six, if not seven (perhaps Nelson will remain neutral) who will decide the compromise law of 1820 to be of non-effect. But the opinions will not be delivered before Friday the 6th of March. We will not let any others of our brethren know anything about the cause of our anxiety to produce this result, and although contrary to our usual practice, we have thought due to you to state to you in candor and confidence the real state of the matter.*

Armed with a knowledge of what the court would rule, President James Buchanan walked down the west steps of the Capitol on March 4th. With the sun high above the unfinished dome and an early spring thaw warming the spectators, he placed his hand on the Bible and received the oath of office from Chief Justice Roger Brooks Taney.

In his inaugural address, the president declared his learned position on the territorial dispute over popular sovereignty, sectionalism, and slavery, and his confidence that the Supreme Court would soon rule likewise.

A difference of opinion has arisen in regard to the point of time when the people of a Territory shall decide this question for themselves.

This is, happily, a matter of but little practical importance. Besides, it is a judicial question, which legitimately belongs to the Supreme Court of the United States, before whom it is now pending, and will, it is understood, be speedily and finally settled. To their decision, in common with all good citizens, I shall cheerfully submit, whatever this may be . . .

No other question remains for adjustment, because all agree that under the Constitution slavery in the States is beyond the reach of any human power except that of the respective States themselves wherein it exists. May we not, then, hope that the long agitation on this subject is approaching its end, and that the geographical parties to which it has given birth, so much dreaded by the Father of his Country, will speedily become extinct? Most happy will it be for the country when the public mind shall be diverted from this question to others of more pressing and practical importance.

The president could not have been more wrong on what the people of the United States considered important, or more naïve in his assessment as to how the public would react to his speech and the soon-to-be-delivered opinion of the court.

Two days later, Chief Justice Roger Taney led his eight black-robed fellow justices into the courtroom not far from where he had sworn in President Buchanan. The courtroom was full and overflowing into the hallways and the crypt beneath the Rotunda. The aged Chief showed clear signs of exhaustion from the events of the past week and the writing of a fifty-five page opinion. He began reading the opinion in a soft, gravely voice that grew nearly inaudible by the time he finished two hours later. Reporters leaned forwarded in their seats to hear and scribbled feverishly to capture the opinion for immediate distribution to a nation waiting breathlessly to learn the fate of Dred Scott. No one was more anxious to hear the result than an obscure black slave in St. Louis.

Dred had always felt most free when, as a young boy named Sam, he swam in the dark waters of the Nottoway, Meherrin, and Blackwater rivers of Southampton County, Virginia. Water buoyed his spirits as much as his body. Surrounded by the waters of Hampton Roads Bay, he had fought and bled for his country. In the Suck of the Upper Tennessee, he had fought for his life. He had fished in the Ohio, dunked his sweetheart in the Minnesota, splashed his children in the Salt, and was born again in the mightiest of them all, the Mississippi. So it came as no surprise to those who knew and loved him that on the day the new president was sworn in, Dred asked permission of his keepers, the LaBeaumes, to embark perhaps one last time aboard a steamer up Old Man River to await the court's decision. None of the places of comfort where he had awaited prior rulings—the courtroom, church, levee, friends' homes—seemed adequate this time.

One day many years earlier, Dred and Roswell Field had been walking along Front Street, watching the endless flow of commerce up and down the great river. They walked far north beyond the levee and the steamships and down to the river's edge. Dred spoke of past regrets and future fears.

"I want you to put your hand in the river, Dred," Roswell suddenly suggested.

"Why for, Mr. Roswell?" Dred asked. "I's been in this here river a hundred times. I even swam across it way up yonder." He pointed upstream.

"I remember something someone famous once said, and I want to share it with you. Now go ahead, do as I ask."

Dred wrinkled up his nose, shrugged, crouched on a large rock, and stuck his hand into the flow.

"A famous Italian artist, sculptor, and very smart man, Leonard da Vinci, said that 'When you put your hand in a flowing stream, you touch the last that has gone before and the first of what is still to come.'"

Dred looked at the small wake his hand made in the water. He pulled his hand out and watched a twig float by. He looked at Roswell and thought for a bit, then slipped off the rock and waded out to his waist, creating a much larger wake behind his body.

"I like what that I-talian had to say," Dred remarked. "And standin' here in this mighty river, with the past flowin' away from me and the future rushin' at me, I feels like a part of eternity!"

On March 5th, Dred and Louis LaBeaume, who was responsible to the court for Dred's charge, boarded the brand new side-wheeler, *Colonel Crossman*, which had just arrived from New Orleans. Dred was introduced to Captain York, the pilot Horace Bixby, and his cub pilot, a young man with thick, curly red hair named Sam Clemens. As Dred explained his experience on board a steamboat and offered to do any job the captain needed, Bixby asked why the name of Dred Scott was so familiar. When LaBeaume told him that he was the famous Dred Scott whose case in the Supreme Court would end the next day, the captain and his crew insisted that Dred bunk in a small room on the Texas deck just below the pilot house, and that he just relax and enjoy the run up to Davenport.

Dred did not sleep as the boat churned north, throbbing to the rhythm of the two side-wheels. He searched out and spent all night with the Negro crew, more than half of whom were slaves. They told stories of the river and of women loved and lost. The river was an oral news source, and the men delighted to learn that their new shipmate was the famous slave who had the nation's capitol in such a dither. They praised him and forced cigars in his mouth, pounded his back, and pumped his hand until he felt like it would fall off. They gathered near the stern of the Texas between the large, covered paddle wheels and passed the early morning hours bundled up in heavy wool and cotton cloaks, warmed from the inside out through the singing of spirituals.

A sweet contentment settled over Dred, and he finally felt that no matter what came with the new day, he would be ready for it. He drew in the cool night air and savored the taste of charcoal on his tongue, then took a swig of the contraband blackstrap alcohol, shook all over as it burned a trail down his gullet, and signaled it was his turn to lead the next call. He started a low soothing hum and the others joined in with soulful murmurs. Booted feet began to stomp on the deck, and hands slapped against pant legs. The men became one with each other and with the rocking, swaying, and thrumming of the boat, and with the river as waves rhythmically crashed against the hull.

"I've got peace like a river in my soul," Dred called.

"I've got a river in my soul," the men responded

"Said I've got peace like a river in my soul," he repeated with a serenity that brought tears to the eyes of his fellow travelers in a world of heartache and despair.

"I've got a river in my soul," they repeated with feeling.

"I've got joy like a fountain in my soul." Dred stood and raised his voice an octave and several decibels.

"I've got a fountain in my soul!" the group responded in kind, and began clapping to the beat.

"I've got love like an ocean in my soul," sang out the slave who had known every sorrow and every joy that life could throw one's way.

"I've got an ocean in my soul," cried out the men, who loved their new friend for his courage in the fight he had waged for all of them.

* * *

It wouldn't be until four days after the decision was announced that Dred Scott learned what the United States Supreme Court had ruled in his case. But by then, it no longer mattered. They were in Davenport, Iowa, and LaBeaume had picked up a newspaper. He walked down to the river, where Dred showed him the spot he had homesteaded for Emerson. Dred watched the great brown river move powerfully by and listened stoically as his companion read the summary of Chief Justice Taney's opinion and several of the more alarming and hurtful quotes. When he was finished, Dred asked for the paper, crumpled it up, and threw it in the water. He watched it flow away and sink.

"That's the past," was all he said, and then he turned and walked up the river. Louis shook his head in amazement and watched Dred move without hesitation toward an unknown future.

* * *

After twenty-five years as Chief Justice of the United States Supreme Court and a lifetime of dedication to justice and the rule of law, Roger Brooks Taney announced the decision of seven of the nine justices that, by law, Dred Scott was still a slave. Eight of the nine justices wrote separate opinions, but it was the Taney majority opinion that, instead of bringing the conclusion and harmony that he and President Buchanan had hoped for, instead lit the fuse leading to the powder keg that would in a few years explode into a great Civil War.

The decision was, by legal standards, a well-reasoned and thoughtful treatise. But because it went so far beyond the question before the court, and was written with such clear and brutal disdain for all people of African decent, it inflamed the passions of Northerners, abolitionists, and Free Soilers more than all of the hated actions of Congress, the chief executive, and the border ruffians combined. In his *New York Tribune* editorial, Horace Greeley used the words "atrocious," "wicked," "abominable," "hypocrisy," and "cowardly" to describe the majority opinion and the man who wrote it. Many agreed with Greeley's conclusion that the decision "has no more weight than given by a majority in any Washington barroom."

Chief Justice Taney ruled against the Scotts on every single point of law. Neither Dred, nor any Negro, bond or free, was a citizen of the United States and had no right of access to justice in the federal courts. The Missouri Compromise was unconstitutional, and therefore, Dred did not become free when he lived at Fort Snelling because Congress had no right to prohibit slavery in any federal territory. He was not free after living at Fort Armstrong in the free state of Illinois, because Missouri law, as established by the State Supreme Court in

Scott v. Emerson, took precedence when he moved back to that slave state.

Half of the fifty-five page opinion addressed the legal issue before the court on appeal from the Circuit Court and the additional questions added by the activist members of the court. Justice Taney then devoted a surprising twenty-four pages to the status and citizenship of a people he termed an "unfortunate race." His words burned deep into the hearts and souls of every freedom-loving American.

> *They [African Americans] are not included, and were not intended to be included, under the word 'citizens' in the Constitution, and can therefore claim none of the rights and privileges which that instrument provides for and secures to citizens of the United States. On the contrary, they were at that time [1787] considered as a subordinate and inferior class of beings, who had been subjugated by the dominant race, and, whether emancipated or not, yet remained subject to their authority, and had no rights or privileges but such as those who held the power and the Government might choose to grant them.*
>
> . . .
>
> *[C]itizenship would give to persons of the negro race, who were recognized as citizens in any one State of the Union, the right to enter every other state whenever they pleased, singly or in companies, without pass or passport, and without obstruction, to sojourn there as long as they pleased, to go where they pleased at every hour of the day or night without molestation . . . would give them the full liberty of speech in public and in private . . . to hold public meetings upon political affairs, and to keep*

and carry arms wherever they went . . . inevitably producing discontent and insubordination . . . and endangering the peace and safety of the State.

. . .

The right of property in a slave is distinctly and expressly affirmed in the Constitution. The right to traffic in it, like an ordinary article of merchandise and property, was guarantied to the citizens of the United States, in every State that might desire it, for twenty years. And the Government in express terms is pledged to protect it in all future time, if the slave escapes from his owner.

Before the year was out, on November 3rd, 1857, Edwin Booth, of the famous acting family that included John Wilkes Booth, took the stage of Wood's Theatre in New York City as the title role in the play *Richelieu; Or the Conspiracy*. In scene two of the second act, Booth, as Cardinal Richelieu, threw down his sword and declared,

> *"True, This! —*
> *Beneath the rule of men entirely great,*
> *The pen is mightier than the sword. Behold*
> *The arch-enchanters wand! — itself a nothing! —*
> *But taking sorcery from the master-hand*
> *To paralyse the Cæsars, and to strike*
> *The loud earth breathless!"*

With the stroke of his pen, Chief Justice Roger Brooke Taney shattered Dred Scott's eleven years of faith in the judicial system of the greatest democratic republic in the history of the world—a nation founded upon the principles of God-given rights: equality and individual liberty.

In so doing, he stuck a terrible blow to Dred Scott and every other person of African descent living in the United States. The courts of justice were closed to them, and the protections of the Constitution did not apply for one reason: the color of their skin.

Now only the sword could restore justice.

The question remained as to which Caesar would pick it up.

Conclusion

A House Divided

*"A house divided against itself cannot stand.
I believe this government cannot endure
permanently half slave and half free."*

- Abraham Lincoln (June 17, 1858)

*"Some o'dese mornin's bright and fair,
I thank God I'm free at las'.
Gwineter meet my Jesus in
De middle of de air,
I thank God I'm free at las'."*

- Slave prayer on marker stone at slave cemetery on
site of Peter Blow Plantation, Huntsville, AL

Epilogue

Rather than heal the growing rift that was splitting the country apart, Chief Justice Taney's controversial and mean-spirited opinion was used by each side to widen the fracture. Newspapers on both sides went on the attack during the spring of 1857. The decision was decried as "inhuman dicta" and Taney as a "mean and skulking coward" by one side of the divide, and on the other "the greatest political boon which has been vouchsafed to us since the foundation of the Republic," and any disobedience to it would be "treason." The White House decided to stick its head in the sand and continually declared that the ruling would result in "harmony and fraternal concord throughout the country." Abolitionists and Northerners used it to inflame the public sentiment and motivate the masses to action, and Democrats called it "the funeral sermon of Black Republicanism."

The latter could not have been more wrong.

By summer, the politicians took up where the newspapers had left off. Senator Stephen Douglas, who had twice run unsuccessfully for the Democratic nomination for president, already had his eye on the 1860 election, particularly since the Democratic president, James Buchanan, had said in his inaugural speech that he would only serve one term. The election was three years away, but the author of the Kansas-Nebraska Act believed, as did the Buchanan Administration, that the Dred Scott decision would end sectionalism, and latched onto it as a campaign platform, which he first tested in a June speech in Springfield that garnered national attention.

Senator Douglas quoted from Taney's decision and stated his own opinion that the Framers of the Declaration of Independence were referring to the white race alone when they declared that all men are created equal. His speech was reported across the country, and newspapers declared that he was without rival for the Democratic nomination in 1860. One man in the audience that day was greatly offended by Douglas's rhetoric and prejudice, and immediately began an intensive two-week study of the entire case so he could publicly respond. An Italian proverb held that "the right men will come at the right time," and Abraham Lincoln was that man.

At 8:00 p.m. on the night of June 26th, the lanky lawyer strode into the Illinois State House, law books under his arm, and publicly dissected Senator Douglas's support of the Dred Scott decision. He wisely did not immediately call for the overthrow of the rule of law nor question the authority of the Supreme Court, but he reasoned that, to be valid, a decision by the high court on a matter of vital public interest, and on whether to invalidate the actions of a sister branch of government, had to be unanimous, without "partisan bias," based on precedent and grounded in historical fact. He picked apart Taney's majority opinion and demonstrated that it failed on all four counts. Lincoln's powerful statements were also reported around the country and catapulted the Republican to national prominence. His words struck a common chord of compassion and patriotism for the common rights of all men as declared by the Nation's founders.

In those days, by common consent, the spread of the black man's bondage to new countries was prohibited; but now, Congress decides that it will not continue the prohibition, and the Supreme Court decides that it could not if it would. In those days, our Declaration of Independence was held sacred by all, and thought to include all; but now, to aid in making the bondage of the negro universal and eternal, it is assailed, and sneered at, and construed, and hawked at, and torn, till, if its framers could rise from their graves, they could not at all recognize it.

. . .

Now I protest against that counterfeit logic which concludes that, because I do not want a black woman for a slave I must necessarily want her for a wife. I need not have her for either, I can just leave her alone. In some respects she certainly is not my equal; but in her natural right to eat the bread she earns with her own hands without asking leave of any one else, she is my equal, and the equal of all others.

. . .

I think the authors of that notable instrument intended to include all men, but they did not intend to declare all men equal in all respects. They did not mean to say all were equal in color, size, intellect, moral

491

developments, or social capacity. They defined with tolerable distinctness, in what respects they did consider all men created equal—equal in "certain inalienable rights, among which are life, liberty, and the pursuit of happiness." This they said, and this meant . . . They meant simply to declare the right, so that the enforcement of it might follow as fast as circumstances should permit. They meant to set up a standard maxim for free society, which should be familiar to all, and revered by all; constantly looked to, constantly labored for, and even though never perfectly attained, constantly approximated, and thereby constantly spreading and deepening its influence, and augmenting the happiness and value of life to all people of all colors everywhere.

. . .

The Republicans inculcate, with whatever of ability they can, that the negro is a man; that his bondage is cruelly wrong, and that the field of his oppression ought not to be enlarged. The Democrats deny his manhood; deny, or dwarf to insignificance, the wrong of his bondage; so far as possible, crush all sympathy for him, and cultivate and excite hatred and disgust against him; compliment themselves as Union-savers for doing so; and call the indefinite outspreading of his bondage "a sacred right of self-government."

The response to Lincoln's speech was overwhelming, and six months later he determined that he needed to provide the people with a choice against Senator Douglas. The following year, on June 16th, 1858, he accepted the nomination of the Illinois Republican Party as their candidate for United States Senate. That night he gave a speech that branded the Republican Party as the party of abolition and left an indelible image on the nation's conscience as to the dangers of disunion.

> *A house divided against itself cannot stand. I believe this government cannot endure permanently half slave and half free. I do not expect the Union to be dissolved— I do not expect the house to fall—but I do expect it will cease to be divided. It will become all one thing, or all the other. Either the opponents of slavery will arrest the further spread of it, and place it where the public mind shall rest in the belief that it is in the course of ultimate extinction; or its advocates will push it forward, till it shall become alike lawful in all the States, old as well as new—North as well as South.*

Lincoln once again focused much of his speech on an attack on Chief Justice Taney's opinion, but first tried to humanize the case. He told of a "negro who's name was Dred Scott" who had been taken by his master to live in a free state and then a free territory, and later brought his case to federal court the same month as Douglas and Congress passed the Kansas-Nebraska bill. In rallying the party faithful to "stand firm," he warned that inaction would lead to defeat.

> *. . . we may, ere long, see filled with another Supreme Court decision, declaring that the Constitution of the United States does not permit a State to exclude slavery from its limits. . . . We shall lie down pleasantly dreaming that the people of Missouri are on the verge of making their State free, and we shall awake to the reality instead, that the Supreme Court has made Illinois a slave State."*

Beginning on August 21ˢᵗ, 1858, in the Illinois town of Ottawa and concluding in Alton, just northeast across the river from St. Louis on October 15ᵗʰ, Abraham Lincoln and Stephen Douglas met for seven face-to-face debates across the state. The main issue of all the debates was slavery, and the Dred Scott case became the focal point of disagreement. People came from far and wide to listen to the debates, and the nation's major newspapers sent stenographers to record every word for publication. Ten thousand people attended the debate in Ottawa, even though the town's population did not exceed six thousand. The popularity of the debates grew, and so did the size of the crowds.

In 1858, United States Senators were elected by the state House of Representatives, and in the November election, while the Republicans won the majority of the popular votes statewide, the Democrats won more seats, and they then reelected Douglas to the Senate.

But Abraham Lincoln was a man inspired with a cause, and he elevated his campaign to the next level. He paid to publish all the Lincoln-Douglas Debates in a book, which sold well throughout the North, and Lincoln's popularity spread.

The country continued to spiral out of control during the year 1859. Chief Justice Taney once again became the favorite target of the abolitionists when he ruled that the Fugitive Slave Law was constitutional, notwithstanding the horrific facts. In 1854, Sherman Booth, the Free Soil editor of the *Milwaukee Free Democrat,* had freed a runaway slave from the custody of a United States deputy marshall. He was charged with violating the Fugitive Slave Act, and after years of litigation, Taney ruled that Booth was guilty and ordered him arrested. The Supreme Court of Wisconsin, fed up with what they believed were improper decisions by Taney, declared his ruling to be unconstitutional and refused to abide by the decision.

In October, firebrand abolitionist John Brown showed up in Virginia with nineteen men and two hundred "Beecher's Bibles"—.52 caliber Sharp's carbines—and attacked the federal armory at Harpers Ferry. He planned to seize the 100,000 muskets and rifles stored there, give them to local slaves, and lead an armed uprising throughout the slave states. During the two-day skirmish resulting in ten deaths, Brown and his men were defeated and captured by a detachment of Marines led by Colonel Robert E. Lee. After a trial that lasted a week, a jury found Brown guilty of murder and sentenced him to be hanged. After the sentence, Brown was allowed to speak. He stood tall and proclaimed, "If it is deemed necessary that I should forfeit my life for the furtherance of the ends of justice, and mingle my blood further with the blood of my children and with the blood of millions in this slave country whose rights are disregarded by wicked, cruel, and unjust enactments, I submit; so let it be done!" On December 2nd, he was hanged by his neck until dead. In response to the sentence, the poet Ralph Waldo Emerson predicted that John Brown "will make the gallows glorious like the Cross."

Slavery, sectionalism, and popular sovereignty continued to be the main issues as candidates began to line up in their respective parties in preparation for the 1860 presidential election. As a result of his growing popularity as a star of the Republican Party, Abraham Lincoln was invited to speak by renowned abolitionist Henry Ward Beecher in his church in New York. When word of the invitation spread, so many people expressed an interest that the Young Men's Republican Union took over and moved the location to the much larger Cooper Institute.

Lincoln solidified and advanced his position as the leading Republican contender for the Party nomination by giving a detailed summary of the history of the Founding Fathers and the original intent of the Constitution. He again assailed the Dred

Scott decision and pointed out a clear factual fallacy when Justice Taney had written that "the right of property in a slave is distinctly and expressly affirmed in the Constitution." Lincoln invited an inspection of that great founding document and promised that the right to own a slave as property was not so affirmed.

The future president assailed the intransigent position of the Southern and slave-owning states that they would destroy the government, "unless you be allowed to construe and enforce the Constitution as you please, on all points in dispute between you and us. You will rule or ruin in all events." Lincoln finished with a moving call to courage that moved those in the packed Institute and propelled him toward the presidency:

> *Neither let us be slandered from our duty by false accusations against us, nor frightened from it by menaces of destruction to the Government nor of dungeons to ourselves. Let us have faith that right makes might, and in that faith, let us, to the end, dare to do our duty as we understand it.*

Propelled by a universal hatred of the Dred Scott decision, and inspired by the leadership of Abraham Lincoln, the Republican Party nominated him in May of 1860 as their candidate for president. The same momentum propelled him forward as abolitionist Northern Democrats and Whigs jumped on the band wagon. A 1860 political cartoon entitled "Political Quadrille, Music by Dred Scott" emphasized the importance of the case to the presidential election. In the center of the parody sits Dred Scott, sitting on a chair gaily playing a fiddle, his feet not quite touching the floor, and dancing around him are four couples. Republican Lincoln promenades with a Negro woman, Southern Democrat John C. Breckinridge dances with the incumbent James

Buchanan who is dressed like a goat, Constitutional Union party candidate John Bell waltzes with an Indian, and Stephen A. Douglas does a jig with a poor Irishman.

Six months later, on November 6th, 1860, Abraham Lincoln was elected sixteenth president of the United States, garnering a stunning ninety-eight percent of the Northern electoral vote.

The two primary factors in the difference between a Republican defeat in 1856 and victory in 1860 were Dred Scott and Abraham Lincoln. The party had grown by 200,000 voters in the free states, but picked up an additional 300,000 votes that had voted for other parties in the prior election. Seventy percent of those votes were from five crucial states that went Democratic in 1856, and all of the sixty-two electoral votes from those five states went to James Buchanan. In 1860, Abraham Lincoln won fifty-nine of them. On March 4th, 1861, a hunched and trembling Roger Brooke Taney issued the oath of office to the tall, strong, new president who had been propelled to the highest office in the land on the strength of his opposition to that Chief Justice's opinion in *Scott v. Sandford.*

If it had not been for the courage and tenacity of the man born on an obscure plantation in southern Virginia, who traveled the nation as Dred Scott, and who would not give up on his quest for freedom for himself and his family, it is unlikely that Abraham Lincoln would have been elected president.

Where was Dred Scott on that overcast March day as the new commander in chief took charge of a nation diminished by the secession of seven states from the Union? Where was the man who, with the help of his close friends, the grown children of his former master, had won and then lost his freedom, but never gave up hope?

On September 15th, 1858, Abraham Lincoln and Stephen Douglas debated the Dred Scott decision in Joneboro, just north of Cairo and the great confluence of the Ohio River where Dred had first felt the mighty force of the Mississippi as he and the Blows entered it aboard the steamer *Atlantic*. While they spoke of the case brought by him, Dred Scott lay in his bed in the small shack on Carr Street in St. Louis and struggled to breathe. He had contracted tuberculosis not long after the Supreme Court declared him to be a slave. On September 17th, surrounded by his wife, daughters, and his white friends and benefactors, he let his mortal body slip away and free his spirit to glide across the River Jordan and into eternity.

But the end was not as tragic as it could have been, for Dred died a free man. Two months after the decision was read from the courtroom in Washington, Dred's antagonist and the defendant in the litigation, John F.A. Sanford, died in a New York insane asylum. Word had somehow gotten out that Irene Emerson Chafee, the wife of abolitionist Republican Calvin Chafee, was the owner of the famous slave Dred Scott, and the embarrassed and unhappy congressman ordered that she immediately get rid of the Scotts by any legal means possible.

And so it was that on May 4th, Taylor Blow bought the Scotts from Irene Chafee for $1,000. On a glorious Tuesday, May 26th, 1857, the Scotts, the Band of Brothers, and all the wives and children of their friends, lawyers, and benefactors, put on their Sunday finest and walked into the St. Louis courthouse for the last time. There Taylor Blow filed the Scotts' Emancipation Papers as 26 Saint Louis Circuit Court Record 263, which read as follows:

> *Taylor Blow, who is personally known to the court, comes into open court, and acknowledges the execution by him of a Deed of Emancipation to his slaves, Dred Scott, aged about [fifty] eight years, of full negro blood and color, and Harriet Scott wife of said Dred, aged thirty nine years, also of full negro blood & color, and*

Eliza Scott a daughter of said Dred & Harriet, aged nineteen years of full negro color, and Lizzy Scott, also a daughter of said Dred & Harriet, aged ten years likewise of full negro blood & color.

* * *

Reverend John Anderson threw a large celebration at the Eighth Street Baptist Church, but when over a thousand happy St. Louis residents showed up, they moved it to a neighboring park. Dred and Harriet strolled proudly under the canopy of oaks, maples, and flowering dogwoods, receiving congratulations from friends and well-wishers. Slaves, free Negros, white abolitionists, reporters, and the curious all wanted to get a glimpse of the famous slaves who had battled the court system for so long, and about whom all of the country was abuzz. Folks just wanted to shake the hands or pat the backs of the couple whose freedom had been denied by the Supreme Court, but was granted by the milk of human compassion.

In the midst of the throng, Dred found the Band of Brothers and pulled them together, and sent Harriet to gather Charlotte Blow and the wives. The group huddled to hear what Dred had to say.

"My brothers and sisters . . ." he coughed several times, then paused to take a breath and regain his voice. He looked each in the eye before continuing. "You is my brothers and sisters, and Harriet and I loves you more than you will ever know. When it seemed that everyone was against us, and when the law and the courts abandoned us, you was always there." Charlotte wept, and the men brushed the corners of their eyes. "I don't know how to thank you, but God does, and I knows that He and his angels are smilin' upon you this day, and will one day welcome you home as His good and faithful servants."

No one spoke as he pulled out a handkerchief and coughed gently into it. He smiled at each of them. "I will be there, too, and will be the first to welcome you home. Thank you, and God bless you!"

The friends hugged and congratulated them, and then parted as Dred led Harriet away. The temperature dropped into the seventies as evening fell. Music from dozens of banjos, fiddles, and make-shift drums filled the air, and the succulent odors of roasted meats and freshly baked breads further uplifted the collective spirit of the community. Dred and Harriet held hands and moved away from the crowds. They smiled when Lizzie darted past in a game of tag, and then disappeared between the thick secondary trunks of a giant sycamore. A distinctive laugh rang out, which they immediately recognized as that of their Eliza, now a beautiful young woman. They could see her with a group of girls in gay print dresses giggling at the attention of several young men.

"Oh, Dred, our daughters is finally safe," Harriet said as she grabbed Dred's right arm with both hands. "This is the first day of a whole new life, and it's only because you would not give up. You is my man, and I loves you so!" She kissed his smooth cheek and snuggled up to his side.

A gust of wind separated a cluster of white and yellow dogwood flowers that fluttered to the ground. Without letting go of Harriet, Dred reached down, scooped them up, and presented them to his wife.

"To the woman who bore me the two greatest joys of my life," he pledged. Then he stopped, took her fully in his arms, and tenderly kissed her lips.

"Dred!" she squealed like the girl she was when they had first met, far to the north. "Shame on you!" she scolded, playfully slapping his chest. "Not here in public!"

"I don' care, "Dred spoke, his voice raising. "I wants the world to know that this here angel of beauty," he fairly shouted, "is now, henceforth, and forever my wife—and I am her man!" Harriet's teeth flashed in a broad smile, and though the nearby crowd quieted to listen, this time she didn't shush him, her heart filling with pride as he went on.

"That's right, y'all heard me," he spoke boldly and powerfully. "I am a man . . . and Harriet is my wife." He paused, and looked around, took in a deep breath, expanding his chest. A steamboat whistle rose from the nearby river, punctuating his declaration.

"God put us together and no man can put us asunder," he said, his eyes burning bright in the midst of the coming night, "because we are FREE!"

* * *

In his first year in office, President Abraham Lincoln appointed Dred Scott's Supreme Court attorney Montgomery Blair to his cabinet as Postmaster General. He then appointed Henry Taylor Blow as ambassador to Venezuela.

On July 17th, 1861, the Civil War began when South Carolina fired on Fort Sumter. On that same day, the Congress of the United States passed the Second Confiscation Act, freeing the slaves of every person in rebellion against the United States of America. For the first two years of the war, the Union suffered one defeat after another.

On New Year's Day 1863, President Lincoln issued by Executive Order the final Emancipation Proclamation, declaring that all slaves in the ten states that had seceded from the United States were henceforth and forever: FREE! Dred was not present in this life to witness the freeing of thousands of Negro slaves by the mighty stroke of the pen that he helped propel into office, but he likely danced a Juba in the courts on high, and Harriet and the girls must surely have thought back on their man with immense love and pride.

Booker T. Washington later wrote of his recollection as a boy of nine of the day he and his family were told they were freed by Abraham Lincoln. His words describe a scene that must have been repeated many thousands of times over the course of the next few years:

> *As the great day drew nearer, there was more singing in the slave quarters than usual. It was bolder, had more ring, and lasted later into the night. Most of the verses of the plantation songs had some reference to freedom. . . . Some man who seemed to be a stranger (a United States officer, I presume) made a little speech and then read a rather long paper—the Emancipation Proclamation, I think. After the reading we were told that we were all free, and could go when and where we pleased. My mother, who was standing by my side, leaned over and kissed her children, while tears of joy ran down her cheeks. She explained to us what it all meant, that this was the day for which she had been so long praying, but fearing that she would never live to see.*

Still smarting over seeing his efforts to preserve the nation by the force of his own pen, Chief Justice Taney began to write an opinion that the Emancipation Proclamation was unconstitutional, but he never finished it.

After terrible losses at Fredericksburg and Chancellorsville, the Union Army intercepted the Confederate Army of Northern Virginia at a small Pennsylvania town called Gettysburg on July 1st. After three days of massive losses on both sides, the gray-clad troops, commanded by General Robert E. Lee, could not breech the line of blue-coated Northerners, and the entire tide of war turned.

On November 19th, 1863, President Lincoln spoke of the eternities at the dedication of the cemetery for soldiers killed at Gettysburg.

Four score and seven years ago our fathers brought forth on this continent a new nation, conceived in Liberty, and dedicated to the proposition that all men are created equal.

Now we are engaged in a great civil war, testing whether that nation, or any nation, so conceived and so dedicated, can long endure. We are met on a great battle-field of that war. We have come to dedicate a portion of that field, as a final resting place for those who here gave their lives that that nation might live. It is altogether fitting and proper that we should do this. But, in a larger sense, we can not dedicate . . . we can not consecrate . . . we can not hallow this ground. The brave men, living and dead, who struggled here, have consecrated it, far above our poor power to add or detract. The world will little note, nor long remember what we say here, but it can never forget what they did here. It is for us the living, rather, to be dedicated here to the unfinished work which they who fought here have thus far so nobly advanced. It is rather for us to be here dedicated to the great task remaining before us—that from these honored dead we take increased devotion to that cause for which they gave the last full measure of devotion—that we here highly resolve that these dead shall not have died in vain—that this nation, under God, shall have a new birth of freedom—and that government: of the people, by the people, for the people, shall not perish from the earth.

On December 14th, 1863, a bill was filed in the United States Senate to support a Constitutional Amendment to abolish slavery throughout the entire United States, and the following April, the Senate passed the proposed Amendment by a vote of thirty-eight to six.

On October 12th, 1864, having served years as Chief Justice of the Supreme Court, Roger Brooke Taney quietly passed away and was buried across the street from St. John's Church in Frederick, Maryland. That same day, Taney's home state of Maryland abolished slavery within her borders.

In January of 1865, the House of Representatives finally passed, by a vote of 119 to 56, the bill for an amendment to abolish slavery. President Lincoln signed it on January 31st, and the very next day Illinois became the first state to ratify the Thirteenth Amendment.

Having been elected the preceding November, Abraham Lincoln was sworn in for a second time on March 4th, 1865, and gave his final speech as his second inaugural address, laying a poignant capstone on his legacy. It may have been written with Dred Scott in mind:

> *One-eighth of the whole population were colored slaves, not distributed generally over the Union, but localized in the southern part of it. These slaves constituted a peculiar and powerful interest. All knew that this interest was somehow the cause of the war. To strengthen, perpetuate, and extend this interest was the object for which the insurgents would rend the Union even by war, while the Government claimed no right to do more than to restrict the territorial enlargement of it. . . . Fondly do we hope, fervently do we pray, that this mighty scourge of war may speedily pass away. Yet, if God wills that it continue until all the wealth piled by the*

bondsman's two hundred and fifty years of unrequited toil shall be sunk, and until every drop of blood drawn with the lash shall be paid by another drawn with the sword, as was said three thousand years ago, so still it must be said "the judgments of the Lord are true and righteous altogether. With malice toward none, with charity for all, with firmness in the right as God gives us to see the right, let us strive on to finish the work we are in, to bind up the nation's wounds, to care for him who shall have borne the battle and for his widow and his orphan, to do all which may achieve and cherish a just and lasting peace among ourselves and with all nations.

A month later, on April 9th, 1865, peace was achieved when General Robert E. Lee surrendered to General Ulysses S. Grant at the house of Wilmer McLean in the village of Appomattox Courthouse. The long national nightmare of slavery and war was over.

On April 14th, the Great Emancipator, "Humble Abe" Lincoln was assassinated by John Wilkes Booth, and he died the next morning. Renowned poet Walt Whitman immediately picked up his pen and poured out the grief of a nation:

O CAPTAIN! my Captain! our fearful trip is done;
The ship has weather'd every rack, the prize we sought is won;
The port is near, the bells I hear, the people all exulting,
While follow eyes the steady keel, the vessel grim and daring:

But O heart! heart! heart!
O the bleeding drops of red,
Where on the deck my Captain lies,
Fallen cold and dead.

O Captain! my Captain! rise up and hear the bells;
Rise up—for you the flag is flung—for you the bugle trills;
For you bouquets and ribbon'd wreaths—for you the shores a-crowding;
For you they call, the swaying mass, their eager faces turning;

Here Captain! dear father!
This arm beneath your head;
It is some dream that on the deck,
You've fallen cold and dead.

My Captain does not answer, his lips are pale and still;
My father does not feel my arm, he has no pulse nor will;
The ship is anchor'd safe and sound, its voyage closed and done;
From fearful trip, the victor ship, comes in with object won;

Exult, O shores, and ring, O bells!
But I, with mournful tread,
Walk the deck my Captain lies,
Fallen cold and dead.

Before the year was out, the Thirteenth Amendment abolishing slavery throughout the entire newly re-United States was formally adopted when Georgia became the 27th state to ratify it on December 6th, 1865.

In 1868, America put a final nail in the Dred Scott court decision when it adopted the Fourteenth Amendment, declaring, "all persons born or naturalized in the United States are citizens of the United States and the states wherein they reside."

On June 17th, 1876, Harriet Robinson Scott went to meet her Jesus and her Dred in the middle of the air and is buried in Greenwood Cemetery in St. Louis.

"Was it right,
While my unnumbered brethren toiled and bled,
That I should dream away the entrusted hours
On rose-leaf beds, pampering the coward heart,
With feelings all too delicate for use?"
— Samuel Taylor Coleridge

Bibliography

"Abraham Lincoln and Freedom - Dred Scott." *Abraham Lincoln and Freedom - Abraham Lincoln's Emancipation Proclamation &13th Amendment.* Web. 28 Aug. 2009. <http://www.mrlincolnandfreedom.org/inside.asp?ID=15&subjectID=2>.

"Abraham Lincoln's Speech on the Dred Scott Decision — Courtesy of TheFreeman Institute . . ." *The Freeman Institute: Arenas of Expertise ranging from Black History, Diversity, Workshops, Keynotes and Retreats to Executive Coaching and Organizational Culture Change.* Web. 28 Aug. 2009. <http://www.freemaninstitute.com/lincoln.htm>.

Ambrose, Stephen E., and Douglas G. Brinkley. *The Mississippi and the Making of a Nation.* Washington, D.C.. National Geographic Society, 2002. Print.

The Antislavery Literature Project — Antislavery Literature Project. Web. 28 Aug. 2009. <http://antislavery.eserver.org/>.

Beecher, Stowe, Harriet. *Uncle Tom's Cabin (Wordsworth Classics).* Minneapolis: Wordsworth Editions Ltd, 1999. Print.

Beecher, Stowe, Harriet. *Uncle Tom's Cabin (Wordsworth Classics).* Minneapolis: Wordsworth Editions Ltd, 1999. Print.

"Brown's Anti-Slavery Harp." *Uncle Tom's Cabin & American Culture.* Web. 28 Aug. 2009. <http://utc.iath.virginia.edu/abolitn/absowwbahp.html>.

Buchanan, Thomas C., Black Life on the Mississippi -Slaves, Free Blacks and the Western Steamboat World, University of North Carolina Press, Chapel Hill, 2004.

Carwardine, Richard. *Lincoln.* New York: Alfred A. Knopf, 2006. Print.

"Confessions of Nat Turner." *MelaNet®: The UnCut Black Experience*. Web. 28 Aug. 2009. <http://www.melanet.com/nat/nat.html>.

Crofts, Daniel W. *Old Southampton, Politics and Society in a Virginia County 1834-1869*. Charlottesville: Universitys of Virginia, 1992. Print.

Davis, David Brion. *Inhuman bondage the rise and fall of slavery in the New World*. New York: Oxford UP, 2006. Print.

Donald, Davidson,. *Tennessee*. Vol. 1. Nashville: J.S. Sanders, Distributed to the trade by National Book Network, 1991. Print.

The Dred Scott Heritage Foundation | Saint Louis | Missouri. Web. 28 Aug. 2009. <http://www.thedredscottfoundation.org/>.

"Dred Scott v. Sandford: Primary Documents of American History (Virtual Programs & Services, Library of Congress)." *Library of Congress Home*. Web. 28 Aug. 2009. <http://www.loc.gov/rr/program/bib/ourdocs/DredScott.html>

"Dred Scott v. Sandford: Primary Documents of American History (Virtual Programs & Services, Library of Congress)." *Library of Congress Home*. Web. 28 Aug. 2009. <http://www.loc.gov/rr/program/bib/ourdocs/DredScott.html>

"Dred Scott v. Sandford." *Touro Law Center*. Web. 28 Aug. 2009. <http://tourolaw.edu/patch/Scott/>.

Evan, Jones,. *Citadel in the wilderness the story of Fort Snelling and the northwest frontier*. Minneapolis, MN: University of Minnesota, 2001. Print.

"Famous Trials - - Prof. Douglas Linder." *UMKC School of Law*. Web. 28 Aug. 2009. <http://www.law.umkc.edu/faculty/projects/ftrials/ftrials.htm>.

Fehrenbacher, Don E. *The Dred Scott Case Its Significance in American Law and Politics*. New York: Oxford UP, USA, 2001. Print.

Fleischner, Jennifer. *Dred Scott case testing the right to live free.* Brookfield, Conn: Millbrook, 1997. Print.

Fleischner, Jennifer. *Mrs. Lincoln and Mrs. Keckly the remarkable story of the friendship between a first lady and a former slave.* New York: Broadway Books, 2003. Print.

Graber, Mark A. *Dred Scott and the Problem of Constitutional Evil (Cambridge Studies on the American Constitution).* New York: Cambridge UP, 2006. Print.

Herda, D. J. *Dred Scott case slavery and citizenship.* Hillside, NJ: Enslow, 1994. Print.

"Historic Fort Snelling : MNHS.ORG." Web. 28 Aug. 2009. <http://www.mnhs.org/places/sites/hfs/>.

"A history of St. Louis." *City of St. Louis Community Information Network - Official Web Site of the City of St. Louis, Missouri.* Web. 28 Aug. 2009. <http://stlouis.missouri.org/heritage/History69/>.

The Holy Bible. Authorized King James Version ed. Salt Lake City: Intellectual Reserve, 2005. Print.

Horton, James O., and Lois E. Horton. *Slavery and the Making of America.* New York: Oxford UP, 2005. Print.

January, Brendan. *Dred Scott decision.* New York: Children's, 1998. Print.

Kaufman, Kenneth C. *Dred Scott's advocate a biography of Roswell M. Field.* Columbia: University of Missouri, 1996. Print.

Kutler, Stanley I. *The Dred Scott Decision, Law or Politics?* Boston: Houghton Mifflin Co., 1967. Print.

Latham, Frank B. *The Dred Scott Decision, March 6, 1857.* New York: Franklin Watts, Inc, 1968. Print.

Lukes, Bonnie L. *Dred Scott decision.* San Diego, CA: Lucent Books, 1997. Print.

Maltz, Earl M. *Dred Scott and the Politics of Slavery (Landmark Law Cases and American Society).* New York: University of Kansas, 2007. Print.

McCutcheon, Marc. *Everyday life in the 1800s a guide for writers, students & historians*. Cincinnati, Ohio: Writer's Digest Books, 2001. Print.

McNulty, Elizabeth. *St. Louis Then and Now (Then & Now)*. New York: Thunder Bay, 2000. Print.

"Missouri Digital Heritage: Collections : Dred Scott Case, 1846-1857." *Missouri Secretary of State Home Page*. Web. 28 Aug. 2009. <http://www.sos.mo.gov/archives/resources/africanamerican/scott/scott.asp>.

Paul, Finkelman. *Dred Scott v. Sandford, A Brief History with Documents*. Boston: Bedford/St. Martin's, 1997. Print.

"The Revised Dred Scott Case Collection." *Home - Washington University Digital Gateway*. Web. 28 Aug. 2009. <http://digital.wustl.edu/d/dre/>.

Rutman, Darrett Bruce. *Place in time Middlesex County, Virginia, 1650-1750*. New York: Norton, 1984. Print.

Sandburg, Carl. *Abraham Lincoln, The Prairie Years - II*. Vol. 2. New York: Charles Scribner's Sons, 1926. Print.

Sandburg, Carl. *Abraham Lincoln, The War Years - I*. Vol. 1. New York: Charles Scribner's Sons, 1926. Print.

Sandburg, Carl. *Abraham Lincoln, The War Years - I*. Vol. 3. New York: Charles Scribner's Sons, 1926. Print.

Schumacher, Alvin J. *Thunder on Capitol Hill, The LIfe of Chief Justice Roger B. Taney*. Milwaukee: The Bruce Company, 1964. Print.

"Scott, Dred | House Divided." *Loading Daily Report . . . | House Divided*. Web. 28 Aug. 2009. <http://hd.housedivided.dickinson.edu/index.php?q=node/6538>.

Simon, James F. *Lincoln and Chief Justice Taney Slavery, Secession, and the President's War Powers*. New York: Simon & Schuster, 2006. Print.

Skog, Jason. *The Dred Scott Decision (We the People)*. New York: Compass Point Books, 2006. Print.

Slaughter, William W., and Chad M. Orton. *Joseph Smith's America A Celebration of His Life and Times*. Boston: Deseret Book Company, 2005. Print.

"Slave missions and the Black church . . . -." *Google Books*. Web. 28 Aug. 2009. <http://books.google.com/books?id=aGGdyAlobAEC&printse c=frontcover&source=gbs_v2_summary_r&cad=0#>.

Sobel, Mechal. *World they made together black and white values in eighteeth-century Virginia*. Princeton: Princeton UP, 1989. Print.

Swain, Gwenyth. *Dred and Harriet Scott a family's struggle for freedom*. St. Paul: Borealis Books, 2004. Print.

Unchained memories readings from the slave narratives. Boston: Bulfinch, 2002. Print.

VanderVelde, Lea, and Sandhya Subramanian. "Mrs. Dred Scott (Race and Gender Issues in Harriet Robinson Scott's Emancipation claims." *The Yale Law Journal* (1997). Print.

"Visit to Dred Scott." *Frank Leslie's Illustrated Newspaper* [New York City] 27 June 1857: 1-2. Print.

Vogler, Christopher. *Writer's journey mythic structure for writers*. Studio City, CA: M. Wiese Productions, 1998. Print.

Williams, Gary M. "Colonel George Blow: Planter and Political Prophet of Antebellum Sussex." *The Virginia Magazine of History and Biography, Vol. 90, No. 4* Oct. 1982. Print.

Wilson, Charles Morrow. *Dred Scott decision*. Philadelphia: Auerbach, 1973. Print.

Woods, Fred E., and Thomas L. Farmer. *When The Saints Came Marching In, A History of the Latter-Day Saints in St. Louis*. Orem: Millennial, 2009. Print.